THE FEATHER

CW01590451

# Other books By Jackie Canessa

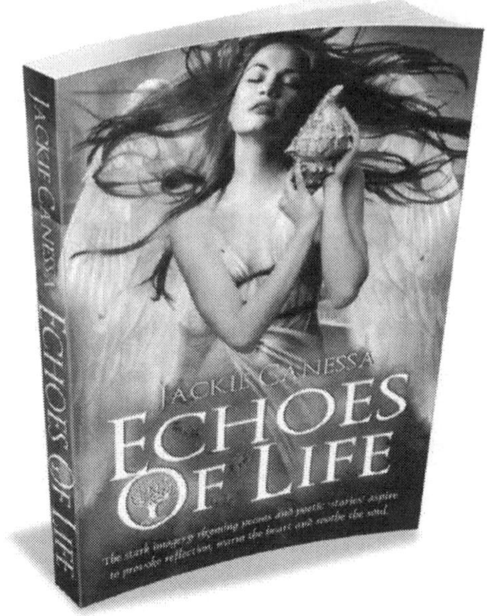


'Can you hear them?
They still breathe in the air,
Listen careful, to the echoing sound,
From all corners, from all walks upon earth,
They rebound...'

Echoes of Life, contemporary poems inspired by social issues, life experiences, spirituality, and the universal language of love. The collection of poems is the result of a life's work began at adolescence, gracefully evolved over the years...

**www.jackiecanessa.com**

*Imagination is the eye of the soul…*

# THE FEATHER

JACKIE CANESSA

*If there is light in the soul, there will be beauty in the person,*
*If there is beauty in the person, there will be harmony in the house,*
*If there is harmony in the house, there will be order in the nation,*
*If there is order in the nation, there will be peace in the world.*

Chinese proverb

*To mum and dad*

## Prologue

Two figures stood on the edge of a cliff, on the plateau of a mountain embedded in a perfect ring of clouds. Magnificent ochre hues tainted the heavens as dimming rays of golden light; a soft diffusion of yellow and orange, cast the last shadows upon the lush green earth. They stood close, whispering, their impatience palpable in the thin air. Two heads kept turning; four eyes kept glancing behind at the glittering forest.

Soon, it would be dark; they needed to get a move on. Impatiently, they headed for the tower situated midway between the edge of the forest and the edge of the mountain. They had nearly reached its entrance, when they saw them. They emerged hastily from behind the hugging trees, one very tall like them, the other shorter.

For a while, the four stood facing each other, whispering among themselves. Suddenly, the short one spiralled up the see-through turret. The other three stood at its foot, whispered some more and then hurriedly made their way back to the edge of the cliff. In minutes, dark indigo crept over the lingering specks of burnt orange, bathing the mountaintop in night.

They stood in a perfect row, on the very edge of the precipice, their hands clasped in front of them, as three pairs of eyes, gazed far into the silver speckled mantle that stretched to infinity. No one spoke; each was immersed in their own thoughts as they bowed their heads to look down at the dark abyss. They stood there for a while, in silence, until a faint roar, a blast of light, announced it was time. Simultaneously, they pivoted on their heels and swiftly headed back to the woodland. As they crossed the shadowed earth and disappeared through the thicket, they were smiling...

Amanda could not remember a storm like this. The wind blustered with demonic rage; rain beat against the ground like bullets fired from heaven and mist hovered impregnable, a thick grey blanket. As she listened to the menacing howl outside, to the violent roar of the sea threatening to break through the building's facade, she began to regret her decision. Remaining alone in the hotel, against her employee's pleas had not been a good idea. There were no guests; the weather forecast had ensured no one would brave the cove this weekend.

She sat in the reception chair, wrapped in her favourite blanket, cupping the steaming coffee that threatened to spill in her shaky hands. The cold made her hands tremble she tried to convince herself; not fear. She kept eyeing the tiffany lamp dangling precariously from the ceiling, as she listened with escalating alarm to the creaking sound of the wooden building that had begun to quake under the wrath of the gods. Her eyes kept eyeing the hands of her watch, willing them to hasten to dawn. Everything seemed worse in the dark.

She did not hear him come in, nor knew how he came in. The hotel had been painstakingly secured; Jason had tied the shutters with ropes he had found in the basement, so they were not be devoured by the wind, swollen into the night, and she had double-checked every door. Yet, there he was, standing at the reception desk asking for a room.

She had no recollection of him crossing the lobby towards her; he seemed to have sprung out of thin air. At the comforting sound of his polite *'good evening',* she had looked up and dazedly asked him how many nights he would be staying. She should have screamed, jumped out of her skin, believing him a spectre, yet she went on to register him as if it were any other day of business. He signed in as Anton, just Anton. On automatic pilot, she handed him the keys to room number seven. He thanked her softly, then, gracefully ascended the stairs to the first floor. He had no luggage, not even a small bag.

The moment she was alone, the storm subsided; the wind dropped from a screaming howl to a whispering whistle and the moon disposed her hazy vestment. Amanda sat perplexed, her nebulous mind, struggling to decipher what had just occurred. *She had fallen asleep...had been dreaming. No one had come in. It was impossible.* Lost in these comforting thoughts... she did not hear him return.

Her eyes rolled languidly over the contours of his face as he probed her across the counter. She had never seen such a handsome face...*chiselled by the Gods themselves*, she thought wistfully, a faint familiar emotion fluttering in her stomach. She gazed deep into his pellucid blue eyes. They were so beautiful...

He was extremely tall, his hair the colour of golden corn. The loose ringlets hang down to his broad shoulders, his perfectly moulded torso evident through his casual clothing. An aura of elegance surrounded him and the expression on his face was extremely gentle. His lips curved into a half-smile.

He placed his palms on the reception counter, and gazed down at her. His gaze was so intense she had to look away, her eyes dropping to his hands; strong smooth hands with long slender fingers tipped with perfectly groomed nails. For a second her hands left her lap. She desperately wanted to touch them, feel them in her own. It was the gentle tone of his voice, which interrupted their journey up to the polished oak counter; they froze in midair then darted back to the comfort of her lap. He wanted an extra pillow.

She stood up hesitantly, incoherent mumbles escaping her quivering lips as she headed uncertainly for the linen room behind the reception area. The sound of his mesmerizing voice, his crystalline eyes haunted her as she clumsily searched the steel shelves of the small cubicle. She felt faint, strangely elated, and suddenly, without any notion of how and when, she was in his room, in his arms, and he was making love to her, love to her soul.

*Seth was longing to finish his daily class. He was edgy and kept tapping his feet underneath the desk willing the bell to ring. The dragging voice of his teacher bored his ears; the constant reminder of the rules brought a yawn to his throat. He enjoyed school but hated this particular class. He did not like to be told how he should do things, of the many things he could not do. Protocol class was a pain. Master Joram was a pain.*

*At last, the high-pitched ringing sound ended the eternal class, he was finally free. Picking up his school bag laden with study books, he rushed out to the schoolyard. Impatiently, he walked the stretch of ivory cobbled paths meandering across the beautiful garden that was the pride of Elder Eldad, the school gardener, to the school gates, and waited for his two friends. Lael and Zeriel were older than he was and were already attending Travel Class.*

*The three friends hurried across the circling forest to the edge of the mountain. Perched on the rim, they gazed down on the luscious green valley divided by the glistening river snaking through its length, down on the pristine white cottages divided in clusters, on both sides of the sparkling rush. Going home was their favourite part of the day...*

The days that ensued were a blur. The cove had returned to its usual haven; celestial blue skies and inviting lukewarm seas once again made it a preferential getaway location for those wishing to relax for a few days and Amanda was back in business. The Seaview was at full capacity most days and booked solid at weekends. It was a cosy two-storey hotel perched on a small cliff overlooking a beautiful sandy inlet thirty minutes from the town. Its enviable and picturesque location and the fact that all its sixteen rooms faced the sea had earned it its name. Amanda had inherited it from her parents when they had tragically lost their lives in a freak car accident two years earlier.

Amanda could still hear their gentle laughter echoing its corridors, whispering her name, calling her their 'little angel'. They had always made her feel special, loved. She had known she was adopted since a young age, chosen among a whole lot of other babies waiting to be 'saved'. Her father had told her incessantly how she captivated him with her angelic smile, by the almost transparent curious blue eyes that had looked up at him from the cot at the maternity ward in St Thomas' Hospital. Her mother had told her repeatedly how they had not slept for days until she had become truly and irrevocably theirs. They both agreed she had been heaven-sent to be the sunshine that lit up their lives.

Amanda would never forget the noble souls that had given her so much; it was a privilege to have grown cocooned in a world enveloped by love. There were still mornings when she woke up thinking the accident was only a nightmare, that her parents were still alive. The thought was tragically fleeting. The reality of her loss materialized as she left the twilight world behind. It was in those first moments of daylight her tired heart wrenched with an agony rendering her almost breathless, and she wished she could curl up in her bed and shut herself out from a world that no longer held them.

The Seaview had been the pride and joy of her father, his legacy to her, and she had insisted on keeping it open against the advice of lawyers, who predicted the business would fail in her inexperienced hands. Within months, Amanda proved them all wrong.

The running of the hotel was her survival tool and eighteen hours of work leaving six hours of sleep, was the only way she knew how to cope with her loss. Maria and Lucy, the domestics, loved her like a daughter. Peter, the handyman who had been a close friend of her father was like an uncle to her and his son Jason, who doubled up as night receptionist and bell boy was, together with Claire, her best friend in the world. Her decision to keep the hotel open had filled them all with joy; the hotel was not only their livelihood but also their home. Amanda knew that even if she had decided to sell it as the lawyers had advised they would have understood. They loved her. They were her family, the only one she had now. They all understood the magnitude of her loss; her parents had been everything to her, her world. The hotel was the only thing left of it now, the only thing that kept her alive. The loving dedication of its staff kept the hotel alive.

Amanda's working schedule was tight, allowing her little time to ponder on the muddled recollection of the stormy night. The only thing she could remember lucidly was waking up in the reception armchair and that the storm was over.

The wind had tamed to a gentle breeze at the first rays of light, settling the seas to a tranquil lull. Ashen skies had gradually shaded a glorious blue with the exception of a few sparse clouds, the last vestiges of the storm. They had prepared well for the tempestuous storm and there had been no major damage to lament. Sporadically, she searched her fuzzy mind for a logical explanation to the bizarre occurrence, but the constant stream of guests and daily 'emergencies' mercifully brought her swiftly back to her busy reality. At the end of each tiring day, her exhausted body attempted to fight sleep. She needed to decipher her vague recollection, but heavy lids soon shut out her preying mind. Asleep, she attempted to catch the dream, which slithered ungraspable, filtered the matrix of her mind without catching.

With each passing day, the disconcerting images began to fade, and her confusion began to turn slowly to an affirmation. She had checked the registration book, scrutinized the room. No one had signed in that night. Room number seven, had not been slept in; it had only been a dream.

It was after a couple of weeks that Amanda began to feel nauseous in the mornings. Initially, she blamed it on stress. She had been overdoing it. Her body was cautioning her to slow down. The nausea persisted. Early one morning, she headed into town to visit the family doctor. She was certain of the diagnosis; the sick feeling in the pit of her stomach was either the result of stress, or a stomach bug.

Amanda made Dr Reynolds check the urine samples, the scan three times; certain his diagnosis was mistaken. Dr Reynolds had been surprised at her insistence but had indulged without comment. He knew better. He had seen this kind of denial before, but each time the result was the same. She was pregnant. He was surprised though that a level-headed girl like Amanda, who had no obvious boyfriend, had gotten herself into such a predicament. The confused and anxious expression on Amanda's face confirmed it was an unplanned pregnancy. Still, he said nothing, asked no questions. He was a family friend, had known her all his life, but he was also a professional. She would tell him if she wanted to, when she was ready. Amanda would never be ready, could never tell anyone, for she did not even know herself what the truth was.

She walked out of the small clinic located in the heart of the Main Street in a daze, her mind in turmoil. As she made her way unsteadily to the car park, she felt her knees weaken and had to sit down on one of the benches placed at intervals down the street. She sat there petrified; rigid fingers clawing her lap, her eyes glued on the paved ground, on oblivion. Her thoughts returned to the stormy night. The blurred images dancing on the fringes of her mind made no sense; she could not piece the scattered memory flashes together. *Had someone broken into the hotel, had she been drugged and raped? That would explain the distorted recollection,* she thought hysterically. The latter seemed the only coherent explanation, yet somehow that possibility did not make sense, did not feel right. Instinct assured that that had not occurred, yet logic was unable to fathom why she was ruling out the possibility. Her head hurt, and her eyes stung with the tears threatening to spill down her blood-drained cheeks. *What was happening to her? What* ***had*** *happened?'* She thought her head pounding, her throat constricting with mounting hysteria. She tried to calm down, rationalize; think of an alternative possibility.

The other possibilities that sprung to mind being preposterously outrageous; a dream had impregnated her, that her pregnancy was some kind of Immaculate Conception...

The moment Amanda returned to the hotel she rushed up the stairs to the second floor and locked herself in her room. She flung herself on the bed and tried to shut her eyes to the world, to confusion. She wished to sleep, curl up in a tiny ball and disappear, wake up again to her 'normal' world. She kept tossing from side to side, trying to get comfortable under the patchwork quilt hoping she would eventually relax into sleep, find peace for a while, but the arms of Morpheus kept eluding her. A knock on her door alerted her to an imminent dilemma, *what was she going to tell everyone? She hated having to lie; she had never been good at lying.* Quickly, she probed her mind for alternatives. She could not find any. Anything would be a lie; she could not convey a truth she did not hold. Two lonely tears slid down her pallid cheeks, she would not be able to conceal the evidence too long. Abortion had been a transitory contemplation. She felt terribly guilty having allowed such a thought, even if it had been an ephemeral one borne out of despair. She could never kill life; God had not made her that way.

At the sound of the insistent knock on her bedroom door, she brushed away her tears, composed herself and got out of bed. It was Maria; she was aware of her visit to the doctor and wished to know what he had told her. The short dark-haired woman walked silently into the shadowy room and gently placed a tray holding hot soup on the night table. Without uttering a word, she headed for the window to the right of the bed and flung the navy wooden shutters open. The afternoon rays filtered into the room, and a crisp salty breeze invaded the musty air. When she was satisfied the room was light enough she turned and confronted Amanda's empty stare. Amanda sat quietly on the edge of the bed as Maria's dark almond eyes probed her. She knew Maria; she was a shrewd woman. She must be cautious. Her mind raced for words that rung with conviction, but she could barely hear herself think, as the rush from her heart pounded fiercely in her ears. For a moment, she was afraid she would break down and confess her outlandish story.

In an effort to gain time, she feebly asked Maria to fetch a blanket from the closet claiming she was cold; her voice merely a whisper. By the time Maria returned with the blanket and laid in on top of her, Amanda had managed to calm down. Serenely, she began to explain, with staged conviction, the doctor's diagnosis to her curious, perceptive friend. Evenly, she claimed her bout of nausea was nothing to worry about, a simple stomach bug that would disappear as soon as she went on a light diet and rested for a couple of days. Amanda watched Maria, waited with concealed apprehension for the dark beads recede, the puckered brow to relax.

Making Amanda promise her she would eat the soup, the petite dark woman left the room in silence. The expression on her face spoke volumes; she had not quite believed her. Amanda lay inert on the bed as dismal eyes stared at the hot soup on the night table that turned as cold as her flesh.

Curled in a foetal position she lay still, engulfed by the night, a hostage to her dark world. She clutched her pillow tight with both hands, and buried her face in the cushioning comfort that soaked her lament. She held on to it fiercely as if it were a life jacket, her only hope in a drowning sea of despair until exhaustion finally surrendered her to sleep. She floated in limbo, until hazy images began to emerge, focus measured into clarity.

She was in his room, lying nude on his bed, flushed, expectant. Rows of candles flickered around her, casting dancing shadows upon her yielding flesh. She felt his eyes lowering down on her, mesmerizing turquoise suns delving deep into her soul. She felt his strong arms pulling her against his chest, the sound of his heartbeat pulsing life into her own. His lips claiming hers as her body quivered with a surge of emotion so intense tears welled to flood her glowing cheeks. Tremors of ecstasy ran the length of her body, as the silver light enveloping her merged with the incandescent white enveloping him. The 'auric eggs' fused into one, the oval energy field exploding with a blinding pure light edged in luminous silver. As she lay in his ardent embrace, listening to his heartbeat echo her own inside the vibrant bubble, Amanda surrendered all that she was, all that she dreamt, all she had ever dreamt...

Although the dream could not be remembered by morning, endured as an impression of a dream, Amanda woke to a strange vitality. The morning sickness had evaporated and tribulation no longer interrupted her sleep. The enigma of her pregnancy was still unresolved but she determined to face the unalterable reality as best she could.

For the first couple of weeks, Amanda hid her growing secret under loose clothing, but by the sixteenth week, even her baggy attire was getting tight. It was time to put her plan into action.

*Seth loved the valley. He had visited the Forest Dwellings, the Mountaintop Dwellings and the Island Dwellings but to him, nothing equalled its luscious splendour. Nestled between colourful hills that run down to meet it, it lay serene, except for the gurgling sound of the crystal gush that ran its course far into the horizon where the sloping multicoloured V held the morning star each day. He loved tumbling down the vibrant carpet onto the emerald lawn that turned to a white quartz cobbled path leading to every dwelling. He loved to float in the crystal waters that lulled him to daydream.*

*He loved his home. The quaint whitewashed cottage circled by the garden his mother lovingly tended to perfection. A tall silver-leafed oak tree with ivory trunk shaded each dwelling's garden and each cradled a tree house built for their young by doting fathers. The tree house was Seth's sanctuary, where he dreamt, where he learned to fly high above the ground lost in magical thoughts.*

*Seth had always been different from the other young ones. He looked different, he acted different. His turquoise eyes always inquisitive, under eyebrows permanently arched in question. His blonde curls eternally dishevelled; his pale skin persistently stained with the soil that clung to his white robe on daily tumbling exploits. His mother lovingly nicknamed him, her 'little rebel', for though he exasperated her with his everyday adventures, that mostly made him late for dinner and exhausted her with his interminable questioning, he was her pride and joy. He was constantly bringing her flowers from the slopes, showering her with kisses the minute he walked in through the door from school. He never complained when she asked him for help with household chores. His rebellious façade hid a warm caring heart.*

*Every night before he went to bed Seth helped his father, a Master in the Halls of Knowledge; a white oblong columned building situated at the end of the valley, fill his bag with the scrolls he took to class each day. His father was a dedicated and responsible man but a bit absent minded.*

After careful meditation, Amanda finally came up with a plausible story. Hoping her tale was credible enough, she left the hotel, early one morning towards Claire's snug cottage burrowed in the dense forest edging the town.

At twenty-one, Amanda was still a virgin. She was not closed-minded. She had simply never been in love. Her chastity was a secret she kept from her close friend, who would have branded her freak of the 21st century. Amanda and Claire were very different. Whilst Amanda was sensible and extremely responsible, Claire was the antithesis. She was impetuous and rebellious. Their parents had been close friends and they had grown up together. None of them had siblings so they had found a sister in each other. Their contradicting personalities did not challenge their relationship. Amanda's serene temperament curtailed Claire's recklessness and Claire's impulsive and fun loving nature ensured Amanda was not a recluse surrounded by books.

Amanda was stunning. With dreamy, almost translucent blue eyes set in an angelical face and golden curls, which cascaded softly to her slender waist. She was even more beautiful on the inside, but her introvert nature made her appear standoffish to men. Claire often chastised her friend on the fact she did not accentuate her womanly attributes. That her irrefutable beauty would make any male fall prey, if she finally engaged the art of flirting.

Claire was a striking redhead, feline and voluptuous with slanted intelligent green eyes that were always alert. She kept urging Amanda to wear makeup, to let her beautiful golden hair loose, to wear some figure hugging clothes that emphasized her elegant curves. Amanda was not interested. She had other priorities. The distance learning business degree she had embarked on and working at the hotel full time left little time for what she labelled as 'superficial stuff'.

Claire was in her garden, painting as usual, on a sunny Saturday morning. During the week, she worked as a bank clerk. She hated having what she termed a 'mediocre job', but it paid her bills. Painting was her real passion, her first ambition in life. She believed herself a free spirit; abhorred the trivialities of life; the restrictions society's fabric placed on her emancipated soul. Her second ambition was finding that soul mate who shared her passionate and feral nature. She talked to Amanda incessantly about the art exhibition she would finally be presenting in the Town Hall in early autumn. She had highlighted 15th October in fluorescent yellow on her kitchen calendar, with the caption 'the beginning of my real life'.

Amanda knew how important the exhibition was to her friend; the Town's Mayor was a close friend of Claire's father and had managed to pull a few strings. A respected critic from the highest echelons of the world of art would be attending, and Claire knew very well that the moment had come to prove she was a talented painter. Fortunately, for Amanda, Claire believed in herself, and she had not had to deal with moments of despair due to faltering confidence. If anyone could fulfil a lifelong dream that would be her friend, and she had to admit Claire's talent was undeniable.

Claire's artistic flare had been evident since kindergarten, but so had her rebellious nature. Amanda could not remember a single occasion when her friend had drawn or painted a picture she had been told to. A lifelong stream of incensed teachers had suffered her artistic 'madness' yet every one of them admitted she would probably become the artist she augured she would be. Her natural talent and stubborn determination would consummate the dream.

The moment Amanda caught sight of her friend, her paint splattered shirt, tousled hair and red, puffy eyes, testimony of her Friday night jaunts, she knew her plan would not fail.

The moment she reached the garden gate, Claire began to excuse herself, claim unconvincingly, her impending exhibition had occupied every spare moment... Amanda was no fool; there was another man in her friend's life, another candidate to be scrutinized as a possible soul mate. She said nothing and smiled inwardly. Clare's predictable self-centeredness would be the unsuspecting accomplice.

The dates matched perfectly. The gods had been merciful on one account. The night of their last escapade together approximately two months earlier awarded the solution to the pressing problem of who had fathered her child. Claire had insisted for days that Amanda accompanied her on a double date. She had met Mark at work the week before, he was a database programmer contracted by the bank to update their IT Network. The moment she had set eyes on the handsome prey, she had gone for the kill.

Mark conveniently had a friend, Lucas. He was a teacher and did not work during the summer months hence, had accompanied his friend to town. Claire had immediately arranged to hook him up with Amanda, claiming to her friend that she **truly** liked Mark, that he was different from the guys she usually dated. Amanda had laughed at her vehemence; Claire always 'truly' liked them all. A couple of dates later she would determine them 'mediocre' and ditch them. Exhausted by her friend's relentless persecution she had finally given in and agreed to the blind date.

The two couples met up for dinner in a cosy bistro off the Main Street. Lucas was a pleasant, nice looking young man, but his stream of corny jokes had made Amanda want to scream, leap out of her seat, head for home, for the book she was longing to finish. She regretted having given in to her persuasive friend. She should have known better. The long stream of dating fiascos should have been argument enough. Lucas persevered with his cliché jokes oblivious to his date's frustration. Amanda kept glancing at her watch, at her friend. Claire, engrossed in her own date, ignored Amanda's hints at cutting the evening short.

Claire had suggested they go to the town's nightclub after dinner. Dance the night away. The minute they walked out of the restaurant, Amanda alleged she had developed a sudden headache. Loud music, flashing lights were out of the question.

Claire, who was flirting outrageously with her latest victim, hopped into a taxi, offhandedly ordered Lucas to take Amanda's home in another taxi, and disappeared without even showing concern for her friend's headache. Lucas, obviously taken by Amanda's beauty, had been immensely disappointed. Disillusion patent on his face, he had hailed the next taxi and taken Amanda home.

During the ride home, neither of them spoke. Amanda pressed her forehead with her hand signalling talking would not help her pain. He did not speak. He was uncomfortable with the situation. They were after all strangers, who had only known each other for a couple of hours. Once outside the hotel Amanda quickly thanked him for a wonderful evening, gave him a consoling peck on the cheek moaning the headache was killing her, rushed inside and quickly shut the door. She had not wished to linger, afraid he would ask to see her again. She did not like hurting people; prolong a hope that was inexistent. Leading people on was not in her nature. Unsuspecting to Amanda, the fleeting encounter would turn out to be the red herring she would need to deflect a 'truth'.

Claire left her brushes on the ledge of the easel and invited her friend into the cottage. As Amanda sat quietly at the kitchen table, Claire retrieved a jug of iced tea from the fridge and sat down beside her. She eyed Amanda suspiciously. She had hardly spoken a word since she had arrived. She looked drawn; her eyes lacked the usual lustre. Something was up.

It was a beautiful day; a pleasant breeze caressed and the skies were a clear, vibrant blue. Claire suggested they drink their tea on the porch. *Amanda could do with some fresh air,* she thought. Amanda, who had become livelier the moment they had sat outdoors, listened attentively to Claire's ideas on her imminent debut. The conversation had changed to other idle matters when, Amanda suddenly looked Claire steady in the eye and spilled the shocking news.

Claire could not give credit to what she was hearing. *Pregnant? How? When? By whom?* She thought frantically, struggling to hold back the screaming questions. Unflinchingly, Amanda began to narrate the convenient story to her stunned friend. She spoke quietly, her confession resonating with required emotional charge, her eyes fixed unwaveringly on Claire's eyes. She told her of the night Lucas had taken her home, how he had stayed the night. Claire could not believe her friend had been so careless, that she had gotten pregnant from a one-night stand. *Amanda, the epitome of responsibility pregnant?* She was gobsmacked.

It was obvious from the onset there would be no father. Lucas had left and was not coming back, had found no reason. Claire mulled over the implications. Amanda would be a single mother, left alone to raise her baby and abortion was not an option. She knew Amanda. She also knew her friend would never tell Lucas. She had not agreed to see him again when he had called. Amanda made Claire swear she would not divulge her condition to anyone, knowing it was a promise her friend would not keep. Amanda knew Claire well; her friend had a big heart but an equally big mouth. Claire would never disclose the father's identity, as that **would** constitute a disloyalty, the rest of the story would spread like wildfire within the walls of the Seaview. The seeds of her plan had been sown; **she** would not have to tell a soul, **she** would not have to lie. Everyone would believe her best friend's story. It was common knowledge Amanda confided everything in her best friend... almost everything.

As hoped, in less than twenty-four hours, everyone at the Seaview knew Amanda was pregnant. After the initial shock, everyone was supportive; impertinent questions avoided. They knew better; Amanda had been through enough. She would tell them who the father was in her own time, if she wished, was the consensus.

The secret out, Amanda began to relax. After the initial shock, the news of a baby filled everyone with new hope and joy. Maria and Lucy doted on Amanda like two expectant grandmothers. Jason was secretly overjoyed there was no father looming on the horizon. *Perhaps now that Amanda was to become a mother she would give him a chance. Perhaps she would finally consider him more than a friend, realise, she needed him, needed a father for her baby...* With these wishful thoughts, he set out to help the woman he loved in everything he could. He covered the reception after lunch so Amanda could lie down, rest for a couple of hours and, together with Lucas, became her shadow. They watched her like hawks ensuring she did not engage in any strenuous activity. Everyone showered her with gifts; a crib, a pram, clothes, soft toys, toiletries, etc., helped her transform the room connected to her own into a beautiful nursery. Amanda had moved from her room in the second floor to room number seven on the first floor. Room number seven was the only one that enjoyed a communicating door to a single room.

Amanda left the hotel early; she had an appointment with Dr Reynolds at noon. She wished to stop in town before going to the clinic and buy some things she still needed for the baby. Her baby, her own flesh and blood, the sound of those words now filled her with immeasurable joy. The initial confusion and shock had numbed her emotions. Subsequently, the knot in her stomach had been a constant reminder of her growing situation. Once the nauseating feeling had subsided, she had managed to block out the reality of her predicament by immersing herself in work. For most of the day, she had consciously forgotten her dilemma, had gone about her chores unperturbed by worry. It was when she had been alone in her room, surrounded by dark, that anxiety gripped her again.

However, the false reality she had immersed herself in during the day had only been possible until her problem had begun to manifest physically; her bulging tummy becoming a perpetual reminder that awarded her tormented mind no truce. Coinciding with her move to the room on the first floor, her emotional state shifted, room number seven had a soothing effect on her. The moment her head rested on the pillow she fell asleep. Sleep was no longer broken, contaminated by nightmare.

As she began to grow bigger, her worries began to fade. Her maternal instinct began to surface, and wonderful unfamiliar emotions engulfed her. She found herself instinctively placing her hand on her swelling tummy, rubbing it gently, wondering what the tiny life forming inside her would look like.

For the first time in a long time, she felt renewed hope and the tragedies of the past began to dissipate like early-morning mist. The ghosts of her past no longer gripped her transition from slumber to reality. The gift inside her enabled her to face each new day with rapturous expectation. As she grew, the love for her baby grew, until finally, she had replaced every dark thought with light.

From the onset, she had chosen to see this life through, despite all her confusion, her fears. The road had been rocky, but here she was, eight months later, ecstatic at the thought of becoming a mother. For the first time in her life, her family would share her blood.

It was a hot August day. A heavenly sky stretched unblemished, and a warm wind kissed her face. She drove slowly, enthralled by the beauty of the tantalizing sea, coasting down to her left. She loved the sea; it resuscitated fond childhood memories. Memories of her parents, the generous souls that had made her part of their lives when her own flesh and blood had not wanted her. She missed them with every cell of her being. She would have given anything for them to be at her side, for them to see the birth of their grandchild. A gentle smile touched her lips as something deep inside her assured her, they would be with her when the time came. They would be watching, protecting them from heaven.

A sudden kick in her stretched womb interrupted the daylight reverie and she caressed her swollen nest lovingly. She was enormous. The doctor had reread the scan repeatedly. His initial suspicion, she might be expecting twins, was unfounded. The second heartbeat had been determined an echo of the first. Soon, very soon she would meet the little stranger who would become her world. A little boy, the doctor had assured her, though sometimes Amanda wondered if he was mistaken. Her instincts on the subject were contradictory; at times, she was certain it would be a boy and impulsively bought a bundle of blue clothes. Unexpectedly, she would change her mind and be convinced it would be a girl. Her drawers were full of blue and pink baby clothes.

As she drove slowly under the warm sun, her golden locks floating in the gentle breeze, her thoughts drifted to the beautiful nursery room everyone had helped decorate, to the rocking cradle that would soon hold her baby, and she smiled.

The smile curving her lips turned to frozen scream as she saw the truck hurling towards her out of thin air...

The sound of her screaming woke her. She was crouched on a white bed, dressed in a white robe, her knees bent. The pushing sensation in the lower part of her womb was uncontrollable, the pain in her back excruciating. The encouraging squeeze of a hand accompanied the waves of pain, the laboured breathing. She turned her head to the side, looked up at the translucent blue eyes reassuring her. She looked down at the foot of the bed and saw, whom she assumed was, the doctor. The transparent blue eyes over the white mask oscillated between the monitor situated to her right and her heaving belly. Realization sunk in; she had survived the accident. They were okay. Her baby was okay. All she needed now was to push with all her might and bring him safely into the world.

Suddenly, the hand of comfort disentangled itself from grip, and the nurse fled the room. Something was wrong. Within seconds, she returned. Two nurses and another doctor accompanied her. They circled the bed, and solemn crystalline eyes glanced uneasily at each other. Something was terribly wrong. 'My baby...' She cried.' My baby...'

*A*fter what seemed an eternity, one of the doctors approached her and sat on her bed, his clear blue eyes grave, his strong fingers curled over her trembling hand as he began to speak. The tempered words echoed the bare white walls to ice her veins. *No!* She thought. *This could not be happening. They had not survived the accident to be separated by death in a hospital bed.*

She fought to regain control of her senses, she had heard wrong... She strained to understand the words he repeated patiently until the dooming words resounded in the air with clarity. There was a choice to be made and without a breath of hesitation she made it...

Amanda opened her eyes, her vision hazy. She blinked, trying to discern the dreamlike surroundings. The sterile white walls had begun to disintegrate, turn to luminous dust revealing a beautiful exotic garden unlike any she had ever witnessed. Delicate flowers of unusual hue and texture edged her hospital bed. Perplexed, she gazed at the coloured array swaying to caress the white sheets in a nonexistent wind. She had never seen such breathtaking beauty, had never smelt such sweet fragrance.

She sat up. The hospital robe was gone, a silken white robe cloaked her tingling body, floated about her in the warm gentle breeze that suddenly brushed the heady air, in the soft mist evaporating between the singular buds. Her ears rang with a fluttering, cooing sound that soon manifested as flying doves amidst the fragrant blooms. They circled over her head for a while then finally stooped to perch on the rocky edge of a gleaming waterfall suspended in mid-air.

The white light that emanated from the gurgling curtain lit up the remarkable garden that stretched endlessly to a silvery blue mist. *What was this place? Was she dreaming?* It was then that she noticed the silhouette emerging towards her from the cloudy distance. As it moved closer, she saw it was a man, clad in a similar robe. She narrowed her eyes, focused on his features as he approached and her heart skipped a beat; he was the man she had seen the night of the storm, the man in her dream...

She gazed at him with swelling confusion. *Who was this man? Why did he keep invading her dreams?* Bemused eyes fixed on his beautiful face, on eyes that had begun to smoulder with a sapphire glow. As she gazed deep into them, she felt a familiar stirring in her soul, a whispering memory trying to reach her from a distant place. It was not until he stood at the edge of her bed that she noticed the white bundle he carried in his arms. Without speaking, he placed it gently on the bed in front of her and backed a short distance away, his eyes smiling at her with infinite tenderness.

The sound of faint footsteps made her spin her head. Two figures headed towards her from the smoky breadth. As they neared, focused rapidly into view, she was stunned beyond words. *It was impossible; her parents were dead, gone...* She felt suddenly faint, her heart beating uncontrollably as she absorbed the scene. Somehow, they did not feel like a dream, a mirage borne of wish. Her parents seemed vividly real as they slowly approached to stand holding hands at the foot of her bed. *What was happening to her? Who had instigated the macabre joke...?*

She looked at the man standing in front of her, and he nodded his head in assent, his crystal blue eyes reassuring. She gazed at her parents. They smiled at her adoringly, their glistening eyes reflecting the golden hue swathing them all, and then smiled down at the gift laid before her. She wished to feel them, wrap herself in their protective love. It had been so long... she had missed them so much...

As she watched them, the impossibility of the scene plunged her further into confusion. Reason wrestled with longing; she was immersed in a dream she did not wish to wake from, a mirage concocted by her yearning soul that had somehow transmuted to solid reality; a miracle. Instinctively, her eyes returned to the fluffy bundle before her. Tears of joy spilled down her expectant face as tentative hands picked it up from the bed and nestled it cautiously in her arms, against her racing heart.

Cocooned in the white cloth was the most beautiful sleepy face she had ever seen, the face she had dreamt of for so many months. She stared down at him, marvelling at the sleeping little being who was an extension of her. With trembling hands and an awed expression, she placed him gently back on the bed, tenderly pulled back at the soft white cloth revealing her son in perfection. Gleaming eyes gazed up at her parents; gleaming eyes returned her gaze. She could not comprehend how it was possible her parents were there, with her, with her baby, but she did not care. All she cared about was that she had been granted her wish had that they were beside her, sharing the most important moment of her life, as she had somehow known they would.

Her confusion, subdued by acceptance, she caressed her son's soft pink flesh, his golden wispy curls. Her heart brimmed with gratitude, with boundless love. As her fingers trailed his cheeks to his chest, his heart, he stirred in his sleep. It was then she saw them; the white silver tipped wings peeping from behind him. He stretched in yawn, and the small wings stretched beneath him. At the sight of the wings, Amanda remembered everything...

Claire was having lunch in a little bistro opposite the bank on the Main Street when, Dr. Reynolds approached her, a troubled expression clouding his habitual smile. Omitting usual pleasantries, he asked her if she had seen or spoken to Amanda that morning. Amanda had not turned up for her eleven o'clock appointment. Claire shared the doctor's concern. Amanda never missed an appointment. Alarm creeping over her face, she rang Amanda's cell phone. There was no reply. She rang the hotel, but strangely, no one picked up the phone.

Without stopping to inform staff at the bank where she was going, she hailed a taxi and headed to the Seaview. Something was seriously wrong. She could feel it in her gut. As she sat in the back of the taxi, her thoughts kept revisiting the most horrendous scenes. *Stop it!* She thought impatiently. *Amanda was fine; Amanda was fine…* she repeated, the mantra helping to dispel the foreboding images.

The taxi had just turned the junction, was twisting down the road leading down to the cove, when suddenly, ahead, in the distance she saw the police had barricaded the road. Her chest began to heave, drum erratically. Her hands began to sweat, shake uncontrollably. As the taxi rolled slowly towards the blockade, she found herself praying. They were a short distance from the barrier, when she saw a lorry lay toppled on its side, behind the makeshift fence. It lay right on the curve, on the edge of the cliff overlooking the quiet seas. Frantically, Claire searched for Amanda's car, but it was nowhere to be seen.

She felt her body relax. *The police had closed the road due to the accident. Amanda had turned around and headed back to the hotel,* she thought relieved. Lost in these heartening thoughts she sank against the leather as the car began to turn around in the direction of town.

As the taxi made the three-point turn, a disquieting thought gripped her. *Why had no one at the hotel picked up the phone?* She barked at the driver to stop the car, jumped out with the dexterity and fury of a wild cat, and raced, adrenalin pumping, in the direction of the barrier. Two policemen intercepted her. Claire fought them, disentangled herself from their grip, raced to the edge of the cliff and looked down. As her eyes drank in the unbearable scene a blood-curling scream pierced the lugubrious air. Before anyone had time to reach her, she plummeted to the ground.

Maria, Lucy, Peter and Jason stood frozen, watched horror-struck from the distance.

Claire was inconsolable. Amanda, her sister, was gone and never coming back. The days following the funeral were a nightmare. She ambled zombie-like, unable to digest the enormity of the tragedy, the unbearable reality. The image of Amanda's car floating in the sea kept haunting her. The fact her body had not been found, added to the tragedy.

The police had been baffled; the sea was dead calm, and the seatbelt had not been unfastened. Witnesses to the accident had immediately called for help, and it had taken minutes for the police to arrive at the scene. No one had seen a body float up to the surface. The divers, who had arrived barely a quarter of an hour after the traffic police, could not understand how there was no sign of the body. The ocean had swallowed her, had swallowed all trace of her. A full-scale search had ensued to no avail.

The funeral service was a traumatic event; the service did not include a coffin.

Like Claire, everyone at the Seaview was devastated. No one could accept Amanda and the baby were gone, cruelly snatched from their lives forever. Jason was heartbroken; he could not believe he would never see Amanda again. He cursed himself for the time lost, for his cowardice. *Life was ephemeral, death, a traitor to the immortality of youth*, he philosophized. *He had not had 'all the time in the world' to tell her how he felt…*

Maria, Lucy and Peter mourned for their lost child. They spent endless days secluded in their respective rooms at the hotel every one of them wishing the Angel of Death had chosen them instead. They were not getting any younger, had weathered many storms in their lives, but this last blow had been brutal. Like Claire and Jason, they no longer had the strength to continue with Amanda's dream. There was no point; she was no longer part of the dream, no longer part of their lives. The hotel was shut down.

A couple of weeks after the funeral, Claire announced she was leaving town, claiming she had had enough of her banking days and was ready to try her luck as a 'real' artist. Everyone knew otherwise. She was running away. She could not conceive a life in the little town that held so many memories of Amanda, of their lives together. She left one day without saying goodbye. She left no forwarding address.

Amanda had had the foresight to leave a will. She had decided to when she had found she was pregnant. *'In case anything happened...'*, she had told them. *'Soon I will be a mother…'* the dooming words still rang in their ears.

The hotel was bequeathed to her 'family' in equal shares. The moment Claire, Jason, Peter, Maria and Lucy left the lawyer's office they made arrangements to sell it. None of them could keep what had become theirs by default. The Seaview had been meant for Amanda's child.

A multinational company that owned a string of coastal hotels bought the Seaview. The only items the 'family' took from the hotel other than personal belongings were Amanda's photo albums, which they divided amongst themselves. A hefty sum was received by each in exchange for their shares.

Jason decided to leave town and travel for a year. He needed to forget, return when he could only remember the good memories. The special moments he had shared with Amanda, his love. He stayed away for five years.

Lucy, Maria and Peter retired, brought three seaside apartments in the same residential complex and helped each other survive their grief. In each apartment, the exact photo of Amanda adorned their living rooms. She was immersed in the sea, her eyes luminously alive, her golden hair floating in the wind, as waves foamed behind her.

Claire did not say goodbye to her friends, could not say goodbye. Her parents had insisted she should stay, that she needed to be with her family. Claire was adamant. She had to leave, escape, if she was to maintain her sanity. The little town strangled her; every corner, every face evoked the past, prompted memories as curse.

Every night was invaded by the same nightmare; she was standing on a cliff, looking down at the coal darkness. Amidst the deafening roar of the ocean she could hear a faint scream, the muffled cry of a baby. It was Amanda, Amanda and her baby calling out to her to save them. She plunged in, desperately searching the murky, agitated waters but could not find them. As she hopelessly explored the muddy turbulent currents she gasped for air, felt herself drown… then, she would wake up bathed in cold sweat, in dread.

It was one morning, after yet another 'familiar' nightmare that she decided to leave. Packing a small suitcase with clothes and a larger one with painting utensils, she called a taxi and headed for the city. She had not wished to take her car; the red mini she had driven so many times around the homely town with Amanda; she had not kept a single memento of her friend.

Claire had no clue where she was heading but the money she had inherited ensured she could settle quickly and safely. She had hated her nine to five job, had wished to devote herself to her painting. The irony was sadistic; now that her dream had become tangible she could not help wishing she was back at the bank. In the 'mediocre' job that had been part of her life, the life she shared with Amanda.

Immediately after the funeral she had cancelled her upcoming exhibition; she could never have managed it without her sister being there. She did not have the strength. Jason had pleaded her to go with him, but she had refused. She needed to get away from everyone she had shared with Amanda. She needed to stay away from those who mentioned her name. Her younger sister's death defied the natural order of things; she must escape a world that was an unremitting reminder of the cruel unpredictability of life. The first nights in the city she had stayed in a Hotel. By the end of the week she was the owner of a loft located in its outskirts. It had belonged to an artist and incorporated a light and airy studio. It was one year before Claire could paint again.

*Seth woke up early. He loved the Seventh Day; no school, no chores, only fun. Most seventh days he accompanied his parents to visit friends in other dwelling lands. His mother preferred the Island dwellings. She loved the sea, the peaceful white shores that edged the perfect circles of pastel flowered lands floating in equal distance to each other. Bridges of light, resembling glowing crescent moons, joined them. Each one joined to a larger centre island. The Halls of Healing, a large dome made of diamond-shaped glass panels, stood at its heart; a huge polished diamond amidst the soft, coloured circles. Domelike-whitewashed dwellings surrounded the perfect round ponds, rimmed by glistening white pebbles. Beautiful waterfalls fed them, the burbling sheets hanging suspended in the air.*

*His mother loved to bathe in the balmy, limpid seas swarming with playful silver blue dolphins; the highly intelligent and spiritual creatures that communicated in the angelic language. She loved playing with him on the shore, searching for seashells of every shape, colour and sound. Seth preferred the ivory conches. He liked the echo of the ocean. His mother preferred the metallic aqua ones, the ones that soothed with the inspiring sound of the violins. The silver starfish that echoed the wishing songs of the universe were also their favourite. They kept a collection at home, proudly displayed on the windowsills. At night, they loved to sit on the porch sharing their sounds.*

*His father preferred the Forest Dwellings. A vast forest located between the valley and the ruby field. Noble trees cradled the wooden dwellings, replicas of his garden tree house built to a larger scale. The trees rose majestic, pinning the forest in a myriad of shimmering colours; silver leaves on gold trunks, purple leaves on brass trunks, emerald leaves on ivory trunks. In a clearing in the heart of the forest stood the Halls of Growth, a circular, three-storey logged building with winding verandas on each level. The Mountaintop Dwellings, a blooming paradise, home to the gentle messenger doves, connected to the Sky Dwellings by a cloudy staircase, housed the Halls of Travel and schools.*

*None of them had ever seen the Sky Dwellings, home to the Golden Palace, where the light was so bright it hurt your eyes. Supermalls, Celestials and Illuminations; non-tangible angels of extreme purity and light formed the angelic trinity, custodian of the Source; the Throne situated at the heart of the resplendent Palace. The Supreme Masters of light were an extension of the Throne, the whole of existence, and shed divine will, wisdom and light down to the next orders of angels able to manifest in the physical realms. Seraphim, Cherubim and Thrones, the Higher Masters of light, the second sphere of angels were also allowed to visit the Sky Dwellings, but only Seraphim were allowed inside the palace. The extremely tall angel's primary function was to keep the Throne in perpetual love and adoration. The crystal gardens upon cloudy soil, surrounding the palace, demarcated the frontier for Cherubim and Thrones.*

*Dominions, Virtues and Powers; the Elders, the third sphere of angels, were allowed access up to the crystal gates of the sparkling garden. Principalities and Arch Angels; the Masters; the fourth sphere of angels, could visit the sky dwellings on extremely rare and special occasions. They must await instructions from the higher angels, on the edge of the bridge of light connecting the cloudy path, to the misty grounds guarding the divine sanctuary. Before they did, they had to prepare exhaustingly in the Halls of Healing in order to tolerate the intense vibration of the elevated dwellings. Angels, the lower order of the triad, could not enter the blinding Dwellings, their low resonation rendered them incapable of withstanding the concentrated light. Seth often dreamed he would go there one day.*

*Lael's father was a Master in the Halls of Healing. Every working day, he travelled to the Islands. Seth and his friends did not know much about their parents' work. The rules prohibited parents to talk with their young ones about the nature of their work, until they matured; graduated from the Halls of Knowledge. They only knew the essentials; Seth knew that his father taught students, as Master Joram taught him. What his father's classes were about, he did not have a clue. He had secretly tried to read his books, but he had not understood their strange language. The secretiveness of the realm frustrated Seth, but try as he may, the secrets remained secrets. The realm functioned with utmost discipline. No one had access to information inappropriate to his or her status. Lael did not know much about his father's work either. He knew he travelled to the Islands, knew he was a healer, how or who he healed was a mystery. He did not even know what the word 'healer' actually meant. Unlike Seth, he did not care. One day he would know, he could wait until then. None of the three friends knew what Zeriel's father did every day in the forest.*

*Each working day, their mothers left the valley for work; some went to the Forest Dwellings, some to the Island Dwellings and some to the Mountaintop Dwellings. Seth's mother remained at home. She took care of her family, their home, the garden she was so devoted to, except for the sixth day when she left for the Mountaintop Dwellings at first light, and returned late at night. He had heard his parents whisper when they had thought he was asleep, knew that his mother was part of 'The circle of light', housed in the Temple of Light. As was the case of the other mothers, Seth had no clue what she did there, or what the 'Circle of light' was.*

*Seth had tried to persuade his mother to share the reason why she left home every sixth day to no avail.* **'When you're older, you will understand the ways of our world... you will have to wait until then'.** *She had repeated often, exasperated by his unappeasable curiosity. Seth had been tempted to follow her, but ultimately, decided against it. His mother did not deserve to be sneaked up on. He was glad his mother did not leave, like the other mothers, to work in other dwelling lands every day. He loved that she was nearly always home waiting for him when he came home from school.*

*Seth had plans for that afternoon. His friends were coming to visit, and his mother had made them an apple pie for tea. She had picked the golden apples from their tree in the garden that very morning. Although it was the Seventh Day, his father had to work. Students were graduating from the Halls of Knowledge, and he would be there for most of the day. Seth could not accompany his father. No one could enter the Halls of Knowledge or any hall until they had come of age. His mother had been invited to attend the graduation, but had not wished to leave Seth alone at home.*

*After tea, Seth led his friends to the tree house. They wished to be alone, talk about their things. They sat on the narrow veranda, their short white robes pulled tight over their thighs, so they would not be grazed by splinters, their sandaled feet dangling over its edge as they observed the gentle doves fluttering playfully on the twinkling surface of the river not far from the garden gate.*

*When Lael and Zeriel heard Seth's adventure proposal for the afternoon, they branded him a lunatic. They would not accompany him; infringe the law, if caught, the punishment would be severe. Seth who was accustomed to having his own way kept insisting, but they would not give in to any of his desperate pleas. It was only when he used the magic word, 'coward', that they finally relented. At the accusation that they were two scared little sissies, they sprang up on to their feet and dared Seth to jump off the tree. Seth grinned with secret satisfaction as he stood up. To the count of three, they jumped off the wooden balcony, spread their wings wide and flew high up into the sky.*

*It was on her first mission, her initial journey to the mortal world, after she had graduated from the Halls, that Amanda had made the terrible mistake. The mistake that had cost her dearly, had separated her from her love. Anton had warned her. He knew how impulsive, sensitive she was and had tried to convince her she was not ready, that she should rejected the elder's request. That she needed more time, that missions could wait until she had fully matured, was ready beyond shadow of doubt. Amanda had disagreed. She had graduated at the top of her class in most disciplines, and when the elders had requested her hall masters to allow her to partake in a mission, she had been ecstatic.*

*Her mission had a name, Christina, an eighteen-year-old, mortal girl who had lost her way. Escaping from an abusive childhood, she had fled to the streets to walk the city's downtrodden areas, become trapped in a web of drugs and violence.*

*From the moment she had laid eyes on Christina, Amanda had felt her terrible anguish, her screaming pain; the light of her soul trapped in her suffering mind, a mind that had lost all hope of ever knowing joy. To Christina, the world was a dark place, with no silver lining. All her life she had suffered. As a child the hands who shared her blood had beaten on her without reason, without mercy, the bruises on her flesh had disappeared but the scars on her young heart remained. At fourteen, she had escaped her abusive family only to become a victim to unscrupulous hands who traded her in the underworld.*

*For days, Amanda had watched her die a little each day, watched the little light left in her soul dull down to an intermittent speck. Impatiently, she waited for her prayer. She wished to inspire her with the hope that would change her desperate life, help her lost soul find its way back to the light. Divine rules dictated no angel could intervene in a mortal's life journey unless invited to do so. Mortals had free will. It was their God-given right. Humans held their destinies in their own hands. It was the law of the universe.*

*Thus, Amanda waited, and waited; frustrated that she could do nothing but watch the wretched girl disappear further into darkness. Time was running out. She knew what was coming. She knew what Christina had bought that afternoon from a drug pusher on a street corner. She knew her intention. She stood in the corner of the dingy motel room that reeked of urine and alcohol, watching the lonely girl with increasing impotence, as she sat on the soiled bed, hugging her knees, rocking back and forth, the fatal needle threatening on the floor. She heard the frail whispers of her soul trying to reach her ravaged heart. She watched the shaky hand pick up the syringe, as tears smeared the dirty, ashen face with sunken, dark rimmed eyes. She watched the needle caress her bony arm, her purple skin...*

*Christina's shaky hands dropped the needle to the ground; wide eyes stared incredulously at the blinding white light emanating from the corner of the dusky room. Amanda smiled, as the whispers from Cristina's soul turned to hymn; as the hollow eyes ignited with hope and tears of joy moistened her flushed face, as she knelt on the floor, her hands clasped in prayer. The young girl's eyes gazed deeply into the eyes of the miracle. The iridescent winged creature towering above her was the most beautiful sight she had ever witnessed. Amanda's eyes locked on the pleading orbs, nodded her head, then spread her wings until they spanned the width of the room. Gently, very gently she enveloped Christina with her soft wings.*

*Yes, she was the answer to her forgotten pleas. Yes, she would protect her, guide her towards the light. No, she did not think of the consequences.*

*Amanda smiled, her eyes closed, as she felt Christina relax in her arms, as she felt her soul glow with the truth, she had always been, her heart pulsing to the beat of renewed hope and faith, as she abjured darkness. Cristina had received the gift of light, a gift that would remain with her for the rest of her days. The light of the source had invaded every cell of her being, ensured the young girl would never be prey to obscurity, to sulphur souls again. Amanda cradled her in her arms, cocooned her in her wings, whilst she whispered her name repeatedly in the tongue of angels. When she was certain Christina was ready, she let go. The moment Amanda released Cristina from her embrace she was plunged into darkness.*

*The next time Amanda saw light, she was lying in a crib in the maternity ward of a hospital.*

*For twenty-two years, Amanda was condemned to walk a mortal, amongst mortals, with no recollection of who she was, whom she had left behind or what she had done. It did not matter that the mortal girl had transformed her desperate life, to one full of hope. She had transgressed the sacred rules of the Angelic realm.*

*It was Anton's desperation, which had finally made the Elders reconsider their punishment. After days of waiting, they summoned to the Mountaintop Dwellings, to the Golden Chamber in the Temple of light. Anton accepted their proposal, agreed to execute their plan. He missed Amanda, missed their life together and wanted her back. Anton knew Amanda would not fail; she would pass with flying colours. Amanda would make the greatest sacrifice a mortal could make, and she had. She had agreed to die so her son could live and had thus earned the right to return home.*

*Anton wished the elders had not summoned him again, had not made him party to the totality of her sacrifice. He wished they had spared him the burden of the secret that burned inside of him. He felt tremendous guilt at having to lie to Amanda, but consoled himself with the fact that he had had no choice. Amanda could never know the whole truth, breaking his oath, would have disastrous consequences for both Amanda and their son. He must protect them.*

*As Anton watched Seth grow, rejoiced at the happiness he brought into their lives, a constant feeling of emptiness tugged at his soul and often wished there had been some other way…*

Christina could not believe what had just happened. Still dazed, her eyes scanned the dark empty room. She glanced at the floor, at the syringe lying at her feet and kicked the deadly tool away from her in disgust. She did not need it any more, never would again. Quickly, she rummaged through her bag, for her purse. *She had enough money*, she thought, as her bony hands counted the crumpled notes. Gathering the few rags she possessed, she rushed out of the room. Frantically, she sped down the corridors of death, zigzagged between the slumped bodies infected with Satan's venom, rushed out the decrepit, putrid building and headed for the bus terminal down the road. With no idea where she was heading, she hopped on the first bus out of the city. After approximately two hours, the bus came to a halt, and the driver woke her up. *'End of the journey honey'*, he called out gently. Still sleepy, she walked into the warm night, into the little town she decided would now be her home.

As she ambled down the narrow, dimly lit streets, veining the sleeping town, she was not afraid. She would never be afraid again. She would make it, all she had to do was keep on the right path, walk in the light and her spirit would remain strong. Since the miracle, her heart felt warm, infused with faith. She was no longer a weakling, a prey for malevolent hands.

She was still a bit shaken by the apparition; she had never been a believer. She had never imagined angels could exist. They did. She had seen one, a beautiful one. Her eyes moistened as she remembered her face, her gentle sapphire eyes, her long golden hair, as she remembered her soothing melodic voice chanting her name. It had sounded so beautiful upon her lips. No one had made her feel like her angel had. No one has shown her love, that she could be loved. The emotions she had felt wrapped in her soft wings were so intense, overwhelming that for a minute she had thought she would faint. The euphoric feeling remained with her as she walked down the sleepy streets, she had never had felt happier. She had never been happy before, she reflected fleetingly, unperturbed.

Somehow, Christina knew she would never see her angel again. It did not matter, knowing she existed was sufficient. Knowing God had chosen her was more than enough. If God had sent an angel to save her, then he too must love her, did not think she was a bad person.

Holding that thought she headed for a diner at the far end of the silent road, sat down on one of the red plastic tables beside the glass façade running its length, and timidly ordered a hot chocolate. She was starving, but did not have enough money for food. As she sat quietly, watching the two storey houses basking in the tenuous glow of neon lining the pavements, she imagined the families sleeping peacefully inside them. It did not matter that she was alone, did not have a family. It did not matter that she felt hungry; her heart was filled to the brim.

She had been sitting quietly for a while when she noticed the waitress kept eyeing her furtively. Eventually, the short plump woman headed towards her menu in hand. Smiling, she handed her the menu and asked her squarely if she wished to eat. Christina's eyes skimmed the menu. '*No thank you. I'm not hungry*', she answered coyly, ravenous eyes contradicting her faint statement. Without uttering a word, the friendly woman turned briskly on her heels and headed back to the bar. Christina stared out the window again, gazed up at the starlit sky. Mesmerized, she watched the twinkling clusters lighting the universe, and she felt herself smile. *She had a friend up there,* she thought wistfully. *One she knew would always protect her…*

The sudden tinkering sound of a plate made her turn around. A burger and fries, a glass of orange juice and a piece of lemon pie, lay appetizingly before her. Surprised, she looked up at the large bosomed woman gazing at her intently. '*It's on the house*'. She declared, before Christina could voice an objection, then headed abruptly back to the bar. The minute she had returned behind the red counter, Christina's hungry hands grabbed the burger and began to devour it. *'Thank you'*, she called out softly, diffidently eyeing the blasé Samaritan and proceeded to finish off the tasty banquet. She had finished her meal when she noticed the motherly waitress head towards her again.

No, she did not have anywhere to spend the night. No, she had not run away from home. No, there was no family. An endless stream of questions ensued, and Christina found herself confessing her pitiful life to the kind stranger. Everything, but her miraculous encounter with an angel, that would remain a treasured secret.

Christina spent the night at the diner, the following day she had a job and a place to live in. A hotel located in a beautiful cove, not far from the town needed extra staff and had hired her immediately. Its owners, a young couple who had decided to leave the perils of the city for the safety of the small seaside town. They were hoping to start a family and wished to raise their child in a sounder, more adept environment.

Christina felt immediately at home in the Seaview. Her life changed dramatically. She put on weight, had a permanent smile on her rosy face and no longer felt an intruder in the world. The staff at the hotel treated her like family. For the first time in her short life, she had a family, felt loved. Every night, safe between the walls of her beautiful room located on the first floor, she read the bible, said her prayers. She thanked her guardian angel for her many blessings.

Olivia, the owner of the hotel, had not been able to get pregnant and after five years of marriage, the young couple managed to adopt a little girl who had been abandoned at St Thomas Hospital in the city. With the help of a family friend, Dr Reynolds, they had realized their most fervent wish. The doctor's help had been decisive in the adoption process. He was an affluent man and had spoken highly of the Caldwell's to Social Services, to the hospital director who was coincidentally a close friend of his. Christina still remembered the first time she had seen Amanda, looked down on her beautiful tiny face as her mother had carried her proudly into the lobby of the Seaview. Everyone at the hotel was immediately taken with the little angel that soon became central to their existence. Amanda's liquid blue eyes uncannily reminded Christina of her Angel's eyes.

Christina worked at the hotel until Amanda was eight years old, until she married Anthony. He was a local teacher who captivated her with his handsome face and noble heart. Her husband's salary had allowed her to leave work and take care of her home, but Christina visited the hotel often. She loved Amanda, had developed a special connection with the gentle and beautiful child. The moment she had set eyes on her delicate face, the almost transparent blue eyes framed by golden ringlets, she had felt the pulling energy. It was a feeling she could not verbalize, a feeling which curiously resuscitated the memory of her angel.

Amanda was eleven when Christina moved to the city. Christina had been thrilled when her husband was offered the post of principal at a public school in the city. She had not wished to leave the little town that had given her a second life, but would have followed Anthony to the end of the world. He was the other half that made her whole.

Christina looked forward to the regular phone calls, to the letters and photos Amanda constantly sent her. As Amanda grew up, Christina marveled at the growing coincidence; Amanda startlingly resembled her angel.

*The edge of the Sphere, the silver curved line that delineated the end of their world, the beginning of other worlds, lay beyond the valley, across the glittering forest, over the crimson fields. They had seen the curved frontier on the Universal Atlas at school. It was not that far away. They would never have ventured, if it had been. Their wings were not large or strong enough to cover long distances.*

*Zeriel and Lael were surprised at Seth's flight deftness Seth had still not attended travel class, yet it was he, who flew ahead and they were the ones who had trouble catching up with him. As they flew in his wake, they marvelled at the sparkling trail, the silver tipped wings shed in the sky.*

*Seth had not told his friends, but he had broken the rules many times. His nightly flight antics were a common occurrence. Since the first day his father pushed him from the edge of the tree house, he had flown. His initiation had been a success. His father had been very proud. His father would not have been as proud, if he had known that since that day, when Amanda and he were asleep, when everyone was asleep, he jumped from the tree house every night and soared over the confines of the valley for a while. Perhaps it was his wings, his friends had thought. They were different from their wings, from everyone's wings. Perhaps the silver tips made his wings stronger.*

*The three friends soared high over the valley, over the vibrant slopes, the lush green flats, the winding turquoise river. Up ahead, the landscape below transformed, and they had to beat their wings faster, climb higher, lest they collided against the sky reaching scintillating trees nailing the forest. They were exhausted. Their wings felt heavy. Perhaps they had been too presumptuous; perhaps they would not make it.*

*Suddenly, they saw it, at the end of the strawberry field that began where the forest ended. They gazed in awe at the convex silver boundary demarcating the end of their world, the frontier to the unknown. Exhausted, they sat on the edge of the forest, and looked uncertainly at each other.* **Were they really going to do this? Were they going to be that brave? It was a mistake; they should all go home,** *thought Lael and Zeriel.*

*Lael was the first to voice doubts, propose they returned home instantly, arguing they had already had their adventure. Zeriel concurred. Seth did not. He did not think the adventure had even begun. He stood defiant before his two friends and told them in a firm tone, he was going ahead with the plan even if they had chickened out.* **He had not come all this way for nothing. They could wait for him at the edge of the forest**, *he thought stubbornly. Neither Lael nor Zeriel said anything. They knew their friend. Once Seth was determined to do something, no one could persuade him otherwise. He was indomitable.*

*From the edge of the forest, they watched him fly over the field that began at their feet and was densely populated by scarlet blooms. Seth flapped his wings vigorously. He flew head on, unflagging towards his objective. Soon, he had become a mere dot on the horizon.*

*He was about to be swallowed by the silver curtain, when a sudden pang of fear gripped him. He shut his eyes tightly and flapped his wings quicker. It was too late for regrets. He would not succumb to fear. Nothing in the world would deter him. He was on the verge of making a discovery he had dreamt of for a long time, here and now lay his chance...*

*Since he had been very young, he had eavesdropped on his parents. Spied on the whispers that insinuated something extraordinary existed outside the silver bubble protecting their world. Curiosity had finally gotten the better of him. Determined, he flew on until the silver cloud of dust swallowed him. It was only then that he slowed down a little, overtaken by fear of the unexpected, by the sudden hindering particles of dust that floated around him grazing his wings. He shut his eyes tighter.*

*The grains continued to scrape his wings for a while longer, and as they stopped, a mellow breeze began to envelop him; the atmosphere inside the dusty lining began to feel lighter, and he felt himself float, the warm air holding him in suspension. As the tepid current carried him forward he relaxed, indulged in the pleasant feeling, in the strange unfamiliar heady smell. For what seemed a long time he floated, until suddenly, he felt the inviting warmth turn ice cold.*

*At the drastic change of temperature his wings instantly wrapped around his torso. He wanted to open his eyes but was afraid of what he would find. He felt himself float down, felt his feet touch soft ground. Slowly, very slowly, he lifted reluctant eyelids, and it was then that he saw it; the place he had heard his parents, the higher angels, whisper about in the quiet corners of the realm; the mortal world...*

*He stood frozen upon the cottony earth, looking ahead across a field, a grassy plain stretching infinitely.. Children without wings were playing some kind of sphere game a short distance away. They were laughing, shouting, kicking the sphere between themselves. He turned his head slightly and the field transformed. Light turned to darkness and men, clad in khaki green, scattered hostile rocky ground, their faces contorted in terror and anguish. Rivulets of fire poured from their hands. Balls of fire rained on them, and scarlet puddles patched the arid earth. The disturbing vision instinctively made him turn away and look in the opposite direction.*

*The field transformed again. Darkness metamorphosed to burning salmon. The field was now a beautiful golden sandy beach bathed by sunset skies. In the distance, a man and a woman held hands, kissed tenderly, delved deep into each other's eyes as they stood on the shore, against the heavenly scenery. He could feel their synchronized heartbeats thundering in his ears, the whispered words of love that rang with truth. He watched them in fascination, felt the euphoric emotion that united them body and soul.*

*A slight movement of the head spurred the next transformation. This time, the beach became a dark street, a gloomy cul-de-sac. Three boys were beating an old man cowering on the ground with wooden sticks. Their faces knotted in cruel twists. The screams of the poor defenceless soul, pierced the night, pierced Seth's soul.*

*The images kept turning, changing. He saw love, he saw hate... hope, despair... mourning, rejoicing..., loyalty, treachery... the fertile earths, the barren... the laughing children, the crying... the living... the dying... He saw man, and he wept...*

*For a long time, he stood upon the now empty field, petrified, like the statues that adorned his garden. He felt cold, tremulous, afraid. His hands covered his eyes and wings curved listlessly over his bowed head. He felt his soul weep, bleed with a thousand excruciating drops at the incomprehensible visions he had witnessed. He could not understand the incongruous nature of the mortal creature. He did not wish to see, hear, feel anymore. He did not wish to remember. All he wished to do was return home, back to the world he knew, back to the world in which there was only room for love. Still blinded by the hands pressing his eyelids, he spun around, sprung his wings open in one mighty swing and thrust back through the cloud of dust. He flapped through the powdered particles vigorously, his thoughts a swirl of confusion, carrying a heart that was heavy as stone. He could not wait to be out of the dusty frontier, back in his world, safely nestled against his mother's bosom.*

*As he spiralled through the misty layers, pushed through the sandy density, he could feel the grains scratching, scaring him. He knew he should slow down. He was damaging his beautiful wings, but he could not. He was too overwhelmed, broken, by what he had just witnessed. He needed to escape, cross the threshold into safety, escape the nightmare.*

*He was nearly home, about to free himself from the damaging ashen granules that tore at his wings when a bright white light blinded him, and an image flashed before his eyes; a blue and green orb hung suspended in space amidst a flickering universe. Suddenly, it began to disintegrate and the particles began to pour like sand, blow away into the distance of space. As it disappeared, mingled screams of terror echoed throughout its surface.*

*At last the opaque grey sky Mercifully turned blue. He was finally home.*

*Unknown to Seth, a feather, severed from his right wing, balanced on the last layer of the frontier, on the thin of the silver curve. It moved up and down, undecided between the two worlds; the glowing tips a mere speck amidst the immensity of the universe, until gently, it began to tip to one side. A rush of burning wind borne suddenly in the vast stillness disentangled it from the few particles trapping it. It floated outside the sphere for only a few seconds then, slowly, began whirling down to earth...*

Michael Jenkins was sitting in his ultra-modern black and silver office, reading the morning paper. He barely had time to read the headlines and quickly gulp down the cup of coffee his secretary had already placed on his desk at nine twenty nine. He liked his morning stimulant piping hot. He was in for a tough morning; Damian Roffe was a tough client, a self-made millionaire, who had turned his father's humble electronics shop to an Electronics Empire.

Roffe was accused of murdering his young wife. Michael prided himself on figuring out his clients. Roffe had been no different. He disliked Roffe the moment he had set eyes on him. The man believed himself to be God. Michael abhorred his arrogance but believed fervently in money, and this god had plenty of it. From the onset Michael knew he was guilty, but this fact did not bother him. He had a job to do and would do it exactly as he did all the other jobs entrusted to him by the firm. Winning was the name of the game. He always won, whatever it took.

The window behind his desk was open. He liked his room aired in the mornings, feel the crisp clean air that floated above the polluted currents one hundred and thirty storeys below. As he folded the newspaper neatly and placed it on the side of his desk, he noticed a feather had floated into the room. It circled towards him unhurriedly to descend languorously beside his glossy slate cup, sharply contrasting the opaque glass desktop. He grabbed the fluffy nuisance and threw it in the paper basket, got up, fetched his briefcase from the top of his metallic black filing cabinet and headed quickly to court. The verdict would be delivered in an hour.

The courtroom was packed, not a single seat was vacant; the tabloids had ensured morbid curiosity. It was time; the judge inspected the verdict, folded it neatly and asked the bailiff to hand it over to the foreman. The ticking clock over the entrance to the courtroom was the only sound that broke the funereal silence, a tense expectancy palpable as all eyes were fixed on the jury. Michael stood impassively beside Roffe as they both faced the jury. Roffe stood rigidly, his expression imperturbable. His phlegmatic facade hid terror; his leg jerking spastically under the table. Michael could smell the fear on him. The fear of being locked up in a place where he would not be God, where God did not exist. He despised the man, wished he could have let the arrogant bastard rot in jail, but money talked, and so had his ex-wife.

She had talked to the police, the prosecutor, to anyone who was willing to listen. She told them that Roffe was in her house, in her bed, at the time the murder had been committed. Her Swiss bank account had fattened considerably that very afternoon. As Michael had expected, the verdict was 'not guilty'.

The concocted alibi was not the only part of the plan that had ensured Roffe's 'innocence.' Michael rang Frank the moment he had hung up the phone with Roffe, who had called him from his car after he had fled the murder scene. Frank, his loyal and extremely well paid private investigator, had got rid of the murder weapon; the gun Roffe had used to kill his wife. Roffe had hidden it behind a stack of books in his library; his fingerprints and the victim's blood all over it. He had erased any trace of Roffe ever owning a gun, being in the house. He had got rid of the car.

The absence of a murder weapon, and the convenient alibi outweighed the prosecutor's argument of motive.

Michael always cut his working day short after a victory. One of the few breaks he allowed himself. He headed straight for the shower, for the hot jets that massaged his tense body after a challenging day. As he relaxed in the soothing rain, he thought of the juicy bonus he had just earned himself. He liked to live well. His loft, decorated by a prestigious interior designer, enjoyed all the technological comforts available. Parked in his garage was his Ferrari... he loved the good life.

At thirty-four he was still single and he intended to stay that way. He did not have the time or the inclination to share his life with anyone. A string of women warmed his bed, lured by his handsome dark looks, by his well toned body; the result of daily exercise at the state-of-the-art gym he had had installed next to his master bedroom, none of them stayed more than one night. Michael had never been in love, did not believe in love. His parents' divorce had taught him love was an illusion, a concoction of romantic novelists.

Michael hated his father, loathed him with a vengeance. He had deserted his mother, deserted him, abandoned them to poverty. His father had been an affluent man,. a renowned city doctor and Michael's early childhood had been extremely comfortable. He had lived in a an enormous and elegant town house run by disciplined staff, had enjoyed every material comfort until his father had run off with his secretary, with all their money. His father had had the audacity, the cruelty, to take a second mortgage on their home condemning them out on the streets.

Michael despised his mother; she was a weakling. After his father had disappeared from the face of the earth, she had gone into a deep depression. She had never worked, did not know how to. She had no idea how to fend for herself, for her child. She could not cope with a life where the kitchen was part of the living room, and the fridge was nearly always empty. Three months after their father had deserted them, Michael had come home from his job filling shelves in the local supermarket after school, when he found his mother's stiff, cold body sprawled on the bed, in the bedroom they shared. She had swallowed a bottle of sleeping pills. There was no suicide note. If there had been, Michael would not have read it. Without informing anyone of the tragedy, he put a bundle of clothes into a small suitcase, took the money he had secretly hoarded under the mattress, and disappeared from the neighbourhood. He did not shed a single tear. He was sixteen years old.

Michael was a survivor. He had learned to survive the world from an early age. His recollection of his childhood was dismal. Before the divorce, he had enjoyed every material comfort but had lacked the attention and love he had so desperately needed. His parents had had little time for him; his father was always working and his mother relayed her maternal duties on a string of expensive nannies he purposely exasperated, until every one of them fled the job. Michael had envied his friends, their families, had felt extremely alone between the walls of his lavish home. He had learned early he could trust no one, could only depend on himself. His foster parents had been good to him. His foster siblings had tried to befriend him. He was indifferent towards both; he could not wait to turn eighteen, could not wait to get out of the rundown house, of the shoddy neighbourhood that reeked of fried bacon and garbage.

Working two jobs, he had put himself through university and become a lawyer. Lawyers earned a lot of money he had decided. His enviable grades, a result of innate intelligence and ravenous ambition, had awarded him entry to the most prestigious law firm in the city; Barns and Ryman. They were also the wealthiest. The firm had a reputation for paying their lawyers exceptionally well; they also had a reputation for being extremely demanding employers. Michael had minded neither. He had no qualms about working hard. He wanted money, lots of it. He wanted it fast. In only a year, Michael proved his worth; his tenacious dedication to the firm and his own particular way of dealing with things, soon made him the highest paid lawyer at Barns and Ryman.

Michael got home about five, fetched the bowl of spaghetti his housekeeper had left for him in the microwave, grabbed a bottle of ice cold beer from the fridge, and sat down to watch the news channel on his fifty-inch plasma. Once he had finished his supper, he headed to his office and fetched his briefcase. He had to read over some documents. An important client awaited him early the following morning. As he opened the black leather briefcase and searched for the document, he saw it, a single white feather that looked exactly as the one he had thrown in the office bin that morning. He did not understand how a feather had ended up in his briefcase, but did not have time to ponder on the odd coincidence; had more important things to think about. Irritated, he picked up the nuisance feather and threw it in the kitchen bin.

Michael got up at eight the following morning; he liked to be at work punctually at nine thirty. After dressing impeccably, in one of his Armani suits, he headed for the kitchen. He placed a bowl of milk in the microwave and went to fetch the mail from his front door. When he had mixed the cereals in the hot skimmed beverage, he proceeded to open the mail between gulps of honey clusters swollen in milk. The spoon nearly fell from his mouth. Embedded in the unopened mail, was another feather, an exact replica of the other two he had already disposed of. He jumped off the black leather barstool and rushed to open the garbage bin. It was empty. *What was is with this feather that seemed to be following him?* The moment the thought had formed, he laughed at the ludicrous assumption; a feather could not follow anyone.

There had to be a plausible explanation. Still, the eerie oddity unnerved him somewhat. Impatiently he snatched up the feather, shoved it down the kitchen drain and ran the water for a while. *There!* He thought to himself. *End of story*! Michael continued eating his cereal and reading the rest of his mail, the feather forgotten. After a while, he glanced at his watch. It was already half past eight. *He had better get going, or he would be late for his meeting, and he was never late.* Picking up the porcelain bowl and the spoon, he headed for the dishwasher, bent down and opened its door. The door was half-open when he saw it; insulated in a glass, bottom up, on the top tray was another white feather.

He stood there staring at it, his mouth agape in disbelief. *This could not be happening... it was a different feather...had blown in through the kitchen window ...into a glass tumbler on the worktop and the house cleaner had put the it in the washer without noticing its unusual content...* He reached out his hand and gently picked it up by the stem walked to his office and placed it in front of him on the desk. He was tempted to dispose of it again but suspected it would be futile. His eyes traced its delicate spine, the wispy white threads, there was something luring about it... He examined it closely, trying to unravel its secret. Gently, he picked it up with careful fingers and placed it on the palm of his right hand. He curled his hand then stretched it. Fascinated, he watched as the fragile spine curved to bounce off his palm, as the airy fluff floated to hover slightly over his open hand.

He felt strange in its presence, the delicate feather evoked sensations he could not quite define. Its lightness seemed to uplift him, its glossy texture soothe him... he would keep it. The moment the choice was made he began to feel dizzy. His eyelids felt suddenly heavy, and his vision blurred. After a couple of minutes, he was asleep, his head pressing down on the stack of papers piling his desk, the feather clasped in his hand.

It had taken a while, but the feather had finally been invited into his life. He slept soundly for a while, and then images began to emerge.

He was sitting in a park, beside him sat the most beautiful woman he had ever laid eyes on, her hand clasping his, she looked radiant. He felt himself smile as he gazed down on her swollen belly, he heard himself laugh as he watched two little boys who strikingly resembled each other, running happily towards him. They jumped onto his lap, into his embrace as they showered him with kisses.

Lost in dream, Michael did not see the tips of the feather begin to glow with a blinding silver light, leave his hand and begin to write on a blank piece of paper that had blown out of the stack beneath his head, curl up in the air and blow out of the window.

Two hours elapsed before Michael lifted his head from the pile of documents. Nebulous fragments persisted on the fringes of memory to leave an impression of a dream. However, the words ***'You have been touched, have been awakened to your truth. When the time is nigh, you will be summoned, and you will come.'*** looping the blank sheet of paper that had mysteriously blown out of the neat stack of papers, rooted in memory.

*Seth flew fast, low, over the ruby speckled stretch separating him from his friends, the two silhouettes on the edge of the forest, a comforting sight. They waved at him vigorously, and Seth felt their relief from the distance. He had no notion of how long he had been gone, and had been afraid they had deserted him. They had waited; beneath the shade of one of the silver-leafed trees on the perimeter until they had sprung to their feet at the first sight of him. As Seth narrowed the distance between them, they spread their wings wide at their sides and bent their knee ready for takeoff. The minute Seth was above them; they sprang up high into the air to meet him, one at each side. Without uttering a single word, without looking at each other, they made their way home. Eyes pinned on the familiar skyline.*

*As he navigated the air currents, Seth reflected whether he should tell his friends what he had just witnessed.. By the time they reached the valley, he had taken a decision. He would tell them nothing. His friends had been right; he should not have trespassed the frontier, disobeyed the rules of the realm.*

*For the first time in his life, Seth understood the true nature of angelic laws. The timeless laws had a sole intention, protecting his world, protecting him. He realized there were things one should not be privy to until one was ready. He had not been prepared to witness what he just had. The enormity of what he had seen had changed everything, had changed him, had changed the questions of the past, replaced them with new ones, ones, he was not sure he wished to know the answers to. Transgressing the laws had cost him dearly; crossing the curved boundary had lifted the veil of innocence from his eyes. His friends would not know until it was time, until divine laws dictated they were ready. He would not burden their souls with the anguish and turmoil that burdened his own.*

*Lael and Zeriel knew something was terribly wrong with Seth the moment they landed on the comforting familiarity of the valley. His face was drawn, his vacuous eyes glistened with the threat of tears and his breathing was heavy. They watched him in silence, as he stood unmoving upon the cobble path leading to his garden, his hands clasped tightly in front of him, his body shaking from head to toe. His wings were slightly ruffled, stained but they made no reference. After a while, Zerial broke the uncomfortable silence, murmured to Lael it was time they left. Darkness would soon claim the skies; they needed to return home before anyone missed them, before anyone knew where they had gone, what Seth had done. Seth remained silent, static, his head hung. Even if he had tried to speak, he would have been unable to voice a word, muted by the cry of desperation that constricted his throat.*

*For a few more moments, Lael and Zeriel stood there watching him, apprehension clouding their eyes. Then suddenly, holding hands they shot up into the air and began to head for their respective homes, further down the valley. They flew swiftly, cutting through the dimming velvet sky in total silence. Neither Lael nor Zeriel ever asked Seth what had happened, what he had seen. Neither of them wished to know.*

Michael never saw the feather again; he searched the whole house, his office but it was gone. As the days elapsed the memory of the strange finding, the haunting words began to fade, trapped in memory to surface fleetingly. As the weeks went by Michael began to change. He began to feel his priorities shift. He began to feel uncomfortable in his job. He began to feel uncomfortable at Barns and Ryman. He began to feel uncomfortable with himself.

Watching Roffe appear in the media made him sick, he despised his swaggering, peremptory manner. Still, the ardent dislike he harboured towards his client was not the cause for the persistent twist in his stomach, the nagging discomfort was a result of the dislike he felt against his own self. His sleep was broken; he kept waking up in the middle of the night haunted by nightmares born of a guilty mind. When he looked at himself in the mirror as he shaved each morning he was disgusted by what he saw, what he had become. The bitter boy had become a bitter man; a man driven by ambition, a man who had acquired every material whim yet had nothing, loved no one, and no one loved him.

His opulent loft was cold and empty, his Ferrari a mere trophy, testimony of his success, his status. No one had ever occupied its passenger seat, accompanied him, laughed with him as he drove down a country lane on a warm Sunday afternoon.

He began to resent the firm, what they represented. To Barns and Ryman he was just a tool, a walking, breathing tool that made money, lots of it, at whatever cost. He suspected they did not even like him, that no one did. The sad realisation was that the latter had never bothered him, until now.

At Barns and Ryman, they had been shocked to hear he had called in sick. He had never been away from the firm, except for the five days annual leave he took religiously each Christmas. Michael did not believe in Christmas, did not like Christmas parties. The festive gatherings reminded him of lavish Christmas parties his mother hosted to perfection. Parties full of strangers where everyone ignored him.

Alarmed, he was seriously ill, the senior partners had sent one of the junior lawyers to his home to check how he was feeling, if he needed anything. They needed him back. The firm was losing money. The young lawyer had found an empty house, that Michael's cell phone was no longer operative.

Michael had left the day before; he had thrown a bundle of casual clothes and one Armani suit into a Louis Vuitton suitcase and driven to the coast. With no destination in mind, he had checked into a small coastal hotel that had caught his attention, after having driven a couple of hours. The homely hotel overlooked a picturesque cove. He had asked for a sea view and had been allocated room number seven, on the first floor. It was perfect. For the first time in a long time, Michael slept like a baby between its elegant walls. When he woke up the following morning, he felt exhilaratingly alive.

Michael never returned to Barns and Ryman. He did not even pick up the few personal possessions he kept at the office. No one at Barns and Ryman ever saw him again. He got rid of everything that linked him to that life, the city, his loft, his expensive car; his bank accounts, and moved to the little seaside town thirty minutes from the cove. For some odd reason, it had seemed the perfect choice. He rented a small office situated at the centre of its Main Street that had belonged to a doctor, who was now retired, hired a secretary, kept some money for a rainy day and donated the rest to different charities, the latter as atonement for his sins.

Alexandra Morgan was tired. She had been working late all week. Every day, there were more cases to attend to; more files piled on her desk; sheets of paper imprinted with the suffering of the innocent. She loved her job, was dedicated to it body and soul, but it was hard. The heartbreak, the monstrosities she confronted day in day out had eroded her faith in humanity. She knew detachment was vital to her sanity, but it was virtually impossible to separate the professional from the human. It was impossible to separate who she was into two different people.

At the end of each draining day, she made a conscious effort to forget the daily tragedies within the confines of her office. Every day she failed. Every night was plagued with the cries of the vulnerable. She felt impotent, in a world where lack of resources impeded the swift hand of justice. Desperate, in a world that harboured the destruction of innocence, was indifferent to alien suffering. The long hours dedicated to her job at the expense of a social life were not enough; there were too many files, too many innocent to save, too many obstacles to overcome, too little time.

She was sitting in the park watching Jimmy swaying silently on the swing. He was such a beautiful child. His sun streaked hair bounced in the wind as he pushed himself back and forth, his tiny feet dangling in the air. She watched his sad eyes staring out into nothingness, and her heart ached. They were waiting for his mother. She was to have an hour's supervised contact with her five-year-old son. Alexandra watched her approach; she was half an hour late. The moment the grubby, stringy woman came in through the gates, Jimmy sprung off the swing and rushed to Alexandra's side, clutched her skirt tightly with his small hands and buried his head in the gabardine cloth.

His mother had bought him sweets and tried to convince Jimmy to take them. Jimmy did not move, did not even look at her and then, as if possessed, began screaming at the top of his voice that she go away. Alexandra whose first priority was the child, took Jimmy in her arms, curtly told his mother contact was over and headed back to her office. Secretly, Alexandra was glad Jimmy had reacted this way, glad of what she would write in her report. She did not trust the woman.

Back at the office, Alexandra gave Jimmy some coloured pencils and a colouring book; she sat beside him and helped him shade the circus elephant in every crayon she had given him. Still affected by the encounter, his shaky little hands scribbled all over the elephant until he eventually calmed down and began to draw with more precision. By the time one of the care workers came to return him to the children's home, he was a happy child. Alexandra smiled as Jimmy ran into the arms of Charlene, a dedicated young care worker who had already won over Jimmy's heart. The twenty-year-old girl had not been working long in the children's home, but Alexandra had already sensed she had the right qualities for a job of such a sensitive nature. The moment Jimmy left; Alexandra typed out and printed the report, sealed it in an envelope and placed it in the Senior Social Worker's tray. The report would not be beneficial to Jimmy's mother; it was obvious the child was afraid of her.

As Alexandra got up to get a file from the oxidizing grey cabinet, she noticed Jimmy had left his favourite teddy bear behind on the floor beside the chair he had been sitting on. She stooped down, picked it up and placed the cuddly toy on her desk. She would return it to Jimmy during her lunch break, before she attended court at two that afternoon. She did not mind. She loved visiting the children, find out how they were doing, and it would not be the first time she skipped lunch. As she picked the bear up before leaving, she noticed a white feather was stuck to its back. *From one of the birds that visited the park,* she thought vaguely. Gently, she removed the feather and threw it in the garbage bin in the courtyard, placed the teddy bear in a plastic bag and headed for the Children's Home in her small car. She could not wait to see Jimmy's eyes light up when he saw his toy; Jimmy was unable to sleep without 'Jacky'.

The court case was a nightmare. Alexandra could not believe what had just happened; the monster had been declared innocent. A highly paid battalion of lawyers had ensured it. She felt bile rise in her throat as she watched him strut out of the room smiling provocatively. She could not hold back her tears as she thought of the two little girls who would again be hostage to his decadence. The system had failed them. **She** had failed them. A whole team in the department had worked with unrelenting dedication, to ensure the prosecutor's office had a watertight case and it had not sufficed. Power and corruption had once again prevailed over justice.

As she opened her handbag to retrieve a handkerchief and wipe away her tears of desperation, she saw it fall. Another white feather that looked exactly like the one she had removed from Jimmy's toy that morning, floated gently to the ground. She stood there looking at it lying at her feet, on the marble floor, wondering how it had found its way into her bag. Other more pressing matters occupied her mind; she did not have time to ponder on trivialities, odd as they might be. Leaving the feather on the cold floor of the courthouse lobby, she headed back to her office, to the stack of pressing cases waiting on her desk.

By the time she got home, she had forgotten all about the feather. She was exhausted and after a quick shower and eating one of the ready-made meals she kept as emergency in her freezer, she headed upstairs to bed. As soon as she switched on the light, she saw it. In the exact centre of her bed, lay another feather, a replica of the others. *What was going on, where were all these feathers coming from?* She thought, a rush of ineffable emotions gripping her. For or an instant, she believed it to be the same feather she had disposed of twice that day, a feather that somehow kept following her. She stood there transfixed; her eyes on the mysterious wisp resting on the floral print. A feather could not follow anyone. It was an incoherent and absurd conjecture.

For a long while she stood at the foot of her bed watching it, unsure what to do, until slowly, she walked towards it, stretched out her hand and carefully picked it up. It felt extremely soft as it caressed her palm, the white silken texture almost luminous. She stared at it, at every delicate detail, captivated by its purity. After a while, she placed it gently on the silver tray that adorned her dresser and went to bed.

The moment the intention to keep it had formed in her mind Alexandra began to feel strangely faint, began falling asleep. The moment her mind had shut out the noise of the world she began to dream a beautiful dream. Children played in a sunflower field, holding colourful ribbons in their hands. They tossed the silken bands up high into the air as their voices rang with laughter, forming a beautiful rainbow that stretched forever into a blue horizon. She sat peaceful on the edge of a field, her long raven hair blowing in the wind, watching their smiles, listening to their hearts sing with joy. Someone sat beside her and held her hand. Her heart somersaulted in her chest. She did not see his face. She did not need to; the hand clasping her own belonged to the man she loved.

Whilst she slept peacefully for the first time in a long time, the silver tray on her dresser reflected the shining silver light glowing on the tips of the white feather. After a while, the feather floated up, landed vertically back on the tray, and began to write on the silver surface. When it had finished etching the tray, the sparkling tips began to dim, until the silver glow faded completely. Gently, it began to float up into the air, began to spiral slowly towards her bedroom window until it vanished in the night.

When Alexandra woke up, she did not remember the dream. Still, the buried vision, echoed from the twilight world to invigorate her. Bouncing with energy, she headed singing to the shower then headed to the closet. As she surveyed her drab office wardrobe, a blood-red dress, reserved for special occasions caught her eye. *Perfect*, she thought, the bold choice matching her elation. She walked buoyantly to the dresser and was about to pin her hair to her nape, when she changed her mind and let her ebony mane loose.

She was about to retrieve her watch from the silver tray adorning her dresser, when her hands froze. The mirror reflected her stunned expression as she read the words etched on the silver tray; ***'You have been touched, have been awakened to your truth. When the time is nigh, you will be summoned, and you will come.'***

*Amanda and Anton noticed a change in their son; he was distant, quieter, not his usual, jovial self. They were worried, had tried to find out what ailed him, but their questioning had led nowhere. Seth had insisted vehemently nothing was wrong, that he was perfectly fine. Both Amanda and Anton knew better than to insist. They knew their son well. Seth would distance himself further if they kept interrogating him. They would have to wait patiently for Seth to confide his worries.*

*For days, they watched him retire to his tree house after school and spend whole afternoons secluded between its timber walls. Lael and Zeriel had not been over to see Seth for a while and Amanda began to suspect her son had quarrelled with his two best friends, and that was why he was sulking. Despite his brazen exterior, Seth was a sensitive angel.*

*Days turned to weeks, and nothing changed. No friends called at the house and Seth's uncharacteristic introvert behaviour persisted.*

*Seth could not forget the images he had witnessed. The turning scenes haunted him, agitating his soul; he could not make sense of the mortal creature who could love and hate with equal passion. Unfamiliar emotions inundated his heart. After his encounter with the mortal world, he had begun to feel strangely connected to the beings that populated the earth. For some reason he could not fathom, he felt part of them, part of their world. His heart beat with anomalous resonations, faint echoes, memories of an earth he had only touched fleetingly.*

*The last vision had been unnerving. He was an intelligent young angel, and he had immediately grasped what the image illustrated; the blue orb disintegrating in space, echoing terrorized screams depicted the end of the earth. Still, he could not understand why the image had been shown to him, if the mortal world was, indeed, facing a catastrophic future. He had no idea worlds could end, or why. He did not understand the intricate and paradoxical nature of its inhabitants, how angels related to them, their world. The only thing Seth knew was the mortal world existed over the curved frontier, that it was a different world from his own, where other 'rules' applied, that he did not wish it to die.*

Marcus could not sleep. The crying of the younger children still rang in his ears. The memory of Brother Jonah's gloating face as he punished them, continued to float before his eyes. A breath of insubordination resulted in a beating by the brothers. He hated the white collared hypocrites. He hated the orphanage. He could not wait to escape the austere edifice. Sequestered by sentinel trees rising on every side in high protective clusters, the stone fortress had been his prison for the last five years. The fact he would not have to wait long was the one thought that consoled him, made his dreary existence bearable.

He was an excellent student and was certain he would win the annual university grant, awarded by a benevolent benefactor to the best student at the orphanage each year. He was undoubtedly the brightest senior student at the orphanage. He had a photographic mind, an intelligence quotient bordering on genius. The generous sum would be set up in a trust for the meritorious student, would pay for every university expense, including food and lodging. Achieving top grades was his ticket to a decent life, winning the award would liberate him from the hellhole that was his 'home'. He could not fail, would not.

The brothers had never beaten him; he had not given them reason to. He had learned the formula for survival a long time ago; *Do as you are told, be invisible.* Marcus had one priority within the dungeon's walls and that was to survive incarceration as easily and harmlessly as possible, to leave with the university grant that would enable him to become master of his own life.

The moment he had stepped inside the walls of St Vincent, Marcus decided he did not need any more beatings. He had learned to control his rebellious nature, had learned to fade into the background, keep to himself, not get involved in other people's problems. He did not mix with the other orphans. Seven days a week he worked in the kitchen so he could eat after everyone else had. He wished to eat alone.

Fraternising occasions avoided at all cost; he did to wish to get close to anyone. He did not have the strength.

Marcus had grown up in foster homes. His biological mother had abandoned him at an old church in a downtrodden part of the city, days after she had given birth to him. He had never been able to find out her identity, and since no one claimed him, everyone assumed there was no father.

He had been moderately happy in a few of the homes, sad and lonely in others, desperate in most. At twelve years of age, no one had wished to foster him anymore; every single foster family alleged Marcus was a strange child. They all coincided in the same thing; he was incapable of adjusting to a family environment. He displayed no emotion, no empathy towards his foster parents or siblings. He was a robot personified. He ate, slept, did what he was told, but never smiled or cried. No one considered him an evil child, just strange. The reality was no one had possessed the sensibility, the patience to delve beneath the mechanical façade. If they had, they would have unearthed the sad truth. They would have discovered an extremely sensitive child. A lonely child, whose heart had been broken a long time ago, had belonged to no one, and no one belonged to it. A heart that was afraid to hope.

The only thing that gave Marcus a sense of joy was reading and writing. He was an avid reader, read everything he could get his hands on. He loved the magic of books, the flipping pages that transported him to worlds where anything was possible. He loved to indulge in daydreams that he later immortalised as stories in the writing pad he always carried with him. His stories incorporated the same theme; a happy ending.

It was on a Sunday morning after church that he found his lucky talisman. On Saturdays, the brothers rested in their dormitories for a couple of hours after lunch, and the orphans played in the courtyard until dinner. Marcus sat under the shade of the only tree that grew in the otherwise barren patio, and opened his new writing pad. It was then that he saw it. A perfect white feather trapped between the blank, lined pages.

He stared at it for a moment and without deliberation decided to keep it, name it his lucky feather. He studied it for a few more moments then placed it gently between the centre pages of the writing pad.

As soon as the feather was sandwiched between the lined paper, Marcus began to feel giddy, suddenly sleepy. The moment his head rested on the thick trunk he was plunged into deep sleep. Then, he began to dream.

He was sitting at a desk, in a bookshop. Rows of books of every size and colour fed the avenue of shelves towering the powder blue, carpeted aisle that stretched endlessly. He looked up and saw a long stream of excited faces waiting impatiently for him to sign the books they carried in their hands. Every book displayed a smiling photograph of him on the back cover.

As Marcus dreamed peacefully under the shade of the lonely tree, the writing pad blew open and the feather began to write. It began to dance, loop upon the blank sheet, its tips gleaming with a bright silvery light. When it had finished tiptoeing the horizontal lines, the glowing light diminished. The feather began to float up into the air, over the tree, until it disappeared over the ironed fence.

When Marcus woke up, bewildered eyes stared at the words on the page that lay open on his lap. ***'You have been touched, have been awakened to your truth. When the time is nigh, you will be summoned, and you will come.'*** He did not remember the dream, but its essence was imprinted on his soul.

Michael felt immediately at home in the quaint town near the coast. Its people accepted him as if he were one of them, had lived amongst them his entire life. Soon, he was an integrated member of the community, respected and loved by every inhabitant of the homely town. A small cottage that had belonged to an artist replaced the expensive loft; she had left town a long time ago but had not wished to sell the cottage, until now. The townspeople had confided the story; its young owner had left abruptly, immediately after her best friend, the previous owner of the hotel on the cove, had died in a tragic car accident. She had been eight months pregnant and had been driving to town when tragedy struck. Her car had fallen over a cliff into the sea. They had rescued her car, but never found her body. Michael had seen her, seen a painting of her. When he had first inspected the cottage, the painting had still hung over the fireplace. *The beautiful woman, with laughing, crystal blue eyes and golden mermaid hair surrounded by foaming sea, had the face of an angel,* he had thought.

The second hand, red Mini, included with the purchase of the cottage replaced his Ferrari. Jeans and sweaters, shirts and sports trousers, for meetings with city clients, replaced all but one of his Armani suits. He had kept one for a special occasion, hopefully his wedding one day.

He would have preferred to stay in the homely and peaceful town every day, but the small town's trickle of work was not enough to earn him a decent living. He had had no option but collaborate with a firm in the city in order to pay his bills. His arrangement with them was flexible and simple; he would choose his clients and pay the firm a twenty percent commission of his earnings. Three days a week, he met with clients in the city. He only changed the days to suit the court's timetable.

Michael's work priorities altered overnight. His driving ambition buried in his past. He chose his cases for other, more altruistic reasons. He refused to take on a case if he suspected clients were guilty, payment for his services derived from immoral sources or were driven by questionable reasons other than justice. The fee did not determine acceptance. If he believed an injustice had been committed, he took on the case, even if it meant he would do it Pro Bono. Those that served to curb social injustices, defend the vulnerable, now appealed to him greatly.

His personal life also changed drastically. He enjoyed barbeques in friends' gardens and loved going for walks in the surrounding forest with his dog; a stray he had rescued from the dog pound. He was a member of the fishing club, presided over local charities and was a member of the panel for the children's home in town and two others in the city. On Saturdays, he coached junior football and now hoped he would marry and raise a family some day. The resentment he had harboured against his parents was gone, the destructive emotion replaced by nostalgia. What could have been if his father had not deserted them, his mother had been able to survive desertion; if they had demonstrated the love he had sought so desperately. He had visited his mother's grave, taken her flowers, cried over it, forgiven her, forgiven himself. He had tracked down his father, called him a couple of times. His father had never returned his phone calls, but the only emotion his rebuff incited was relief.

Michael had grown to love his leisure time, every Friday he was glad to see the weekend arrive. He planned them carefully so he made the most of them. Weather permitting, if he was not fishing with friends, he was hiking or camping in the forest with his football team. In rough weather, he stayed in the cosy cottage watching films from his collection of oldies, cooking new dishes his friends devoured at candlelit dinners by the fireplace or catching up with his reading. He read any genre, except law. The simple pleasures in life like going for a walk, playing with his dog on the beach or conversing with his friends were the things that now made Michael happy.

He was sitting by the sea, in the cove, watching his dog fetch the ball he had thrown in the tranquil cobalt waters, thinking how perfect his life was, how much it had changed, how much he had changed. When he now shaved in the mornings he liked his reflection, the person he had become. Gone was the ambitious ruthless and resentful man he had once been, in his shoes stood a better man, a happier man. Nala, his golden retriever, sat beside him, panting, the red rubber ball clutched between its teeth. As Michael affectionately patted his wet muscular back, his thoughts returned to the day it had all changed, how extraordinarily easy it had been to build a new life. He had been amazed at the fact he had not encountered a single obstacle that had hindered the life he had pursued, the life that now filled him with joy and serenity of spirit.

His thoughts wandered to the perfect snowy feather that had entered his world and changed it forever, had converted him from eternal sceptic to ardent believer. Michael had no doubt the fluffy intruder had been a gift from heaven. One he should not waste. The mystical message echoed in his mind from time to time and he often wondered if the time would ever be 'nigh'.

They verdict would be announced any time. Sandwiched between the crowd of expectant journalists, Arianne St Claire kept pushing forward, as the mass of bodies, hailing microphones threatened to swallow her. At precisely 3pm, the doors to the courthouse flung open and Roffe walked out. Before his lawyer announced the verdict to the sea of microphones, inches from his face, everyone had known; the goading smirk on Roffe's face revealed he had been found innocent. In a brief statement, Michael Jenkins, Roffe's lawyer, proclaimed *justice had been served,* then hurriedly followed his client into the limousine parked at the steps of the courthouse.

Arianne searched her bag for her phone. She called the newsroom, informed them of the outcome and then made her way to a cosy café she had discovered opposite the courthouse. She was famished, her stomach hurt. She desperately needed to eat something, the only thing she had had all day was a coffee. The café was full but for a small table in the corner, quickly she rushed to claim it before anyone usurped it. She ordered a coffee along with a cheese and ham croissant, and whilst she waited, checked her diary for her week's appointments.

She loved being a journalist. She loved playing detective; she loved writing. She had been extremely lucky; fresh from university she had landed a junior journalist post in a reputable newspaper in the city. It was a great place to work in. It's editor, William Steger, was an exceptional man; he was also a good boss, demanding but fair. Her colleagues had all been excellent people; they had made a great team. As she sipped her coffee, she reminisced about the past, the friends she had left behind. She had been sorry to leave but being a reporter for a prestigious TV station had been an exciting challenge.

The station was a different world; she had not made a single friend. Everyone backstabbed everyone. Channel 6 was a nest of ambitious vipers. Arianne had been shocked at the treacherous environment, had been tempted to leave after she had only been working a week. She could not quit the job; her prior position had been filled by someone else and she had rent to pay as well as a car loan. Returning to the God forsaken ghetto was not an option. She had escaped that world. She would never go back; there was nothing... no one to go back to. Hence, she had stayed, learned to play the game. *If you cannot beat them, join them,* she had determined quickly. The fact that she was beautiful and intelligent made her a target of envious co-workers, but she had soon learned to counteract the undermining ploys.

Arianne had been a beautiful child and had grown into a stunning woman. Her delicate features resembled a doll's and her petite frame carried itself with quiet elegance. She had amber slanted eyes and a soft sensuous mouth that required no lipstick. Her hair, the colour of honey, hung in soft waves below her shoulders. Her dainty hands caught everyone's attention. They were beautiful hands but the little star at the base of her right thumb was what drew people's attention to them. Initially, everyone thought it was a cute tattoo. On closer inspection, they were fascinated to discover the perfect little star was nature's creation.

Arianne had learned fast to survive the hostile world of TV journalism. She devised a set of rules that helped her stay ahead of the game, kept her in the winning lane. Every day she was the first one at the office and the last one to leave. She kept her enemies closer than they suspected. A recording device, a sophisticated piece of equipment disguised as a brooch, was always pinned to her chest and she paid her informants extremely well, the subsidy out of her own pocket. Her implacable discipline quickly paid dividends; soon, she was a respected and reputed reporter with a string of successful scoops under her belt. She was no longer the amiable journalist, the integrated team player she had been at the newspaper. She had become colder, distant. Her sole ambition, being, advancing in her career, she had adapted to the hostile environment. She trusted no one, knew no one trusted her.

She moved in a world where loyalty was nonexistent, treading on corpses, the lonely road to the pinnacle.

Arianne enjoyed her success, enjoyed her comfortable life, but sometimes, when she lay alone in the dark, a whispering voice warned her she was betraying her true nature too often, selling pieces of her soul to the devil. Soon, there would be nothing left of the Arianne who had vowed to be an eternal seeker of the truth. Before long, there would be nothing left of the naïve debutante who had been inspired with philanthropic ideals, of the girl who had grown under the virtuous auspices of the convent and vowed to uncover the injustices of the world. She had been a victim of such injustice; a terrible truth lay behind her beautiful face, a truth so horrendous that had made her flee a nightmare in the dead of night. However, darkness dissolved to light and she was back in the game, the ominous murmur forgotten.

When Arianne had drunk the coffee and finished devouring the delicious snack, she drove to the state prison; she was interviewing a recluse on death row. The sadistic murderer had killed seven women. The station was running a new show on notorious killers and had entrusted Arianne with the thorny interviews. At five sharp, she waited outside the prison grounds for the guard who would be escorting her to interview the dangerous prisoner. She was extremely nervous. It was the first time she tackled a story of such nature.

As she followed the guard down the long narrow corridor to the cell, she felt sweat trickling down her temples. The thought of confronting evil, a sadistic killer who had coldly raped and murdered seven women, one of whom was seven months' pregnant, sent shivers down her spine... curled her blood. Iron bars would separate them; four guards would accompany her at all times. Still, the mere thought of speaking to such a vicious and coldblooded criminal, looking into the eyes that had relished in such gruesome acts, made her sick.

They were nearly at the end of the long white corridor when she informed the guard she needed to go to the rest room. She needed a few minutes...

She stood in the tiny cubicle facing the small square mirror with no frame. She opened the tap and ran the water for a while. Her fingers filtered the cold spray then joined to cup the icy water. She splashed a few scoops on her face, as if she were dispelling the remnants of a bad dream. *She must calm down.* She thought anxiously. *She needed to see this job through.* For a few minutes, she stood there, her head overhanging the basin. As she lifted her head she saw it, stuck on the mirror was a perfect white feather. She looked at it, her bewildered expression staring back at her. There were no windows in the minuscule toilet. *Where had the feather come from*? The knock on the door jolted her back to her imminent reality. She flushed the toilet she had not used, straightened her clothes with her sweaty palms and headed out the door leaving the feather stuck to the mirror.

Within minutes, she was inside a light blue painted room. empty, except for the chair and table placed in its centre. She sat down, positioned her notebook, pen and tape recorder neatly on the table and waited nervously for the prisoner to arrive.

As she waited for the sound of footsteps to echo the corridor, she stared at the small cell opposite her; at the chair placed in its exact centre. As she watched the tiny prison, she tried to imagine what being locked inside the confining room would feel like, an image of a bird desperately flapping its wings in its cage flashing before her. Her eyes roamed over each bar separating freedom from captivity until startled eyes fixed on a corner of the grey tiled floor.

As if possessed, she shot up from the chair raced to the cell and curled quivering hands on the cold rods. Transfixed, she stared at the feather, twin to the one stuck on the mirror lying on the floor, twin to the one stuck on the mirror. Without offering an explanation, she grabbed her working tools, fled the room, dashed down the interminable corridors and escaped the high-voltage enclosure to the sanity of the free world.

Once home, Arianne headed straight for the shower. As she crouched on the white porcelain base, her head resting on her knees, she tried to relax her body under the spraying jets. Her body continued shaking despite the heated rain pouring over her. The first feather had unnerved her, the bizarre coincidence of the second one scared her out of her wits. After a while, her body began to loosen under the comforting flow, the notion that the feather had been an omen, a sign for her to escape prison had begun to seem ridiculous.

The long, hot cascade managed to cleanse away some of her fear, her confusion, but the apprehensive clench in her stomach persisted. She headed straight for her bedroom, quickly changed into a pair of silk pyjamas and, knowing she would have trouble sleeping, selected a book from the bookshelf outside her bedroom door. Reading always did the trick. She rested her head on the satin pillows and made herself comfortable under the silken quilt, placed the book on her lap and opened it. The moment she opened the cover she saw it, another feather, exactly like the others, was stuck to the first page.

Shaky fingers stroked it, whilst disbelieving eyes scrutinized the length of its spine. It was the same feather. Something strange was happening to her, three feathers were too much of a coincidence. It was an omen, a sign she was walking the dark side too often. With trembling fingers, she picked it up and examined it closer. The minute the feather was in her possession, she began to feel strangely calm. Fear and apprehension melting away.

As she inspected the fluffy threads, the flexible backbone, she pondered on the fact that her first instinct had been partly correct. The feather **was** some kind of omen, but the more she thought about it, the more she was convinced it was not a menacing one. Gently, she placed it inside the pages of the book and rested the book on her chest. The moment

Arianne accepted the feather into her life she drifted off into deep sleep and her dream began.

She was sitting in her living room, on her couch, watching television. Suddenly, a close up image of her face appeared on the screen. She looked beautiful; perfect hair, perfect makeup, perfect smile. Suddenly, the image pixilated then sharpened to illustrate a second image. She was sitting in a boardroom surrounded by men in suits. They were smiling, congratulating her. At the foot of the long, polished table, a chart illustrating the channel's ratings for her prime-time-show, projected on the wall. They were colossal. Her cell phone rang. Her eyes lit up, and her heart fluttered, as she listened to a husky voice speak her name.

Arianne did not see the white feather's tips glow with a silver light, push open the book nestled on her chest and scribble on the open page. When Arianne woke up the following morning, she was both startled and intrigued by the mysterious message written over the black-and-white print that read ***'You have been touched, have been awakened to your truth. When the time is nigh, you will be summoned, and you will come.'*** The dream had evaporated, but its spirit lingered in memory as wish.

*Seth was awake when his mother came into his room. Darkness had begun to recede, heralding the morning star about to greet the valley, reign over a new day. Amanda sat on the edge of his bed and gently took his hand. She sat in silence, looking at him, her crystalline eyes radiating with tenderness.*

*Eventually, Amanda had known, had realised the enormity of what her son had done. At first, she had thought nothing of the stains in his wings, but insistent ashen specks had clung to its silver tips after lathering them vigorously with starlit soap night after night. On closer inspection, she had realised what the specks were, where they had come from. Her son had crossed the frontier to the first world, the mortal world. He had transgressed the ancient laws of the realm...*

*For days, she considered what to do, what to say to her son. For nights, she worried about certain repercussions. She walked around the cottage in a frenzy, continuously peeping out the windows, dreading the coo of the messenger doves, scanning the garden for that scroll that would condemn her son's fate. When she realised there would be no request from the Elders for Seth to appear before the Seraphim in the Temple of Light, Amanda's fear turned to confusion. Nothing, however trivial, was a secret to the higher angels; that an infringement of such magnitude had gone undetected, was extremely strange.*

*After debating every option, considering every outcome, she came to a decision; she would talk to her son, make him understand...*

*Anton had already left for the Halls of knowledge and Seth was having breakfast in the porch, his satchel on the empty chair beside him. She had not wished to involve Anton, she preferred to talk to her son alone. She watched him from the door, her eyes lingering on the stray curls hanging over his forehead, as he silently scooped the rainbow cereals. Her heart went out to him; she missed his smile, the talkative rambunctious angel who exasperated her every morning at breakfast. Slowly, she walked towards him, sat on the chair across him, took a deep breath and without hesitation confessed to her son what she had done and the cost of her transgression.*

*She told him how she had succumbed to human tragedy, how she had gotten involved in a human's life without being asked to do so. She spoke about how she had given in to impulse without thought to consequence. She had not been ready to encounter man and the intricacies of his journey towards the light. She had not respected their free will. She had been arrogant, viewed herself above divine law. She had not understood that she had had no right to interfere in the lessons humans must learn on their own.*

*She told him how she had come to understand the importance of their divine laws; that they were the instruments that protected their beautiful world. She told him about the human journeys, about their own responsibilities towards humanity. There were reasons for the suffering, for the joy humans encountered. She had learned to trust in their merciful realm, had finally understood the wisdom of their divine laws, laws she would never question again.*

*Like him, she still had many questions, questions that remained unanswered, but she now believed the answers would arrive when the time was right, when one was ready.*

*Seth listened carefully and silently to his mother's words. He knew why his mother* **had** *confessed her disobedience of the sacred laws. She knew what he had done, she had somehow discovered he had transgressed the curved frontier into the mortal world. She knew what he had seen. She had wished to comfort him, make him understand she would always be at his side, guiding, protecting him. She had wished to warn him...*

*Seth trusted his mother implicitly, if she told him the answers would come, then they would come. All he had to do was walk the path of knowledge as fast as possible, so he would not have to wait long for the 'right time'.*

It was seven thirty when John Taylor finally left the station. He finished work at five, but lately he had been more and more reluctant to go home early. Things at home were a mess. His wife Eva was more often than not in a foul mood. His children, Aaron, six, and Jeannie, ten, were always whining and fighting. Eva was permanently scolding them, scolding him. She kept complaining he was never home, that he had no time for his family. John knew Eva was right. He was never home; he made a point not to be.

He loved his wife, his children and wished with all his heart he could go back in time, return to the days when his family had been happy; he had been happy, 'clean'. He wished he could confide his troubles to Eva, but he was too ashamed. She had always been so proud of him, trusted him. He feared if he told her the truth, she would abhor him, leave him and take the children with her. He had tried to confess many times but had choked on the words that would condemn him in her eyes.

Since adolescence he had wanted to be a policeman, his uncle was a policeman. It had been his uncle who had saved him, saved him from his father, from the beatings that had nearly ended his life. He had never told a soul about the beatings; his mother had made him swear he would not disclose their terrible secret, claiming that if he did, his father would kill her.

For years, he had suffered the abuse, had listened to his mother being beaten in the dead of night. He hated his father, hated everything he stood for. Impotence, that in everyone's eyes he was the perfect family man, a highly respected member of the community, suffocated him.

He hated his father's cold bloodedness, his conniving nature, his capacity to lie, to pretend he was not the monster he metamorphosed into in the privacy of their home. He was Jekyll turned to Hyde at the first sips of the venomous potion that burned his breath.

It was after his last beating; the brutal assault that sent him to the intensive care unit, made him balance on the edge of death for days, that his father's abominable nature was revealed. His uncle had been shocked to discover his brother's 'secret'. Everyone in the community had initially assumed the boy had been lying. It was impossible that John Taylor, a civil engineer of notable prestige, an upstanding member of the community, a devoted churchgoer, had committed such a deplorable act, had inflicted such brutality on his own flesh and blood.

When John had been released from the hospital he had gone to live with his uncle. His testimony, supported by his mother's, had ensured his father's incarceration, and he be placed in his uncles' custody.

John had implored his mother to stay with him, but she had refused. '*Your father needs me…*' she had told him weakly. Ignoring everyone's advice, she had sold their home, bought an apartment near the prison grounds, so she could visit him every day, and waited patiently for him to serve the three-year sentence.

John had been devastated that his mother had decided to remain by her father's side. He had not understood why she had not grabbed the chance to escape his brutal clutches, get rid of him once and for all. His mother was mistaken. His father would never change, was not capable of change; a leopard did not change its spots.

Contrary to his gullible mother, John understood his father was devoid of conscience, empathy. He had never loved him or his mother. He was an egocentric sadist incapable of noble emotions. Contradictory emotions thrashed his young soul, battled against each other to scar his heart; he felt both compassion and anger towards his mother.

His mother had been wrong. She should never have made him a silent accomplice to the beatings; she should have protected him, protected herself. She should have gone to the police, exposed her father's vile acts, not waited until he dangled on the precipice of death. Still, he was grateful that she had ultimately spoken, testified against her husband, ensuring finally, his father would never hurt him again.

John knew his father would not forgive what his mother had done, would not forget her betrayal. The moment his dastardly father set foot on freedom, he would beat his credulous mother to a pulp. John knew his father well; revenge was the one thought that consumed his nights in captivity. His father would utilize his mother, would be charming, trick her into believing he had changed, forgiven her for her treachery when she visited him in prison, when she brought him the things he needed. The moment he was released from prison, he would shed his benign disguise and transform into the beast he had always been. John wished his mother would realise the man who had beaten her, since they had gotten married, would keep beating her until 'death do them part'.

After the scandal, John Taylor senior was finished in the community and when he had finally served his sentence, John's mother moved away with him to another city. The scandal had ensured his banishment from a community that had once held him in high esteem.

Whilst his father had been imprisoned, John had called his mother every day, visited her on a couple of occasions with his uncle. When his father returned home, his mother told him not to call her anymore. John understood what she had meant; if he did, his father would punish her severely. Since that day John lived in constant fear. Every time the phone rang he jumped, dreading it was the police calling to inform him that his mother was dead, that his father had killed her.

John's life changed radically the moment he went to live with his uncle. For the first time in his young life he was happy, felt safe. With time, he learned to forget, block out his parents, his wretched past from memory. His mother had chosen her life. He had the right to choose his. He had the right to be happy. He could not, would not, allow her weakness, her inability to keep herself safe to consume him, to cloud the sunshine that now lit up his life.

Gregory could not come to terms with the fact he had missed the signs, that he had been so blind to his nephew's misery. Guilt weighted heavily on his shoulders. He was a policeman. He defended the vulnerable. He should have been more observant, more vigilant. He, of all people, should have been able to detect something was not quite right, was terribly wrong. He had visited his brother's home often, but had never detected the slightest anomaly, the slightest breath indicating the man sharing his blood, the man he had known all his life, hid an execrable secret. His brother had seemed to have the perfect family life; his family had seemed to be happy. Margaret, his sister in law, had always been cheerful, amiable, the perfect hostess, a doting mother and wife. Too perfect Gregory had thought.

John, though a quiet child, was always pleasant, well behaved and, as far as Gregory gathered, a happy child. He had assumed John Junior's timidity, his reluctance to bond with him, was a result of an introvert nature.

John's teacher was, coincidentally, a good friend of his and had often relayed how well his nephew did in school; he was a bright student and a fabulous sportsman. With hindsight, Gregory had detected a few bruises on his nephew's legs from time to time but had attributed the latter to his sporting endeavors.

John's excellence, both in the academic and sporting fields, could not, unfortunately, be attributed solely to natural talent. His father's authoritarian and tyrannous attitude ensured he was number one. Number two meant more beatings. If John had to name one thing he could thank his father for it would be the sporadic happiness he found in school. To his classmates, John was a hero. He was good-looking, the perfect student and an unbeatable sportsman; all the ingredients to make him the most popular boy in school. John took none of his friends home, not even when his father insisted and his refusal provoked another beating. John never allowed his father to pollute his 'other world'.

The moment he lived with Gregory, everyone had been invited to his home. None of his friends ever mentioned his parents, his 'past', to John; they loved him, respected him, knew better. John never mentioned his parents to anyone again. They belonged in the past, a past he no longer allowed to infect his world. Secretly, his friends whispered among themselves; they despised his father, had contempt for his mother. They agreed John was a brave and loyal young man, that had kept his suffering secret in order to protect his weak mother.

The years he spent living with his uncle revealed another side to life, another side to man. His uncle was a good man, an honorable man, who struggled to keep the innocent, the vulnerable safe. At home, he was a gentle, caring man of affable demeanor. At work, he was disciplined, implacable to those who threatened to destroy the safety of his world. His meticulous and diligent investigations ensured that those who cheated the law were swiftly placed behind bars. John had only been living a couple of months with his uncle when he decided to follow in his footsteps. He would join the police force; make his 'father' proud.

After only a couple of years in the force, John was promoted to Inspector. He never heard from his parents again. They had moved incessantly through the years until his uncle had lost track of them. A ringing phone was no longer a cause of distress to John, as far as he was concerned his parents were dead, had chosen to depart from his world a long time ago.

John was about to turn the knob of his front door when he changed his mind and decided to sit on the steps of the porch for a while. As he stared ahead into space, the urge to flee into the night, return to the station and sleep on the small sofa in the corner of his office grabbed him. He remained seated on the wooden plank. He was shattered, his overtired body unresponsive. His day had been grueling, frustrating, another endless day where hard work and exhaustive investigations had led to futility. John did not understand the world anymore, did not understand a society that had allowed the hand of justice to become so sluggish. Another heinous crime had gone unpunished; another fleet of overpaid lawyers had 'gotten away with murder'. Damien Roffe had been found innocent; his defense team headed by a ruthless Lawyer, Michael Jenkins, had ensured his 'innocence'.

It had not mattered that the neighbours had seen what had resembled his car, parked outside his house, at the time of the murder. That they had heard his familiar voice. It had not mattered that they had heard his wife's screams before the gun had been fired; that two passersby had sworn they had seen someone of his stature, his characteristics, fleeing the scene of the crime. That his wife had blatantly been unfaithful to him, that she was battling for a hefty divorce settlement; he had a motive.

The defense had argued vehemently; there was no murder weapon. No one had seen his face. No one had been able to relay the car's registration number. He had an alibi. Everyone involved in the case strongly suspected, the alibi, Rolfe's ex-wife, had been paid to lie. John and his team had checked every bank account, every bank statement, every possible financial link but had come up empty handed.

This was not the only case that had seen an unjust end; there was a long string of other 'unpunished' ones. The longer hours he worked, the harder his team endeavored to present watertight investigations to the prosecutor's office, the less they seemed to achieve desired result. Criminals; from petty thieves, drug offenders to murderers; pedophiles returned to the streets, a few after serving hardly any time, many having served no time. Every day he and his men placed themselves in danger, struggled to place criminals behind bars, cleanse the streets that were home to their families. Every day they watched those streets plagued by more criminals hunting for vulnerable prey. John had lost faith in justice, in a God that had forgotten to endorse its execution.

Sister Julia sat in the small chapel; slender fingers rubbed the silver cross resting on her chest. A soft smoky light suffused the room as rays of warm light filtered through the arched narrow window to fall softly over the altar. She was restless again. Her mind was troubled; her soul was troubled. She was in desperate need of prayer, of guidance, of answers that reaffirmed her waning faith. Seeds of doubt had bloomed into thorns to pierce her temples; her migraines were getting worse by the day. She remained quietly still, except for the wishful fingers that moved up and down the crucifix in steady rhythm.

She gazed at the Virgin standing on the altar amidst vases laden with the fresh gardenias, carnations and chrysanthemums the sisters picked from the garden in the predawn haze. Pearl candles edging the tiny chapel, cast chatoyant shadows creating the illusion she was real. As she watched her face, her flickering eyes, Julia knew what the heavenly mother was thinking and they prayed in unison for the salvation of the world.

Julia had joined the convent as a novice at seventeen. Since she was a young girl, she had wished to become a nun but it was not until she was sixteen years old that she announced her decision to her adoptive parents. On the eve of her sixteenth birthday, she had confessed her plans to marry God. Her parents had been shocked, had tried to dissuade her with a hundred different arguments; they wished her to go to university, get married, bear them grandchildren, have a 'normal' happy life... When the arguments had failed, they had resorted to subtle coercions but nothing they said could convince Julia, make her deviate from the path she had set foot on a long time ago.

Martha and Frederick Lewis had adopted Julia soon after they had gotten married and realised they would not be able to bear children of their own. Since they had set eyes on the baby abandoned in the hospital, the beautiful little girl had become their most precious treasure.

Her desertion was a mystery; someone had abandoned the newborn baby in the hospital's chapel one night, nude and wrapped in an immaculate white blanket. The events of the night remained an enigma; security staff had locked the doors to the chapel and there had been no sign of a break in. The staff at the hospital had conducted an exhausting investigation that had cleared personnel of all suspicion. No one had broken into the chapel; no one had left the baby on the front bench. No one had seen anyone entering the hospital carrying a baby.

To Martha and Frederick, the little baby was a gift from heaven. They did not care who had abandoned the beautiful baby girl or why. The only thing they cared about was she had become their child. In the beginning, they had feared someone would claim her, that her desertion had been the fruit of desperation, but the weeks rolled by and, mercifully for the Lewis', no one claimed the little soul. When they had eventually signed the adoption papers, when she had finally become irreversibly theirs, they had relaxed. Worrying thoughts no longer interrupted their sleep. The cry of their baby was the only reason for their sleepless nights.

Martha and Frederick had envisioned another life for their only daughter but nothing they said could alter Julia's resolve. Once she had told her parents, she told her friends. She had gone crazy was the immediate and unanimous reaction. Initially, they thought it was another of her zany jokes until they had realised she was dead serious. When the realisation had fully sunk in, they were flabbergasted. They could not believe she was actually going to become a nun. She had gone mad they insisted, (still incredulous) no one became a nun anymore, not in the 21st century. Julia could not be dissuaded. She ignored her parents' incessant arguments, ignored her friends' claims that she could not be happy living the life of chastity and sacrifice; she forgave her classmates' cruel jokes. In her ears, the only thing that rang was the voice of the Father calling her name.

Julia did not fit the 'nun' stereotype; she was a fun loving sociable girl, an excellent student with a promising future; a beautiful young girl who already enjoyed a string of admirers. Julia had understood their concerns, had listened patiently to the well-meaning advice, but remained strong in her conviction. Devoting her life to God was the only life she wanted, had ever wanted.

Sitting on the wooden bench, her hands clasped in prayer, she was no longer certain if a life serving God, was the life she should be living, the life she was suited for. Perhaps everyone had been right. Perhaps she was only a dreamer. She had so wished to devote her life to serving the Father, help shed light on the evils inundating the world with his divine guidance. Change so many things... help so many people... and she had failed.

Her thoughts strayed to the public school located in the beggarly, decrepit neighbourhood downtown, where she taught during the day. The school was a nightmare; a concrete jungle where only the fittest survived. Guards were posted on every entrance and framed metallic detectors kept concealed weapons out.

Fights were a daily occurrence in the decaying yard. Girls were getting pregnant at a younger age every year and drug pushers lingered outside the building's gates waiting to pounce on susceptible prey. Terrorised teachers quit their jobs overnight. Replacements lasted a term at most; they had had three different principals in two years. The learning institution was chaos. The world was chaos. Still, she held on to her faith and remained in the school. She did not wish to renounce, did not wish to accept God had deserted her, had forgotten the neglected building that was the only hope for the many children whose sole shot at a decent life was through education.

Many of its students had been born into poverty; many were victims of rage. Born into defunct family environments, they indulged in violence because violence is what they knew, what they had been victims of most of their young lives. Each day was harder than the previous. Each day she resisted the temptation to flee within the confines of the convent, to pray for the world from the safety of the sanctuary.

The principal had separated the willing students from the disruptive ones. Only three classes out of the whole school were dedicated to teaching. The rest of the classes' function was to keep pupils off the streets. To Julia, the segregation was less than ideal, but it had been necessary if any student was to survive the educational ladder. She felt guilty that they had needed to resort to such measures. She understood better than anybody, it was the lost that needed to return to the flock. She prayed endlessly for direction, for divine intervention, but every day she became more desperate, everyday she felt her faith weaken, for every day the school deteriorated further.

The sound of the bell interrupted her desolate thoughts; she sprung to her feet, rushed out of the chapel and ran down the long bleak corridors towards the kitchen. Breakfast was served at six thirty on the dot. Mother Agnes ran the convent with a stern hand. Tardiness, whatever the reason, was intolerable as far as she was concerned. At seven thirty, after she had helped Sister Mary with the washing, she headed for school in her small, second hand car, a gift from a fellow teacher who had fled the school after one term. As she drove down the meandering road to the town below she prayed again for a miracle.

Leroy, the bald, burly negro security guard, greeted her at the door. No one had arrived yet. As usual she was the first. She headed straight for her classroom, she had a lesson to prepare before the nine-o'clock bell rang. As she walked into the room, she saw it; stuck in the exact centre of the blackboard was a perfect white feather. She sighed to herself, wondering who had been the joker who had stuck it there. Very fitting, she smiled, remembering the previous day's lesson as she detached the feather from the board and placed it in the first drawer of her desk.

They had been discussing the story of Icarus, a character in Greek mythology. Daedalus, Icarus' father, had fashioned a pair of wings out of wax and feathers, so he and his son could escape from Crete. Overcome by the giddiness that flying lent him, Icarus had soared too close to the sun. The wax had melted, and he had fallen to the sea. *If only she possessed a pair of wings*, she thought wistfully, *a pair of strong wings immune to the rays of sun with which she could fly straight to heaven. Then she could confront God, ask him why he had forgotten her, forgotten them all...*

With this wishful thought, she returned to sit at her desk and began to prepare the morning's lessons. Surprisingly, the day went smoothly, with no significant disruptive incidents reported. Punctually, she left the building at five p.m. and drove home. Mass was scheduled at seven every evening. She had time for a quick shower. She was exhausted, her legs ached and another migraine threatened; the blinding lights hovering over her left eye nearly always announced an attack. Without undressing, she lay on her bed and closed her eyes, attempting to thwart the escalating headache. Sometimes, though rarely, she could prevent an attack. Thankfully, the throbbing pain in her temples began to subside, until it had faded out completely. She glanced at the clock on the wall over her dresser; the only decorative element allowed other than the crucifix hanging over her bed, over every bed in the basic convent.

*It was already six, she should be heading for the shower*, she thought as she stretched her arm unconsciously towards the bible resting on the bedside table. *What was she doing?* She realised. *She had no time to read. If she wished to clean away the sweaty reminders of her exhausting day, change into a crisp clean habit, she must head immediately to the communal showers down the hall.* Her actions contradicted her thoughts; her hand was already clutching the Holy Book. As soon as the black, leather-bound book was in her possession, she noticed the stem of a feather protruded its bottom. Carefully, she pulled it and the book flung open to reveal the perfect white feather compressed in its centre pages. It looked exactly like the feather she had unstuck from the blackboard that afternoon. Holding the feather in her hand, she read the first words on the open page, '*I am Gabriel. I stand in the presence of God, and I have been sent to speak to you…*'

Tossing the bible on her bed, the impending mass forgotten, she headed towards the small chapel as fast as her feet could carry her, a beaming smile illuminated her face, hope floated in her eyes as she knelt, hands clasped in prayer on the red carpeted floor beneath the Holy Virgin. Joy streamed her blushing cheeks; wonder fluttered her heart as she gazed lovingly at the Mother. '*Thank you*' she whispered softly.

Thinking back, John did not quite understand how it had all begun, how he had allowed himself to be convinced. It had been an arduous, disastrous week full of the usual futile struggles. He was having a couple of beers with his team after work on a Friday afternoon when Sam, one of the veteran policemen, had suggested jokingly that they took the law into their own hands, became vigilantes. 'We will not fail, where the system has', he had stated, his fist in the air, mimicking a cartoon hero.

What began as a joke quickly turned to a debatable idea, the latter evolved to an only option which ultimately led to a unanimous secret pact to cleanse their streets of the corrupt, the degenerate, the vile.

Three months had elapsed since their first furtive mission. Many others had followed. Drug pushers had been arrested with false evidence; with drugs that had been stolen from police custody and planted in their possession. Small time delinquents had been beaten ruthlessly and, fearing for their lives, had fled the streets they patrolled. A week earlier, on their last mission, they had trodden the dark side. A pedophile suspected of molesting several children and raping a seven-year-old girl, had been hunted down and executed. They had manipulated the crime scene to represent Sam as having shot him in self-defense. No one had questioned their testimonies.

After the 'sin,' John had hardly been able to sleep, had avoided going home early. Confusion, guilt and shame consumed his every thought. He could not bear to look his wife in the eye. *She knew him well. She would discover his secret…* he had thought despairingly every time she neared him. A part of him felt there was justice in their acts, a whispering voice warned he had turned into someone he detested; he had turned into his father.

On two occasions, induced by a guilty subconscious, he had ambled torpidly to his uncle's doorstep. His uncle had finally retired, married the widow of an ex-policeman and his warm hearted and hospitable wife had invited him to dinner.

On the two occasions, he was unable to finish his meal, unburden his conscience. The words he longed to voice had remained unspoken; he had been too afraid, too ashamed to confess he shared more than blood with his father.

His thoughts trailed to Eva, his beautiful wife, to his children. *He was such a fool, hadn't his uncle, life, taught him anything?* He felt small, ridiculous; a nescient fool under the immensity of the heavens bathing his guilt. The image of his wife's innocent eyes dawned in the night and he finally understood what he must do. The time had come to confess his iniquitous deeds. He must come clean, irrespective of penance.

His ignoble acts would remain unpunished no longer. He could not allow his opprobrious acts to corrode his soul, destroy the good in him. He must expiate his sins. Exile from the police force, imprisonment was a certainty, but the latter was pittance in exchange for his soul. An image of his uncle replaced his wife's. He would be devastated. His uncle had given him a chance in life, taught him to be a decent, honorable man. He had entrusted him with the execution of justice, and he had betrayed him, had betrayed them all. He was a despicable and arrogant fool. There was no righteousness in his deeds, no justification. He was not above the law, no one was.

His thoughts drifted back to Eva. She would be watching television in the living room, the kids asleep. His dinner, as usual, would be waiting for him in the microwave; she never waited to have dinner with him these days, had stopped doing so a long time ago. The thought of facing her sent a bone deep chill down his spine. He stood up, sat down again. *He wasn't ready... not yet. He would wait for a while longer... wait until she was asleep... He would tell her in the morning…* holding the thought, he closed his eyes, reminisced of a not too distant time when they had all been happy, when there had been no shame in his heart. Then he prayed, asked God to give him strength, to forgive him for his sins.

He was half asleep, steering his thoughts to nothingness, his head resting against the wooden balustrade.

Suddenly, he felt a light tickle on his face. He rubbed his face, opened his eyes, and he saw it; upon his lap, nestled vertically between his legs, lay a perfect white feather.

He gazed up to the heaven then lowered his eyes to the feather again. God had heard him, had sent him a sign…two careful fingers transferred the brilliant feather to his chest pocket and, suddenly invigorated with courage decided to go inside the house. The time had finally come to confess his sins to his wife.

His body felt heavy as he tried to get up. It became suddenly limp, unresponsive. He felt lightheaded and slumped back against the timber handrail. Within seconds, he had fallen into deep slumber, his head propped against the wooden rods.

The moment his eyes closed, he began to dream; he was standing on the stage of an auditorium, the audience packed with uniformed men, fellow officers, a trickle of civilians. He turned his head slightly and the Commissioner stood dignified beside him. Suddenly, everyone in the auditorium stood up to applaud. A thunderous roar echoed throughout the large hall as the tall, white bearded man pinned a medal on the lapel of his uniform jacket. His eyes roamed over the standing ovation. In the first row, flanked by uniforms, stood his wife gazing adoringly up at him, her eyes bristling with pride. By her side stood his two proud children, they beamed up at him, their small hands clapping with unbridled enthusiasm.

Lost in the dream, John did not see the tips of the feather begin to glow with a blinding silver light, did not see it snuggle out of his pocket and float to write on his front door, did not see the feather lift up in the air and blow away into the night shedding a diamond trail.

A couple of hours elapsed before John woke up and climbed the steps to his home. He had no recollection of the dream, which anchored deep in memory, imperceptible to conscience, but the words; ***'you have been touched, have been awakened to your truth, when the time is nigh, you will be summoned, and you will come...'*** implanted in his soul.

Tremulous, euphoric, he reread the mysterious message repeatedly. As the enigmatic words resounded in the night, John wondered what God had in store for him, what he must do to regain his favour.

As usual Ethan was in his room, his eyes glued to his laptop. For months, he had been striving to create a new search engine, one that would revolutionise the internet. It would be faster, more powerful, more accurate, invulnerable to viruses. He still needed to surmount a few obstacles, but his keen mind always managed to overcome them. A few more days, maybe weeks and his masterpiece would be ready. No one knew what he was working on. His creation was a fortified secret.

A brilliant hacker himself, he knew how tugging at a thread of information would dismantle a secret. Thus, his invention remained clandestine until it was time to reveal it to the world. The internet was a thriving nest to virtual pirates, but he had ensured no one would be able to spy on him. He had created a firewall that equated NASA's. His IQ determined him a genius. There were few concepts he did not understand, could not learn to understand. His parents were proud of his outstanding academic achievements, but lately they had begun to worry. They did not consider his seclusion healthy. He hardly ever went out with his friends anymore; he spent most of his days sequestered in his room. He would have had his meals in his room had his mother allowed it.

Ethan rushed home from school every day, eager to continue his work. It was not that he enjoyed a hermitic existence, except for his high Intelligence Quotient; he was just like any other seventeen-year-old boy. The excitement of his project was what kept him away from his friends, the fun. He would have time to socialise soon. Hopefully, a month at most. Right now, he could not afford to sacrifice precious time. He wished to be the first, the best.

He had been interested in computers since an early age; he liked machines, what they could accomplish, what he could teach them to accomplish. Whilst his friends chatted on the internet, he traded information with hackers. Whilst his friends downloaded music, he downloaded tutorials, surfed the net for the information he needed. Part of the information he required lay at the touch of a button, the rest and most valuable was in his head. The search engine he was creating was different from anything on the market, not only would it search quicker than any engine but it could also communicate quicker and safer with other sites. Advertising companies would pay hefty sums to advertise on his user interface. The income derived from the adverts would allow him to subsidise sites devoted to free legal music and media downloads, virus free. The latter would return profits from adverts. Everyone would use his search engine, his downloading sites. Record companies and movie companies would hail him their saviour; piracy would cease, talent justly remunerated. This would only be the beginning. Numerous innovative ideas had already been drafted in his mind.

It was Friday afternoon; he had received a text message from his friends informing him there was a party at a friend's house that night. Ethan texted them back declining the offer, claiming he did not feel well. He did not wish his friends to call the house; if they did, he was sure his parents would force him to go. They had been on his back lately, nagged him constantly to socialise more. His seclusion was unhealthy, they had insisted. The immediate lie out of the way, he concentrated on work. He was getting more excited as the days rolled by, as he neared completion. He was impatient to see the end result.

He was so engrossed calculating data, he kept ignoring the beeping sound alerting him he was about to run out of battery power. *One more calculation, one more alteration*...the screen went black. '*Shit!*'. He hoped he had not lost important data... He kept a couple of backups on independent hard drives but hated to lose even seconds of work. *Eight beeps, eight beeps, before the battery ran out*, he thought frustrated. Chastising himself for yet another miscalculation, he opened the first drawer of his desk and retrieved the power cable. He had a brilliant mind, but he was hopeless at practical matters. He plugged in the cable. Nothing, his laptop was dead. He switched on the light to check power supply. The bulb lit up. He fetched his old laptop from a shelf behind him and inserted its power cable in the same socket. The laptop worked fine. He tried his laptop again, nothing.

Quickly, he unplugged the power cable, was about to check the plug fuse when the familiar purring sound startled him. He lifted his head, glanced rapidly at the screen. Disbelieving eyes fixed on the intermittent light expanding from its centre. He sat frozen, the power cable dangling from his limp hand, the power indicator of his laptop off, his palm resting on the dead keyboard. '*What the hell ...*' he murmured through clenched teeth, his privileged mind in disarray. Slowly, the flashing dot at the centre of the screen began to expand further, began to focus steadily to an image. Ethan stared hypnotized as the image sharpened. A perfect white feather spanned the totality of the screen.

*He had been hacked,* was his immediate thought, but the idea was soon discarded. It was impossible. His firewall was impregnable. He watched the image demoralized, perhaps he was not the best, there was someone better. Rage and impotence engulfed him. He stood up brusquely kicked the chair to the floor, rushed into a clean pair of jeans and sweater, took some money from the jar he kept in his closet, and ran down the stairs. As he ran out the front door, he called out to his parents, who were preparing dinner in the kitchen; he was going to a party. As Ethan hurried across the front garden, his parents watched him from the kitchen window. The moment he had disappeared around the street corner, they smiled at each other in relief.

His friends were overjoyed to see him; he had not hung out with them for some time. Claiming he was feeling better, he walked with his friends towards the makeshift bar and got himself a beer. He did not usually drink alcohol, but tonight he would have a couple of drinks. He needed to tame his hyperactive brain, drown his frustration. After a few beers, he felt himself loosen up, he was an appalling dancer but braved the dance floor with a girl he had had an eye on for some time, had intended to ask for a date once his work was finished. His magnetic looks; smiling sea green eyes, dirty blonde hair, square dimpled jaw, and toned body made him extremely popular with the opposite sex and if it were not for his 'passion', he would have played the field more often. After cavorting to the rhythm of the pounding beat for a while, he felt sick. Excusing himself politely from his eager dance partner, he headed to the garden. He needed fresh air.

He sat on the grass, under a tree, wishing his head would stop spinning. He felt bile rise up his throat, and threw up on the base of the tree. The dizziness persisted so he decided to lie back on the grass for a while, wait for the giddiness to subside. He was sprawled on his back. His eyes closed, when he felt something tickle his cheek. Mechanically, he waved a heavy arm above his face, scratched his cheek lamely as he yawned. He was close to sleep when he felt the tickle again, this time on his other cheek. Reluctantly, he opened his eyes; a feather, exactly like the one that had appeared on the laptop's screen, hovered above his face. He sat up quickly, the bizarre coincidence disquieting him, the dizziness gone. *Some joker had thrown it over him,* he rationalized, as his eyes searched the garden for the culprit. There was no one around. After a while, he looked down at the feather that had floated to the ground and landed at his feet.

Its whiteness contrasted the olive carpet, *a perfect specimen,* he thought vaguely. He picked it up with two fingers and examined it; there was nothing special about it. Birds flew over gardens. Feathers fell in gardens. The fact that it was the second feather he saw that day was a mere coincidence, an acceptable variable in the laws of probability. Holding that thought, he stood up and returned to the party, leaving the feather behind on the grass. As he chatted animatedly with his friends, he kept visualizing the first feather, kept wondering who the magician hacker was.

He got home late but his parents said nothing, they were delighted he had finally decided to act normal. He had a quick shower; hating the lingering smell of alcohol and then headed for his room, for his laptop. He switched it on. Mercifully, the screen displayed his usual desktop. He decided to check the data he had been perfecting before he went to bed. It was then that he noticed it. Peeping from under the keyboard was another feather, exactly like the others. His heart raced, pounded his chest with fury. The feather seemed to have materialised out of the screen. Something strange was definitely going on. With extreme care, he picked it up, put it in a plastic sleeve and locked it in the drawer of his desk. He would resolve the enigma tomorrow he thought, as his exhausted body pulled him to bed.

The moment Ethan accepted the feather; he began to feel sleepy. Soon, he was fast sleep and the dream began...

He was watching television, a tall modern building filled the screen. Hanging over its revolving glass entrance was a 3D silver and white logo that spelt 'Quill'. He watched himself spin out the revolving doors, dressed in an expensive dark suit. Reporters avalanched the four bodyguards surrounding him as they ushered him to a black limousine. The moment he stepped into the car, he was greeted by a dark haired man impeccably dressed in a dark grey suit that seemed to know him extremely well.

Ethan did not see the feather's tips light up, did not see it float up, disappear into the screen and begin to write. Did not see it emerge from the screen and float out of his bedroom window, its silvery trail curling high in the night. When Ethan switched on his laptop the following morning, he nearly fainted; a flashing message on his desk top read ***'You have been touched, have been awakened to your truth. When the time is nigh, you will be summoned, and you will come.'***

When John woke up the next morning, he headed straight for the front door. The mystical words were still there. Quickly, before his wife, the kids woke up, he headed for the kitchen, wet a cloth and cleansed all trace of the baffling message. Intuition told him the message was meant for his eyes only. He rushed up to his bedroom and searched the pockets of his uniform; the feather was gone. He searched the porch, the lobby, the steps leading up to the second floor, his bedroom, the bathroom... Disappointed, he returned to the kitchen, made himself a cup of coffee and waited for his family to join him..

Eva was the first to meet him. She was in a surprisingly cheerful mood and greeted him with a peck on the lips. John at the breakfast bar, cup in hand, staring at her, whilst she happily potted around the kitchen making scrambled eggs on toast for everyone. In minutes, the children came running into the sunny room, into his arms and showered him with kisses.

John could not believe the sudden change; he had regressed to the happy past. He rubbed his eyes, pinched himself on the arm. He was not dreaming.

As they ate breakfast, Eva and the kids debated on what do for the rest of the day. It was a beautiful summer's day, a barbeque for friends and family seemed a good option, or swimming and fishing in the lake. '*What would you rather do darling?*', whispered Eva in his ear, ignoring Aaron's excited '*lake, lake*!' and Jeannie's '*barbeque, barbeque!*', '*Errrm... whatever you wish sweetheart*' he whispered hesitantly.

John could not get over the miraculous metamorphosis; his family life seemed suddenly perfect overnight. His wife looked radiant, more beautiful than ever. His children kept showering him with affection, laughing with him, with their mother. There were no words of reproach, no fighting, no arguing. The unanimous decision was finally a barbeque and after tidying up the house, Eva and the kids left for the supermarket to buy food and drinks leaving him to prepare a quick lunch, mow the lawn and clean the porch and pool.

As he vacuumed the bottom of the pool, gazed into the clear blue waters, he kept revisiting his family's sudden change of behaviour. He felt happier than he had for a long time. He had missed his family. He revelled in the miraculous transformation, felt hopeful again, but the jubilant thoughts were short lived. A wave of dread swept over him as he realised he must confront his wife, confess the secret burning in his heart. The unexpected turn of events had weakened his resolution; he did not wish to destroy what promised to be a happy day, the kind of day he had not had, in a long time, his family had not had in a long time. His wife's, his children's good-humoured attitudes still baffled him, but he was adamant he would enjoy the 'miracle' while it lasted, even if it was only for a day. He would tell her tomorrow...he would be ready then....

Eva had invited everyone; Gregory and Margaret, every member of his team, their wives and children, their neighbouring friends. John was pleasantly surprised every one of them, without exception, had been able to make it on such short notice. It was an extraordinary coincidence no one had other family plans for the day. The children invaded the pool the minute they had changed into their bathing suits. The women helped Eva to place food and drinks in the long table he had helped her place under the porch and most of the men hang around the barbeque area, cold beers in hand, whilst he and Gregory grilled steaks, burgers and sausages for everyone.

John kept glancing covertly at his accomplices wondering how long their friendship would last after his confession. He would make an individual confession but the latter would trigger an investigation that would inevitably uncover their collective sins.

He watched their families, his family, and felt sudden desperation; they had all been such fools. His blood flamed as he watched them, merrily drinking beers in his garden. Like him, they were no different to those they hunted. He glanced at Gregory, who had moved away to chat animatedly with Eva by the pool and he wished tomorrow would never come...Gregory, his beautiful wife...they would be devastated, ashamed of him...

It was then that the unimaginable happened; he needed to fetch more burgers from the freezer and, as he crossed the perfect lawn to the house, he noticed Gregory was in deep conversation with his 'partners in crime', at the far end of the garden. The seven men whispered among themselves, thoughtful expressions conveying the conversation was of a serious nature. For a moment, a frightening thought attacked him; *Gregory justified their deeds. He knew, someone had told him. He had become a silent accomplice, encouraged their acts.* The ridiculous thought was soon discarded; *it was impossible, Gregory was not 'in on it'. He was not that kind of man, he was not like them, him. Gregory was Gregory.*

He hastened to the kitchen, to the window meters away from them and eavesdropped on their conversation. He strained his ears, tried to make sense of the fragmented conversation...*No it was impossible...Gregory was agreeing with them, dishing out advice, condoning the means that justified the end.* He listened to his uncle's words of admiration in shock; he was openly proud of the high level of detentions, the swift eradication of crime. He kept shaking hands with them, patting them on the back...a smile beaming from ear to ear... John could take it no more, it was time to confront the 'righteous' clan. Someone must remind them of the oath they had sworn to when they joined the force. He must put an end to the madness. Abandoning the platter of burgers on the kitchen counter he headed their way, hands clenched at his sides, knuckles white.

Before he could utter a word, express disgust, Gregory placed an arm over his tense shoulder and began to congratulate him for their outstanding results. '...*I'm so proud of you son... proud of the man you have become.*' He told him, hugging him closer. His last words puzzled John; *Proud of the man I have become?* He glanced at Eva, she was sitting on the edge of the pool watching the children, blissfully unaware of the drama meters away. Their eyes locked briefly and she blew him a kiss. An unnerving thought invaded him as he absorbed the surrealist scene; something strange was happening to his family, to his world...

He would say nothing, admit to nothing, until he discovered what was going on... Instinct told him the feather had something to do with the sudden change of attitudes, the uncharacteristic behaviours. It was a bizarre thought he admitted, still, it was what his gut told him. He had learned to trust the sinking feeling in his stomach; it had saved his life, those of his men, on more than one occasion. He would wait until he was back at work on Monday. He would confront his men then...

Despite the confusion, the looming confrontation, it had been a wonderful weekend; he had enjoyed his 'new family life'. He had played and laughed with his children until exhaustion had rendered them sleepy, having to carry them up to their beds. Alone at last, he had made love to his beautiful wife. She had fallen asleep in his arms and, for a moment, he had felt the luckiest man alive.

Monday morning he got up early, kissed his family goodbye and headed impatiently for the station. The minute he arrived at the station, sat at his desk, he summoned his men to an urgent meeting. The impromptu reunion was nothing like he had expected, could ever have imagined. When his men had abandoned his office, returned to their tasks, he lowered the blinds of his office, told his secretary he was not to be disturbed, locked his door and began to cry like a child.

He had learned to believe in God, believing that miracles were possible was another thing. That a miracle could happen to him, to those around him, was unthinkable and yet, a miracle **had** happened. The foolish 'mistakes', the unjustified deeds had been erased from his life, from all of their lives. God had spared them, had miraculously cleansed them of their sins. They had never made the wrongful pact; crossed to the dark side. He had just read the files, the proof. God had blessed them with a second chance.

Indeed, their achievements had been spectacular, unprecedented; they had resolved cold cases that had remained unsolved for years. They had found missing people they had given up on ever finding. They had arrested criminals with the necessary evidence to have them locked behind bars, many for good... In three months, they had miraculously wiped their streets of crime. Their success unspoiled by unlawful means. Gregory was still Gregory.

His thoughts drifted to the feather, to the night when he had been imploring God to give him strength. God existed. He had answered his pleas, had cleansed his soul, given him back his family, his life. For a moment he wondered if someone else had found it, if the feather had found someone else...

Inspector John Taylor could not wait for the time to be nigh. God had already forgiven him, but he was impatient to repay him for the second chance he had been miraculously awarded.

*Seth stood tall on the raised platform as the Higher Master of light handed him the certificate scroll and placed the golden book insignia to the chest of the long robe worn by mature angels. (Angels matured at the equivalent of 25 mortal years and did not age further) Seth watched his parents as they smiled at him proudly. They had reasons to be proud, he had graduated top of his class. He looked at his mother, his eyes gleaming with gratitude. She had understood he had been dying and she had saved him. He owed everything to her. Her revelations, wise counsel had made him understand he should learn from his errors, learn to be patient. The realm would answer his questions when the time was right. Since that night, the enlightening conversation, he had striven to conform, had endeavoured to seek his answers on the right path. He had striven to block out the soul shattering images, learned to wait...*

*Graduating from the Halls of Knowledge top of his class had been his first objective. His rebellious antics well in the past, he had dedicated long afternoons to the pursuit of his goal. Achieving first place in the final exams meant he could learn in every hall, be experienced in a variety of disciplines and not be restricted to only a couple, as was the case with other graduates. His first choice were the Islands.*

*It was in the Islands that he had his first dream, his second bizarre contact with the mortal world. What happened to him that night by the shore had no logical explanation; his study books did not portray such happenings. As far as he knew, no one had shared a similar experience and he had begun to think his overactive imagination was simply playing tricks on him. Initially, he had been tempted to confide in his Master in the Halls of Healing but, instinctively, decided against it. He was afraid his confession would be counterproductive to his studies, would tarnish his spotless curriculum.*

*When meditation class had ended for the afternoon, he had headed for the peaceful shores that edged the circular lands. He had sat on the ivory sands listening to the gentle swish of the tides, to the loving thoughts of dolphins gliding over the warm indigo waters and had thought of his mother, wondered what she would be doing at that precise moment. A burning sensation on the top of his right wing had interrupted his nostalgic stream. He had spread his wing and curved it forward. The edge of his wing glowed with silver light. He had pulled the wing close to his eyes, the glowing outline, the concave dent, depicted a feather was missing.* ***It was impossible****, he had thought perplexed.* ***His feathers regenerated immediately...***

*He had not had time to analyse what was happening to his wing, why one of his feathers was missing. A bright light had swarmed him and he had found himself floating outside the sphere, looking out on the same field he had seen when he crossed the frontier as a young angel. He had remained motionless, afraid to turn his head; he had not wished to see what he had seen the last time.*

*Nothing had happened for a while and then suddenly, the field had transformed, become the inside of a house. He had stood beside a man who had fallen asleep over a heap of papers covering his desk. A white feather rested on the palm of his sprawled hand...*

It was noon when Alexandra woke up the following day. She had gotten home late the previous night, had had to catch up on her busy schedule and had left the office at ten. Thoughts of the mysterious feather, the cryptic message had haunted, distracted her all day.

She had not heard the alarm go off at eight; she always got up early on Saturday mornings to go jogging in the park. Still sleepy, she slid out of bed thanking her lucky stars it was the weekend; that she was not late for work. Clad in her favourite pink and white stripped pyjamas she headed, yawning and stretching, towards the bathroom. She had slept like a baby and felt extremely relaxed, she had forgotten the pleasant feeling. She had not felt this rested in a long time.

She was about to get into the shower cubicle when an image of the feather exploded in her mind and the puzzling message surfaced the murkiness of slumber. She turned around abruptly and headed back to the bedroom. Her pulse racing, she headed for the dresser. The message **was** inscribed on the silver tray, she had not dreamt it, yesterday **had** happened! She searched for the feather, searched everywhere but it was gone.

For the rest of the weekend she mulled over the enigmatic message. Every time she recalled the words, goose bumps crawled over her skin. She had no idea what the mystifying words meant and was both afraid and eager to find out. The baffling message excited her, unnerved her. A million questions attacked her impatient mind. She was dying to share the extraordinary mystery but instinct advised against it. The encounter with the feather would remain a secret. The feather was gone and no one would believe her anyway...

Alexandra arrived earlier than usual at her office Monday morning; she wanted to catch up with some of the work she had not managed to complete on Friday. Blocking out the mystery, she made herself a strong cup of coffee and fumbled through the stacks of files crowding her desk. One of them caught her attention. She stared at the names printed on the manila cover and recalled how badly that particular case had ended. Her heart knotted as she remembered the two little angels they had been trying desperately to save and had failed to keep safe. She blinked back tears as she remembered their tragic eyes, their desperate expressions when their father, the vile monster, had claimed them, taken them back to his lair. Loopholes, shrewd and ruthless lawyers used to their advantage, continued to plague a system that advocated protection of the vulnerable.

Alexandra did not understand anything anymore, everyone had been convinced the girls would remain in the safe haven, in the Children's Home Social Services had placed them in months before. She strived to block out the grotesque images lacerating her soul but the horrid scenes insisted. Slowly, she opened the file. *She should not be torturing herself this way,* she thought, but her hands moved with a life of their own and eyes dropped on its contents. Slowly, she turned the pages until innocent imploring eyes stared up at her. The image tore at her heart and she squeezed her eyes. The image persevered, would not disentangle itself from culpable memory and she began to cry desolately. She whimpered like a child as the faces of the innocent she had been unable to save, endured in her mind's eye.

For a long time her sobbing echoed the walls of the shabby office, impotence strangling her breath. Eventually, she began to calm down. Wearily, she lifted her head and reached for box of tissues she kept in the second drawer of her desk. As she dried her swollen eyes they involuntarily darted back to the black-and-white photograph. Her mouth dropped in disbelief, her heartbeat throbbing in her throat; twin innocent faces were smiling radiantly up at her. Before she had time to react, digest the inconceivable transmutation, the phone on her desk began to ring.

She listened in awed silence to the words being spoken, her eyes wide with incredulity. The moment she hung up the phone she fled the office and headed to the police station. As she drove through the traffic congested streets, beads of gratitude slid down her warm cheeks, the police officer's words blessing her ears. The girls were waiting for her, waiting to return to safety. Merely an hour ago, the police had arrested their father and, this time, no jury on earth would proclaim him innocent. Detective John Taylor and his team had ensured it.

Slade Alston sat on the edge of his white Italian, leather sofa in the centre of his spacious, minimalist attic. His sharp eyes dissected the overlapping layers of black-and-white photographs covering the oval glass coffee table. One by one he picked up the glossy prints, scrutinized them and placed them in one of the two piles on the side table. One stack comprised those he would keep, the other, those he would destroy. Those that were perfect, those that were not. As discerning eyes roamed each image he recalled the moment he had taken the snapshots, what he had felt then and compared it to what he felt as he studied them. If the image did not reflect a déjà vu feeling, they were discarded. To Slade, photography was not merely about capturing a moment, taking the perfect shot; it was about capturing the emotion of the moment, emotions he immortalized to be enduring testimonies of life.

As he flicked through the remaining photos, one of them caught his eye. He had taken it the previous day wanting to finish the reel and had developed it in his dark room that night. He had forgotten all about it, forgotten the quick shot he had taken of his dog Gizmo basking in the sun on the corner of the terrace, surrounding the luxurious apartment. The toy terrier was a gift from his sister Sadie who had insisted he kept one of the two puppies she had rescued from a friend. Her capricious friend had bought them on a whim and decided shortly, the yappy dogs were a burden. He had not wanted a dog but was unable to refuse his kid sister anything.

He smiled as he stared at the image; he was a cute little dog. On closer inspection, he realized a feather was nestled between its front paws. *Strange,* he thought. *He had not noticed it when he took the shot.* Placing the photo on the good pile he stretched his arms, rubbed his tired eyes and slumped back on the large sofa. He lay there, his eyes closed, his thoughts veered to oblivion. Suddenly, on impulse, he stood up and headed out to the terrace.

The moment he set foot on the cold mosaic he saw it; a perfect white feather lay on the corner where the dog had been sleeping. He stooped down and carefully picked it up. *A bird had dropped it,* he thought casually and tossed it over the wall into the dusky skies.

The evening was invitingly pleasant so he decided to have his usual club sandwich and glass of wine outdoors. He was sitting quietly, sipping the wine, gazing at the twinkling lights stretching the city when he felt a tickling sensation on his bare feet. He searched under the table but found nothing. He was about to pour himself a second glass of wine when he felt it again. This time he stood up, pushed the rattan table to one side and searched the floor around him. He found nothing. It had been a long day and, after finishing a third glass of wine, he retired to bed. He was dozing off when he felt the familiar tickle on the soles of his feet. He pulled the grey satin sheet off him. As he flung the sleek fabric to one side, a feather floated in the air to fall on the floor beside the bed. *How strange... the breeze must have carried it back up and it had somehow stuck on his clothes...* He was beat, the several meetings he had had that afternoon had worn him out.

He hated to wait in lobbies, hated to wait to see if his photographs were of interest. He loved working freelance. As he brooded over the wasted journeys, he questioned his nomadic existence; perhaps it was time he resigned himself to a conventional life, he conformed. He was too impatient, arrogant, he admitted. He was a magnificent photographer, his photographs were always of interest, he only needed to wait for a while. Unlike him, people had schedules, adhered to a priority-synchronized world. *He would change,* he thought dismissively, as he walked idly out onto the terrace, feather in hand.

Sadie had been urging him more and more to accept one of the positions offered to him by prestigious newspapers, magazines, modelling agencies, kept arguing it was time he quit his vagrant existence. *Perhaps she was right,* he thought gravely. *Perhaps it was wrong of him to spend so much time away from her.* Job offers had become more and more succulent over the years but he had refused every one of them. It was not because he did not need the money, he did not wish to be tied down; belong. Once he had belonged, fit perfectly in a perfect world, but that world had been destroyed, would never exist again.

Sadie and he had had the perfect childhood. Their father had been a wealthy businessman and their mother was the only daughter of an even wealthier one. When they had married their father's real estate business had complemented the construction empire their mother had inherited. She was an only child, the sole heir to the Carrington fortune. Her father Thomas Carrington had become a widower the day she was born, and had never remarried.

They had grown up in a beautiful mansion, edged by a lake an hour from the city. They had never wanted for anything, but above all had never wanted for love. Isobel and Desmond Alston had doted on their children but ensured their privileged environment had not spurred two spoiled little brats.

Unlike most of their friends' offspring, Sadie and Slade were affable, down to earth children with solid values. Slade idolised his father, adored his mother and hoped one day to create a family in their image. Their parents were deeply in love and, unlike his friend's parents, openly demonstrated this love. They were forever kissing, hugging, joking with each other. Slade, who had developed a passion for photography from an early age, immortalized the constant displays of affection and stuck them among hundreds of other snapshots illustrating their enviable family life in the rapidly expanding collection of albums that stacked his bedroom shelves.

The childhood utopia was shattered one night when they were asleep. Two men jumped over the high fence that surrounded the grounds to the mansion, hacked the alarm, invaded their world through a window on the ground floor at the rear of the building. Isobel and Duncan Alston were sound asleep when two bullets shattered their skulls. Sadie and he were miraculously spared. Their bedrooms were on the third floor and the cold-blooded assassins had already spent too much time trying to open the invincible safe in the walk-in wardrobe, next to the master bedroom, to hunt for more prey.

The moment they had heard the gunshots, Sadie and Slade had hidden behind the rows of clothes inside their closet. Slade, who always obeyed his father, executed his plan to perfection. He had immediately grabbed his sleepy sister, dragged her whilst covering her mouth, into the long closet and shoved her into a far corner, behind the row of coats. They remained huddled, trembling with terror, confused, until the police had finally rescued them from behind the protective veil.

The nightmare that ensued was still a blur in Slade's memory. The only lucid memory that surfaced his chaotic mind was the blast of two gunshots. The one thought that kept protruding his agonized warp was that his parents had died for nothing. That somewhere out there, two strangers, two evil and callous men, had taken the two people he loved most in the world from him. He was only fourteen years old.

A couple of weeks after the funeral they had left to boarding school; the proviso included in the will. Slade had not contested the stipulation; he no longer had a family. Remaining in the mansion, in the scene of the crime under the tutelage of an estranged aunt, who had emerged into their lives sporadically, was not an option. Somewhere, in the depths of memory, remained the idea his aunt had hurt his father in a terrible way...

Boarding school became their new life, except for the summers they were forced to spend in their aunt's new home. Slade was no fool, knew his aunt's displays of affection were fake. The only thing his aunt cared about was the generous sum she received for their up-keep every month, the expensive home she had inherited so Sadie and he could continue to enjoy the standard of life they were accustomed to.

Their inheritance remained in the capable hands of the company board until Slade was old enough to take over the business. The day he turned eighteen Slade sold the mansion, brought a luxurious attic in the city and had his fleet of brilliant lawyers get him his sister's custody. Slade could still recall the glimmer of relief in his aunt's eyes the day they had said goodbye and left for the city. He never saw her again, never returned any of her desperate phone calls after his lawyers rescinded the lifelong monthly sum. He had no pity for hypocrites, for those that betrayed his father. The only thing he regretted was leaving her the luxurious house. He had had no option. His astute aunt had insisted on having the property deeds transferred to her name in exchange for agreeing to supervise, tolerate them during the summer.

When they had both earned their business degrees, honoured their father, Sadie took over the family business under the guiding hand of the board. He left to travel the world.

Everyone had expected him to take over the business; assume his father's role. He was a shrewd intelligent young man but, to everyone's dismay, he had not set a foot in the company. During the two years he had spent waiting for his sister to finish her degree, to mature, become independent, he had studied photography, the only thing that distracted him in an otherwise uninteresting world. The distraction soon turned to an obsession, the obsession to a profession.

Unlike his sister, who had finally managed, after considerable therapy, to overcome her traumatic past, he was still a prisoner of the tragic memory; anchored in the 'could have been'. He had refused therapy, decided it would make no difference, would change nothing. No one could help him. No one could bring back his parents.

Unknown to his sister, he kept his collection of family memoirs hidden in his study. Every day he flickered through his 'other life'. Initially, staring into the vivid remnants had killed him. With time, he had managed to dismember the images, block the pain and keep only the true essence of that fragment in time.

When Sadie had finalized her university studies, he had given her the keys to the adjoining attic apartment he had secretly bought a few days after he had purchased his, waited until she had settled happily in the company and left to travel, capture the world and the emotions in it.

As his bare feet tread the cold roof of the city, he thought of all the places he had been to, of all the faces he had met. He thought of the paradisiacal lands, the savage ones, the peaceful, the war-ridden, the beauty and destruction he had immortalized. His photographs had captured the essence of each destination, the emotion of each inhabitant in a world that had already begun to become small.

Feather in hand, Slade walked to the glass wall, fencing the terrace, and blew the feather out into space a second time. He was about to turn around, return to bed, when a sudden gust returned it back over the glass panel onto the chilled floor. Frustrated, he picked the feathery pest once again and delivered it back into the night. Again, the feather blew back over the glass. Impatiently, he grabbed it from the floor, pushed his arm as far as it would go down over the glass and released it. To his amazement, it floated back up to land on the tessellated floor again. Irritated, he attached a piece of string to the feather, bound a stone from one of his flowerpots to the string and flung the ridiculous thing high over the transparent boundary. *There!* He thought. *End of problem!* Before he had time to reach the sliding glass doors connecting the terrace to his bedroom, he heard a stone hit the floor behind him. He turned around slowly, as he suspected the feather had returned. He had sensed right; there was something very odd going on with the feather. A persistent breeze was not what kept bringing it back.

He untied the 'little fellow' with careful fingers, sat down on the terrace's floor and began to caress its silken body. As he watched it closely, he felt a strange emotion stir inside of him. The feeling was almost like the ones his family albums incited. Quickly, he rushed inside, grabbed his third eye and switched on the lights in the terrace. He placed the feather on the ground and flashed at it repeatedly. When he was satisfied he had taken enough shots, he picked it up, placed it on the empty pillow to his left, and got into bed. The moment the feather entered his life his eyes began to feel heavy. The moment he was asleep, he began to dream.

He was standing in a large hall, in a stage; hundreds of people filled the curved seats below. The room roared with applause as someone handed him some prestigious photography award. His sister stood proudly in the front row, holding the hand of a decorous young man. Beside him stood a woman, the most beautiful woman he had ever laid eyes on. A younger man held her hand. His eyes rested on her Mona Lisa smile, on the enigmatic eyes gazing adoringly up at him, on the sensuous lips mouthing the words *'I love you'*... Slade's memory was unable to snapshot the dream, but his soul immortalized its emotion, the déjà vu feeling perennial within its walls.

Slade did not see the feather lift from the pillow, scribble on it, its tips smouldering, float over the terrace into the night, a twinkling trail painting the darkness. The moment he woke up the next morning, he turned his head. The pillow was empty. The feather was gone. To his amazement, the words ***'You have been touched, have been awakened to your truth. When the time is nigh, you will be summoned, and you will come...'*** sprawled the slate satin pillow.

Alexandra felt euphoric. The girls were safe. She could not believe it; could not believe God had finally heard her desperate prayers. She was still perturbed by the photograph's uncanny transformation; she had gone back to the office, looked at it again, thinking that perhaps she may have been daydreaming, that the altered image was a figment of her wishful imagination. It was not. Two smiling faces kept staring up at her. *She* ***had*** *witnessed a miracle,* she concluded. *One she would also keep secret.* Once again, the little voice inside her head whispered, heeded, she should tell no one. She had henceforth taken the photograph from the file, sealed it in an envelope, taken it home and locked it away where no one would ever find it.

As the days went by, other miracles followed. Unexpectedly, the office's expenditure budget increased considerably, and two more Social Workers, excellent professionals, were recruited. Good people devoted heart and soul to their jobs. In the same week, an IT Company, located a couple of doors down their street, reallocated to a newly built office building and donated computers, monitors, a photocopier and trendy office furniture to their office; everything in top notch condition. The budget allowed for a paint job and modern blinds for all the office windows. The donated cabinets allowed better filing organisation, and they had been able to decorated the small playroom at the back of the office. A 'Magical garden' had been the chosen theme, appealing greatly to the children who visited. Overnight, the office had transformed into a modern, cheerful and efficient environment, easing daily struggles.

The bright surroundings seemed to resound with a lucky vibe; the local community suddenly became interested in the nature of their work and volunteers flocked to their offices. Some offered to help with the twenty-four-hour child line; others donated toys and other useful items to the Children's Homes. Neighbouring companies donated TV's, DVD's, gaming consoles and PC's. Carers in the home were ecstatic;

their tight budget had not allowed even the slightest luxury, and everyone joked Christmas had arrived early.

The local community was not the only sector that made donations. Neighbouring companies contributed generously, allowing two more children's homes to become a reality.

Alexandra was overjoyed at the sudden bout of good luck, but the most important miracles were yet to come. Overnight, difficult cases had sudden solutions and children were removed from hostile environments effectively. Witnesses to abuse no longer feared testifying in court. A string of coincidental events lead to suspicions which when confirmed, allowed children to be removed from dangerous habitats into safety, miraculously before they had suffered irreversible damage. The hand of the law became swift; police work flawless, bureaucracy expedient, and an extremely vigilant community allowed little breathing space to abusers an uncaring society had once ignored. As more children in need of a safe haven reached them, more money flowed into their coffers, allowing more homes to be opened and cope with the growing demand.

It was a beautiful morning. Alexandra, as usual, was the first to arrive at the office. She went through the pile of files stacked on her desk and one by one, remembered what had happened to the children regarding each case. A smile illuminated her face; every child was safe, a hopeful future augured for them all. Clasping her hands in prayer, she gave thanks to God for his gift, for the perfect feather that had flown into her life and touched it with magic. The feather's message remained entrenched in memory. Every night when she retired to bed, she wondered with nervous anticipation if the following day would see a resolution to the enigma.

When Marcus woke up, the feather was not in his book. He searched the entire yard but could not find it. He questioned the children insistently, but no one had seen it. The sound of the bell, announcing it was time for supper, cut his search short. The laughter died down at the first toll, and sombre faced children walked in a quiet line to the grim dining room. When they had all reached their allocated seats, they sat down in silence. Marcus headed for the kitchen.

He was busy peeling potatoes when he heard the first scream. He covered his ears to deafen the shrill sound. He did not wish to know who had screamed or why. It was none of his business; he got along fine being invisible. Dirty hands muffled the second scream that pierced the silent hall. Unexpectedly, his body tensed and anger boiled inside of him. Without thinking, he flew out of the kitchen and raced into the dining hall. The scene he confronted made him physically sick; one of the younger orphans was crouching in the corner at the far end of the long room. Brother Jonah towered over him, the punishing leather strap in his raised hand ready to strike again, his face consumed by hate. Marcus noticed the bloodstain on the terrorised boy's cheek, his fists clenching with rage. He ran towards them. Frightened voices whispered Charlie had done nothing wrong, had accidentally toppled his glass of water. At the sound of these words his nails dug deep into his palms, but Marcus felt no pain. He could only feel anger burning inside of him. Within moments, he rammed into the aggressor, who immediately lost his balance and fell helplessly onto the floor. With a succession of swift movements, Marcus retrieved the strap from the Brother's shaking hand.

He stood over the squalid, bald man sprawled on the floor, the leather strap threatening in his raised hand. Dark, menacing eyes told Brother Jonah of Marcus' intention and he instinctively covered his face. Marcus loomed over him, breathing heavily, whilst the despicable coward crouched defensively. As he watched him squirm on the cold floor, all the hate, rancour, grief and frustration buried in his young heart exploded. A prolonged and frightening howl, akin to that of a wolf, escaped his fired throat and resonated from the sterile walls, as clenched fists stretched over his head towards the ceiling. When the last drop of air escaped his lungs he hung his head, dropped his arms and began to sob quietly. No one spoke. No one moved. No one dared.

Brother Jonah, stood up quickly, eyed Marcus with contempt and retrieved the strap from his limp hand. Raising the strap, he ordered him sternly back to the kitchen. *Charlie was waiting... he would deal with Marcus privately...he had been waiting for him...* Marcus remained quietly still. Brother Jonah moved closer and, inches from Marcus' face, ordered him back to the kitchen again in a low, menacing tone, his eyes burning liquid hate. Marcus remained unmoving.

The room was silent except for the controlled breathing coming from the dining table. Two long rows of frightened eyes remained fixed on Marcus who was standing wilted, chin on chest, in the corner of the room. Without warning, Brother Jonah raised his arm and swung the strap violently in the direction of Marcus's head. Marcus' quick reflexes avoided the aggression; with a brisk movement of the arm he grabbed the weapon in mid-air with his left hand and twisted the brother's arm backwards. The gaunt, beady-eyed coward writhed in agony until he finally opened his clenched hand dropping the strap on the floor. Marcus grabbed Brother Jonah by the throat with his right hand and pushed him against the wall.

Marcus' strong arm kept him pinned to the cold stone whilst intimidating eyes probed the Brother's terror. Marcus, his breathing irregular, the veins in his temples swollen, throbbing, watched the pitiable dastard squirm against the wall as he silently vowed he would never let him harm another child again. The blood-drained fingers clutching the Brother's throat constricted further as he neared his lips and whispered into the unholy man's ear. He did not want the children to hear him threaten the brother; whisper between clenched teeth he would kill him if he did not disappear from the orphanage immediately.

The moment Marcus released him, Brother Jonah fled the building. Marcus watched, rage still blazing in his eyes, as he scurried across the hall, out of the door like a scared rat. The dark determination in Marcus' eyes had told him he should not push his luck.

Cheering and clapping filled the room the moment the scrawny oppressor escaped the room. Every child, except for two of the older ones who had run to assist the injured orphan, rushed to surround Marcus. Their small hands clung to him as they showered him with hugs and kisses, as they chanted his name. Marcus remained stiff in their midst, disconcerted in the sudden flood of affection. In one moment, he received all the kisses and embraces denied throughout his life.

As he felt the eager hands, their lips, as he listened to the praising chant, he felt his body relax, surrender. The shield of ice surrounding his heart melted and, all of a sudden, he found himself returning their embraces, kisses, the tears he had restrained for so long suddenly liberated. A warm feeling invaded his heart, infused his veins. For the first time in his life, he felt reciprocal love. For the first time in his life he felt special, a hero in one of his stories.

When the clamour died, he sat the children at the long dark table and instructed them gently but firmly what they must do. They did not have much time; he was sure brother Jonah had gone to the police with his version of the story. Without uttering a word, they rushed to do his bidding. Whilst the rest of the children raced up the stone staircase to the their dormitories, two of the older boys locked the two brothers resting in their rooms. The rest of the brothers had gone to the city cathedral as they usually did on Sundays. Without wasting time, the children ripped the sheets from their beds, bundled the few clothes and personal belongings they owned in them, and raced to meet Marcus in the lobby.

Cautious, none of the children followed him, Marcus slid quietly into the kitchen and took the money he knew the brothers kept hidden in a jar at the back of the pantry; the money destined for kitchen supplies. He was no thief but had no alternative; they needed money for bus fares and food. As he shoved the wad of notes into his pocket, all trace of guilt disappeared. The sum was compensation for the banquets the brothers had enjoyed at the cost of the children's meagre meals. Part of the penitence they must pay for their sins.

Marcus told none of the children he intended to head for the city to visit a woman he had met a long time ago. He had not had much time to think about options, but a viable one had abruptly burst in his head. The distant image of her gentle eyes had suddenly popped into memory. She was the only one he could turn to; the only person in the world he instinctively trusted.

When the police and the rest of the brothers arrived at the orphanage, they walked into an empty building. Scattered on the floor of the lobby were heaps of torn, grey clothing.

Most of the children slept all the way to the city, to the last station near the building that was their destination. They had to catch two buses. Marcus led one and Jordan, who was the same age as him, the other. The buses had slightly different routes but intersected at the desired bus top. Jordan led the first one, Marcus the second fifteen minutes later. The bus driver had eyed Marcus, the trail of children, suspiciously, but had curiously accepted them into the bus without interrogation.

Night was nearly upon them. When the second bus arrived, everyone followed Marcus as he quickly led them down the lonely obscuring streets in silence. They had no money for a hotel and even if they had been able to afford one, nearly one hundred children, travelling without adults was extremely suspicious. Still, no one asked questions. They trusted their heroic leader.

Marcus had thought it best that no one knew where they headed. He had been afraid someone would spill the beans if the authorities had intersected their flight and had not wished to implicate his friend unnecessarily.

As had he had suspected, the gates to the yard were locked. He had only been in the building once, a long time ago, but somehow he had clearly remembered its location. The gates were not too high, he decided, after inspecting them hurriedly. Propping the younger children on the older children's shoulders, they jumped over the ironed gateway onto the silent patio. One by one, Marcus and Jordan caught them in their strong arms. It was cold, so they huddled in a corner under a small porch leading to the entrance of the building. They heaped the bundles of clothes under them and covered themselves with the sheets. Marcus instructed the older children to hold the younger ones in their arms for body warmth. Some of the children had had the foresight to strip blankets as well as sheets from their beds. Luckily, the blankets were wide enough to cover the sleepy human mountain.

Marcus could not sleep, a kaleidoscope of thoughts racing his mind. He did not know how it had happened, did not understand how the torment of his past could be gone in a second. He felt reborn, filled with energy, oddly courageous. Gone was the embittered selfish individual he had been until that very afternoon. He no longer wished to be invisible; to be an island. He wished to be part of the world and wanted the world to be part of him. Shout his name from the city's rooftops. Tell everyone he was alive. He was free.

As he contemplated the children's sleepy faces, his heart went out to them. For the second time in his young life, he felt love fill his heart and tears well in his eyes. As he stood watching the innocent breathe from the corner of the yard, he pondered on the ramifications his actions would have. He was not afraid for himself, but for the children, afraid of the repercussions, the impulsive exodus he had led would carry.

The image of his lucky feather interrupted portentous thoughts and he knew then, without a doubt, everything would be all right, that they would all be safe. The message the feather had left, the one still inscribed in his notepad, floated before his eyes. Whatever it was that feather wanted from him would be a small repayment for the children's safety, his rebirth.

As soon as Arianne opened her eyes the following morning she remembered the feather; she sat up quickly and searched for the book. It had rolled off the bed and lay at its foot. Frantically, she fanned its pages; the feather had disappeared. She searched everywhere; under her bed, inside it, every inch of the room. Nothing. Disheartened, she placed the book back on the bookshelf. She had taken a few steps when she heard the book hit the floor behind her. Startled, she turned around. The book lay open at the foot of the bookshelf, as she bent down to pick it up, she saw words had been scribbled over the print of the right-hand page.

She read the words aloud, repeatedly. She memorised each word then returned the book to the shelf and calmly headed towards the kitchen to have breakfast. She was suddenly ravenous and devoured three buttered toasts between gulps of strong coffee. As she voiced the message a last time she smiled, fortunate to have been the receptacle of such mystery. She would keep the encounter with the feather, the unsolved message, a secret.

Her decision had nothing to do with the fact that no one would believe her, that envious co-workers would accuse her of concocting the story, claim she had written the message herself, that she would do anything to be famous... It had nothing to do with the fact that the feather had disappeared, no evidence to contest it had even existed. Intuition warned she should tell no one.

The feather, the message was only the tip of the iceberg, but she would be summoned and could not wait for the time to be 'nigh', to uncover what promised to be the scoop of the century.

The weekly prime time programme on serial killers was an instant success. Against her boss' advice, she had moulded the setting, given it a different perspective. She refused to interview the killers behind bars and arranged to hold the interviews face-to-face separated by a small table. The chained feet concealed under the table, out of the camera's path would be the only thing restricting the heinous men. Two armed guards placed strategically in the room, so they too, would be invisible to the camera, would protect her.

Arianne was a petite woman with delicate features but under the apparent fragility lay strong determination. Her audacity, her exquisite beauty, had instantly captivated the audience; 'An angel amidst devils' made the headlines of every reputable newspaper the morning following its launch. The camera had immediately fallen in love with her; she had courage, charisma, a rare beauty, all the ingredients for success. The night of her debut, ratings had been meteoric

Arianne's intent had been clear from the onset; she knew the show was a great opportunity for her, and though she wished it to be successful, something more important had become her priority. She did not wish to give the sadistic killers the fame they so desperately wished. Arianne was no fool, knew attaining widespread notoriety was only that reason they had agreed to appear on the show. They would not use her. She would use them.

Initially, she interviewed them without cameras, studied their profiles, their reactions, weighed their egos. Satisfied she had mapped their weaknesses; she returned to the station, sketched a preliminary interview, polished it up and returned with the camera crew.

Her interviews were sensational. She started slow, her questions simple, 'innocent', and then began to accelerate the tempo, raise the stakes. Unflinchingly, she delved into every detail, every gruesome element of their modus operandi and exposed their macabre signatures to the fast expanding audience. The cameras induced them to brag about their victims, the innocent people they had tortured, callously killed. She fed their egos, induced them to expose themselves, keep talking until they had portrayed themselves as the vile monsters they were. When she had achieved her goal, she swiftly changed the mood of the interview. Cameramen altered the lighting; turned the unusual set blue shadowed and sepulchral, and she began to attack them, provoke them, humiliate them until each one of them crossed the line and had to be restrained, sometimes, inches away from her. Every one of them fell into her trap, proved to the world they were exactly where they should be, awaiting the same fate as their victims.

Every interview was hard, every night after the programme her sleep was haunted by nightmares; the last one had been the hardest. As soon as Arianne had entered the room, she had felt the chill in the air, after only two minutes, she had fled the room, bile burning up her throat. She never returned. The interview never saw the light of day, never would. The depraved savage that had abducted and killed fifteen children remained 'anonymous'.

Seven days later, on the 15th of the month, at precisely 15.00 hours he was executed. The time and day eerily coinciding with the number of lives he had taken; the victims 'present' in the execution room.

However, Arianne had already achieved her goal; she had turned what would have otherwise been a sensationalist macabre programme to gruesome reality viewers, society instantly abhorred. Love letters to death row corridors stopped after the first programme aired.

After the gripping shows, her cache soared and leading channels competed to have her onboard. Overnight, she became a star, the newscaster for channel 6, the host of high-rating shows. Her programmes pulled large audiences; her face plastered on billboards across the city, on city buses...

Arianne was proud of her success, but her ambitions had changed. **She** had changed. Fame was now a mere tool, one she would employ to help her change the things she wished to change. Julia was her number-one fan.

Contracts gave her full power over the high voltage shows; every single one of them carried her indistinct signature. Social evils were exposed with stark imagery intended to provoke civilian reflexion and involvement. Thorough investigations, possible with the help of a team of young altruistic journalists, selected personally and carefully, uncovered corruptive webs that weaved the city's underground, revealed injustices to a propagating, empathic audience. Every one of her contracts included an indisputable clause; ten percent of the show's earnings would be destined to social causes. Luckily, for all concerned her altruistic visions paid high dividends. All her programmes became leading prime time emissions.

Each night, millions of people followed Arianne's shows. Each night, Arianne was thankful for the decreasing airtime dedicated to crime. Each night, Arianne thanked the magic feather for the miracles that surrounded her life. Each night Arianne wondered when she would be summoned.

*Seth's second experience was in the forest lands where he had learned to become one with all living things, that all beings were connected to each other, to the same divine energy emanating from the Source; the throne in the Golden Palace. The first time he had heard the voice of the forest he had been startled; awed he had understood their whispers, their eternal language. He had meditated long to make the connection, had been eager to engage the ancient angelic tongue that communicated with all living things, the one he had been unable to decipher in his father's scrolls. Still, when he finally succeeded, he had been surprised; he had never imagined forests could speak. Every evening after class, he went for a long walk amidst the glowing foliage. He loved listening to the whispering revelations of the timeless trees, the poetic inspiration of the delicate blooms that flourished in their shade.*

*Seth hoped to visit the tree of life one day, enter its hollow trunk and listen to the whisper of the ancient souls that echoed its aged walls. He had read about it at school. The millenary tree was revered by the realm, protected by Dominions; spirits of wisdom. Infinite souls of light, wisdom who had reincarnated the terrestrial world, lived many lives rested inside its cavity. Nevertheless, visiting the tree of life, listening to the souls' murmurs, their infinite worldly knowledge was an honour reserved to a chosen few; angels who had earned the right by accomplishing an extraordinary mission.*

*He was sitting alone on the terrace of a fellow student's tree house, watching the morning star drown behind the robust trees, thinking of what he had learned that day. The Halls of Growth held many secrets, secrets that were unlocking one by one. He could not wait to engage the language of the creatures that inhabited the glittering lands. As he sat on the edge of the wooden veranda, he indulged in the memory of the grounding technique of that morning. Remembering the experience recharged him with vigour.*

*He had sat upon the emerald cushioning ground and formed a circle with seven other students. Slowly, they had spread their wings until their tips had touched each other's. As per their Master's instructions, they had breathed rhythmically, deeply, visualized roots growing from the soles of their bare feet.*

*The veined roots had dug deep into the ground, spread fast throughout the exuberant earth to join the roots of every tree standing proud in the forest. The tingling sensation was immediate, ebbed through their feet up their bodies to pulsate their temples. They had connected with the source, with Mother Nature. Their bodies resonated with creation's unmistakable vibration, and the angel circle had begun to lift from the ground. Suspended in mid air, their bodies and wings had begun to glow, shine with the purified life of the source, the light responsible for the origination of every being in the universe. They felt their bodies nurtured, cleansed, revitalized. They felt love emanate from their souls towards each other, towards every living creature in the coruscating woodland. As light seeped up the burrowing roots, they grew stronger and the light of their souls intensified. Feeding on the light would prepare them for the missions that lay ahead, the dark paths they would have to tread, the burning light, their protecting shield.*

*As he gazed at the lofty trees, felt their own unique vibration, as he listened to their gentle voice echoing with wisdom, he smiled. His mother would be proud of him. He was becoming the wise and strong Angel she wished him to be. Lost in the assuaging thoughts it happened...*

*A bright light engulfed him suddenly and, once again, he floated outside the sphere, onto the field. This time the field became a room. Dusty pink flowered curtains draped its windows; a lilac hue dyed its walls. On a brass bed, covered with a quilt in the same floral pattern, a young woman was asleep. On a dresser, resting on a silver tray lay a perfect white feather.*

When Ethan woke up he headed straight for his desk, unlocked the drawer and retrieved the plastic sleeve, it was empty. He searched the entire room, the feather had vanished. Deflated, he sat at his desk and absentmindedly rolled the screen with his mouse, his mind on the feather. His eyes checked data, altered data; checked data again, removed data. After a while, he felt hungry and headed downstairs to the kitchen to make himself a sandwich. Carrying a tray with a peanut butter sandwich, some crisps and a diet coke he returned upstairs to his desk.

The moment he sat down his eyes glued on the screen. *'Nah it couldn't be...'* He scrutinised the information; reread every word, number, quickly tested the software. Every function executed with precision. He could not believe it. He had done it. He had finally linked the pieces together. His creation was ready, was perfect.

He gazed at the screen, scratched his head, willed memory to exhume the steps he had inadvertently taken. He shut his eyes tight, squeezed his mind but was unable to rescue a single drop of information. He hung his head in dismay; beating his forehead with the palm of his hand repeatedly. He would not be able to reveal his revolutionary software. He could not explain the final steps. He would be branded an imposter. He was finished.

Hypnotically, his eyes moved sideways to the open notebook on his desk. To his amazement, detailed explanations scribbled in his handwriting covered its centre pages. Every step taken in making his dream a reality was miraculously noted down.

Ethan could not wait to reveal the secret to his parents, explain at last why he had become a recluse, a social hermit of late, but decided to wait until he had tied up all the loose ends. *He needed a lawyer, a cheap one. He must copyright his software.* He thought excitedly. *He could not reveal his masterpiece until he had legalised exclusive rights. It would be suicide.* He scanned the yellow pages and decided on a small ad. The bigger ads belonged to more important, expensive firms. During the last year, he had saved most of his pocket money; the money his family had given him for his birthday. He hoped the amount would suffice.

He needed a plan; a plausible excuse that ensured his visit to the legal firm located in the small town near the coast, raised no suspicions. He could have chosen a firm in the city, there had been other small ads, but the simple black-and-white advert had inexplicably drawn him.

His best friend Simon became the unsuspecting accomplice. Coincidentally, his parents owned a two bedroom flat in the area. Coincidentally, Simon had casually told a mutual friend he would be away the weekend. Simon was ecstatic that Ethan had asked to accompany him, relieved his friend had finally decided to have fun again. He had missed him.

Early on Saturday morning Ethan packed a small bag, hid the money he had saved in a pair of socks, knowing his mother would check his bag as usual,, and waited for Simon to call. At eight thirty, the phone rang. It was Simon. His mother was indisposed; his parents had cancelled the trip. The plan was ruined. His pulse racing, Ethan counted the money again. As he scanned the yellow pages again, he decided he would go alone. He called a few hotels in the area. One of them was moderately priced. He would risk it; take the money, destined to legal fees, and hope for the best. He had no option; he must move quickly. He could have told Simon to cover for him but had not wished to hurt his feelings; Simon would have been devastated if he had known he had an ulterior motive to visit the coast.

He did not wish to blatantly lie to his parents, so he said nothing. Saying nothing was better than lying. Hurriedly, he bid his parents goodbye, walked out of the house and raced around the corner to the bus stop. Three and a half hours later, he was lying on the bed of a hotel room. The room was spectacular, the view breathtaking, amazingly cheap considering its luxurious decor. He had asked for the cheapest room but had been allocated an upgrade. Room number seven was the only vacant room in the hotel, the pleasant receptionist offered nonchalantly.

The moment he had walked inside its beautiful walls he had felt the uplifting energy, the faint buzz that made his flesh tingle. With two hours to kill he decided to have a short nap. He set the alarm on his phone to 2pm and was asleep within minutes. The moment he shut out the world the dream began. He was lying on the bed. A white and silver light hovering above him. It descended, enveloped him and transported him to the cove, the shore. He hovered above diamond twinkling sands, over vibrant turquoise seas for a while, then the bubble of light deposited him gently on the arched shore.

A young woman sat a short distance from him on the gleaming sands gazing into the ocean. Unexpectedly, she turned her head in his direction and smiled at him. The moment he met her beautiful eyes the beat of her heart sounded in his ears. The moment he smiled back at her the beat of his heart joined hers. When Ethan woke, he did not remember the dream but a strange emotion lingered in his heart for the rest of the day. He had taken several moments, several times to analyse the feeling, and had come up with the same outlandish conclusion every time. It was a crazy thought; contemplating the farfetched notion was insane. People could not fall in love in a dream. ..

Ethan arrived early. His appointment was not until 5pm and it was only quarter to. The hotel was located thirty minutes from the town and he had needed to get a bus so he had left the hotel at three thirty. He had stopped to grab a bite in a small cafe a few doors down from the lawyer's office, but his excitement had curbed his appetite and he had only managed a few bites of his sandwich.

As he sat in the small reception room, he kept worrying he would not have enough money to pay for the copy-write. *He should have slept on the beach instead of spending part of his cash on the hotel,* he thought apprehensively. The voice of the receptionist interrupted his anxiety. As he was followed the vivacious, young woman into the adjoining office his hands began to sweat.

The man behind the desk was nothing like Ethan expected; he was dressed in a jogging suit and looked as if he had been doing just that. He shook his hand cordially, invited him to sit down and introduced himself as Michael Jennings.

The moment the feather blew into Slade's life, he began to change. His life began to change. For the first time in a long time, his sister looked happy. Sadie had coped well in the last few years, had seemed satisfied with her job, the attic she had so carefully and tastefully decorated. She dated from time to time, but moaned to Slade none of her suitors were what she was looking for. His sister did not have to spell it out. Slade understood what she meant. She wanted what their parents had had. He had had various relationships himself, but his continuous globetrotting and inability to commit emotionally condemned them random. He had never been in love; never met someone like his mother.

Despite their vast wealth, Sadie and he repelled extravagance. Raised by down-to -earth parents, they understood the important things in life were those money could not buy. Their attics had cost a fortune, but Slade had not chosen them for their spacious luxury, the heated rooftop swimming pools, their amazing views. His concern had been security. The attic apartments were roof to the safest skyscraper in the city, in the world. The colossus was the vision of Andre Lessard, the world-renowned architect who had sought to build an impregnable haven of luxury for the richest, most affluent people in the country.

Every apartment had a state-of-the-art safe embedded in the floor of the living room that rose with the touch of a button. The glass, exterior walls of the building were bombproof and an intricate security system veined the entire building rendering it unconquerable to the shrewdest hackers. The security guards that protected the invincible glass tower were all ex-military elite with impeccable credentials, handsomely paid for their loyalty. It had cost millions to build; it sold in twenty-four hours. Slade was away for long periods at a time and had wanted his sister to sleep safe whilst he was gone. Since the tragedy, her safety obsessed him.

His travels had helped to alleviate the nightmare that kept him moored in the past, his lens distracting his attention to other sources. His untimely inheritance gave him the freedom to go wherever he wished. He explored the five continents, captured their beauty, their ugliness, but never in first class. He wanted to feel, portray the real world, the people that inhabited it. Every two months he returned to the city, to his sister, and stayed for a week. He spent every moment with her, except those he dedicated to selling his photographs. He did not need the money, he pursued recognition, reaffirmation he was good. The income, derived from his freelance work, was anonymously donated to victims of crime. By the end of the week he was longing to get out of the urban jungle, return to the freedom of an unpredictable and ever-changing world.

Curiously, since his encounter with the feather, the city had ceased to strangle him. He felt oddly relaxed; uncharacteristically at home. Slowly, he began to ease into the beat of the city, meet up with the few friends he had in the bustling metropolis and, unconsciously, one week rolled into another. Without noticing, notable time had elapsed and he had not flown what had begun to feel more like his 'nest'. It was after a couple of weeks that the extraordinary began to occur...

He had finally decided to photograph in situ, the studio he had had installed at home. A team of interior decorators, with experience in photographic technology, had turned a large portion of the spacious living area to a photographer's paradise. His prestige as a photographer was already prevalent, and he soon had to hire a personal assistant to handle his rapidly cramming agenda.

He was finalizing the details for the afternoon shoot when the three models arrived. As Laurel, his energetic assistant, escorted them to the set at the far end of the attic, Slade could not help admire the three ravishing beauties. *No wonder they were the most sought-after models in the world*, he thought, as expert eyes studied every angle, every shadow, facial bone structures that were a photographer's dream.

Rain Forrester was an African beauty with melted ebony skin and lustrous coal eyes. A long, raven mane and sharp, feral features offset by a full, sensual mouth. Alyssa McDermott was a startling redhead with almond emerald eyes. A spray of freckles painted her face, giving her an ingenuous charm, contrasting with the sensual, voluptuous body that moved with subtle erotic dance under the tumble of red curls. Chloe Jermaine, the youngest of the three, was a golden siren. The almost oriental eyes over Slavic cheekbones were a rare shade of purplish blue, and Nordic blonde hair hung sleek down the length of her back, over the graceful, yet insinuating pale body that moved with elegant serenity.

They were the chosen queens who would launch 'Wings', the awaited new perfume by the famous fashion designer, Lulu. Her marketing director's instructions had been clear, and Slade hoped he would be able to grasp the marketing concept in the first shoot. The exotic yet fresh perfume must portray purity and sensuality merged into one.

After welcoming his muses for the afternoon, Laurel ushered them to the guest bedroom where makeup artists awaited. Two hours later, three sparkling and sensual angels with a hint of devil sauntered onto the set, ready to be immortalized. Slade detested his sets to be overpowering and always opted for a minimalist yet effective decor. The striking trio contrasted stunningly against the coiling, glossy scarlet fabric that draped as backdrop and onto the floor. White and silver dust snaked their otherwise nude bodies, and large glittering gossamer wings curved slightly over their heads as they posed against the crimson cold in feline stance.

The scene was breathtaking; three ravishing, star speckled angels, pure, except for the glossy blood-red lips that pouted at the hovering lens and matching coated finger nails scratching the scarlet satin. Red and white; sensuality and purity; 'Wings'.

The shoot was a huge success; the visionary and powerful images immediately captivated Lulu's marketing director. Slade Alston was a genius.

Slade could not believe the resounding success of 'Wings' Thousands of winged- topped, scarlet diamond speckled bottles sold overnight and an image of the seductive angels crowned the heart of the city; the heart of every major city in the world. The TV ads based on the photo shoot were spectacular and highly effective. No one but Slade knew the magic concealed behind the ingenious creation...

The first extraordinary incident happened immediately after the shoot. The moment he had finished flashing his camera Laurel had taken over and helped the models transform back into the humans they had been three hours before. Without stopping to rest he had headed straight for the dark room and revealed the photos. As examining eyes lingered over the contrasting images he remembered the expression on Rain's eyes. For some reason, her eyes had unnerved him. They were beautiful, deep and dark; the 'dark' made him uneasy. There was a mystery to them, he intuited, and not necessarily an alluring one. *Stop trying to see more than exists,* he had admonished himself, as the lens had zoomed repeatedly on them. Rain had not flinched as the mechanical eyes prodded her. She had remained calm, returning the expressions he requested. He had expected no less, she was after all a professional of international fame.

As his eyes fixed on the glossy image, on her eyes, he tried to relive the sensation her eyes had evoked during the shoot. Again, he felt it, the same odd feeling.

It was then the miracle happened. Astonishingly, the images began to blur, focus again. Incredulous, he watched the white and silver dust sweep leisurely over Rain's dark flesh until the metallic grains contracted to form a small heart in her abdomen. *It was impossible...what the...* He was hallucinating. *Images could not move...* He closed his eyes, opened them wide; the silver heart was still there.

During subsequent days, he kept checking at the image. The tiny sparkling heart remained on her stomach. The image **had** transformed. It was not the result of stress or rampant imagination. For days he pondered the imponderable, racking his brains for a coherent explanation. There was none. For days, he paced the attic floor, unkempt, chain smoking, hardly eating. Every hour on the hour, he looked at the image, hoping it had returned to its original form. Every hour on the hour, the twinkling heart induced him further to insanity. Thankfully, his sister was away on company business allowing him to digest the shocking transmutation without untimely interference. *He should tell someone, Sadie... He would destroy the image, forget he had ever seen it, 'become alive'...it was the only evidence he had he was not crazy...perhaps it happened again...he should keep it...* After days of oscillating deliberation, he decided he would keep the 'miracle' a secret.

Early one morning he had been looking at the image again, when a sudden thought struck him. The more he lingered on the suspicion, the more he trusted it to be a possibility. Craving to confirm the intuitive hypothesis, he rushed out the attic like a maniac and headed for the media library.

Anxious eyes searched newspaper and magazine articles until, finally; he found what he was looking for; Rain Forrester's eyes **had** concealed a dark secret. She had been raped when she was 14 years old. Rendered unable to bear children in a vicious attack, that had nearly cost her life, by four members of a street gang that had terrorised the beggarly slums where she had grown up. Paparazzi had uncovered the ugly story and news of her tragic past had made tabloid headlines. When she had broken up with her first serious boyfriend, an actor of mediocre talent and scarce recognition, he betrayed her. The story that he had broken up with her because she was unable to bear children again made headlines.

A week after Slade's sad discovery, news that the international model was pregnant made tabloid headlines once more. This time, Rain did not mind the exposure, did not mind the world knew her conception was fruit of a one-night stand.

Everyone immediately knew the story, she could not bear children had been an added tragedy, concocted by unscrupulous Paparazzi who had wished to earn an extra buck. Slade knew otherwise. Two days before the story of Rain's pregnancy was exposed, Slade's lawyer had tracked down the doctor who had saved her life after the brutal assault. They had paid him handsomely for the information, the succulent 'donation' destined to innovative hospital equipment. Reassured him legally, no one would ever divulge his name or the information he had entrusted them with. The contract also ensured he would not tell a soul.

Only four people in the world knew Rain's conception was a miracle.

The next miracles occurred shortly after. The snapshot he took of the city's new Mayor saved the charismatic politician's life. When Slade had revealed the photograph, the image transformed before his astonished eyes; the Mayor sat in his office, smiling up at Slade when sudden shadows began to dance over him. The shadows kept elongating, shrinking, mapping his expensive suit until they shrank to form a small heart in his chest. This time the tiny heart was split in two. This time Slade needed no investigation to confirm his suspicion. He knew exactly what he must do.

With the pretext of showing him the photographs, he called the Mayor, who agreed to meet with him the following morning. Slade arrived sharply at ten, accompanied by his doctor. The Mayor's first reaction was to brand Slade Alston a lunatic; he was only forty-two years old. He had never been ill in his life... He was about to call security, evict them from his office when Slade quickly retrieved a check from his worn, leather satchel and placed it before him on his desk. *For worthy causes...for the city*, he told the Mayor evenly, the luring string of zero printed on the check a refutable argument. The Mayor instantly agreed to the check up, agreed to the contract that impeded him from telling a soul of their conversation earlier that morning. Thinking the acclaimed photographer was another crazy artist, that it was the easiest money he had ever raised, he accompanied Slade's doctor to his private clinic a few blocks away. Two hours after the check-up he was already undergoing the heart surgery that saved his life. When the Mayor called to thank him, to ask how he had known, Slade had answered casually: *'A hunch, your face was the same colour as my grandfather two days before he died of a massive heart attack'*. What the Mayor did not know was that Slade Alston had never met either of his grandparents; that they had both died before he was born.

From time to time Slade had other similar episodes that saved, changed people's lives. Every time he clicked his camera he wondered, with thrilling expectation, if the 'target' of his lens would be one of the 'lucky' ones. Every night, when he laid his head against the scribbled pillow, he wondered who was responsible for his 'luck'.

Alexandra had never felt as happy as she did at present. Things at the office were running smoother than ever. They had recently inaugurated three more homes and cases advanced satisfactorily. It had been a long time since she enjoyed some time to herself and so decided to have a four-day break, by the sea. She deserved it. For the first time in years, she felt she could take time off without feeling guilty. Mercifully, stacks of urgent files no longer heaped her desk; the innocent no longer waited endlessly for salvation.

She had booked herself into a pretty hotel by the sea lured by the beautiful scenery. The choice of location had been accidental; one of the office cleaners had retrieved a magazine from the rubbish bin, forgotten to take it home and left it on her desk. Idly, she had skimmed its pages during her coffee break and was instantly drawn to the advert, the photo of the two-storey hotel with whitewashed walls and navy blue shutters resembling a large beach house, perched on a small cliff shadowing a perfect cove. She had asked for a room with sea views and looked forward to some reading time in the idyllic surroundings. She could not wait to feel the warmth of the sun on her skin as she listened to the gentle roar of the waves; immerse herself in the vibrant blue waters.

She got up early Thursday morning, placed the small suitcase she had packed a week before in the boot of her car and headed cheerfully for the coast. She arrived early and her room was not ready. Whilst she waited for hotel domestics to finish attending to her room, she sat on the terrace overlooking the perfect bay and ordered a glass of wine. She had not minded the delay. She was not wearing a watch.

It was a glorious day. The skies were clear, except for the few clouds patching it at distant intervals, and a friendly breeze rocked the ocean. As she watched the curling waves wash the shore she thought of her childhood days, the distant days when she had been so happy, when her parents had still been alive. Her thoughts drifted back to their last summer together, to the beach house where they had celebrated her ninth birthday. Her parents had bought her a surfboard and her father, who was an excellent surfer, had patiently introduced her to the thrilling sport. Vivid thoughts of her father's strong arms steering the board behind her as they rolled over the waves laughing, carefree, brought a timid smile to her lips.

She missed her parents. She always would. In the beginning after they had disappeared from her life, victims of an air crash accident, their memory had occupied a broken heart; fortunately that changed. Fond memories now dwelled in a heart that had learned to heal with the passage of time. After her parents were gone, no relative had wished to take on the responsibility of caring for her and, consequently, she had been placed in a Children's Home. It was a good home; the Care Workers were good people, devoted people, who had ensured she had grown up a happy child, a balanced child, with a chance for a good future. They had been her family, as were the children who shared the home with her. She had lived at the Children's Home up until she had left for university. She had wished to become a Social Worker herself; help children no one wanted, save those in perilous environments. She wished to give them the opportunities she was fortunate to have been given.

As she sat on the inviting terrace, the sun kissing her skin, Alexandra thought of the times she had doubted, thought she had made the wrong career choice. Her job had been hard, desperate at times. Her heart had suffered constantly with the frustration of not being able to do more. Through the years, there had been occasions when her unwavering dedication had nearly faltered. In times of desperation, she had allowed herself selfish thoughts; her life was nothing more than an endless struggle. She had sacrificed many things, abandoned them by the wayside in aid of other people's needs. She had no husband, no children of her own, a social life that was virtually non-existent and she was not getting any younger.

Mercifully, her doubts were gone. Her world had changed. The rocky road had recently ironed out, become a silken highway into a promising destination. As she squinted her eyes, filtered the blazing sun already at its apex, felt its warm embrace, she thought of the feather, of the miracles it had created in her life. She did not know why, did not even understand how, but did not care. She was simply grateful it had found its way into her life.

The polite young receptionist, who had welcomed her to the hotel, interrupted her thoughts. Her room was ready. When she glanced at the key the young woman had placed on the table, beside her glass of wine, she smiled; room number seven, *her lucky number.*

Alexandra sat alone on the compact sand, her bare feet dipping the shore. Gentle waves crept up to lap them as her eyes fixed on the infinite azure. It was a beautiful late spring morning. The ascending sun had already begun to warm the golden sands and the sea would be inviting by noon. The small beach was empty. It was only nine thirty. She had slept like a baby and had been awake by eight. She loved her room. The moment she had crossed the threshold she had walked into a fairytale.

It was light and airy, decorated with tasteful and comfortable elegance; sophisticated and inviting at the same time. Beautiful, silver, floral wallpaper covered the wall behind the brass, four-poster king-size bed draped in a luxurious satin silver quilted bedspread trimmed in lilac. Sheer pastel lilac curtains dressed the French window brandishing a view of the sea and vases filled with fresh lilies adorned the whitewashed dresser matching an ornate oval brass mirror. The en-suite, decorated in complementing tones was exquisite. The beautiful, oval bath nestled in a raised platform underneath an arched window allowing the joy of sea views, a surprising extravagance. The elegant tub surrounded by an array of silver candleholders bearing ivory candlesticks and delicate glass jars, filled with lavender scented salts, had invited her to soak in its aromatic waters for over an hour the night before. She could not wait to repeat the experience; relax in the foaming, warm water, surrounded by candlelight whilst gazing out to the ocean, listening to the gentle roar of the dark waves.

The room had an almost magical quality, a luring nature, a quiet yet invigorating pulse, a sanctuary where daily turmoil was forgotten. As she had floated in the fragrant waters, as she had soaked the revitalising energy of the room, she had wondered about the people who had rested between its comforting walls.

Alexandra sat on the shore, hugging her knees, as dreamy eyes drank the placid ocean that echoed the peace in her heart when she heard a dog barking, in the distance, disrupting her serenity. A man with his dog had just turned the corner rocks into the cove; he walked languorously down the shore whilst the dog raced ahead of him. It splashed into the water, retrieved the small red ball floating in the sea, a short distance from the shore and waited, his tail wagging happily. Soon, the man caught up with it, took the ball from its mouth, as the dog nuzzled against his leg, then patted it affectionately on the head.

Even from a distance, Alexandra discerned he was a good-looking man. As he neared, she noticed his smile, a relaxed grin that complemented his deep blue, laughing eyes. Dark, unruly hair hung just below his nape giving him an unconventional edge. As his feet splattered the shore, his hand kept pushing a stray lock away from his eyes. She gathered he was in his mid thirties, like herself, though his toned torso, visible through his open white linen shirt, could have well belonged to a younger man. For a moment she hoped he was a guest of the hotel and secretly blushed. As soon as he was standing next to her, he bent down, stretched his hand confidently and introduced himself as Michael Jenkins.

Looking back, Alexandra could not quite remember how it had all happened. He had sat down beside her on the lukewarm sands skirting the gentle ripples and without notion of time, they had talked for hours. She had felt comfortable, relaxed in his company, oddly at ease. The refreshing treat of the previous night, the enlivening tingle that still lingered in her skin, seemed to have altered her spirit, uninhibited her, and she found herself pouring out her heart in a way she had never done before.

The impetuous confessions had been highly atypical; an introvert by nature, Alexandra had shrunk further into her shell as life had taken its toll. Past tragedies, recent ones, that had, until lately, surrounded her life had made her prisoner of numbed emotions with no voice. Still, for some peculiar reason, the voice she had quashed long ago had recouped its freedom, as Michael's beautiful smiling eyes had looked deep into her own. The conversation had continued over lunch, over dinner. They had shared their tragedies, their dreams... For the next two days, they were inseparable.

It was Sunday night, her last night in the hotel, the enthralling cove. As she combed her long black hair to a shine, she thought how much she would miss him; it would be some time before she would be able to come back. She stared at her reflection in the oval mirror and her dusk, grey irises gleamed with the memory of his compelling eyes. For a moment, she wished she could stay with him on the beach, remain on the sandy curve fed by crystalline seas forever.

The knock on the door awoke her from her wishful reverie; *it was probably hotel staff that had come to inform her Michael was waiting in the lobby,* she thought vaguely. He had suggested they had dinner in town, told her he would be picking her up at nine. She glanced at her watch, it was five to nine, then glanced at her reflection one last time. She looked ravishing in the stylish, burnt orange organza gown. She had worn the striking gown once at a colleague's wedding. A last minute frivolity included in her luggage. The tight bodice accentuated her tiny waist, the full skirt draping elegantly to the floor. Silk stilettos, heeled in glass matched its colour. A silk shawl, trimmed with small rose buds in a lighter tone, covered her bare shoulders. Her skin had already developed a healthy tan and accentuated the vibrant colour of the evening dress, her dark hair falling sleek to her waist. She resembled an Indian princess, a fitting guest in the regal room.

The moment Alexandra opened the door a rush of anticipation gripped her. The moment she delved into Michael's intense blue eyes she knew what would happen next. What she had hoped would happen since she had first laid eyes on him. Michael gazed at her with open admiration, his eyes aflame with raw passion. Silently, he took her into his strong arms and began to kiss her, devour her. Between ardent kisses murmurs that she was the most beautiful woman he had ever come across caressed her ears.

With lips crushing hers, his muscular arms around her waist, he pushed her impatiently towards the edge of the four-poster bed then stopped, backed away a little and hungry eyes drank her. Slowly, he approached her again; eyes locked on hers, fingers slowly peeling the sheer fabric with gentle, sensuous movements. As parts of her flesh were revealed, he kissed them. Alexandra quivered, her skin tingling as his sensual lips claimed bits of skin. When he had undressed her, he lifted her in his arms and laid her on the centre of the bed.

He sat dressed on the edge of the bed and revelled in her nudity, took in every curve, every detail, every shade of skin. Eager hands began to caress, explore. They moulded over the contours of her face, her neck, her shoulders, her breasts... then moved down her body... Alexandra gasped as she anticipated his next move, her body trembling with excitement, her mind willing him to claim her.

His hands stopped trailing her body, he stood up, lifted her effortlessly from the bed as her arms curled around his neck, pulled back the silver bedspread with one hand and nestled her nude body under the covers. Alexandra watched him disconcerted as he made his way to the bathroom, her body quivering, moist, under the satin cover, her breath racing with anticipation at the impending climax.

Her eyes blazing, pupils dilated, she watched him enter the room, laden with candles he placed strategically around the room. When he had lit those that had blown out as he had moved them around the room, he disappeared again. When he returned, he was naked. As he crossed the soft grey carpet unhurriedly towards the bed, ravenous eyes trailed his bare toned skin. *He is so beautiful,* she thought, her incensed body curling under the covers as she felt desire contracting her womb. His eyes glued on hers he flung the blanket to the floor and knelt before her on the bed. Gently, his hands circled her delicate ankles and he pulled her towards him. Languidly, he began to caress, creep up her legs then returned to massage her feet in a circling, tantalizing motion. One by one he kissed her coral painted toes whilst Alexandra purred on the bed, arched her body like a cat.

Suddenly, he was on top of her, embracing her tightly; kissing her hard, until gently, very gently, he claimed her. Slow, circling movements soon became insistent and surrendering bodies rocked in unison under the magical candlelight. Their bodies spent; they gazed into each other's eyes in wonder, as quivering lips whispered words of love. Room number seven was again witness to a match made in heaven

Michael stared at the young man sitting opposite him trying to imagine the reason for his visit. He guessed he was no more than seventeen. *What could he possibly want from him?* He was a tall, neatly dressed handsome-looking boy with intelligent sea green eyes and did not strike Michael as being the kind of boy who would be in any serious trouble. Still, one never knew. Michael had to reassure his potential client everything they discussed would be confidential before he timidly divulged the reason for his visit.

Michael listened in utter fascination to what Ethan was telling him, what he had created. The boy was a computer whizz, a genius. As he listened attentively to his requirements, he understood. The boy had no idea, did not understand the magnitude of his enterprise, the repercussions his invention would have on the virtual market. Copy writing the software would not suffice; there were other equally important legal measures that must be taken.

*Ethan Larson would become an easy target to vultures that preyed upon the world of business,* he deliberated. *He needed protection; he would not allow the boy out of his sight. Coincidence had not sent Ethan his way...*

Michael could not help but smirk at the irony of life. Only months before he would have been such a vulture. He would have preyed on Ethan's gullibility and inexperience, conning a fortune out of him. As he reflected further on the quirk of fate, he realised the latter would never have happened. Ethan would never have visited the 'old' him. He was destined to meet the 'new' him. He burned to ask Ethan if he had encountered a feather, but checked himself. His question would have seemed ridiculous. Though a redeemed one, he was still a professional. The outlandish question would have driven Ethan out the door. He would have thought him a nutter.

As Michael explained the imminent steps, Ethan kept worrying he did not have enough money to pay for the legal services the excited lawyer listed. Plucking up courage, he asked him about costs. Offhandedly, Michael mumbled he did not have to worry about money; they would come to an agreement, one that suited them both, his head bowed, his hand racing over the notebook. After he had finished jotting down points, comprising a list of tasks, he picked up the phone and called Ethan's parents. He needed to see them, explain the importance of what their son had done, was about to do.

Once he had escorted Ethan to the bus station and watched him return safely back home, he returned to his office. When in town he usually retired early, but today was an exception, he had tons of work to do. The first task was drawing up a contact with his young client. He knew exactly what the terms of agreement would be. He would ask Ethan for a small percentage of his company as payment for his services, his guidance.

The intention of the contract was twofold. The percentage would mean a huge amount of money, monies he would designate to altruistic causes. He also wished to keep an eye on the company, an eye on the kid.

*Seth could not wait to be home. As usual, on the Seventh day, he woke up as soon as the morning star shed its first sunbeams on the forest. He flew fast. His wings had grown considerably. They were stronger, faster. As he sliced the air, the sterling tips scattered a silver trail in the celestial sky. He soared high, his turquoise eyes reflecting the landscape below. The glittering foliage soon turned into the colourful, sloping carpet where he had tumbled happily with his friends many times.*

*He missed his friends. Wished they had not distanced themselves from him after the fateful day. He had tried to rekindle their friendship, but every time he had suggested to Lael and Zeriel they hang out together, they had come up with feeble excuses. Seth was secretly hurt. He endeavoured to justify their behaviour, tried to understand they did not wish to become accomplices to his deed. Still, he had another perception of friendship.*

*He gazed down at the perfect, round clusters that were home to those who had seen him grow up; those who loved him, those he loved. He wished for a moment he was still the innocent angel he had been before his deed. He slowed down, stretched his wings wide and began to glide, descend gently over the sparkling river. As he skimmed the surface, a shoal of glittering rainbow fish swam close to it, led the way home. His lips curled in smile; the melancholy that clouded his eyes vanished. His mother, as always, was already in the garden waving excitedly up at him.*

*The moment he landed on the white cobbled path, she ran to him and took him in her arms. They embraced for a while, synchronized heartbeats echoing the singular bond that united them. He had only been gone for six days but to Amanda, the days he was away seemed like an eternity.*

*Seth put his arm over his mother's shoulders, kissed her cheek, and led her home, holding her close. His father was still asleep so Seth rushed to his room to wake him. He sat on the bed, watched him sleep peacefully for a while, then kissed him on the forehead. He missed his father, missed going fishing with him in the river, blowing the star kites high in the sky over the strawberry fields, ensuring he did not forget his scrolls... Anton stirred in his sleep, murmured something illegible and turned on his side. Seth and Amanda's chuckles finally woke him up. At the sight of his son, Anton's face beamed with a wide smile. He sat up immediately and ruffled Seth's golden locks playfully, as if he were still a child.*

*Seth narrated his experiences in the Islands and Forest Dwellings to his parents as they dined on the raised porch, overlooking the garden. Amanda and Anton watched their son with swelling pride, listened attentively as he told them about the healing techniques he was learning in the Halls of Healing, of the 'lake of light' located in a cave behind the gigantic waterfall situated on the north end of the centre island. Every evening after lectures he bathed in the revitalising pool with his classmates. Its waters shone with a golden light that emerged from deep below its surface, and a golden speckled mist surrounded its smooth rocky edge. Pure white sands surrounded the kidney shaped lake, stretching evenly to the shimmering brass walls of the cave.*

*Everyone had been amazed at how quickly Seth's feathers regenerated the first time they had engaged in the healing meditation, the visualisation of purple light swathing their wings that enabled their revival, re-growth after strenuous flight manoeuvres. Whilst other angels had to wait a considerable while before their wings regained their lustrous texture, Seth's rejuvenated instantly. Whilst other angels had to wait for a considerable while for a single feather lost in flight to grow back, Seth's feathers regenerated, sprung to full size immediately.*

*They had marvelled at his capacity to regenerate. The Masters had never seen anything like it and news of his 'talent' soon reached the Elders. Their answer had been simple; he was one of the 'lucky ones', and denied further explanations. Seth was curious to know more but refrained from asking for clarifications he knew would not be given and relished in the fact he was one of those 'lucky angels', had been blessed with a special talent.*

*Excitedly, he told his parents about the morning choir in the chamber of music where they lifted their spirit, sang in unison to the melody of starfish swinging from its domed ceiling, of the healing classes where they were learning to work with various curative lights. Soon they would undertake their first missions and light was the weapon that would keep them strong when they visited the shadowlands; the physical underworlds. The spectrum of coloured lights would not only heal their ethereal bodies but would also nurse different parts of the willing, ailing souls they encountered.*

*Seth understood the need for healing light to be shed upon the mortal world he had secretly visited, understood it better than the Masters could imagine.*

*With open wonder, Amanda and Anton listened to their son's enthusiastic portrayals of his life in the Halls, listened quietly to the experiences he shared with them. They shared their thoughts; their 'little rebel' had grown into a fine angel.*

*Seth sat on the ledge of his tree house's terrace; he no longer fit comfortably inside the horizontal, log walls. Gazing up at the twinkling heavens, he thought of all there was still to learn, of the mysteries to be conquered. He had not told his parents that he was having problems in some of the classes, with some of the teachings. He had not wanted to alarm them. He did not intend to argue the rules, but was not whole-heartedly convinced by some of them.*

*He had learned angels were different from physical beings, from humans, that their world was very different to their own. Sometimes, when the Masters spoke about mortals, he felt a sudden urge to speak out, to defend them. He knew the Masters were justified in their argument; man had made a mess of their world, but did not agree with the majority view that humanity was beyond hope. He had seen them, peeped through the looking glass. He had seen the destruction man was capable of, had been witness to their hate, greed; their vanity, cruelty..., but had also seen their capacity for love under a sunset sky, on the edge of the sea. A distant beat echoed that love, whispered to him across time... He did not wish their world be destroyed.*

*Angels must be detached; passive observers to mortals' journeys upon the earth school and never interfere unless invited to do so. Physical entities possessed free will. The latter was sacrosanct. Seth knew he must remain detached, that he must adhere to the divine ruling no matter what. The angelic realm would exile any angel who transgressed the law. A shiver ruffled his feathers as he thought of his mother's exile, of his own reckless transgression, miraculously undetected by the Elders.*

*To this day, the lucky escape remained an unnerving mystery. With time, his mother had relaxed, realised Seth would not be summoned to the temple and the ominous clouds that dimmed their happiness had dispersed. He had been lucky; he would not take the fortunate escape for granted. He would not tread where all angels feared to tread. He resolved to comply with, respect the heavenly commandments and accomplish his missions with honour. He would make his mother and father proud. As Seth spread his wings and soared over the valley towards the mountain, a whispering question persisted.* **Could he be trusted when the moment arrived?**

*It was in mid-air, that the next confusing episode assailed him. He had barely left the cottage, was still flying over the dawning valley towards the Islands, when he suddenly felt dizzy and lost his balance. His wings tripped under him, he spiralled clumsily to the ground and tumbled over the cushioning grass to the edge of the river. Brushing off the blades of grass that had stuck to his wings, he stood up quickly and turned to face the river. The gleaming stream had disappeared, and he was floating outside the sphere again, in the same familiar field.*

*He stood motionless; the usual apprehension replaced by expectancy. Curious eyes watched the field transform to a stone-paved courtyard. Children dressed in identical, grey clothing played in a grim patio. His eyes strayed to the lonely tree at the back of the courtyard, near the imposing iron gates surrounding the dreary enclosure. A young man slept in its shade. On his lap the open pages of a writing pad revealed a white feather.*

*Unexpectedly, the field altered a second time. He stood in a beautiful room watching a woman sleep; in her hand an open book revealed another feather.*

*When Seth was returned to the shore of the gurgling stream he felt the burning sensation on the edge of his right wing. This time he did not curve his wing to inspect its edge, he already knew what he would find.*

The moment Slade Alston saw Arianne St Claire's face fill the screen he was captivated. There was something about her... an inexplicable quality that drew him to her like magnet. To say she was beautiful was an understatement. She was bewitching. From the moment his eyes gazed into hers, Channel 6 was the only news channel that resonated in his diaphanous attic.

It was a long time since Slade had dated a woman more than once, since he was interested in anything other than work or in his sister. Sadie kept urging him to find himself a girlfriend. He needed a woman to put some order in his life. He had crossed the thirty's threshold for some time now. He was getting old, she often joked.

Slade was an extremely attractive man; tall, lean and muscular with shaggy, dirty blonde hair, vivid green eyes, a square jaw and an enticing smile. Most days he tied his unruly mane in a ponytail; he hated the nuisance locks that interrupted his work. Sadie called him sissy every time he asked her for the hair bands he kept loosing. He would always justify his 'feminine' look with; *I'm an artist...'*

Women were drawn to him like bees to honey, and it was not because he was rich. Slade enjoyed the opposite sex intermittently; a relationship was not a priority in his agenda. It never would. The only constant woman in his life was his sister; the most important woman in his life was dead.

Slade dated occasionally but never made promises he could not keep; he never promised to see them again. As his eyes fixed on the face luring him from the screen, he wished he could meet her. For the first time in his life, Slade Alston was not afraid to make promises.

Coincidentally, an opportunity materialized. A friend photographer had left the country unexpectedly to attend a family funeral and asked him to cover a couple of important pending jobs. One of them was a photo shoot of Miss Arianne St Claire at Channel 6. *'Miss',* the word sounded heavenly... Offhandedly, he agreed to the spur-of-the-moment favour. His casual manner deflecting the truth; he was as excited as a fifteen year old.

He was a sack of nerves when he set foot on the set. As he waited for the rising star of the most powerful station in the country, he kept smoothing his ponytail, kept glancing across the polished ground for a sign of her. Twenty minutes had gone by and she was nowhere to be seen. *He had merely an hour to conduct the shoot,* he thought despairingly. An assistant producer interrupted his escalating frustration. Curtly, he informed him the shoot had been cancelled, that Miss St Claire was indisposed.

As Slade crossed the visitor's car park and headed towards his Porsche one thought prevailed; *Perhaps it was best. He did not need complications*...the butterflies in his stomach contradicting the statement. When he turned on the news that evening, Arianne's face stared at him, spoke to him from the screen. She looked ravishingly healthy.

Synchronous incidents led Slade to nearly meet the woman he watched religiously, on his sleek plasma every night, three more times. The hit-and- miss situations seemed bizarre; for some unfathomable reason it appeared they were not destined to meet. The notion seemed ludicrous, but after a third hopeful encounter was impeded the suspicion solidified.

He had waited to see her for over an hour the last time. This time no one had turned up to give him an explanation. Initially, he had been frustrated, angry, but eventually resigned himself to the fact that the rude omission was a stringent declaration they would never meet. When a fourth possibility had arisen, he had not bothered. He already switched to another channel.

Ethan could not believe his luck; his instinct had not failed him. The black-and-white advert had led him to the right firm, the right man. Though young, he was not ignorant of the dubious reputation surrounding some lawyers, the excessive fees some of them conned out of clients, especially gullible ones like him.

He had warmed up to Michael Jenkins the moment he had begun to speak. He could not explain the steadfast feeling, but he trusted him immediately, implicitly. The small percentage of his company's profits in exchange for legal services seemed just. The arrangement caused him great relief; he no longer needed to worry about money.

He was euphoric; the proposed arrangement implied his company would do well, Mr. Jenkins, Michael as he had insisted he called him, believed in him, in his creation.

Ethan was impatient to see his parent's reaction. When Michael had insisted on informing his parents himself, he had not contradicted him. He dreaded telling them, confronting them on his own.

As he watched the familiar landscape looming ahead, announcing he was not far from his home, a sudden thought struck him; he had seen few guests in the hotel, it was not full to capacity, as the receptionist had claimed. He could not understand why she had upgraded his room, had lied.

Julia woke up earlier than usual. As she drove down to the city she felt more alive than she had felt in a long time. New hope filled her eyes as she understood her world was about to change. She felt a lightness of spirit she had not felt in a long time, her eyes beamed with expectation, she could not wait to see how the day unfolded. The moment she got to the school's parking lot, she felt a rush of exhilaration. It had already begun to happen. The miracle was materialising, as she had had no doubt it would. As she walked briskly towards the school's entrance, she observed the students bypassing her on the grass-rimmed path.

Their tread was eager. Their faces illuminated by smiles. They were all neatly groomed and carried study books in their hands. As she caught their eyes, every single one of them greeted her with a polite '*good morning*'. *This was going to be an interesting day,* she thought. When she left for the convent at the end of the day, Julia had to admit, the miracle had spun more magic than she could have ever imagined.

Julia sat alone in the chapel, her hands clasped in prayer, her eyes brimming with joy. Her faith renewed, excitedly, she confided the extraordinary events to the Virgin, who now seemed to be smiling knowingly down at her.

The moment she had set foot on the school campus, she had breathed the change in the atmosphere. Every pupil had made their way obediently to class and the usual rowdy school had been silent, except for the brisk patter of footsteps heading for their respective classrooms. She had smiled inwardly as she had confronted the incredulous faces of the teachers roaming the corridors on their way to class. Shock had been the unanimous expression. None of them had understood the sudden submissive behaviour, the drastic changes in appearance.

At ten thirty, she had joined the other teachers for their usual coffee break in the staff room. She had been impatient to see them. As she had anticipated, all of them had remarkable stories to tell. Amused, she had listened to the unusual tales;

how the classes had miraculously evolved smoothly, how pupils had been attentive and participated excitedly in lessons. How every single one of them had done their homework, received new homework with enthusiasm. Many students had suddenly volunteered to join extracurricular classes that had had to be suspended due to lack of interest. A group of older students had even offered to give the school a fresh coat of paint arguing it was in dire need of a facelift.

Students, notorious for their violence and rebelliousness, had transformed overnight to perfect models of behaviour. No one could give credit to the sudden miraculous transformation. Everyone had been baffled by the unprecedented change. Everyone had backed the same theory; the surrealist scenes they were witnessing were a diverting ploy, part of a Machiavellian plan. They needed to be extra alert, everyone had concurred vehemently. They must report the slightest hint of menace immediately if they were to thwart the diabolic plot that was being brewed by the school's troublesome leaders.

After a couple of weeks, everyone resigned to the idea that their suspicions had been unfounded. Students continued behaving immaculately. Classes evolved more than satisfactorily and participation in extracurricular events flourished. Volunteers buried all trace of graffiti under a fresh coat of cream paint and students who had never taken an interest in their education became extremely adept students. Everyone mixed with everyone else. Cliques and gangs ceased to exist, obliterating discrimination and fear from the school's social framework. Bullies no longer hunted the corridors and toilets of St Christopher's.

The magic spun at the school had a domino effect. Parents began to take a serious interest in their children's education, and the recent parent's evening had been a resounding success. The principal was ecstatic and proudly announced the school board's intention to improve the yearly budget considerably. The overnight success of the school had reached the higher echelons of the educative system. Their hard work, the unprecedented and drastic improvement of the school, was being rewarded.

The miracles were not restricted to the confines of the school. Parents were able to provide adequately for their children's necessities. Those that were unemployed found a job. Those who were on a poorly paid one found one with a higher salary, but the biggest miracle of all, was the change in the children's family environments. Every family home became a caring nest and children did not feel the need to roam the streets aimlessly after school. Each stray sheep had returned to the flock.

Julia prayed in the chapel for a while longer, thanked the Virgin, God for the miraculous gifts. She thanked them fervently for not abandoning her, abandoning them. As she basked in the candlelight, she smiled peacefully. She was strong again. Faith filled her heart; she now viewed the future with hope.

Memory strayed to her childhood; to the days in the park, she had heard God's voice calling her, whispering her name, as she swung carefree, as she was one with the wind. The invisible voice had stirred her young heart, awakened her to the knowledge of the path she was destined to lead. The early recollection imprinted itself on her soul, whispered she would be part of something wonderful, magical one day. That day had finally arrived. With that joyous thought, Julia finished her last prayer and retired to bed.

When Julia woke up the following morning, she remembered the night's dream: she was praying quietly in the garden when the gentle breeze caressing her suddenly turned to a gust. At the sound of rustling leaves, she looked up and an intense white light blinded her. Awed, she watched as the radiant light slowly began to dim, take solid shape to reveal a tall beautiful angel. Without speaking, she gazed into his eyes and offered him his feather back. The celestial being's expression told Julia he had not expected her to see him.

Michael could not believe he was in love. He was overjoyed to admit he was wrong; love was not fiction, romantic novels had not portrayed a wishful illusion. He felt more alive than he had ever felt; he walked in a cloud, a pink one. Everyone in town commented on his sudden euphoria; on the eternal smile stretching his handsome face. Eventually, he had confessed to friends, his sudden happiness had a name. Alexandra.

Since the revelation, everyone was on his case. Everyone wished to meet the special woman who had stolen his heart. They had all assumed he had met her in the city, during one of his weekly visits. No one guessed he had met Alexandra at the cove. Secretly, he was dying to introduce her to the people who had become family, but it would have to wait for a while. He would be spending a lot of time in the City. He was up to his eyeballs in work. Alexandra had recently been promoted to Senior Social Worker and her agenda was tight.

As he sat in his city office waiting for his next client, his mind lingered on the magical night they had made love for the first time. He could not wait to see her, hold her in his arms., smell her, love her again. He closed his eyes, visualized every detail of her face, every inch of her flesh...

He had called her early that morning, woke her up with a sexy '*hello beautiful*' and had arranged to pick her up after his afternoon appointments. He had booked an intimate table in a cosy Italian restaurant, near the circular park; the green bull's eye of the city. An assiduous client to the homely pasta house, he had fast become an appreciated client. With time, he had become a close friend to the owners of the charming venue. The excellent food was not the reason he had chosen it as a first formal date, he had not been able to resist showing off Alexandra.

He wished he could have accompanied her back home, he had not wished to separate himself from her, but had already arranged to meet Ethan's parents later that morning. It was a meeting he could not cancel, Ethan depended on him. The thought that he was in for a rather interesting meeting, consoled him. He could not wait to see the expression on the Larson's face, when he delivered the news.

*Seth loved the Mountain Top lands; the sky reaching plateaus laden with exotic shrubs and flowers, the luminous white limestone cliffs that shone with speckled dotted lights, when the daylight star bathed the southern face of the lofty paradise. On the four corners of the plateau, midway between the forest crowding its centre and the precipice, stood four towers, the tall glass cylinder turrets revealed a spiral staircase. At the top of each tower, in the centre, was a circular platform etched with golden wings; the insignia of the 'travelling angels', where travel missions initiated.*

*Each tower was the launching point to different destinations, to other worlds. A cloak of energy wrapped them. The pure light was so powerful that it was impossible for fallen angels to enter the realm through the cardinal portals. The purity of the energy awarded safe passage to angels travelling to and from worlds, ensured no negativity filtered through, threatened the heavenly vibration.*

*Seth thoroughly enjoyed his stay in the Halls of Travel. Understanding different atmospheric densities and frequencies of diverse worlds, dimensions, fascinated him. He was equally passionate about flight techniques, especially those that enabled him to pirouette the skies at great velocity. In the mountain, in the Halls of Travel, he learned to polish his wings with stardust wax that enhanced flight manoeuvres; to vault high in the air and catch the halo in the 'seven a side' game that was a weekly ritual. The swift game perfected flight technique, enhanced dexterity and Seth was always in the winning team. He loved the races that began in the mountaintop and ended in the forestlands where he was a strong contender. He had no idea why the tips of his wings were unlike any other angels', why they were silver; but they seemed to help him cut through the air faster.*

*The fascinating framework of the realm was slowly revealing itself; teachings in the different learning halls were connected. The more he learned in the Halls of Healing and Halls of Growth the stronger and more spiritually elevated he became. The stronger his wings grew, the higher he could soar. Healing protected him, prepared him for missions, rendered him invulnerable to external damaging forces when he crossed frontiers. The fact that his feathers regenerated so quickly meant he would have to wait less time than other angels between missions did. His 'gift' enabled him to be the first in his class to learn the teleportation meditation that allowed him to defy long distances. With time, he would be able to engage in a more elevated meditation that would allow him to teleport instantly. The meditation did not involve engaging speed of light, but subatomic particles of energy.*

*He learned the perspective of time, how a second in his world could equate a lifetime on another world, another dimension. He learned about different frequencies, vibrations, what they denoted, what they presaged. High pitched resonations, pulsations signifying entities of light, and low, dark entities. Day by day, Seth grew stronger, wiser; each day his aspiration became more tangible, visiting the Sky Dwellings one day no longer seemed an impossible dream.*

*The following encounter occurred on the Mountain Top Lands. On the edge of the northern cliff, whilst relaxing into the meditative technique he would be using on inter-dimensional travel. The moment his breathing slowed down and his eyes begun to feel heavy it happened; suddenly he was bathed in light, floating outside the sphere once again. The experience was different to the others. This time he did not see the field, he was standing in a garden shadowed by a church crowning the plateau of a small mountain.*

*On a wooden bench, in the centre of the harmonized garden, sat a beautiful young woman, her face radiated a gentle serenity. Boundless love emanated from her pure soul, a soul recently liberated from torment, from doubt. She was dressed in a long black tunic, a silver cross hanging from a black cord resting on her chest.*

*She sat silently, a soft smile touching her lips, her eyes. On closer inspection, he noticed she held a white feather in her hand. Its tips glowed with bright silver light. Seth stood still, watching her, afraid to make a sound that would perturb the perfect scene.*

*Unexpectedly, she raised her head, delved deep into his eyes, slowly lifted her arm and offered him the feather. She had seen him.*

Her prime-time-show about to begin, Arianne had ten minutes. The night's theme was prostitution, the traffic of flesh, slavery in the twenty-first century. As usual, the investigation had been impeccable, meticulous, in keeping with her customary pragmatic portrayals depicting the austere tragedy of vulnerable victims. She gazed at her reflection as she retouched her makeup and brooded on how her life had changed. She had come a long way from the innocent and lonely girl no one had loved. She had come a long way from the broken girl who had fled a nightmare into an uncertain world, at the tender age of fourteen. Her thoughts wandered back to her mother... *What would her mother think of the woman she had become?*

Arianne had grown up in a ramshackle neighbourhood, in a dingy council flat on the second floor of a dilapidated building. She hated the place. She hated having to pinch her nose as she raced up the steps to her front door in order to curb the nauseous reek of alcohol and garbage, of human faeces. The rundown four-story edifice was home to drug pushers and prostitutes, a string of suspicious-looking strangers permanently queuing on the rotting stairs.

Her mother was a waitress in a shabby little cafe that stung with tobacco and greasy food. She worked six days a week and got home late every evening. The moment she walked through the door, the threadbare flat was impregnated with the rancid stench clinging to her clothes. From a young age, she had learned to fend for herself, clean the tattered house, cook meals, wash and iron her own clothes etc. When her mother finally got home, she was too tired to devote any time to housework, to her. After she gulped down the food Arianne had lovingly prepared, she went to bed without even saying goodnight. A sad and lonely Arianne watched television until ten, the self-administered curfew. She had school the following day.

Arianne felt alone in the world and silently envied the other children in school. She wished she had a family, even if it was a one-parent one.

Her mother was a bitter selfish woman, who blamed the world for her miseries and had given up on life. She worked, ate, slept and watched television on weekends until beer and wine knocked her out.

Since she could remember, Arianne had tried desperately to please her mother. She kept the house clean, had a hot dinner waiting for her on the table every evening, never asked her mother for anything except for vital necessities and never got herself into trouble.

Despite all her efforts, her model behaviour, she never received a kind word. Since she had been born, her mother had made her feel unwanted, a burden, the cause of all her unhappiness. The reason her father had deserted them.

At school, Arianne was a different child. She loved learning and was an excellent student. She was a curious child who loved books, loved to write. When a renowned journalist had visited her school, as part of a prospective career talks programme, she had decided there and then, she would study journalism. Despite her desolate life, her callous upbringing, she was an extrovert child and had many friends. Friends, she never took home.

She had never told any of them where she lived. She had implored her teachers not to tell anyone. Her mother's continued absence from parental meetings had raised an eyebrow, but Arianne had never given anyone cause to suspect she was being neglected. When the teachers had asked why she did not wish her friends to know where she lived, she had claimed she was ashamed of her neighbourhood. When they had asked why her mother never turned up for parental meetings, she had told them her poor mother worked long hours and was unable to take time off, that her boss was a stern man. Her teachers had understood her embarrassment but had not been entirely convinced with her explanations regarding her mother's continued absences. Mrs. St Claire had never visited the school. Still, they had agreed to the request. Arianne seemed a happy child, and they had detected no other problems.

Her creative imagination came up with a plausible story; her father was an undercover cop, hence why she could not disclose their address. Everyone thought she was lucky to have such a brave dad. None of her friends imagined she had no father, that she did not have a mother, at least one that acted the part.

Arianne fit perfectly in her 'school world', she was always impeccably groomed; her honey blonde streaked hair tied back in a neat ponytail, her uniform clean and ironed, her school satchel and books immaculate. She was just like any other kid, better than most. No one suspected that after the bell rang at the end of every day she returned to a world of isolation, that weekends were a nightmare she could not wait to escape Monday morning.

When Arianne was thirteen years old, her mother changed. She began to take pride in the house, in her appearance. Her eternally sullen face became cheerful overnight. She became interested in her daughter. She asked Arianne about school, if she had done her homework. Arianne was profoundly confused at the sudden metamorphosis but equally ecstatic that her mother had emerged from her long depression, had finally noticed her.

Two weeks later, Arianne discovered the reason for her miraculous change. Her mother had a boyfriend; a younger man she had met at work. She was heartbroken. For a short while she had been happy, had believed her mother was capable of loving her, that she was finally well. Her mother had only wished to pretend; make-believe she was the perfect housekeeper, a doting mother. Her mother had wished to ensure nothing, not even her nuisance daughter, disrupted the budding love affair.

Arianne disliked Joey the minute she set eyes on him, the moment she saw him standing at the door carrying a cheap bouquet of flowers. He had an arrogant air about him, a disingenuous demeanour. His eyes were beady, probing, menacing. As he swaggered into the room and kissed her mother obscenely on the lips, she had felt sick, nearly retched on the living room floor.

Reluctantly, she sat down to have dinner at the table, the dinner she had prepared whilst her mother had dolled up and listened with mounting rage to her mother boast of her academic achievements. She had never read a single school report. Arianne had forged her signature on every one of them.

Arianne stared down at her food, toyed the peas with her fork, uncomfortable under Joey's persistent glare. She did not trust him. Mumbling she had homework to do, she excused herself politely from the table and disappeared to her room. As she lay on her bed, listened to her mother's hypocritical laughter, to her lies, heartache spilled down her cheeks.

She was half-asleep when the creaking sound of her bedroom door alerted her. Before she had time to raise her head from the pillow, the nightmare was upon her. Terrorized, she shrieked her mother's name repeatedly, her desperate cries piercing the stale air as wanton hands abused her in the dark. Her mother never came. She was comatose on the couch, a result of the bottles of cheap wine she had washed down.

Small clawing hands frantically tore at her attacker but her fragility was no match for the forcing hands of the decadent stranger who took away her innocence with one brutal thrust.

He left as suddenly as he had come in, in silence, closing the door of her room stealthily behind him. Arianne sat in the dark, frozen, vacuous eyes fixed on space, on the darkness that had always prevailed in her world. She huddled in the corner of her bed, dead, unable to digest the enormity of what had just happened. Her pyjamas barely covered her flesh, but she did not feel the nocturnal gust seeping through the cracks of her window pane. She did not feel anything.

It took a couple of hours for the monstrosity of the ordeal to sink in. The aberrant images eventually forced themselves through sanity's frontier into memory and a silent scream escaped her tortuous soul as she wrapped her cold arms over her violated body. She shut her eyes, struggled to suppress the repulsive recollection but the vision, the feeling of clammy hands destroying her innocence, insisted. Tears spilled loneliness, shame, insanity on the sullied sheets as she hugged her knees, rocked her aching body, as she scratched her arms in an effort to divert pain, a shiver of ice trailing her arched spine.

The sinking disgrace, the deathly turmoil eventually turned to algid determination, to blazing survival. Her body quivering, she crawled out of the bed and headed unsteadily to the shower cubicle next to her room. She scoured her desecrated flesh under the sparse rain wishing to erase all trace of humiliation, sacrilege, then hurriedly returned to her room. Numbly, she changed into warm clothes, packed her bare belongings into a rucksack, took the money intended for the weeks shopping, stashed away at the back of the first drawer of her mother's dresser, and fled into the night. As she had tiptoed down the corridor to her mother's room, she had caught a glimpse of the two bodies sprawled, stoned, on the frayed grey sofa. For the first time in her young life felt the fury of hate. For the hundredth time in her young life, she wished she had never been born.

As she ambled dazed across the intimidating neighbourhood, her brutal assailant's face floated before her; the narrow rapacious eyes, wicked lips... She had not trusted Joey, had sensed something sinister lurked behind his gaunt boyish face, his charming grin, but had never suspected his depraved intent. *It was her mother's fault...she had brought the degenerate beast to their house....* Rage consumed her young heart, as she tasted hate again. Her mother was a selfish and despicable being. Her heart crowded with so much bitterness it did not allow a morsel of love for her own flesh and blood.

She wandered the threatening streets aimlessly for hours, her body feverish, her face biting with cold as tears trickled down her ghostly cheeks. Again, the sickening images haunted her; Joey's smell, his bony hands upon her flesh...She could not eradicate the image of her mother knocked out on the couch from her mind. She hated her. She was no mother. She had never been one.

She was dog-tired. Her feet could not crawl another inch. Desolate, she sat in a bench, in a park she had unconsciously invaded. She had no idea how long she had been walking, how far she had ventured. Her eyes roamed the unfamiliar surroundings. She had no idea where she was. As her swollen eyes trailed the trunks of the trees ahead of her, she noticed a church's steeple towered over them. Dragging her numb feet, she headed resignedly towards it. *It would be safer to spend the night in a church,* she thought wearily. Luckily, the door was open. An elderly priest, with failing memory, had forgotten to lock them before he retired to bed after evening mass. Aching feet slid down the centre aisle to a polished oak pew at the front row below the altar. Crestfallen, she sank her knees into the red cushion of the kneeler.

As she sat silent, hugging her rucksack, her eyes fixed on the huge crucifix hanging above it. As sleepy eyes rested on Jesus' bloodstained temples; on the wreath of thorns crushing them, her head begun to hurt, pounded with questions; *Why hadn't God saved his son...? Why hadn't he saved her? Why hadn't he woken up her mother? Why had he given her a mother who did not love her? Why had he abandoned her all her life? Why had he allowed her to be born? She had never done anything wrong...*

After battling with God's abandonment, persistent repugnant images for some time, exhaustion finally won the war and she fell asleep on the wooden bench, her head resting on her rucksack.

A soft voice woke her the next morning. When she opened her eyes, Arianne thought she had died in her sleep, that God had rescued her, taken her to heaven and she was staring up at the face of an angel. She had never seen such a beautiful face, such radiant, gentle translucent blue eyes.

For a while, her face was the only thing she saw until slowly her surroundings focused into vision. Confused, she looked around her, she was still in the church. A few meters away, an old priest stood looking at them his hands clasped in prayer. She turned her face, looked up the 'angel' realised the gentle whispering voice belonged to a nun, a nun with the face of an angel. Her name was Sister Julia.

*The next encounters occurred in mid-air. Seth stood on the Southern platform feeling both anxious and exhilarated. Today was his first important flight; he would cross the frontier to the mortal world officially. He had prepared well. Early that morning he had flown to the Islands where he had bathed in the healing waters of the lake. He had then flown swiftly to the forest where he had engaged in a grounding meditation that made him one with the eternal trees that colonized the edges of the crystal pond. The previous day he had visited the guarded woodland for the first time. A Cherubim, a childlike angel, guardian of celestial records and member of the celestial choir, had accompanied him.*

*Seth was the first of his class to earn such unprecedented honour and had been thrilled. He had been dying to see the secret and heavily guarded grounds. His classmates had been impressed. As far as they knew the woodland enclosure were only accessible to angels of higher triads. Their Master had ambiguously shrugged off impertinent questions insisting other angels had visited the sacred precinct before Seth, that their friend was not an exception. Seth had not believed him. The Master was evidently lying, furtive eyes had given him away. The question was why? As he had followed the Cherubim deep into the forest he had been tempted to probe him but resisted the temptation. He was impatient to discover what lay behind the tall golden fence guarding the mysterious grounds, he had earned the honour, had after all excelled in all the disciplines.*

*The moment they had crossed the imposing gates he was overwhelmed by the breathtaking landscape; violet blades swished back and forth caressing the stems of crystal roses that spouted in bunches amidst the lavender fields stretching to dusty pink mounds surrounded by purple palm trees. Ahead, in its centre, ancient glittering mauve and powder blue willow trees brushed the rippling surface of a perfect round pond to drink the pools of eternity, fed by the gentle fountain of youth sprouting its core*

*The zesty liquid travelled the rooted mesh to feed the trees, so they breathed with the wisdom of eternity, the timeless universal language, with the life of the endless cascade sheltered by the gilded fenced compound. The cherubim invited him to take a few gulps from the crystal goblet awaiting him on a small white column behind one of the leafy curtains meeting the translucent waters. The revitalising energy had immediately provoked a tingling sensation throughout his body, his wingspan.*

*The wings had become remarkably luminous and his feathers had lengthened. Flashes illustrating creation exploded in his mind's eye. The endless vast spun around him giving birth to galaxies, planets, solar systems, nebulae, stars... which mingled, shrank to form a small ball of light that disappeared into his forehead. Celestial choirs merged to form a single soft voice that sang his name, the harmonised whisper of inspiration echoing in his soul to render him breathless.*

*When he left the enclosure, he had changed. He felt physically stronger. His mind expanded, his trail of thinking startlingly lucid; he was one with the judicious source that had created him.*

*Lightheaded, electric, he had returned to the mountain to raise his vibration further in the music chamber, located near the southern face of the mountain, behind the thicket hugging the plateau in a semicircle. The marble white vaulted building was invisible to the eagle eye. Thick foliage weaved the entirety of the domed roof. The elaborately gilded arched doors, framed by ivory stone columns coiled with golden wisteria, led directly to the silver and white room. Hundreds of Silver Star fish hung from the convex ceiling, swayed gently as they echoed songs of the universe. A white, velvet chaise longue stood in its centre, circled by six arches supported by marble columns engraved with music notes and cherubs playing lyres.*

*He had relaxed on the cushioning fabric, waited to reach acceptable flight level vibration, his eyes closed, his ears soaking the soul- reaching melodies that bathed him in ecstasy. Before leaving the room, he had reached for the small piece of paper that popped out from the slot at the top of the columned pedestal beside the chaise lounge, and placed it in the pocket of his white robe.*

*As he had neared the clearing to the southern precipice, he had spotted his guide between the trees. Anael, a Principality belonging to the fourth sphere of angels, waited by the tower. Principalities were watchdogs of the earth, directly responsible for the success of mortal missions entrusted to Archangels and angels. They were also responsible for the recording of such missions in the Travel Book housed in the Halls of Travel. Seth glided to the ground, walked up to him, reached into his robe pocket and placed the small piece of paper in his outstretched hand.*

*For a second the expression on the towering angel's face had alarmed him and he had been afraid his vibration levels were incorrect. He had looked forward to his initiation for a long time. Without saying a word, the tall and sturdy angel with equally robust wings wrote something on the back of the paper, folded it, put it in his pocket then silently led him up the spiralling stairs. The journey would be short. He would only be crossing the sphere for a fraction of a second, would remain in the density of the frontier briefly. He would then return to the platform to be escorted to the Halls of Healing where his endurance ratings would be noted and sent to the Halls of Travel.*

*Seth was ready. His wings stretched wide, his eyes pinned on the luring skyline. To the count of three, he jumped high into the air and began to soar across the clear skies, towards the southern frontier. This time he was not scared, this time he knew what he would find on the other side. This time he would not be transgressing the law. He was no longer the ignorant, irresponsible and naive angel who had delved into the unknown, without thought to repercussions. His thoughts regressed to the day he had defied the realm. Silently, he thanked the universe for being an ally.*

*He had flown for a while when he discerned the silver curve delineating the end of the realm and flapped his wings energetically. Drinking from the crystal cup had fortified him, he flew faster than he had ever done; the stretch to the gleaming barrier had not tired him in the least. Without warning, an invisible force pulled him forward and a flash of light blinded him again. When the light vanished, he was floating outside the sphere. The familiar field emerged and predictably transformed. He stood in a small room. A young man sat at a desk watching a perfect white feather dancing on a screen. He hardly had time to absorb the image when the room began to spin around him. The circling images becoming swirling rings of colour. After a few moments, the colourful tornado slowed down and the palette of colours began to take form, reveal a second image. A uniformed man sat on the steps of a house, on his lap was another feather. Again, before he had time to assimilate the vision it disintegrated, the coloured particles sprinkling to the ground. In moments, multi-coloured beams sprouted from the grass. The rays of light began to entwine, fuse to reveal a third image. A man slept soundly on a huge bed, beside him, on the empty pillow, lay yet another feather.*

*The invisible force pulled him forward a second time and he found himself flying towards the silver curve again. He had nearly invaded the grey cloud when out of the corner of his eye, he caught a glimpse of the familiar field, the light emerging at its far end. Conscious curiosity was the enemy, that he must not succumb to temptation; he fixed his eyes on the dusty layer, continued his journey.* **He should not, could not stay. He must return to the platform, he must not challenge the realm a second time...** *He slowed down, hesitated, temptation defying duty...*

*Without realising, he spun around and faced the field. The light moved nearer, dimmed to become an amorphous shadow. The shadowed mass traversed the field in his direction, moved slowly through the cold dusky field, the grey ground, the outline splitting to reveal the silhouettes of seven people. As the figures advanced, the indistinct image sharpened to reveal the mortals in his dreams.*

*Each carried a feather in his hand. The moment he recognized them, the vision evaporated and he was thrust back through the coarse boundary. He flew in tight spirals, the silver tips of the wings taut, like metal. He sliced the air, a spinning torpedo, his wings undamaged.*

*The strapping angel was waiting for him on the platform; he stood at its centre his compact mass of feathers unperturbed by the draught whipping the turret. Seth descended apprehensively on the circular base, readied himself for harsh reproach. Surprisingly, innocuous eyes and a docile expression greeted him. The angel's easy manner, his relaxed smile, told Seth his vacillation had gone undetected. He relaxed, dropped his wings leisurely and returned the angel's smile.*

*Disturbed by the image; the seven faces staring at him on the field, he followed the principality down the winding stairs onto the grassy plain. As he trailed behind the guide, the small note he had given him before accidentally fell from his pocket to the ground. Quickly, he stooped down, picked it up, was about to return it, when he realised Anael was already in the air, on his way back to the Halls of Travel.* **He would give it to him later,** *he thought, digging the rectangular strip of paper in his pocket. He was about to jump into the air when curiosity gripped him again.*

*He retrieved the note and unfolded it. His eyes on the forest, the note burning in his clenched hand, he waited a few moments. debated whether he should read it...he lowered his eyes, stretched his hand. A puzzled expression clouded his face as he voiced the words 'vibrations are disconcerting'.*

Alexandra had been reluctant to leave Michael. She had nearly cried when she had said goodbye to him outside the hotel. She already missed him. The memory of his flesh upon her flesh still made her quiver. She could not wait to see him again.

She had fallen asleep the moment her head had touched the pillow. Her sleep comfortingly invaded with a dream of him. Alexandra couldn't believe it; she was in love. The kind of love described by romantic heroines. She had long given up on ever finding love.

She had dated through the years, but the men who drifted into her life had not fit the bill, understood the nature of her work, the long hours she dedicated to the children. Her inexistent love life, however, had failed to convert her into a cynic. She believed in love, unfortunately, she was not to be the receptacle of it. She had consoled herself with the fact that love came to her from other quarters. The children adored her.

Untarnished by scepticism she had indulged in romantic reveries, fantasised often she was a princess trapped in a castle turret, waiting for her prince to save her from her solitary existence, visualised passionate encounters with the man of her dreams. The dreamy illusions had served as an escape valve, liberated the inbred need for amorous love. Recently, she had reconciled with the fact that her prince would never exist, that the man of her dreams was a desperate concoction to fill the void inside her. She had been wrong. Her prince existed; his name was Michael.

She was, as usual, the first one at work, to park her car behind the grey flaking building and walk around to the front gate. The moment she reached the iron gate, she saw the human mass under the porch leading to the front door. *Who were all these children? What were they doing in the yard?* She thought anxiously, the shaky key missing the lock repeatedly. After several attempts, she managed to insert the quivering key in the lock and free the chain. Quickly, she swung the gate open and rushed towards the sleeping mountain. Bewildered, she stared down at the heaving mound, at the heap of sleepy faces. As her eyes roved over the worn grey blankets covering the overlapping bodies, as she struggled to understand what was happening, a hesitant voice from behind whispered her name.

He had grown up, but she knew him instantly. It was Marcus, the boy she had helped out of the Hudson foster home years earlier. She remembered him clearly; he had been her last case before the department transferred her to another district. She remembered someone telling her the Social Worker who had replaced her had found him a more adequate home, and had heard nothing of him since. She stared at him confounded. *What was he doing in the patio, why were all these children with him, where did they all come from?* There were nearly one hundred children huddled on the yard's floor.

Marcus walked shyly towards her, the moment he reached her side he began to cry. Between broken sobs he began to spill his story; what his life had been like since he had last seen her, before he had met her...the suffering of the children at the orphanage, what had happened the previous day, his fears...

Alexandra listened quietly, her heart constricting in her chest. After Marcus had finished speaking, delivering the explicit account of misery, she took him in her arms. They hugged in silence, the sound of waking yawns echoing throughout the cold yard. After a while, Marcus relaxed, stopped crying. Alexandra disentangled herself gently from his embrace, gazed tenderly into his frightened dark eyes and placed her hands on his stooped shoulders. She reassured him; the ordeal was over. He had come to the right place.

Quickly, she opened her bag, retrieved her phone and dialled Michael's number.

Marcus had been right; his instincts had not betrayed him. Alexandra would help him, help the children. Whilst Alexandra made pertinent calls, he waited in the yard. As he watched the sky, his thoughts drifted to the feather, his lucky feather. He wished he could have kept it, that the wind had not stolen it. An image of the feather curling high over the city floated before him. Perhaps it was not his to keep; perhaps wise winds had carried it in their invisible arms to spin magic in someone else's life...

The hungry pleas from the children brought him back to reality. The children were famished, had ate nothing since the previous day; he still had some money left... As he stepped into the office in search of Alexandra, adult voices rang in the yard. He looked out the office window; four women were cheerfully distributing breakfast rolls and glasses of milk among the ravenous crowd. He swung a glance at Alexandra. She was in deep conversation with some lawyer, but nodded at him conspiratorially. Marcus returned the smile, they were in capable hands.

That night they slept in a hotel, supervised by Alexandra and two junior Social Workers. They would be staying there until the department resolved what to do with them. Marcus slept like a baby, strongly reassured by Alexandra they were never going back to the orphanage, to hell. Coincidentally, that same week a Children's Home had been inaugurated. It was big enough to house the one hundred orphans. A whole block of flats had been destined to the cause; a generous proprietor had refurbished and relinquished one of his properties to the department, with the sole condition it remained a Children's Home for life. 'The Rainbow Home for Children' located in a small town, edged by woodland, two hours from the city became their new home.

It was a three-storey building with thirty three-bedrooms and ten, two-bedroom flats. They had been fully reconditioned, with newly equipped kitchens and bathrooms. Word that help was needed spread like wildfire throughout the local community, who instantly flocked to the home offering to help. The flats were ready in twelve days. A department store miraculously donated soft furnishings, TVs, toys, books, clothes... everything needed to turn the empty flats into homely nests. In return for their generosity, the store had requested that a banner with their logo was displayed over the home's main entrance, predicting the media would have a field day with the extraordinary story. The media had turned out en masse, awarding unbeatable exposure. The vision they had held that a 'caring' store would lure more clients was proved right, news of their altruistic involvement catapulted sales to record level.

Volunteers helped to transform the flats into comfortable homes and offered to care for the children until more Care Workers were recruited. A picture of children flying coloured ribbons hang above the four entrances of 'The Rainbow Home for Children'. 'Welcome home' banners hang over them. A cheering mass welcomed the thrilled children as they descended from the buses and headed into their new home. They cried unashamedly, overtaken by emotion; they could not believe they had been so lucky. They were walking in a fairytale dream, one where wishes did come true. Marcus proudly led the four separate groups into the building then helped Social Workers split them into family groups. They had needed his help to ensure friends were placed with friends, age groups respected and siblings remained together. By the end of the day, they had settled in the newly formed family units.

Alexandra enrolled the children in a school located only twenty minutes by bus from their new home, that remarkably comprised the resources to accept them all. The contemporary edifice was located on the fringe of the charming town, on the edge of the forest skirting it. The modern glass and white brick, four-storey building loomed against the exuberant woods holding a shimmering lake, visible through the natural avenue of trees. Weather permitting, outings to the forest were a daily occurrence, picnics, botanical expeditions, fishing, swimming and other outdoor games being part of the curriculum.

The children were fascinated with their new learning surroundings, with the natural playground that was an extension to the school's yard. The fresh open space, breathing with life, with freedom, diverged greatly from the stark stone, paved yard, the sterile fortress that had suffocated their will.

Every one of them adapted, without problem, to the new environment. The children at the school welcomed them warmly and soon every orphan had made a friend. Although the children established immediate affectionate bonds with Care Workers, no one came close to what they felt for Marcus. Since their liberation, Marcus had become their leader, their confidant, their hero. They idolized him. As far as they were concerned, no one could fill his shoes. He had freed them from torment, led their exodus to the Promised Land.

Marcus had difficulty acclimatizing to some aspects of his new life. Whilst he adapted well to school, made friends and settled smoothly in the home, he was still uncomfortable with the open admiration, the constant praise the children conferred. No one had bestowed such devotion on him before. No one had ever made the slightest effort to enter his world. It took some time to accept so many loved him.

Late at night, in the intimacy of his room, he unbridled his emotions; wept softly on his pillow, his head buried on the cushion that muffled his crying. His tears were not tears of sadness but joy. Throughout his life, no one had shown him affection, the feeling he was the most loved person on the face of the earth overwhelmed him. Every night before he dozed off to sleep, he thanked the feather. He thanked a God he had never known existed, until now.

Arianne spent the next four years in a girl's convent school. Julia was responsible for the arrangement. Social Services had wished to place her in an orphanage, a public school but Julia had argued the all-female environment and the spiritual and peaceful surroundings of the convent were better suited to Arianne's needs. She needed to feel safe, be cocooned in a world that soothed her agitated soul, assuaged recollection of her nightmare...

Julia had quickly discerned Arianne was exceptionally intelligent and St Mary's outstanding curriculum would mould her to become one of the numerous high-flyer graduates that left the convent for university each year, would empower her to become the young woman she was meant to be.

When the authorities had contacted Arianne's mother, informed her daughter refused to return home, she was indifferent, muttered a vague '*I understand...*' and slammed the door on the Social Worker bearing the message. It was evident Arianne would be better under the caring tutelage of the sisters.

Before leaving for the convent, Arianne had confessed to Julia the real reason that had made her a runaway. Loneliness, sorrow, had not made her escape the grungy apartment in the middle of the night. Her negligent and indifferent mother was not the cause. She had been raped.

Julia was devastated, knew what the savage assault had done to her young soul. For a long time, she had rocked the poor child in her arms, reassured her softly she was the victim, that she had done nothing wrong. That God had led her to the safe haven of the church, to her. That no one would ever harm her again. She had tried to convince Arianne to press charges, but she had refused. She did not have the strength to relive her ordeal. Julia had understood and had not insisted.

Five weeks later Sister Julia was in for another shock. Arianne was pregnant. With her help, arrangements for her baby to be adopted the moment she gave birth were made. Arianne had decided she was too young to be a mother. She had wished her baby to grow up in a safe and loving environment, with a father, a mother. She had wished her baby to have the life she had been denied. The reality was she had been terrified. Haunting doubts had kept her awake every night. Her baby was the fruit of brutality, depravity and she had feared she would be unable to love him/her. She had been afraid she would become her mother.

On the 22nd January, Arianne gave birth to a beautiful and healthy baby boy. The moment it had left her aching body, he was bundled in a blue blanket and rushed out of the room. Arianne had not wished to see him, see his face. She would never have been able to give him up if she had.

A cruel twist of fate prevented her baby from living the life Arianne had dreamt for him. An inexperienced nurse placed her son in the wrong cot, under the wrong nametag. Five days later, he left the hospital in the arms of another fourteen-year-old girl who had coincidentally given birth that night.

From the hospital, she had headed straight for an old church in the outskirts of the city and deposited the newborn baby on the cold steps leading to its arched wooden doors. The moment she had abandoned him to the night, the frightened girl had hopped on a bus and left the city.

Ethan sat between his parents, waited nervously for Michael to spill the news. On edge, he kept rubbing his hands under the desk, his eyes fixed on Michael. He did not wish to confront his parent's expressions as they digested the news. They had been hurt at his lie; had thought him safe with Simon's parents. They had still not forgiven him. He had never lied to them before. They had not raised him that way.

His parents had no clue of the internet, no idea of what it was he had created. He prayed Michael would be able to translate what he had done was important, revolutionary. He hoped the lawyer's explanations would suffice. He fervently wished them to support him, his dream. He wished them to be proud of him. He did not wish to go solo. The dream would mar without their support. They must understand the importance of his creation, the impact he, Michael, envisaged his software would have on the virtual world. *They would reprimand him, tell him to forget the ridiculous idea and devote his time to his studies, his friends...* he thought anxiously.

Corinne and Johan Larson did not interrupt Michael as he explained the intricacies of what his son had done, was about to do. Ethan glanced at them surreptitiously. Their expressions were frustratingly noncommittal. With aplomb, Michael stressed the importance of their son's creation; the astronomic sums of money his software could yield, the imperative need for everything to be legally watertight... His parents remained quietly pensive, as he explained the agreement he had made with their son. He would keep a small percentage of the company as payment...

They watched Ethan, Michael, blankly, then looked at each other. Frustration gripped Ethan as he was forced to witness the silent language his parents often engaged in... He wished them to speak, kill the uncertainty choking him. He could not bear to look at them any longer, turned his head to look at Michael. He discerned a flicker of smile in his eyes... Hesitantly, he looked at his parents... They beamed proudly at him, nodded their heads in unison signalling the lawyer they agreed with every word pronounced.

When the meeting ended, Michael invited the thrilled family to lunch. Excitedly, he confided his immediate plans to Ethan, the legal steps leading to the disclosure of his creation, to the world.

Both Corinne and Frederick were glad Ethan had chosen Michael; he was a good man with good intentions, they agreed. He would protect their son.

Ethan was ecstatic; Michael's dynamic explanations, obvious expertise and charisma had immediately won over his parents. His subtly persuasive argument that Ethan had had the foresight, the maturity to do what needed to be done, had not intended to disrespect them, had helped to patch the fissure in their relationship.

'Quill' was publicized a month later. As Michael predicted, powerful advertising companies offered the anonymous young entrepreneur succulent contracts to advertise in his user interface and the search engine became the number one portal chosen to navigate the virtual highway. Michael took Ethan under his expert wing, guided him every step of the way. With Ethan's approval, he hired an initial team of experts, ten graduates fresh out of university. Soon, the ten turned to fifty, by the end of the year the company employed a fleet of whizz kids who were thrilled to be part of the fast expanding innovative company. He acquired excellent office space in a modern high-rise tower in the hub of the city. Initially, they leased one floor, within two months they had leased a further five. By the end of the year they owned the building.

Office space on the top floor was converted into two flats, a spacious two-bedroom, two-bathroom apartment for Ethan's parents and a three-bedroom, two-bathroom apartment for Ethan. The stunning ethnic-eclectic flats enjoyed every comfort and surrounded an oriental roof garden with a large heated swimming pool and Jacuzzi constructed to resemble natural ponds. Ethan only stayed in his flat when Michael and

Alexandra visited; otherwise, he remained in his parent's apartment during university breaks.

Michael and Ethan become inseparable. Michael presided over the company's board until Ethan finished university. Ethan wished he could have started work in the company straight away but understood a good leader must possess advantage over those he led. Knowledge was power.

Ethan left for university knowing that his company was in safe hands. Quill's success attracted the media like magnets but Michael ensured Ethan's anonymity. Ethan would continue to enjoy a normal life until he became Company President. The world knew the young genius existed, but no one had ever seen him. His identity remained a well-guarded secret. That Ethan remained incognito until he had matured had been his parents' only prerequisite and Michael had concurred. When Ethan finished his studies, had time to grow up like any other young man he would take over Quill, until such time, he would remain anonymous.

Continuous attempts to sabotage the intricate security web that protected his identity failed. Michael, the company, had hired the best security team money could buy. No one ever saw Ethan or his family enter or leave the apartments. Michael had instructed a discreet and highly regarded construction firm to build a secret riser, install a lift, that reached up to the attic apartments. The high-speed lift was accessible through an adjoining building that had clandestinely become property of Quill. A concealed door in its underground parking area connected the two buildings via a secret corridor. The lift was located at the end of the latter. The construction firm was sworn to legal secrecy. Three floors beneath the apartments remained empty, the voids of space insulating sound.

Ethan's parents agreed to move from their home in the suburbs to the apartment so Ethan could control his company. They had had no choice; their son could only nurture his 'baby' when everyone had gone home. Meetings with Michael were scheduled for weekends, when Ethan returned home; no one had access to the buildings then. Initially, Michael and Alexandra had slept at Ethan's flat every Friday and Saturday night Ethan returned home on university breaks.

Alexandra watched Marcus get on the bus with tears in her eyes. He had not said much before leaving, he was not a demonstrative boy. Alexandra was not fooled, under the impassive surface lay a tumult of emotions.

She understood the dilemma that afflicted his young heart. Marcus was torn; excited at the prospect of leaving for university, sad at leaving the children. The children were his family; he had never had a family. He would miss them, would make them proud. The children worshipped him; he must become someone they respected, a role model to follow. He had responsibilities.

Alexandra remembered the first time she had met Marcus; he had been nine years old when he had collected him from his latest foster home. He had not spoken much during the two-hour drive to her office, except to tell her that one day he would have lots of money and would buy himself a big and beautiful house. A house where he would not have to live with people that didn't really want him, that didn't really wish him to be part of their families.

When Alexandra had asked how he would accomplish this, he had told her, self-assuredly, that he would go to university and become a famous writer. Alexandra had thought it remarkable that a child his age was so clear in his goals, understood that a good education was a powerful survival tool.

As the bus moved away, her eyes remained riveted on his face. Marcus sat on the back seat, stared at her soberly through the rear glass. He had not kissed or embraced her when he had said goodbye moments before, but Alexandra was not surprised, the only recipients of Marcus' open affection were the children. Alexandra watched the bus roll slowly over the tarmac, move further away down the avenue and sighed to herself. She hoped with all her heart Marcus adapted well to his new life, made good friends.

She had begun to walk away, towards her car when the bus screeched to a halt. Alarmed, she turned around, wondering if the big blue bus had broken down, when she saw

Marcus jump off. He stood still, looked at her seriously across the heated asphalt, then began to run in her direction. Before she had time to determine what afflicted him, Marcus had thrown his arms around her, locked her in a strong embrace, whispered *'I will miss you too,'* let go off her as abruptly as he had avalanched upon her and run back to the bus. Alexandra did not have time to look into his eyes but knew they were flooded with tears.

As she returned to her office, Alexandra recalled the events that had led Marcus to her and her heart burst with pride. He had evolved into a fine young man despite the early setbacks, despite the pain. Alexandra marvelled at the way he handled the children. The Care Workers were lost without him, could not wait for him to return home during university breaks; Marcus made their lives a lot easier.

Whenever there was a problem with a child, Marcus was always ready to guide him, support him, protect him, scold him if need be. Marcus showered every one of them with unconditional love, devoted his spare time to their needs. The children were his priority. Alexandra understood why Marcus was their hero, the father figure they all craved, the idol they wished to emulate. She had no doubt most of the children, if not all, would follow in his footsteps. Mercifully, an optimistic future awaited them all.

As she walked through the park, her thoughts drifted to Michael, how important he had become in all of their lives. He had been instrumental in ensuring the children's safety. He was a brilliant lawyer and an even better man. The moment she had called him the morning she had found the children on her doorstep, he had sprung into action. Within hours, the children had been placed under the tutelage of the Social Works Department, the orphanage under investigation. He had also managed to pull a few strings ensuring brother Jonah would never work with children again, even if the charges against him were dropped as a result of ecclesiastic influence.

Michael had been repulsed by Alexandra's account of the children's suffering in the hands of men claiming to be servants of God. He had been appalled at the hardships inflicted on children who did not possess the power to defend themselves. Like Alexandra, Michael was extremely proud of the young man who had had the courage to defy the heartless men who had treated the children like convicts; the stone grey building had been a prison not a refuge. The thought that those 'holy' men had ill-treated children simply because they belonged nowhere, had no one to protect them, made his stomach churn. Alexandra could not thank Michael enough for his help, for understanding what the children meant to her. Michael was also a hero in her eyes, a knight in shining armour that had saved her in more ways than one.

With hindsight, she realised she had fallen in love the moment they met. The moment he had smiled into her eyes on the cove, but would never have guessed they would be so perfect for each other. They shared the same ideals, priorities, vision of life. A magical connection existed between them, a match made in heaven she had often thought, one she hoped would last a lifetime.

*Seth had been unable to shake the images he had seen on the field and had trouble concentrating on his studies. The masters had admonished him repeatedly in class, but he could not quash the questions that shadowed him. He could not wait to retire to his room, for the last class in the Halls of Travel to end. He needed to think...*

*As he lay on his bed, starring up at the logged ceiling, he kept mulling them over.* **Who were these mortals that kept invading his dreams? What did they want from him?** *As he pondered on the questions further, he realized he was not sure if they were the only ones that wanted something, if the feeling was reciprocal. If they were the ones pulling him across the frontier or he was the one pulling them into his dreams. As far as he knew, mortals did not have the capacity to magnetise him. ...* **He must be the one luring them... but why?** *For some reason he felt connected to them; it was a subliminal sensation, one he could not quite fathom.* **Why did each of them carry a feather? Was it the same feather he had lost?** *The burning depiction of a feather on his wing pointed in that direction...*

*The questions spun like a tornado in his head...whizzed around him, whipping his mind, hurtling him deeper into confusion. He wished he could catch them, match them to answers one by one. The assumption that the feather they held was the same feather he had lost, seemed a logical one, but he could not be certain. He was not even sure if the visions were real, if they were only dreams. Something strange was happening. He needed to resolve the riddle, what the apparitions meant. He would tell his mother about the dreams, the visions. His mother would help him unravel the mystery. Wrapped in the hopeful thoughts, he fell into dreamless sleep.*

Ethan enjoyed his new life at the university; he loved learning. His brain was like a sponge's that was never squeezed. It absorbed and retained every drop of information. Sometimes he wished he could have stayed home, run his company but understood the need for the detour. He had created software, a user interface that had turned to a successful company. The company employed people who depended on it, Quill was their livelihood; he had to ensure its solidity. Knowledge was the tool that would keep him ahead of the game, his subordinates, the competition.

As intended, Michael made substantive donations to charities from his share of the company. Ethan followed suit. Ensured donations did not come solely out of Michael's pocket. He instructed Michael to donate a generous sum of the company's dividends at the end of each financial year to worldwide charities. That donations continued to alleviate the less fortunate would ultimately be his responsibility.

Ethan devoted most of his time to his studies but, heeding his parent's advice, he made it a point to socialise with his new friends every Friday and Saturday night. His parents had insisted he made the best of university life. They knew their son well, once he took over the company he would devote himself to it body and soul and allow little time for enjoyment.

It was Friday night and he had arranged to meet his friends at a music pub frequented mostly by students. The alcohol was cheap and the music was good. He arrived early, ordered a beer from the bar and sat down at a table in the corner, near the small dancing area. He was a pitiful dancer but enjoyed watching his friends contort to the beating rhythm trying to impress girls.

He was sitting leisurely sipping his beer, minding his own business when a group of students entered the pub and headed for the bar. They were clearly drunk. He shifted his body slightly, avoided eye contact with the rowdy group and continued enjoying his beer.

Suddenly, one of them broke away from the sniggering crowd and swayed to his table, called him a geek and poured a pint of beer over his head. The cold liquid spilled down his shoulders, his back. He had not expected the sudden assault and before he had time to react, the drunken bully had already returned to his group of jeering friends. Before he had time to unleash anger, confront them, another student, who had been sitting quietly two tables behind him, rushed towards the bar and swiftly knocked two of them to the floor. The remaining two fled out the door, fearing they too would end up with a broken nose. Ignoring Ethan, he walked back to his table, finished his drink in one gulp and walked out of the pub. Everything happened so quickly Ethan had hardly been able to digest the incident, remained in a state of shock. Secretly, he was grateful the anonymous student had intervened; he hated violence. Still, why a total stranger had involved himself in a conflict that was not his concern baffled him.

For days, Ethan searched the campus for the heroic student. Eventually, he spotted the dark unruly haired man reading under a tree near the campus' perimeter. He headed in his direction. At the sound of Ethan's '*hello*,' the young man looked up and a pair of dark broody eyes confronted Ethan's timid stare. Ethan introduced himself, tentatively offered his hand. Indifferent eyes dismissed it and continued reading. Ethan towered over the aloof student, uncomfortable, uncertain. After standing awkwardly for a while, he sat on the grass beside him. He remained silent for a few moment until eventually, he managed a faint '*thank you*.'

At the sound of his shy whisper, the intimidating student shut his book brusquely, stood up, blatantly exasperated and walked away, ignoring him. Disconcerted by his antisocial behaviour, Ethan remained rooted to the spot, his eyes fixed on the rude and unfriendly student storming away. He watched him perplexed, trying to rationalise his puzzling attitude until he disappeared across the grass into the library building. Disheartened, he stood up, was about to walk away when he noticed the notebook at the foot of the tree. He picked it up and inspected its contents. The first chapter of a novel filled its pages, scribbled on its cover was the name Marcus.

Alexandra's life could not be better; her professional life ran smoother than it had in years. The daily miracles continued; help came the department's way from unexpected quarters and coincidental events ensured children were continuously and swiftly placed in safety. Michael's professional life had done a three hundred and sixty degree turn. His fortuitous involvement with Quill permitted him to donate large sums of money to those in need. Alexandra's children were top of his list.

Alexandra liked Ethan the moment Michael had introduced him to her. She had been pleasantly surprised by the affectionate relationship between Michael and his protégée. Ethan was extremely affable, highly intelligent and equally modest. Alexandra could not help admiring this last quality in him, he was extremely down to earth, had no airs despite his huge achievement, his immense wealth. From the onset, he had treated her with the same affection he bestowed on Michael. In no time, Ethan had become the younger brother Alexandra wished she'd had.

Alexandra loved visiting Ethan's apartment on weekends when he was home. She was thrilled to spend time with the two most important men in her life. Michael apologised profusely for leaving her alone in the apartment whilst Ethan and he spent weekend afternoons dealing with company matters, but she did not mind. She was happy to spend time with Ethan's adorable mother, learning gardening tips, catching up on her reading or simply relaxing in the Jacuzzi or swimming pool. She could see why Ethan was emotionally balanced, amiable and noble. Corinne and Johan had done a great job raising their son. Loving and coherent parents, they had instilled the sound morals and values that made Ethan the person he was, the man he was fast becoming.

Their dinners in the garden's terrace were the highlight of the weekend; exquisite food and charming company were infallible ingredients for pleasurable evenings after a hard day's work. Alexandra was eager to learn about Ethan's university life, and gently scolded him for not enjoying himself more. She reminded him repeatedly that once he became CEO of Quill, he would have little time for enjoyment, especially in the first years. Ethan reprimanded her jokingly that she sounded just like his mother, but was secretly pleased Alexandra was genuinely concerned with his life.

During their last weekend together, Ethan had confided an unpleasant episode to her whilst Michael had gone to see a client. He told her about the bullies that had harassed him without reason, whilst he had been waiting for friends in a pub near the campus. How another student, a stranger, had defended him. He had wished to thank him for his noble gesture but the student had rudely ignored him when he had approached him on campus grounds. '*He was probably having a bad day'*, Alexandra had advised, certain that they would cross paths again and he would not be as hostile then. He only needed to be patient. Patience was not one of Ethan's virtues.

Alexandra understood Ethan's compelling desire. She had come to know him well. She knew of his aversion to violence, to conflict of any kind and was conscious of the fact that Ethan was secretly pleased he had not been forced into a fight. When Alexandra retired that night, she could not help thinking about the timely coincidence. Providential synchronicity blessed their lives. The latter would have been reaffirmed if Alexandra had known Ethan's opportune avenger's name.

*Before Seth had a chance to express his concerns to his mother, he suffered another bizarre episode. Early on the Seventh Day, his wings spread wide; he dived from the northern face of the mountain and skimmed the steep cliff. He had nearly reached the valley's multicoloured slope when a bright light blinded him, engulfed him and he began to float in a warm bubble. After a few moments he began to descend, landed on soft ground. The minute his feet touched ground, the light vanished. Once again, he was standing on the familiar field.*

*The field was instantly flooded in darkness and children began to materialize from the shadows. They emerged slowly, from every corner of the field. As the small crowd moved closer, he realised each child cupped a candle in his hands. The crowd of ten soon turned to twenty, a hundred, a thousand... Before long, the field was a carpet of faces shadowed by flickering light. Seth remained still, disorientated, his limpid eyes drinking the contrite expressions bathed in dancing shades, the glistening eyes mirroring the crackling flames sheltered by small pallid hands. Their blazing eyes implored him; the gathering of early souls tore at his heart.*

*He felt their sadness, despair, their pain. Wishing to embrace the avalanche of wretchedness, he spread his wings wide, but his wingspan was not large enough, a drop in the ocean against the tide of anguished innocence flooding him. He felt impotent and his soul spilled silent shame. He could not reach them all...*

*He could not bear their torment any longer, when a rush in the air, a subtle murmur of hope, originated at the core of the sombre mass and spread outwards to reach every child. The echoing ripples lit spectral faces with smiles, ashen flesh turned rosy as the lights in their delicate hands became vibrant, taller. In moments, beaming smiles, vigorous flames, killed the cold darkness transforming the field into sunny day.*

*A rain of white feathers suddenly flooded the field, until fluffy silken plumes covered every inch of ground from clear skies. The scene was unreal, a snowy carpet beneath a warm celestial sky. The minute the feathery rain ended, the throng of children began to chant his name.*

*Jubilant, Seth listened to the high-timbre voices that rang like a heavenly choir. His eyes rested on their joyful expressions and peace invaded his soul. He shut his eyes, revelled in the voices ringing with laughter, with hope...The second he opened his eyes he was back on the cliff waiting to jump.*

*As Seth flew home, the scene preyed heavily on his mind. This time he had not been floating outside the sphere before he found himself on the field. This time the images felt different, more dream than vision. He could not erase the intense scene from memory; the children's faces, their eyes.. their initial sorrow, the merciful transformation from despair to joy...*

*He was certain the vision held a message of great relevance; he could feel it in his soul.*

*What that message was, he had no idea.*

Arianne arrived early at the charming hotel shadowing the cove; she had booked three rooms, one for herself two for her crew. Room number seven on the first floor had been her unconscious choice. With an hour to kill before her team arrived, she decided to have a short nap; she was in for a long day. The moment she saw the room, she fell in love with it. She had not expected it to be so luxurious, welcoming. The moment she set foot in it, she felt her spirit uplifted.

There was a strange pulse in the room, a vibrant breath that invigorated her. Immaculately decorated in silver and white tones, the furniture exquisite and the view breathtaking; the room was a dream. The moment she saw the sunken bathtub surrounded by silver and glass candelabra she changed her mind, replaced the quick nap with a hot relaxing soak. As the scented water caressed every inch of her tired body, she gazed out of the arched window towards the ocean.

The sun bounced upon the rippling seas, the twinkling glimmer heaving as gentle waves washed the shore. The salty mist floated into the room, the cool breeze mingling with the scented aroma. She was thrilled she had come. The discreet opulence of the room, the luxurious bathtub, the particular energy of the room had a comforting effect on her usually high-strung body; it was a long time since she had felt so relaxed yet so uniquely alive.

Her life was a rollercoaster ride, by the time she had habituated herself to the rhythm of a show a new project materialised and she had to acclimatise to a frenetic tempo again. The first few nights were frantic; she hardly slept, ate, was highly strung. Insomnia and a poor diet were the price she paid for her enormous success. The disparate sensations, the energizing yet calming pulse of the room, made her feel more lucid and balanced than she had in years, at that moment, immersed in the foaming warmth, she felt strong enough to take on the world.

Arianne was glad that she had the chance to work again as a field reporter. Her assistant had called in sick in the last minute and she had jumped to fill her shoes. The channel's executives had argued someone else should do the job, that **she** was a star, but she had insisted.

Arianne had felt an inexplicable compulsion to cover the story. She was dying to meet the heroic young man who had freed the orphans from a life of tyranny, led them to safety. She was dying to show the world the generosity of those who had made their new life possible. As she stared down on the indigo ocean, at the dawning skies, she visualized the feather, thought of the magic it had spun in her world.

Audiences sensitized to her shows and citizens had begun to implicate themselves actively in the quest for social change. The brutal depiction of subjugated minorities, neglected injustices, struck a chord and those who had selfishly detached themselves, turned a blind eye to daily tragedies surrounding them, were forced to pay attention. As she dried herself with the spongy grey and silver edged towel, she felt strange, giddy. A tingling sensation invaded her body and a sudden euphoric feeling seized her. As she dried her hair, she looked at her smiling reflection on the ornate mirror. At that moment, in that room, she felt the happiest and most privileged woman on earth. Wistfully, she thought of the feather again, wondered if it was blessing another person's life.

Arianne stood with her camera crew outside the Children's Home. The whole town had turned up for the event, the expectant crowd impatient. They could not wait to see the children's faces when they saw their new home for the first time. The camera crew focused on the two buses laden with exited children as soon as it turned the corner down the street. They had been the first to arrive; Arianne, as always, ensured the best spot.

As soon as he stepped out of the bus, Arianne deduced that the young man who led the children to their safe haven was Marcus. As he ushered the excited children into the building, to the sound of cheering and clapping from the well-wishing crowd, the dark-haired hero intrigued her. A beautiful, raven-haired woman, who she suspected was Alexandra, the Social Worker she had spoken to on the phone, accompanied him.

Social authorities prohibited cameras entering the building; children's intimate surroundings must be respected. Senior Social Workers had agreed to Marcus' interview once the children had settled in their new home. In the meantime, Arianne interviewed the generous proprietor and the department store's manager, the benefactors who had enabled the dream become a reality. When the interviews were completed, they took some more footage of the building and headed back to the hotel.

Arianne had an early dinner. She could not wait to be back in the beautiful sanctuary. She could not remember feeling so peaceful, alive, anywhere else. She had begun to undress when a faint knock on her door startled her. Thinking it was Jerry, the head cameraman, she flung on the embroidered silver bathrobe and headed for the door. The moment she opened the door she froze. Marcus was standing in the corridor.

She remained static, speechless, as she prodded dark eyes that revealed nothing. They stood staring at each other in awkward silence until, finally, she ushered Marcus into the room. Hesitantly, Marcus headed for the window at the opposite side of the room, stared into the night. Arianne watched him confused. *What did he want, what was he doing in here?* Marcus seemed to have heard her thoughts, turned around abruptly, lowered his eyes down to the carpeted floor and began to excuse himself weakly for having interrupted her evening.

Without the slightest glance in her direction, he began to head for the door. Arianne intercepted him, stood defiantly in the threshold; she burned to know why he had come. Finally, reluctantly; Marcus retreated into the room. He walked slowly to the bed and sat on its edge. Clouded eyes told her he had no idea why he had come.

For a while, the two strangers shared the edge of the bed in silence, unable to find words befitting the moment. Arianne did not know what had compelled Marcus to seek her in the middle of the night. The only thing she was certain of was that, for some reason, beyond comprehension, she did not wish him to leave.

Marcus could not remember the reason that had lured him to visit this woman, this stranger. He had nothing to say to her... He felt uncomfortable, miles from his comfort zone. He did not dare move as he sat beside her, his arms inches from hers. Resisting the impulse to run out the door, he remained on the bed, watched her out of the corner of his eye. *What was it about this woman who stirred such confusing emotions?* He thought, wishing he had not given in to the sudden urge that had propelled him out of bed...

Chaos fogged his mind. He wished to speak, struggled to find words between thoughts ceaselessly interrupted by a galloping heart. He wished Arianne to speak, dissolve the layer of tension suffocating him. She remained silent. Furtive eyes darted to the delicate hands resting upon her trembling lap, then stealthily roamed the elfin contours of her face. *She was so beautiful...*

A sudden headache attacked him, the pound in the base of his skull expanding to his throat. His heart seemed to have disentangled itself from the rib-protected cavity, was travelling up his oesophagus... Suddenly, his flesh tingling with the elating quality of the room, his hand pressing the base of his cranium in an effort to attenuate the relentless throb, the words he had been striving hard to find suddenly began to gush forth and he found himself confessing his tragic childhood to the stranger sitting to his right.

Between gulps of breath, he shared the miseries of his past, the long years he had felt unloved, how he had been damned to walk the earth sequestered in an unfeeling shell covering a heart he had converted to stone. The torrent of words spilled from his soul until the last drop of lament had been delivered.

Arianne drank every drop of his bleeding heart, the stream of wretched grief reviving her childhood tragedies, loss of innocence, the desperate loneliness she had suffered, the sacrifice she had made...

A sudden pain attacked her temples and it was Marcus's turn to be a silent witness to her liberation. When every burdening word had abandoned her tired soul, she reached for Marcus's hand and held it tightly. They sat on the cushioned ridge in silence, the headaches gone, the beating of their hearts echoing the soothing pulse of the room, the sweep of the ocean on the dark, cold shore.

Neither of them understood what had just happened, neither of them cared. For the first time in their lives, they felt strangely at peace. As Arianne remained motionless on the bed, her hand clutching Marcus', she had a weird thought; the room had encouraged their confessions...

*Seth and Amanda were sitting out on the porch, listening to the sound of sea shells as they exchanged daily anecdotes. They had been sitting chatting animatedly for hours when Amanda suddenly claimed she was sleepy and stood up. Placing a soft kiss on Seth's forehead, she headed towards the front door. Before she crossed the threshold, Seth jumped to his feet, grabbed his mother gently by the arm and whispered he had something important to tell her. Amanda turned slowly to face him, trying to camouflage the panic that had begun to shade her face. Avoiding his eyes, she sat down on the whitewashed steps beside him and reached for his hand. Cloaking alarm, she looked at her son, the tender expression of her eyes willing Seth to confide his troubles.*

*Seth did not know where to begin.* **His mother would not understand him this time, she would think he had gone mad,** *he thought anxiously. Amanda scanned her son but remained silent. Whatever it was her son was about to tell her she knew it was important. His eyes were unusually dark.*

*Plucking up courage, Seth told her about his visions, described the encounters with the mortals. The strange emotions the visions, the dreams incited. He told her of the burning outline; his missing feather... Amanda remained silent, listened attentively as he described every bizarre scene, analysed the feelings he described when he had confronted them. Finally, Seth stopped talking, looked at his mother intently, then resignedly rested his head on her lap. Amanda caressed his unruly curls for a while, she needed time to assimilate the information, find the words that would make her son understand what she thought was happening...*

*She took a deep breath, exhaled the nippy air slowly, playing for time, whilst tender hands continued to soothe his golden locks, his soul. She inhaled deeply again, slowly released the long gasp of air and began to explain to her son what she knew, what she thought was of relevance.*

*Her words paced, she told him about the visions, the dreams she knew other angels had had. Dominions had written about them, recorded them in the Sacred Book. As far as she knew, visions heralded changes in other worlds, dimensions. They had helped the realm interpret 'happenings', imminent changes in the worlds surrounding the realm. What Amanda did not tell Seth was that the visions happening to an angel was unprecedented. Presaging dreams had only occurred to angels of higher triads.*

*The Elders, Dominions and Powers were custodians of the Sacred Book, carefully guarded in the Golden chamber housed in the Temple of Light. No angel was allowed access to it. The elders had surprisingly unlocked the secured glass cylinder and, coincidentally shown it to Circle of light members recently. It was the first time they had seen the ancient book, devoted to the understanding, the protection of the sacred laws of light, up close.*

*Light was the lungs of the realm, the energy that kept their world, the reason their world existed. The light, the 'source', must be protected at all cost from the fallen angels that threatened to replace it with darkness. Fallen angels, angels banished from the realm for defying the source, lurked in the shadowlands, a dismal world deep below the realm, a world with a deathly vibration. As precaution, light was distributed in levels of intensity throughout the realm, the higher planes, progressively enjoying a stronger intensity of light. That was why the Sky Dwellings home to the source was restricted to a select group of angels able to tolerate the intensity.*

*It was impossible for fallen angels to infiltrate the realm through the higher planes due to their low resonance. Warrior angels zealously guarded the lower planes. The moment an infiltration by the black feathered angels was detected, the celestial army curbed their invasive attempts. The scaly winged angels, with prominent bloodshot eyes, were no rivals for the divine elite force bearing burning swords.*

*The Sacred Book narrated battles forged, extraordinary happenings in the realm. Its golden trimmed pages recorded the slightest variation in light intensity, the subtlest invading threat. Other Circles of Light existed throughout the realm, other higher angels kept the Sacred Book updated. Coincidentally, the elders had read a passage devoted to prophetic visions and dreams. Members of the Circle of light were bound by secrecy; nothing spoken in the temple was to be revealed.*

*Amanda did not wish to defy the laws again, betray her sacred vows, but had no choice. Something was happening, something of great relevance concerning the mortal world, but most importantly, something was happening to her son. She agreed with Seth that the visions were definitely trying to convey a message, that the feather he had lost was perhaps a vital piece of the puzzle. She wrote down everything he had told her. She needed to review each detail. She needed time...*

*They would speak again the following Seventh day, when he returned home, in the meantime she would try to discern what they must do, if they should tell the Elders. A load of his chest, Seth kissed his mother goodnight and retired to bed. After a while, his mind rested, and he fell asleep.*

*Amanda remained on the porch a while longer. Though her mind was exhausted, her body weighed down with worry, she knew she would have been unable to sleep even if she had tried. As she listened to the rush of blades swaying in the nocturnal gust, she wished she could have confided the pieces of the puzzle she already held. She wished she had the courage to hell her son the truth about his conception... She would tell him the next time they met. She would be ready then...*

*She was not one hundred percent sure but strongly suspected the mortal world felt Seth's presence. Somehow, the feather he had lost connected him to the physical world, revived the distant bond. Conceived, having lived in a mortal womb for eight months, listening to the beat of a human heart, the beat of the world around him, he had felt part of it, its inhabitants since.. it seemed the feeling was reciprocal.*

*Sleep eluded her all night. When the first rays of the morning star filtered through her bedroom window announcing her son had already left, she prayed for him, prayed he was strong enough to face whatever challenges awaited him. She augured a major shift in both worlds. As she stepped onto the dew-beaded grass, a sudden warm gust enveloped her; the winds of change were already blowing and she began to pray again.*

Marcus was first to be interviewed. Arianne had felt nervous at the prospect of seeing him after what had happened between them the previous night and had wanted to tackle him first, get the uncomfortable meeting out of the way. In spite of her inner turmoil, she listened in quiet admiration as the young man timidly related his heroic tale, taking down every detail. Alexandra, his social worker, was second to be interviewed; Arianne could not believe the stream of lucky coincidences that had made the Children's Home a reality. Too many she had thought. She was glad she had come, witnessed the extraordinary 'happy ending'.

Neither Arianne nor Marcus referred to their freakish encounter, both felt ashamed at their impulsive behaviour. Their emotional outbursts seemed incongruous in the light of day, their uncharacteristic conduct a source of mortification. Once the interviews were completed and the crew determined they had enough footage for the documentary, Arianne thanked Alexandra for her hospitality and returned to the city. Arianne and Marcus did not say goodbye. Other than in the interview, they did not engage in eye contact.

As the van sped down the highway, Arianne's thoughts kept returning to an image of Marcus. She could not get him out of her head. She had nearly cried when she had gotten in the van to leave and felt ridiculous. As she had relived the moment in her head, she thanked God she had been able to restrain her tears. Her crew would have questioned the inappropriate display of emotion. She was no stranger to emotionally charged scenarios and she had never cried, always the detached professional.

The memory of the unorthodox encounter kept visiting her, confusing her, she could not make sense of the bizarre meeting, the candid confessions. Marcus was a total stranger. She could not understand why she had dispensed emotions without reserve, why the uninhibited confession had been mutual. He was someone she would never see again. *Then why did she feel she was going to miss him, already missed him...?*

Arianne relaxed into her seat and closed her eyes. She wished to sleep, shut out her turmoil, but Marcus' mysterious dark eyes kept preying on her mind. For some reason that escaped explanation, she felt connected to him... She had never felt this way about anyone.

She covered herself with the travelling blanket she always carried in the van and snuggled into her seat. Divagating thoughts to the extraordinary documentary they would air the following week, the interest the story of the heroic young man who had liberated one hundred orphans from the clutches of unholy men would foment, she snuggled further into the seat and eventually dozed off. She slept the whole way to the city, did not wake up until Jerry shook her arm gently and told her she was home.

A long hot bath cleansed away the fatiguing tension of the past two days, and after eating a bowl of fruit, she headed for bed. Mercifully, she fell asleep the moment her head touched the silken pillow. Minutes later a peaceful smile curved her lips as she dreamed of Marcus's intense dark eyes.

The day before Marcus left for University the children, with the help of Social Workers and Carer Workers, threw him a farewell party. Everyone was thrilled Marcus had achieved the scholarship he had dreamed of for so long, but were sad to see him leave. They showered him with goodbye presents. The children bought him a beautiful silver pen set and a trendy leather satchel. Social Workers and Carers chipped in to present him with a top of the range laptop. When it was time to say goodbye, the children hugged and kissed him, blinded by tears. Their small hands clung to him desperately and for a moment, Marcus was tempted to stay. Eventually the Carers managed to calm the children down, made them understand Marcus was not abandoning them; was only leaving them for a while. He would return on holiday breaks... Marcus' excitement at the new life enfolding before him was blemished by the heartbreak he felt at leaving his family behind.

Marcus loved life as a student, loved every module of his literature degree. He made a few casual friends in classes and met up with them occasionally, but mostly he was a loner. He spent the majority of his free time at the library, researching, devouring books or in his room devoted to writing. He had begun to write a novel and hoped to finish it by the end of his first year of studies.

Marcus' broody dark looks and mysterious demeanour attracted unrelenting attention from the opposite sex but he was not interested in frivolous flirting. Marcus had grown from a detached child to an introvert and sensitive man. His noncommittal façade hid emotions that run deep. One-night-stands would be more damaging than pleasurable. He did not wish to become invisible again but was determined that nothing would stand in the way of his studies, in the way of his future. The children needed him...

Marcus had agreed to meet up with a group of classmates for a drink. He would have preferred to stay in his room writing but had finally given in to their insistence, warning them he would only be staying a while. He was the first to arrive. His lectures had finished earlier than expected and after a quick shower and change of clothes had headed across the campus towards the chosen pub, located twenty minutes from the university. He had an hour to kill and decided to kill it drinking a cold beer. He knew that if he had begun to write he would never have left his room. He sat at one of the tables at the back of the room against the wall, drinking the vodka and lemonade he had finally decided on. As he took small sips, his mind raced with new ideas for the next chapter of his novel. Most of the tables were empty, a couple of students drinking at the bar.

Writer's eyes discerned the scene and began painting it in his mind, the exercise prompting metaphoric, stark imagery descriptions. Lost in the imaginative portrayals, he vaguely noticed a group of four students had entered the pub. It was only until the slurred cacophony interrupted his literary embellishments that he fixed his stare on them. Sagacious eyes instantly perceived they were trouble. The bawdy crowd ordered drinks from a reluctant bartender who finally gave in to their demands and stood at the bar swaying and roaring with laughter. Unexpectedly, one of them walked unsteadily towards a table situated at the edge of the dance floor and poured a pint of beer over a student sitting quietly drinking a beer and swayed back to the mocking crowd.

Without thinking twice, Marcus shot up from his seat and leaped to the bar. He detested bullies, had sworn he would never let anyone fall prey to them again. Fury burned his eyes as images of Brother Jonah's vicious attack on the innocent orphan plagued him. With two expert swings, he knocked two of them to the ground. Before he had time to engage the remaining two they fled out the door, abandoning the two cowards, with bleeding noses, cowering on the floor. Adrenalin still rushed his veins as he returned to his table, gulped down the remainder of his drink and left.

He had not wished to engage conflict but had had no choice; once, he had been a silent spectator to the pain of others and had sworn it would never happen again. An image of the feather floated before him and he thought how finding it had changed him. Shortly, he felt shame at his primitive behaviour but shrugged off the negative emotion. He was visible now, part of the world. He had responsibilities. Karma was a bitch; he was a mere tool to the invisible force.

The words racing the screen came to a sudden halt; interrupted by an insistent knock on his door. *This better be important*, Marcus thought exasperated. He hated being pestered by trivialities when he was writing. He hated abandoning the magic world when the muse whispered in his ear. Grudgingly, he separated eager fingers from the keyboard and stood up. The moment he opened the door, a stubborn foot wedged itself in the doorway. He stared at the intruder as he reluctantly stepped back, his eyebrows raised in question, his dark eyes revealing distinct irritation. Ethan's defiant expression told Marcus he did not intend to leave, had no intention of being ignored a second time. As soon as the door opened wide enough the inopportune visitor slipped into the room.

Marcus and Ethan sized each other up, Ethan's wavering '*thank you*' breaking the prickly silence. Marcus did not intend to engage in conversation and murmuring flippantly, he had no time for idle chatter, began to usher Ethan towards the door. Ethan ignored him, headed towards the desk situated beneath the only window in the room and placed the notebook he carried on the grey surface. Ignoring Marcus, who remained by the door, he began to read the words that filled the screen, turned around after a few moments and offhandedly stated: '*so you're a writer then.*' Marcus realised he would have to entertain the imposing guest, satisfy part of his curiosity. He had returned his book; he guessed he owed him a few moments.

Surprisingly, Ethan did not refer to the unfortunate incident at the pub. Casually, he began to question Marcus on his writing. What the novel was about, if he had finished it, and a dozen other annoying queries. Although Marcus did not really wish to talk about his literary project, he found himself answering the questions one by one. When Marcus had satisfied his curiosity, Ethan smiled enigmatically, scribbled something on a sheet of paper he picked up from Marcus's printer and headed hastily towards the door. Before he left the room, he stopped at the door, turned around abruptly and informed Marcus, in a matter of fact tone, he would be hearing from him again. A bewildered Marcus stared down at the empty corridor, unsure of what had just happened. He could not believe he had just given details of his work to a total stranger.

The moment Ethan returned to his room he wrote Michael an email. As he typed the message, he pictured Marcus's insolent eyes. He had not quite figured him out; his impudent exterior did not match the sensitivity conveyed in his writing. Marcus intrigued him, a melancholic charisma exuded from him. Despite their differences, if Marcus had been willing, they could have been friends.

By the end of the day, he had received a reply. The pertinent arrangements had been made. Ethan stared at the email, a satisfied smile on his face.

Unknown to Marcus his courageous deed was about to be repaid.

Two days later, minutes after Marcus returned to his room after university lectures, a courier knocked on his door and handed him a large white envelope. He read the sender's address at the back and was surprised to find it was from a legal firm he had never heard of. Nervously, he tore it open and scanned the documents. He could not believe his eyes. A publishing company was offering him a contract for his novel; the marketing package surpassed any writer's expectations.

The publisher was a subsidiary company of Quill, the internet mogul; Quill's user interface would be the primary marketing tool. His mind raced for a logical explanation. He had not confided he was writing a novel to anyone …he had not finished editing it... *Ethan! It had to be. He was the only one who knew, had seen his work...*

The last page of the document confirmed his suspicion. A clause headed 'important' stated that he was never to mention Ethan's involvement in the matter. If the condition was breached the publishing contract would be declared null and void. He read the clause repeatedly, a single question occupying his mind. *What was Ethan's involvement with Quill?*

The moment Michael received the email from Ethan he had spurred into action. Before the day was over, the publishing contract was ready for dispatch. Michael had to read the email three times before he could assimilate its contents

Initially, Michael had not made the connection, missed the astounding coincidence. He had picked up the phone to make the pertinent calls when it dawned on him; Ethan's Marcus was Alexandra's Marcus. Phone dangling in hand, he had skimmed Ethan's email to the student's description. The young writer Ethan described so graphically was unmistakably Marcus. It could be no other.

Michael liked the young man. They were not close, had met fleetingly on two occasions, but Alexandra spoke often and highly of him. Marcus preferred having Alexandra to himself when he returned home on university breaks; he was that way with her. Michael understood. Marcus had a rough time growing up and did not trust people easily.

When he had finally digested the extraordinary coincidence, what the publishing contract would mean to Alexandra's protégée, to Alexandra, he had swirled in his chair and shrieked yes! Yes! Yes! Excitedly he had dialled Alexandra's number and told her the amazing news.

Alexandra had been dumbfounded by the coincidence. '*Another miracle*', *s*he had whispered incredulously, as she had rambled to Michael about the faint possibility of their respective protégées becoming so importantly entwined in each other's lives. Indeed, Marcus and Ethan attended the same university, but there were hundreds of students. The campus was extensive and their choice of curriculum could not have been more different. Michael agreed.

Extraordinary coincidence, miracle or not, the fact was Marcus had defended Ethan, had spared him the violence Ethan abhorred and Ethan had given Marcus the greatest gift anyone could give him.

*As Seth flew towards the mountaintop, he thought how fortunate he was to have a mother like Amanda; she was always there for him, guiding him. She was different from the other mothers; approachable, unorthodox. Their bond was manifestly special, his mother's uninhibited displays of affection towards him had raised more than one eyebrow from mothers who reared their offspring with the regimented discipline of the realm.*

*When he reached the paradisiacal plateau, he headed straight to his dormitory in the Halls of Travel. He did not have classes until later in the afternoon and decided to take a short nap. The moment he fell asleep, he began to dream.*

*A flashing light transported him to inhospitable land. He stood alone on the parched wasteland, cracks veined across the yellowish arid earth into the distance. Suddenly, children began to appear out of nowhere. They walked wearily, aching feet treading dusty ground, some of them fainting on the hostile terrain. He turned his head slightly and saw some of the children dug desperately into the earth, tiny bleeding fingers raked the scorched ground in search of water. Soon, the vast sterile plain swarmed with children. They were covered in dirt, protruding stomachs manifesting extreme hunger, the tone of their skins very dark. He looked into their eyes as they scavenged the barren earth, imploring dark rimmed eyes with drained expressions. The vision inundated his soul with desolation, with insufferable agony and he felt his body begin to quiver.*

*The dark fleshed swarm with sunken eyes crawling over dusty ground came to a sudden halt and grimy faces stared up at him. Again, the children began to chant his name. As the chorus of voices rang throughout the sterile plain, the field began to transform. The sallow earth began to spring a vibrant green mantle that soon covered every grain of the deathly desert and the sound of rushing water began to ring in his ears. As the mass of children parted down the middle to the sides, a gurgling stream born in the horizon began to zigzag the fertile earth to reach his feet.*

*The children jumped into the clear waters, cupping their hands, drinking its life. The field became alive; trees laden with an array of fruits popped out of the earth and children swiftly climbed up the steady barks to tear the appetising crop from yielding branches. Their eyes had stopped crying, their bellies flattened and grateful smiles adorned their innocent faces. A rain of white feathers fell from the warm skies and snow peaked trees contrasting the lush green terrain again revealed a surreal landscape. Before Seth could speak, the vision disappeared and a new one emerged.*

*He stood in the same field until it altered. Light became darkness and a whimpering sound echoed in the distance. As the soft sobbing gathered momentum, scattered spotlights beamed down on the beds that had invaded the dark. Terrorised children huddled in their corners, hid under them. Again, their anguish, their terror consumed his soul. Fraught, he tried to run towards the beds scattering in the dark but could not lift his legs; an invisible force glued them to the ground. As the cries of the children became louder, hysterical, silhouettes of men appeared in the distance. The gelid air filled with screaming dread as the menacing shadows moved closer to the beds.*

*Seth battled with his legs, willed them to move. He tried forcing them with his hands into step but they remained cemented to the ground. As he perceived the predatory silhouette's depraved intention, his desperation grew and he tugged at his legs frantically. The dark shadows were feet away from its prey when suddenly, the invisible force that had pinned him to the ground, released him. Swiftly, he lunged towards the enemy, his wings spread wide, his eyes incensed. The moment he was upon the destructive shadows, they vanished. Quickly, he turned in the direction of the children and his rigid body slackened. They were sound asleep on the beds, peaceful expressions manifest on their rosy faces. Each held a white teddy bear in his hand. Each teddy bear held a feather in its paw.*

*He had not recovered from the frightening vision when a third confronted him. This time the field became a long dark street.*

*Stacks of cardboard boxes lined both pavements. It had begun to drizzle, the thin spray dyeing the manila ceilings a dark brown. All of a sudden, children began to crawl from underneath the cardboard shells into the cutting night. They scurried into dark alleys, the brumal air turning to frost as they exhaled, in search of plastic bags, anything that would protect their humble abodes from the impending shower. Seth watched them, his heart aching as bare little feet prowled the icy slabs, as they trembled with cold under the torn rags that barely covered their freezing, numb bodies.*

*Mercifully, he was not to be tortured further by the desolate apparition; before the children had time to scavenge rubbish skips at the end of the lonely road, the boxes began to shake fiercely and the cardboard began to expand. The cardboard became wood and the wood transformed magically into houses. A charming avenue of perfectly clipped trees now stretched before him; two rows of beautiful houses faced each other down its length. The children played on the perfect lawns, flawlessly groomed, happy. They waved their hands, beckoned their parents to come out of the house, to look up at the blue skies patched with fluffy clouds. As mothers and fathers invaded the front gardens, cotton white clouds dissolved into thousands of feathers to rain on them. The moment the white rain covered the verdant grounds the vision disappeared.*

*The moment he was back in his room, in his bed, he rushed to the edge of the mountain, dived off the eastern cliff and headed in the direction of the Islands, to the lake. The visions had made him dizzy, weak. He needed to heal. He needed to think. As he floated the golden waters sheltered by the glistening cave, he kept retracing the altering images; the children's faces, the intense emotions they had provoked. Suddenly, one vision preponderated over all the others. A second before he had emerged the dream, he had become a detached spectator, a mere bystander looking into the dream and watched a younger version of himself. Suddenly 'he' spun around. The young angel had no wings.*

*Seth immersed himself in the golden pool, stretched his body under the curative liquid, then floated again on the soothing warm waters, his wings sprawled at his sides. He stared at the glossy bronze ceiling replaying the images, searching for answers.* **Why did the mortals carry a feather? What were the dreams with the children trying to convey? What did the random vision illustrating a younger version of him with no wings mean? ...**

*The visions were unquestionably heeding something significant, the visions, dreams, were somehow connected... It was logical to assume the feather each of the mortals held, the children held, had something to do with the feather he had lost. It was probable that, in a way that escaped him, the feather connected them to him, connected their worlds... The dreams depicted the suffering and hope of mortal children, but how did he fit into the picture? What did the children want from him? As he immersed his body under the water, soaked the healing light, his convulsing mind began to tame.*

*His thoughts returned to the vision he had had of the beautiful young woman sitting in a garden who had startled him. Suddenly it struck him; unlike the other mortals in his dreams, she had seen him, had been expecting him. She had interacted with him in the dream. He could not wait to see her again.*

*Since he realised the nun had seen him in the dream, been waiting for him, every time he thought of the beautiful young woman, he was instantly transported to an elegant silver room. He did not have to visualise coordinates, cross the frontier. He appeared in the room the moment he lingered on her face, absorbed her serenity. Each time was the same, a sudden silver edged, white light blinded him, dimmed down and he was in the room.*

*He had flown out of its window, seen he was in a hotel overlooking a beautiful cove. Coincidentally, room number seven was always empty when he invaded it. The first time it had happened, he had been frustrated. He did not wish to traverse the frontier unnecessarily. Challenge the rules for no reason. He had sat on the bed for a while and soaked the revitalising energy in the room, wondering if the young woman had ever been inside its beautiful walls. He was about to fly into the sky, return to the frontier when he had a sudden idea.*

*Thinking of the young nun brought him to the room; thinking of his mother would perhaps return him home. He visualised his mother's face, repeatedly, but nothing happened. Impatiently he flew out the window, into the night and towards the curving light. Quickly, he spiralled through the thick layer of dusty particles. In moments, he was back in the mountain. As he glided over the green plateau edged by woodland, he realised he had just found an immediate portal into the mortal world....*

Arianne could not get Marcus out of her head. Memory kept resuscitating the outlandish encounter. She had gone over every detail a hundred times, still, she could not comprehend what had lured Marcus to her that night. She was no more than a coincidental visitor to his life.

She explored her emotions, determined hastily she felt admiration for the heroic young man, empathised with his tragic past. Her early life was full of parallel calamities; like him, she was no stranger to loneliness or rejection. Her assertion was evasive; she was skimming the surface. The coherent analysis was only the tip of the iceberg, deeper emotions tugged at her heart. An inherent need to care for him, protect him, birthed deep inside her, the consuming need illogical.

His dark melancholic eyes kept revisiting her dreams, her waking hours, until the shocking realisation became a lucid thought. Her life would never be the same again. She needed Marcus to be part of her life.

Arianne could not concentrate at work; the impulse to call Marcus kept distracting her. She wished to see him again and was frustrated she could not concoct a plausible excuse that would allow her to be near him. Marcus was underage and under the tutelage of the Social Works Department. She was just a journalist who had interviewed him; she had no business asking to see him. Showing a personal interest would have raised many eyebrows. Marcus was only seventeen years old but looked older and was an extremely handsome young man. Her interest could only seem professional. She would think of a way...

The orphanage was still under investigation and the confiscated files in the possession of the authorities. Arianne's reputed professionalism opened the necessary doors. The relevant files were released into Social Services' custody so she could examine them.

Arianne had done her homework. Marcus helped Alexandra at the office three afternoons a week. The scholarship award would not pay for the little luxuries students craved and he wished to earn some money before he left for university, Alexandra had confided. Arianne had plotted well; coinciding on the professional field would not raise any suspicions. No one would guess her true intentions. If the orphanage had been involved in adoptive illegalities, she would be killing two birds with one stone.

The stacks of documents were already in Alexandra's office when Arianne arrived. Alexandra had to leave for court urgently and was not able to wait for her. A helpful receptionist ushered her to the office and explained the documents, piling the side table beneath the window, were ready for her inspection. The confidential files were not to be removed from the room under any circumstance and no copies to be made. Arianne got comfortable behind Alexandra's desk and proceeded to examine the files. There were tons of records to check, Children's histories, birth certificates, etc.

She had been inspecting documents for nearly two hours, when she came across Marcus's file. Though intrigued, she placed it to one side. She must continue checking documents, raise no suspicions... Everything seemed to be in order, there was nothing to alert illegal adoptions had taken place at the orphanage. When she considered she had examined enough documents for one day, she stood up, stretched her tired body, headed for the small kitchen two doors down the corridor and made herself a cup of strong coffee.  She placed the coffee on the desk and picked up Marcus's file. Taking small sips of the piping hot beverage, she began to read Marcus's life history and the events that had led him to the orphanage.

Tears filled her eyes as she read the details of his hard young life.  Marcus had not exaggerated. His confession was a true reflection of what she read. Her heart ached for him, ached for a distant memory of her own self.  She could not imagine someone leaving a defenceless newborn on the steps of a church, in an empty street in the dead of the night plagued with perils. No wonder Marcus had felt deserted. He belonged nowhere, had no roots, no surname. As she kept on reading, she froze; Marcus had been born in the same hospital she had given birth, on the same night. The eerie coincidence unnerved her and her imagination ran riot for a moment.

Thank God, her son was safe. Julia had secretly updated her on his welfare, assured her son had been blessed with a wonderful family and had grown up to be a fine young man. Arianne wished Marcus's mother had done the same for him. No child deserved such cruelty.

Through the years, she had thought constantly of her son, often imagined what he looked like. Giving him up for adoption had been a difficult decision; contradictory emotions had inundated her at the time of his birth. Part of her had wanted to keep her child but the horrendous events that had led to his conception battled against her maternal instinct. It had been easy to succumb to the sister's arguments that the baby would have a better chance in life if placed in a loving and stable family nucleus. Still, she had never forgotten the real reason for agreeing to the adoption. The latter had haunted her to this day. Guilt seized her again, as she remembered how she had dreaded the thought of rejecting him, become like the mother she hated; blame him for his father's sin.

By the end of the week, she had concluded the investigation. The orphanage was clean as far as illegal adoptions were concerned. As she drove home, her heart felt heavy, her plan had failed. Marcus had not turned up at the office the whole week.

She was a fool; she should not have gone to so much trouble. Marcus was not part of her life. He would never be. She had been crazy to think otherwise. He was just an orphan she felt sorry for.

*Seth was standing on the eastern tower; he had prepared well for his first mission to earth, but felt anxious. That he was the first angel in his class to attempt a mission was not the reason for his unease, something else bothered him... He wished he could confide the confusing visions to the Masters but was afraid of their reaction, the consequences his confession would detonate. He did not wish to jeopardise his formal initiation into the mortal world.*

*He stood on the circular platform, his mind plagued by the turmoil the visions incited.* **He must calm down. He would never forgive himself if he failed,** *he thought frustrated. He had spent many hours trying to raise his vibration frequency to an admissible level and it had not been easy. For some reason the report kept reading erroneously. His master had been frustrated, had been about to cancel his mission when Aneal appeared, inspected the report and, practically ignoring his Mater, instructed Seth to follow him up to the platform. Seth was greatly relieved, he had to heal twice as long as the other angels did.*

*The delay determined he was last to fly off the platform, senior angels, already executing missions, had long left. A Virtue, his guide on this occasion, stood behind him, beside Anael, as he stretched and contracted his wings repeatedly, prepared them for imminent flight. The day before, Anael had briefed him on the mission, drummed the coordinates of his destination into his head, reminded him of the perils that awaited those who did not follow exact orders. When Seth checked the coordinates of his mission, in one of the volumes of the Universal Atlas, he had glimpsed at different other locations in various worlds. Each world, each dimension, began with a different three-digit number. 777 was the earth's; the first world through the frontier. As his eyes had roamed the silver laminated pages, he had felt a surge of excitement, there were so many places to see, to discover...*

*The mission would be short. Once he crossed the frontier, he would teleport to the coordinates with the meditation technique he had perfected in the last week. He had been the only angel to grasp the technique the first time around and felt confident he would be able to execute the mission successfully.*

*A praying congregation awaited him in a little church, on the outskirts of a bustling city. They had been praying fervently for help; their community recently plagued with violent gangs that had chosen to parade their streets. He would join them in prayer. Help to raise the frequency inside the church, its surroundings, until a column of light, barely visible to the human eye reached up to heaven. The column would serve as a bridge between the two worlds. Light from the divine source would beam down; the spiritual frequency would spread from the holy building to resonate throughout the vicinity. The concentrated pulse would protect the praying community from the dark souls who would be unable to tolerate the increased vibration and disappear from their streets. The mission was elementary; it did not involve an apparition or revelation. Seth was overjoyed that the small group of believers had pleaded for divine intervention and hoped the dawdling prayers increased.*

*The moment Seth traversed the last layer of the frontier he shut his eyes and engaged in the teleporting meditation. The latter would de-materialise his ethereal configuration and reconstruct it at the memorized coordinates. He visualised the coordinates. Nothing happened. He desperately wanted to open his eyes, but it was prohibited. He must not open them until he felt the dizzy spells announcing he had engaged the time tunnel that ensured safe passage to his target. He visualised the coordinates repeatedly but different coordinates insisted. Suddenly he felt his body pull forward and the dizzy spells began, he knew he had engaged the tunnel, but he had no idea where the supplanting coordinates were taking him.*

*As he travelled down the coiling, silver passageway at the speed of light, a series of visions flashed before him. The first blast of light created images of him crossing the frontier as a young angel, a feather dangling on the silver curve, on the last layer between the two worlds. The second illustrated the burning silhouette on the edge of his right wing, focusing on the dent that indicated a feather was missing. The third flash, the seven mortals holding a feather, their faces beaming. The fourth, children standing on a field, chanting his name as a rain of feathers bathed them in hope. The fifth depicted an image of his younger self without wings, the sixth, a beautiful young woman eagerly waiting for him in a garden. The seventh burst of light showed Seth pointing to a building at the far end of the garden, his mother standing on the steps leading to its entrance. The last blast revealed the inside of a church. At the bottom of the altar lay a single white feather. The last vision seemed different to the rest, more 'realistic'. Intuition told him the vision was not connected to the others.*

*When the image dissolved, he was propelled towards the ground. The moment his feet touched the moist grass the beautiful mountaintop garden materialized around him. Directly, in front of him loomed the convent. His mother stood at the foot of the ancient building. He was not surprised to see her. The flashing images had heeded she would be waiting.*

*The succession of images had cleared doubts, he was now certain the feather the seven mortals held in their hands, was the same feather that had broken from his wing and invaded the mortal world. That the young woman in the garden awaited a message from him, that that was precisely the reason why she was the only one that could see him. He had felt her vibration, had understood her nature. She was an elevated soul, one that understood the ways of the divine. The message he must deliver, was still unclear.*

*The children in the dreams were telling him to liberate them from suffering...*

**Why had they chosen him? How could he deliver hope if he had no idea what he must do?** *He thought gravely.*

*As he walked eagerly towards his mother, he hoped she would be able fill in some of the missing blanks. As he neared her, he scanned the garden grounds. The young nun was nowhere to be seen.*

*Amanda waited for Seth a short distance from the entrance to the Halls of Travel. She stood behind one of the silver-leafed trees circling the glass pyramid building, the Sacred Book close to her chest. As she waited for her son to appear, she gazed at the beautiful glass wings pinned to the peak of the glass triangular hall and hoped her son would soon wear the prized glass, one winged brooch denoting he was officially a 'Messenger', the title given to angels travelling between worlds.*

*A second brooch would complete the pair of wings indicating he was also a 'Guardian'. Possessing the full pair meant he could execute missions allocated from Mission books; missions of key nature. The Mission Chamber was situated on the third last level of the pyramid. Prayers from other worlds, dimensions were recorded in the books, in volumes arranged in alphabetical order pertaining to different worlds.*

*Satellite stars spread throughout the universe, picked up prayers and transmitted them to the celestial receiver; an orb of light suspended in the centre of the top level of the pyramid. Messages floated inside the orb until retrieved and recorded in Mission books. Reclining chairs circled the orb and Cherubim lay back in the white cushioned seats until their foreheads immersed in the glowing sphere. Prayers were absorbed, etched into memory, thousands of pleas immediately extracted from the orb in a single sitting. Cherubim recorded them, telepathically inscribed the vast numbers simultaneously in pertaining volumes, the supplications to be distributed among Messenger- Guardians. The number of prayers had regrettably seen a huge decline in the past century.*

*Amanda had been waiting for a while, when a series of unfamiliar coordinates invaded her mind. Involuntarily, she engaged the time tunnel to land on a mountain, outside an old convent. Perplexed, she scanned her surroundings. She had no idea why the forces of the universe had transported her to the beautiful garden at the foot of the holy building.*

*In the distance, under a tree a young woman sat praying, bible in hand. At the sight of her, Amanda began to feel lightheaded, a peculiar serenity, akin to 'awakened' beings, radiated from her. She felt purity emanating from her soul; she was a fervent believer, a soul devoted to the propagation of the source. A strong urge to near the young woman, to know her, invaded her, but she resisted the temptation. She would not fall prey to temptation again. She would not chance exile, jeopardise her life, be separated from those she loved. She would not fail her family, Seth. Her son needed her, now, more than ever.*

*She closed her eyes, blocked the image in an effort to allay the odd sensation that had suddenly beset her. When she opened them, the young woman had disappeared. Amanda was confused, coordinates were never spontaneous, the involuntary transportation was highly anomalous. She did not understand what had just happened, why she had been taken to the mountain. All she knew was the nun fit the description of the woman in Seth's dream.*

Two weeks later Julia saw the angel again. This time it was not a dream. She was reading in the garden, wrapped up in a novel that had caught her attention in the little bookshop, located a couple of streets from the school. She usually traded second hand books in a local charity shop. New books were an extravagance she could not afford on her small allowance, but the title had sparked her curiosity and had made an exception. A talented young author had written the instant best seller. The moment she read the first two pages, she realised it was not curiosity that had made her purchase the novel. It was not coincidence but a God incident that had lured her to the bookshop that afternoon. Quickly, she had searched the back of the book for the publisher's details. She must meet the young author; ask him about the source of his inspiration.

Lost in conjectures, she did not perceive the sudden light radiating from behind the tree, did not hear the angel appear from behind its thick trunk and walk towards her.

It was not until she heard the gentle voice trailing a high-pitched echo whisper her name that she spun around to face him, a beaming smile greeting his gentle eyes. This time, the angel was not startled by her presence. He had come to see her, knew she was waiting for him.

Slowly, he narrowed the distance between them, his wings bouncing gently behind him, his eyes shining with limpid lustre.

Awed, she watched the garden disappear around them as spectral rays merged to form a glittery shroud. They stood in the dazzling veil, facing each other until they were invisible to the world, until earthly sounds quashed to silence but for the sound of their harmonized breathing.

The moment the celestial messenger had delivered his message, the light diminished and she was back in the garden, in the crisp cool air engulfing the small plateau.

Ethan could not wait to return home. As he stood outside the student halls, he thought of the enormous challenge awaiting him. He glanced at his watch impatiently. Michael would arrive any minute. Together, they would head to his apartment and review the statement he would be delivering at the press conference the following day. He could not wait to disclose he was the mastermind behind Quill to the world. Arrogance was not the reason for his impatience, but an innate sense of responsibility.

He would be eternally grateful to his friend, his mentor, for protecting, expanding the company whilst he had been partially away. The time had come for him to take his rightful place, lead Quill into a promising future. As intended, Michael would resign the post of president, become vice president. Together, they would face the challenges that lay ahead. The media, the world, would finally be party to the sought after secret; they would finally know his name, him.

Michael and he made a good team. They shared the same altruistic vision; their intentions born of identical ideals. They were not bound by ties of blood but considered each other family, trusted each other implicitly. With hindsight, Ethan was glad his parents had imposed the condition that he finish university before devoting himself to the company. He had enjoyed his student life, had time to mature. Becoming CEO of Quill at only eighteen years of age would have been problematic. He would have been too young to be taken seriously. Employees at Quill would have questioned his leadership at the slightest setback and the company would have suffered. Michael had kept him abreast of everything that went on in the company, had not taken major decisions without consulting him. There was no detail of Quill's evolution he did not know, did not understand.

The press statement would ensure the corporate world knew he had been the sole creator of the search engine, that he was the founder of Quill. They would be made aware of his close involvement with the company during the four years he had been away; how he had devoted every weekend to the business, been the vital force behind the company's success. It was imperative that everyone knew the company had been in his capable hands since its creation, so they would trust him with its future.

Quill's headquarters was a hub of excitement the day the young president delivered his statement to the world. Michael had given strict instructions for the employees to assemble in the large conference room situated on the last floor of Quill's headquarters.

The fleet of employees waited, intrigued for Ethan to appear on screen. As they witnessed Ethan's press statement and the lengthy interview that ensued, everyone had been impressed with the young man's curriculum, obvious genius and humility.

Arianne was awarded the privilege of interviewing Ethan. The extensive interview had revealed a modest, young erudite. The new president explained his reasons for remaining anonymous, why he had not wished the world to know his identity until that moment.

He was a natural orator and a curious audience listened attentively as he described the concept behind Quill, as he talked at length of the company's plans. He spoke openly of Quill's donations to charitable organization, to social and environmental causes, stressing the need for wealthy companies to follow suit. Sharing prosperity with the less fortunate would not hamper benefits, expansion, believing generosity attracted prosperity. His company was a marked example.

The audience was fascinated by his charismatic demeanour, altruism and the early press hailed the unassuming and philanthropic genius a corporate visionary, a serious contender to Bill Gates.

A thunderous applause greeted Ethan and Michael as they entered the reception. An even louder roar echoed throughout the elegant dining room at the end of Ethan's inspiring speech. The reception was held in the most luxurious hotel in the city and the company spared no luxury. An exotic banquet was set up at the far end of the dining hall, a Swarovski champagne fountain adorned its centre. Silver and white tablecloths draped the oval tables scattering the polished champagne marble floor. Silver candelabra and orchid centrepieces decorated each one. Ten six- tier chandeliers, suspended by gilded chords, bathed the room mellow amber.

Everyone had turned out in their finest array. Immaculate tuxedoes and exquisite evening gowns complemented the opulent setting. For days, everyone at Quill reminisced about the wonderful evening, a night to remember.

Employees had been bowled over by their young President and enthusiastically congratulated their promising leader on the future vision he held for the growing company. They thanked him effusively for his imminent plans to grant proficiency bonus payments at the end of each financial year. News of the latter was the unexpected gift that crowned an already magnificent evening.

Ethan shook hands with every employee at the reception, held in his honour that evening. Everyone praised his initiative to seek them out individually.

From the day Ethan set foot in the building officially, he was their idol. Every employee at Quill revered him. News of the generous bonuses rewarding hard-working employees spread like wildfire throughout the corporate world and working for Quill became every graduate's dream.

Michael, Alexandra and Ethan's parents accompanied Ethan to his apartment when the exhilarating night had ended. The excitement of the night had rendered them sleepless and, between cups of coffee, they had recalled the magical night's events until dawn. Ethan could not believe how superbly things had turned out, how employees had received him with open arms. He had been extremely nervous. He had not confided his fears to anyone but had been terrorised at the thought of rejection. He needed his team to accept him, trust him, if he was going to keep Quill number one.

When everyone had retired to bed, Ethan stood out on the terrace watching the dawning heavens. As he gazed up at the golden layers of light painting the new day, his thoughts drifted to the magic feather that had made his dream a reality. '*Thank you*', he whispered up to the waking skies.

Michael left early for the city; he was meeting Alexandra at Ethan's apartment. He had important matters to discuss with his protégée and they would be staying at his apartment, as they usually did, when Ethan was home for the weekend. He was glad Alexandra accompanied him whilst Ethan and he discussed business matters. He liked to have her near him. Alexandra did not mind the long days devoted to work, an independent woman, she always found ways to amuse herself. She did not wish to sleep alone.

Ethan hired a chef on weekends and Michael thoroughly enjoyed dinning out on the terrace with the woman he loved and the young man who had become like a son to him. Ethan's parents joined them for lunch on Sundays but devoted their evenings to the theatre. Ethan always got them the best seats.

Michael sat by the pool, drinking a glass of sherry. Ethan had popped over to his parent's apartment and Alexandra was relaxing in the Jacuzzi. As he contemplated the universe, he felt the happiest man on earth. Again, he reflected on the ironies of life; once he had been an ambitious man whose sole objective was to make money. The moment his values had changed, money had become last on his list of priorities, he had become richer than he had ever dreamt he would be. That he would someday part with a large percentage of his money, that making donations to worthy causes could make him so happy would have been unimaginable. The donations had become consistently larger. The more he donated, the more money the company made. He made. His generosity was rewarded with abundance. He had inadvertently tapped into an endless pool of wealth and was conscious of the fact his former self would never have made the discovery. The universe was wise; it rewarded those moved by high intention.

He had been blessed in more ways than one; Alexandra was perfect for him, he could not have fallen in love with a more beautiful and noble woman. He loved that she was proud of him and told him so almost daily. Alexandra was not interested in the material; she was a deep and empathic human being of spiritual pursuit and wholly supported Michael's altruistic enterprise. Michael had become her department's most generous benefactor. His sumptuous donations had enabled the construction of more children's homes, and a university scholarship trust ensuring the children in care pursued higher education had been set up thanks to this generosity.

Alexandra was his life. He wished to spend the rest of his life by her side. As he fingered the little velvet box hidden in the pocket of his trousers, he felt a rush of excitement. He glanced at his watch and willed the hands of time to move faster. At exactly midnight, he would be popping the question. Everything was ready for the witching hour, Ethan his willing accomplice. He stared up at the sparkling sky, at the full moon presaging new beginnings and took a deep breath.

Michael watched Alexandra as she walked slowly towards him. His heart skipped a beat. She looked radiant in the simple silk dress that hugged her curvaceous silhouette, her hair, a silken coal mantle down her bare back to her waist. The moment she neared him, he took her into his arms and kissed her passionately. Whilst he tasted her, trailed her sensuous lips, he thought how fortunate he was she had chosen to love him.

Ethan's arrival interrupted the romantic moment. He was famished and, without further delay, they sat to dine on the beautifully laid table on the terrace. As they enjoyed the superb dinner prepared by Pierre, Ethan's Chef, they shared weekly anecdotes, the sound of their laughter ringing throughout the rooftop oasis. Ethan could not help but smile inwardly as his friend kept glancing at his watch. Michael was conspicuously edgy and Alexandra kept giving him sideway glances.

Alexandra was distracted complimenting Pierre for his exquisite dinner. Grabbing the timely opportunity, Ethan raised a thumb at Michael reassuring him everything was ready. It was a perfect night and no one was in a hurry to retire. They were sitting on the sun lounges edging the heated pool, drinking champagne, when the escalating roar of a helicopter startled them. Within moments, roaring rotors emerged from below. In seconds, the helicopter rose over the glass wall. A whirling gust invaded the peaceful terrace as the iron bird hovered above them.

On cue, Michael and Ethan moved away from Alexandra, left her standing alone at the edge of the swimming pool. All lights dimmed except for those lighting the pool a vibrant green. The two friends smiled conspiratorially at each other, then back at Alexandra's startled face staring up into the sky; at the helicopter shadowing her. She was a vision, her long lustrous tresses floated wild around her, the vibrant emerald lighting of the pool casting scintillating aqua hues on her sapphire robe as the sound of violins filled the air.

Before she had time to turn around and face them, the skies began to pour red petals. The moment the crimson shower began, Ethan tapped Michael affectionately on the back and discreetly slipped to his apartment. Three was definitely a crowd.

Michael's heart raced as his eyes absorbed the magical scene. Alexandra twirled excitedly, her arms stretched up to the sky as the scarlet rain caressed her. Soon, the ground became a red carpet, the pool a crimson lagoon. As the last petals fell from the sky, from the helicopter above, Michael walked towards her. The moment he reached her side, he noticed her eyes were sparkled with emotion. Alexandra was about to speak when Michael put a finger on her parted lips. Gently, he took her hand and led her towards the entrance of the pool. By the time they reached the circling steps into the red-stained waters, the helicopter had disappeared. The poetry of violins emanating from speakers, those which Ethan had secretly installed the day before, hushed to background whispers.

Michael retrieved a remote control from his pocket, smiled as he gazed at Alexandra's flushed face and pushed a button. The domed glass cover of the pool began to slide towards them, cover the pool's length to stop a few feet away.

Taking off their shoes, they walked into the pool. Michael pushed the button a second time and the cover continued to close behind them. At the touch of another button aluminium blinds began to creep over the sides of the curved ceiling until only the glittering sky was visible.

Eyes locked, they undressed each other, their hands languorously peeling the layers of clothing. Holding hands, they walked naked into the sea of petals. For a while, they floated in silence in the centre of the pool, listening to the murmuring melody of violins whilst soft petals caressed their bodies. Michael squeezed Alexandra's hand as they shared a thought; *they were privileged to have found each other.*

Suddenly, Michael let go of Alexandra's hand, stood upright in the water and after kissing her hard on the mouth told her to close her eyes. He waded to the entrance of the pool, fetched the remote control and retrieved a velvet box from the pocket of his trousers sprawled on the edge of the pool. Quickly, he waded back to her, kissed her wet lips again and told her to stand without opening her eyes.

Moving a few feet away, he pushed different buttons; the water in the pool began to drain at an amazing speed. Hot air replaced the warm water as the curved ceiling parted over them. Four blowers, camouflaged in the decorative rocks, strategically placed on each corner of the pool, began to pour a second scarlet shower up to the open gap.

Michael watched Alexandra's naked glistening body under the gentle red spray. Parts of her flesh began to shade crimson, as the soft magenta rain stuck to her body. Mesmerised he waded across the red cottony sea towards her, knelt in the silken layers and softly told Alexandra to open her eyes. Burning eyes locked on the small blue box Michael held in front of her. With trembling fingers, she opened the round velvet box and gasped at the sight of the impressive diamond ring set in platinum, nestled on ivory satin.

Before Michael had a chance to speak, she whispered '*Yes, oh god yes*', her pupils dilated with rapture. Michael stood up, carefully slid the diamond ring on her slender finger and gazing lovingly into Alexandra's fervid slate eyes, whispered '*I will marry you too.*'

As Michael lifted his fiancée in his arms, gently deposited her on the silky-smooth bed and began making passionate love to her, he did not notice Alexandra's look of astonishment as she analysed the scene. Alexandra was bowled over at the astounding coincidence; Michael could not have chosen to propose to her upon a more magical carpet, even if the feathers were scarlet.

Again, she was tempted to tell Michael of her feather. She had wanted to share the magic visitor's impact on her life many times. Every time she had been on the verge of confiding her secret, intuition had whispered she should not tell him. She had grown to believe that if she did, the magic in her life, and of those that surrounded her world, would disappear.

Julia could not get the young author out of her mind. She needed to see him, ask him about the 'Magic feather'. The uncanny coincidence as far as Julia was concerned was a providential sign. She had long stopped believing in 'coincidences'.

Julia devoted her spare time to research him on the internet, until finally, she found what she was looking for. The talented young writer was due in the city the following week. He would be signing copies of his recent best seller, 'Miracle' in the largest and most prominent book shop in the city.

A week later, after school, she headed for the city. To her dismay, as she neared the bookshop, she saw a queue of people coiled the entire circumference of the building. She stood near the entrance, weighed if she should join the endless string of admirers, and ultimately decided to leave. She did not have the time, the patience. She would find another way, another day. She stared disheartened at the never-ending line of enthusiasts a few moments longer; the 'Magic Feather' close to her chest, then began turning around. She was about to make her way back to the underground parking where she had left her car, when the security guard suddenly called out to her; '*Sister, sister, wait up*!'

Before Julia had time to speak, the tall muscular man grabbed her gently by the arm, lifted the cordoned barrier and ushered her through the revolving glass doors. '*I am sure you're very busy doing the lord's work.'* He smiled. '*No time to waste on queues that take away precious time*,' he continued, his boyish smile inconsistent with his menacing physique. '*Thank you*,' Julia managed faintly. As she followed the line of excited readers down the long aisle, sandwiched by tall bookshelves, she could not help but smile. *The lord works in mysterious ways,* she thought.

The moment Julia saw the young author she could not but help smile again. He was so handsome, accomplished. Marcus greeted her with a reserved smile, stretched out his hand. A hint of confusion touched his eyes as he realized the book was not his latest bestseller, but ignoring the 'mistake', courteously accepted the novel. He was about to inscribe the short dedication on the first page when his hand froze. His eyes widened incredulously as he read the words: '*when did you find the feather?* He stared transfixed at the yellow post-it stuck at the top of the page. A telephone number was scribbled beneath the daunting message. Eventually, he managed to pull his eyes away from the note and he glanced up at Julia, an expression of bewilderment shrouding his handsome face. Julia returned the smile, raised her eyebrows in question but said nothing.

Visibly shaken, Marcus looked behind her at the long line of impatient fans, then, avoiding Julia's inquisitive eyes lowered his eyes to the open book before him. Julia remained silent as she watched him intently. Hurriedly, Marcus scribbled his signature on her copy of 'The Magic Feather'. Julia whispered a soft 'thank you,' turned swiftly on her heels and disappeared down the crowded aisle.

As she walked down the busy street to the underground parking, she smiled again. He would call her.

Marcus sat pensively in a bench under the shadow of a pin oak, his vivid mind instigating possible scenarios. He regretted having called the disconcerting nun the night before and was about to flee the scene when Julia approached him from behind and sat next to him.

*'So?'* She asked softly. Marcus ignored the monosyllable, waited for her to speak again. He had nothing to tell her…

Julia prodded him gently, cautiously.

Marcus insisted 'The magic feather' was the fruit of imagination, that though he assumed she believed in miracles, given the nature of her vocation, his book was pure fiction.

As he spoke, Julia examined the subtlest expression. He was lying.

She understood his reticence. She had told no one of her own finding. After Marcus promised to send copies of his books as a gift to the school, they shook hands warmly and parted ways.

She had been a fool to think Marcus would confide his finding. She had never told a soul about her own miraculous encounter believing the magic would fade. Marcus had intuited the same.

Julia could not sleep that night. Her thoughts kept reliving their conversation. As she dissected their brief meeting, one thought overshadowed the rest; *she had already found one, she was certain there were others…*

Marcus could not sleep that night. A single thought kept disturbing his sleep; there were others…

When Julia returned to the convent that evening, she retired early to bed. She wished to sleep, award her agitated mind a breather. She could not sleep. Marcus' face kept intruding her thoughts. On impulse, she picked the novel from the night table and studied his photograph on the back cover.

She explored his face, the dark eyes conveying a compelling melancholy … It was then the miracle happened…

Amazingly, the photograph began to transform before her very eyes. It began to blur, until it became a swirling grey cloud. With bated breath, she watched the whirling shadow light up, spin faster over the glossy black cover until a continuum of colours began to stain it. The tenuous image began to sharpen, shape, slow down, until an image materialized.

A younger Marcus sat alone under a tree in an otherwise barren yard, abject eyes staring into space. The image perfected, a small caption, indicating the name of the photographer who had taken the photo, unstuck itself from the bottom edge of the page, floated up and began to hover, expand over Marcus' face until it stamped itself on it.

The minute Julia finished school the following day she headed for the city, for Slade Alston's studio, his attic apartment in the Crystal Haven.

*The moment Seth saw his mother's austere face; he knew she had something of utmost importance to share with him. She carried a book.* **Surely, his mother had not had the audacity, the recklessness...?** *Panic pounded his heart. The Sacred Book was painstakingly guarded, sacrosanct to supreme angels.* **What was her mother doing with it? What was she doing here...?**

*Amanda, ignoring her son's anxious expression, signalled Seth to sit on the steps leading to the convent, the book nestled in her arms. Seth began to voice concern... Amanda interrupted him adamantly. There was no time...*

*She took a shuddering breath and opened the book. Quickly, she fanned its pages to the folded page. An impatient finger slid down the golden script to the passage she had found on visions. '...Angels blessed by visions, by dreams are chosen by the universe: to do its bidding...'*

*Seth read the words aloud, processed the implications of the divine passage then stared questioningly at his mother. Amanda nodded solemnly then whispered,* **'yes my son, the universe is calling you...'**

*Before he had time to debate the inference, his mother breathed deeply again and, without time for an extenuating prelude, began to narrate the events of his unconventional birth...*

*Seth listened in controlled silence, his eyes wide with incredulity his turbid mind labouring to decrypt the stupefying information.* **The words filling the dawning night were impossible, his mother would never lie to him...** *he thought, probing his mother's eyes for confirmation.*

*The theft, the vatic scripture forgotten, he struggled to digest the mind-blowing disclosure as his mother's grave expression told him she was speaking the truth. The impossible words hammered his mind, boggled his world. That his mother had kept vital information surrounding his existence was beyond his comprehension. They shared a special bond; they told each other everything...*

*Before he had time to voice his disenchantment, his anger, Amanda began to cry softly. Between sobs, she confessed the reasons for her 'betrayal'. She had not wished him to feel different to other angels. The choice to keep his mortal conception a secret stemmed from her need to protect him. She had wished to tell him many times, she whimpered, her face shadowed by guilt, but had been afraid. He had been a rebellious child, thinking himself different to the others would have accentuated his inherent rebelliousness. The time had come to tell him the truth. He needed to understand his true nature so he could understand part of what was happening to him. Destiny was knocking on his door...*

*What Amanda did not tell her son was that the elders had prohibited her ever telling him, any angel. That the passage she had read out to him was incomplete. '...Angels must report any visions, dreams, immediately to the elders...' She had not wished to frighten him, confound him further.*

*Though he was still disconcerted, hurt at his mother's overdue disclosure, as Amanda's incredulous story surrounding his birth had unfolded, Seth had begun to understand some of the incognitos that had bewildered him for so long; he* **had** *felt different to other young angels ...*

*His mother's epiphany explained his curiosity with the mortal world. His dreams, his visions, gained clearer perspective. Conceived in a human womb, exposed to the mortal world, the earth had become part of him and he had become part of the earth. The heart that had beaten echoing his own, the womb that had cocooned him in unconditional love had avowed the possibilities of humankind, of the goodness inherent in every human being. The light of the source existed in every form of life, sometimes dormant, sometimes half-awake, sometimes wholly alive...*

*The beat of human hearts had echoed his since then. Hope had attached to his soul and never faded... He was not the selfish defiant angel he had thought himself to be. Rebelliousness had not lured him to seek answers beyond the angelic realm, a force greater than him, had enticed him to cross the forbidden barrier...*

*He had hoped his mother had held the clues to solve the conundrum, but he could never have imagined she had held them for so long, their nature...*

*Without warning, an image of himself without wings surrounded by the desperation of innocent children flashed before him. This time he was able to interpret the vision ...*

*He had only been a child when he had exposed himself to the perplexing tragedies of the mortal world, his soul infested with images of violence, of destruction, of the carnage capable by man. His young soul had mourned for a long time, until he was finally able to bury the traumatic experience in the deepest recess of his soul. However, the child in him had never forgotten..., the feather he had lost, had unknowingly invaded the earth, was the catalyst that resuscitated the dormant bond to his other world.*

*He had been destined to see, understand the suffering; the road to perdition humanity had embarked on. He had tried to detach, adhere without questioning to the laws his world advocated but, from time to time, a whispering voice inside of him questioned what he was struggling earnestly to believe in.*

*That the missions were dawdling, that humanity was beyond salvation was a screaming secret in the realm. He had heard the whispers, the Elders, the Masters, the Supreme Angels, all agreed humanity had lost faith in prayer. Until now, he had not argued, had not defied their views, had learned to accept, to wait, yet deep in his soul was the deep-seated knowledge that humanity was not beyond hope.*

*As he watched the tree trunks melting in the forest dusk, the last beams of light drowning in night, he suddenly understood where the goodness of humankind, the light of the world, still prevailed untouched, where the power to transform the world lay...*

*The dreams he had of the children was what told him. He had finally unravelled the visions' intention. The children were the purest testimony of humanity, their souls filled with light. The gleaming shield remained strong against confounding egos, but they were in danger, the world was in danger. Man had failed to protect their legacy, their future...*

*Thousands of children died of hunger each day, roamed the streets trying to survive, suffered the abandonment of their progenitors; many falling prey to those who traded their innocence, their organs, to satisfy the dream of immortality of the rich... even the most progressive, sophisticated societies failed to ensure the safety of the vulnerable.*

*The memory of innocent eyes ablaze with hope tugged at his soul. Suddenly, he was terrified, afraid of himself, of the rebelliousness that had pushed him to defy the laws of the realm once. Still, if he did not intervene, did nothing to help the innocent, they would grow up to be replicas of those that had destroyed their innocence, diminished the light in their souls. Nothing would change, the world would be condemned.*

*The vision of himself without wings manifested again, he understood what the depiction intended to convey. In the image, his human heart predominated, his 'other' self was not feeling the world that had seen him grow up but the world in which he had been conceived. The mortal heart was echoing the agonizing cries of the children, listening to their prayers of hope.*

*He was the only one who understood the two worlds. He knew the divine laws forbade that he got involved in human journeys, but he was part mortal, divine laws were no longer the only ones applicable. His soul could not listen to the desperate cries of the children and do nothing. He was convinced there was still goodness in man. He had witnessed their capacity to love, had seen it burn under a vermillion sky. His early soul had felt it in his mother's womb. His human heart had pulsed with the heart of those that had surrounded his mother's world. Unlike the Masters, the Elders, the higher angels, he still harboured hope for the mortal creature that had lost his way...*

*The struggle of man for perfection, his elevation to higher planes, was dictated by his learning capacity on the earth school, his spiritual advancement by the insurgence of the soul against the ego. The earth school had become a sombre place. Temptation lurked in every corner of the globe. Man had lost his way, forgotten his 'truth', had become blinded to the light of the source. He needed to remind man; save the children. The passages in the sacred book his mother had read to him, were heeding him to change things. The future of the mortal world lay in his hands. The universe was calling him...*

*Every child was at risk, even those lucky enough to be born into a protective loving environment. Children were continually bombarded with images of violence and became delinquents at a younger age. Progress was a double-edged sword. Whilst technological advances aided humanity, others served to propagate violence, tug at the already fragile fabric of morality holding society. Children who survived the streets of sorrow grew up into adulthood hating the world, their fellow men, more often than not became replicas of the men they had loathed.*

*No longer prey, they became hunters and the viscous circle was ensured, rendering man to doom. The elevated souls inhabiting the earth had no chance against the wave of corruption that swept the earth, against the tide of temptation that enticed lost souls, those with low spiritual frequency to the shadowlands, the abode of fallen angels. They would never have a chance without divine intervention.*

*The path towards his destiny illuminated before him. He had to save the children in order to save humanity, even if he had to take on the two worlds.*

*Suddenly, he knew who would be aiding him in his rebellion...*

Slade glanced again at the next appointment. *Sister Julia? What would a nun possibly want from him?* He thought intrigued. The minute Julia walked into his apartment, Slade realised she was nothing like he had expected. As she crossed the living room towards his studio, his desk, he marvelled at her graceful poise, her angelical features, her crystal blue eyes. He had to fight the urge to grab his camera and begin to click at her. He desperately wished to roam his lens over the perfect curve of her face, capture her virginal beauty. For a minute, he imagined the body under the unflattering habit. *For God's sake man, get a grip on yourself, she's a nun,* he thought, hoping the holy woman could not see the shame that burned his face.

Julia was forty-one, but Slade would never have guessed. No one could have. Amazingly, she did not look a day over twenty-five. The 'young' nun stared at him unflinchingly, held out her hand and equably introduced herself as Julia, Sister Julia. Slade invited her to sit down and for a few moments, they eyed each other in silence. Slade sat awkwardly, avoiding her intent eyes, wishing she would speak.

*So*? She asked after what seemed like ages to Slade. He did not understand what she had meant by the sterile question, what she was doing sitting in his studio, why she kept looking at him strangely across the desk. The atypical pious woman intimidated him. His hands clasped under his desk, he kept fighting the urge to stand, escape the room. Curiosity kept him riveted to the seat.

So? The monosyllable again. '*Shall we talk about the photographs?'* Julia asked softly, subtle defiance shading her eyes. *The photographs? What on earth was she talking about?* He thought, his mind reeling. Without waiting for an answer Julia opened the worn, black satchel she had placed on the floor beside her, retrieved 'The Magic Feather' and placed it on the desk before him.

Slade recognized it immediately; he had taken the photo on the back cover. Marcus' publishing company had hired him to take the picture of the young author who had recently taken the literary world by storm, a couple of months before. Tentatively, he turned the book. The photo had transformed. The nun sitting opposite him knew of the miracles. There were 'others'...

For a moment, he was tempted to ask her about the feather, but said nothing, he was not supposed to...

Slade listened in awe to what the young nun had come to explain, to ask of him. The time was finally nigh...

*Amanda had watched Seth closely as he read the passages that spoke of visions, observed the subtlest twitch of his face, listened to every whisper of broken breathing. His eyes had narrowed; he had become suddenly pensive as he had read the words she had underlined with her slender finger. He had said nothing, but Amanda knew he had understood. The end of the journey was near. A journey that had began a long time ago.*

*Amanda had felt the apprehension in his soul, but had also felt the courageous beat in his chest. She had to steal the book, Seth had needed to read the sacred words himself, telling him would not have sufficed. She had wanted her son to know the nature, the importance of what was happening to him. She had wanted to show her son that for some unfathomable reason, one he should not question, the universe, the source, had chosen him, as it had chosen others before him.*

*Amanda had ached for her son as she had disclosed the secrecy surrounding his conception. His eyes had dulled, become confused, smouldering cobalt pools as he had stared at her accusingly. He had never looked at her that way...Amanda had been afraid he would never forgive her.*

*Seth had a hard time assimilating he had not been born like other angels. That Amanda and Anton had not fused in spirit to become guardians, 'parents', of a new light. That Supreme Masters of Light had not summoned them to the temple of light to present them with the tiny, glowing orb that would become a baby angel the moment it rested on their united palms. Seraphim had not supervised the 'birth' ceremony...*

*Perspiration beads had slid down his forehead, his chest heaved to broken breathing, the ocean of his mind fighting to appease the roaring waves confounding him as he struggled to accept he was 'different', that his mother had lied to him. Amanda feared he would swoop into the sky and disappear.*

*He had stayed, his hands clutched tightly, his wings listless, his intelligent eyes distant. She had wished to soothe his pain, had understood the truth had hurt, but time had run out. He needed to know the truth if he was to understand what was happening in his two worlds.*

*The Sacred Book burned in her hands.* **She must return it before the elders missed it,** *she had thought, masking fear. She had taken a huge risk, one she would certainly pay dearly for if caught. Once again, she had no choice, had no time to ponder on consequences. Her chest tightened with the knowledge that this time she might not be so lucky. Still, in her eyes, her action was justified. Transcendental matters were at stake.*

*When Seth had finally calmed down, he had looked at her, his eyes indicating the antiquity of his soul, the corners of his mouth weakly quirking upwards. He had opened his arms wide and Amanda had nestled in their warmth.* **'Everything would be alright'** *he had whispered into the golden locks floating in the temperate wind, caressing them.* **He knew what he must do...**

*Amanda had listened to the words and the fear of losing him had faded like breath on glass turned milky by sunlight. She had buried her face in his chest and revelled in his protective embrace. For a moment, she was not afraid.*

*The prophetic words had served to confirm the veracity of visions, resolved they were a universal calling that must be heeded. Knowing the truth surrounding his birth had finally made him comprehend things, he could not have understood otherwise. The determination in his eyes had confirmed he had untangled the enigmas, had found the answers to the questions that had besieged him.*

*Gently, Amanda had disentangled herself from Seth's forgiving embrace, there had been no time for questions, there had been no need. She trusted Seth. Holding hands, they had walked to the edge of the mountain. It was time for her to leave, time for Seth to face his destiny.*

*As mother and son had stood on the edge of the mountain, looking out to the unpredictable horizon that had begun to turn dark, a sudden rush of wind born below reminded them both the winds of change would soon be turning to storm.*

*The moment Amanda vanished from sight, Julia emerged out the main doors of the convent. Seth watched her, enthralled, as she walked with the delicacy of a ballet dancer towards the small garden, sat on one of the benches and immersed herself in a book.*

*He towered above her, invisible for a few moments, revelled in her unearthly beauty, in the familiar feeling of completeness that invaded him the moment he neared her. Angels loved all living things, but the emotion that emanated from his soul towards her was deeper, different. As he gazed at her, his lips curved to an easy smile, thankful one of his feathers had found her.*

*The time had come for him to tell her why he visited her, explain the magnitude of the mission they would be embarking on, what she must do...*

*When Seth confided the identities of those she must call, those chosen, Julia could not believe the astonishing coincidence.* **It was a small world,** *she had thought.*

John as usual, was in his office at lunchtime, when his secretary informed him Slade Alston wished to see him. John glanced at his watch with irritation. His next meeting was due in an hour's time. He had a busy schedule laid out for the afternoon. As the new Commissioner, his duties were extensive, exhausting, and he had wished to take a small nap before immersing himself in the frantic rhythm of the long afternoon ahead. He had wished to tell his secretary to inform the untimely visitor he was busy but found himself acceding to the impromptu appointment. He knew Slade Alston vaguely; the Mayor had introduced the famed photographer to him at his birthday party. He did not quite know the photographer's relationship with the Mayor but, as far as he knew, they were close friends. .

John had no idea what Slade Alston could want from him but the moment he walked into his office, and sat down opposite him, he knew the visit was not a trivial one. The expression on the man facing him was sober, he had come to relay something of importance. Skipping the usual formalities, Slade Alston rushed to tell him why he had come, what they must do...

John sat in silence, keyed up, his sweaty hands sliding nervously back and forth, smearing his polished desk as he listened carefully, his heart raring to words pervading the room...

The moment Slade had uttered the first words, he had gotten up, locked the door, lowered the blinds and informed his secretary to cancel the afternoon's appointments, all his appointments for the week. She had begun to argue, '*The Mayor would not be pleased at the short-notice cancellation... the...*' He had cut her short, insisted she did as ordered, ignoring her puzzled expression.

An hour later, the two men left the building and headed for John's house in Slade's Porsche. Quickly, John traded his uniform for a pair of jeans and sweater, packed a small suitcase and informed his wife he would be away on business for a couple of days.

The moment they reached Slade's apartment, they began their work. There was much to do and they did not have much time.

Three days later, they headed out of the city. After two days in the seaside hotel, they returned home. They had accomplished every instruction on the list Julia had given them. All they needed to do now was wait. As they patiently rolled down the congested highway back to the city, they indulged in idle conversation. Both John and Slade agreed the cove was a beautiful place, that the hotel was very charming, that room number seven was stunningly elegant, blessedly peaceful, peculiarly invigorating. Neither made reference to the dream.

Each had thought it best to keep the strange vision private; dreams were after all just dreams. At the first touch of light, the dream had seemed silly, a mirage borne of a susceptible subconscious to the extraordinary witnessed.

If they had shared the dream, they would have been shocked they had both dreamt of angels floating inside a white and silver edged bubble.

Julia remained awake the whole night, pacing the room, looking out the window, searching the skies for light to brush the night proclaiming day.

The moment darkness turned a glowing teal she tiptoed barefooted down the shadowy corridors, across the hazy garden to her car. She had rolled her car silently to a safe distance from the convent the moment she had been certain everyone was asleep. She had not wished the sisters to interrupt her getaway. She had not wished to lie.

Whilst she drove down the waking mountain, the cold breath of early mist on her face, Seth's message resounded in her mind. She felt privileged the angel had chosen her, God had chosen her. Suddenly, she felt ashamed, humbled that despite the moments of wavering faith, she was one of the chosen.

By the time she had descended the mountain, turned the junction to the highway, the sun had began warming the crisp morning air, warming her heart. She felt closer to God than she ever had.

As she joined the growing traffic out of the city, she glanced at the book on the empty seat beside her and smiled. Soon, she would be meeting them all. Soon, they would all be meeting her

Slade and John had already returned to the cove; the others would follow shortly after. She had still to unravel the mystery of the cove, why it was the chosen location. The only thing her angel had told her was the room was a portal to the mortal world.

She had done a bit of investigative work herself. She had checked the hotel's history and had been sad to find that the quaint hotel shadowing the perfect cove had a heartbreaking history.

A young woman had been its previous owner. She had died tragically, her car had collided with a lorry and fallen over a cliff, into the sea. They had never found her body; her disappearance was a mystery to this day. The fact she was eight months pregnant added to the tragedy. Julia had found the newspaper article in the town's media library; her photo printed with the obituary.

At first glance, Julia had been stunned at the striking resemblance between the young woman and herself, but the image was slightly blurred and she soon discarded the comparison. On impulse, she had checked the hotel's registry logs. Amazingly, Arianne, Alexandra and Ethan had all been guests of the Seaview, of room number seven.

The room held a secret, other than being a portal to the earth... *She did not have long to wait*, she thought, as she approached the gates to the Hotel's car park. *The time was nigh. The world summit was nigh...*

Julia stared at the young receptionist as she checked room availability. Room number seven was 'coincidentally' vacant. Julia booked herself in for three nights paying cash in advance. Carrying the bulky telephone book, she had asked the receptionist for; she headed to the room on the first floor. The moment she entered the room she felt herself relax, the room felt strangely natural to her, like home.

It was stunning, the views spectacular. She was not accustomed to luxurious surroundings and wished she had time to soak in the inviting tub she had discovered in the en-suite bathroom. Unfortunately, there was too much to do.

Quickly, she changed into a pair of grey slacks and sweater, tied her long hair in a knot at her nape and sat on the small round table near the window. She searched the yellow pages, made a list of the numbers she needed and began to make calls.

The courier arrived thirty minutes later and handed her the small box, the order she had placed to Plumes and Co. via email two days earlier. Julia instructed him to wait in the lobby whilst she organized the delivery. Ten minutes later, she handed him the five padded envelopes and returned to her room.

As the pleasant young man made his way back to his van, the tingling sensation he had felt in the beautiful room lingered. The buoyant mood accompanied him all day, for the first time he enjoyed his tedious job.

The moment the courier had disappeared, Julia returned to her task. A couple of hours later, five receptionists confirmed delivery. The moment she had ticked the five company names on her list, she phoned her two accomplices.

Julia felt suddenly tired. There was nothing left to do but wait for the others to arrive so she decided to rest for a while. As she got comfortable on the pillow, curled on the bed, her thoughts wandered to the angel. As she remembered his handsome face, his soulful eyes, an image blasted in her mind; the angel's wings enveloped as her head rested on his chest. His sweet breath warmed her face, his arms curled round her waist, steadied her, as her legs turned to water. Alien emotions suffused her and an overpowering impression they were connected, belonged to each other, occupied her soul.

The nonsensical hallucination shook her to the core. She leapt off the bed and grabbed her bag. Frantically, she searched her tattered leather bag for her black beaded rosary, curled it around her hand, knelt at the foot of the bed and began to pray. She felt deep shame. *What was wrong with her? She was a nun. He was an angel. A divine messenger sent to her by her God!* She thought desperately, as trembling fingers counted the black beads; *one bead one Hail Mary... one bead, one Hail Mary...* As she delivered her prayer to the Virgin, her mind returned involuntarily to the perturbing images.

She had only counted three beads, when she stood up suddenly and headed for the beach. Barefooted, she walked towards the shore, tread along its edge for a while, then sat down. As she watched the trail of footsteps on the moist, packed earth, she thought of her life, the things she had given up to become a soldier of God. The recent miracles, the honour she was one of the chosen, had restored faith, but she could not help question if her life was really all she had ever dreamt it to be. The nuance of abandonment, the inexplicable emptiness touching her soul like fingerprints on a windowpane, had recently intensified… Quickly, she admonished herself. *She was being ungrateful God had bestowed enough.*

As bare feet stretched to caress the dark waves licking the shore, her parents' words of warning echoed in her befuddled mind. *Someday, she would miss having a husband, a family...* the premonitory words lacerating the stalwart conviction vehemently professed.

Her trail of thought was blasphemous. She could not believe she could allow such thoughts. *God had chosen her, and she felt completely fulfilled doing his bidding. She did not wish for another life, never would.* Resolute in this conviction, she got up brusquely and headed back to the hotel. As she walked briskly to the terrace bar, she wondered if the emails had been received.

Hurriedly, she walked to the bar, asked the bartender for a coffee, then headed for the internet station in the lobby. She took a few sips, placed the hot cup on the table and logged into the email account she had opened a few days earlier. There were five emails in her inbox. As per her instruction, the packages had been delivered to recipients on time.

The mission accomplished; Julia decided to grant herself the luxury of soaking in the enticing bathtub. As she soaked in the scented, foamy waters, relaxed under the magical candlelight, her thoughts divagated to the disquieting images. The moment she closed her eyes, envisaged the angel's face, the overpowering emotion seized her. Her heartbeat accelerated as sleepy eyes visualised him standing at the foot of the bath, looking down on her. The dreamy image infused her bloodstream with warmth, a familiar smell from long ago, far back in the brain, mingled the steamy aroma, saturating the room, to make her lightheaded.

It was not until she realised her heartbeat was not the only one echoing in the room that she understood the vision was not a mirage. The angel was not a figment of her imagination; he was actually standing in front of her!

She stared at him wide eyed. *What was he was doing here?* She thought, her mind in disarray. She had not expected to see him until the following night. His eyes delved deep into her own and she felt herself blush. Quickly she cloaked her naked body with the foamy water. Feeling her embarrassment, Seth turned around and walked back to the bedroom. The moment he was gone, she got out of the bath, clumsily unhooked the luxurious bathrobe hanging on the bathroom door, wrapped herself in it and vigorously combed the dripping curls hanging down to her waist. Trembling hands raked her tresses as she stared at her reflection in the mirror. As she towel dried her hair, she kept hoping the apparition was fruit of a dream, that the angel was not waiting in the next room. The disruptive emotions the image had wreaked, still afflicted her. She was dreading confronting him...

For a while, she stared at her ashen reflection in the mirror until, eventually, she managed to calm down. Hesitantly, she treaded the rich carpet to the bedroom, praying he was gone. The moment she set foot in the room, she saw him sitting at the edge of the bed, his head buried in his hands and her pulse raced again. Julia stood stagnant by the door, staring at him, afraid to make a sound, when a sudden feeling of dread gripped her dispersing her own agitation. Something was wrong...

The Angel seemed to have read her thoughts, raised his head, searched her eyes and whispered '*what do you feel for me?*' The faint dreamlike words blew Julia away. She stared at him, uncomprehending, her body feverish. Before she had time to react, voice a sound, he stood up and spoke again. '*Perhaps I should leave...*' he whispered, walking slowly towards the window. On impulse, Julia rushed to his side, clasped her trembling hand around his and whispered '*don't go.*'

In silence, they headed back to the bed, the angel towering behind Julia, and sat down at its foot. Neither of them spoke. They sat there, staring into space, drained by confusion.

Fighting shame, Julia broke the awkward silence. Her face burning, she began to unbolt the confusing feelings, the deep emotions his presence incited. The inexplicable intrinsic conviction that they were somehow connected, that they had known each other long before they had met on the garden, perhaps in another lifetime... As she spoke, she realised the irrationality of her tremulous acknowledgement. *This is madness...* she kept thinking.

Unable to contain the gush of words escaping her heart, she continued, her eyes on the floor. She wished to search his eyes for reassurance but did not dare look at him, her cheeks afire. As the torrent of words kept flooding the pulsing room she had a strange sensation. She was both speaker and listener, a bystander, an invited eavesdropper to the irrepressible affirmations. Somehow, the dual perspective gave her the strength, allowed her to continue her confession. The beat of the room encouraging...

Her words soft, paused, she spoke of the first day she had seen him. How she had not been surprised. She did not know how or why, but she had known he would come. As the statement reverberated in her mind, understanding glimmered with lucidity of day; she had been waiting for him all her life...

Her eyes glazed as she recalled the daydreams she had indulged in as a girl. The scenery kept changing but the theme was always the same. She was the lucky girl visited by an angel. After their first encounter, he became her best friend in the world. Throughout the whole of her life, she had felt his presence. Suddenly, she was ready to answer his question. She had loved him all her life...

When she finished speaking, she raised her head timorously and gazed deep into his eyes. Liquid, aquamarine eyes glistened as he whispered '*I know.*'

The moment Michael set foot in his office, Jenny informed him an urgent package had been delivered. Michael accepted the padded envelope, absentmindedly left it on his desk and proceeded to the small kitchenette to make two coffees, one for himself, the other for his energetic assistant. He had offered her the post of Private Secretary at Quill, but she had gratefully declined. She was getting married in autumn, to a local police officer who would never have agreed to transfer out of the seaside haven into the city. Michael had raised her pay, equivalent to the job offer.

He sat in the reception room drinking his coffee, listening to Jenny's weekend adventures. When he had finished the vital stimulant, and Jenny had returned to her desk, he left the office in search of the early press at the newspaper stand, around the corner to his office. As he strolled down the town's bustling street, he recalled his unsavoury meeting in exactly one hour. Unfortunately, Quill allowed him few visits to the town he considered home. Today, it had been imperative that he allocated time to visit the homely town. The townsfolk delegated their legal dilemmas to him; he could not let them down. Since he had established himself in the community, and being the only lawyer in town, none of them visited city lawyers anymore. It was lucky for him that requests were rare.

A friend was coming to see him that morning. He was getting divorced, after twenty-five years he had thought had been bliss, and was devastated. Michael was sorry for him, his children, but had not been able to convince his unsympathetic wife to agree to matrimonial counselling before taking the drastic step. He could only imagine what Terry was going through and hoped he never found himself in his shoes. Alexandra had just agreed to marry him and he was euphoric. He feverishly hoped their union was insusceptible to life's onerous challenges.

The meeting lasted until lunchtime. He had invited Terry for lunch but he had been too upset to accompany him.

Ending his marriage with a mere signature on a piece of paper had been more than he could bear.

He was on his way out the office to the pasta house down the street, when the padded envelope caught his eye. He vacillated a second but decided to open it after lunch. He was famished and about to devour his favourite dish, cannelloni with spinach, when his cell phone rang. He smiled happily as he stared at the caller's identity. It was Alexandra, calling to inform him she would not be able to see him that evening, something important had cropped up and she would be working late. Michael was disheartened, but understood her commitment to work.

He was in no mood for a solitary evening and decided to call Ethan. His friend would be delighted; he stayed at the magnificent villa he had purchased recently, he was dying to show off the prized property. Ethan was not at the office. He had already left. He called his cell phone but there was no answer. Michael was not surprised; Ethan continually forgot his phone at home when he was at work and vice versa. His young friend had an extraordinary memory when it came to intricate data but was extremely absentminded when it came to banal matters.

His plan thwarted, he decided to head for his city apartment, he had city clients awaiting him the following morning. The unpleasant meeting had demoralized him, drained him. He would order a pizza and watch a film.

He had almost forgotten the envelope when he noticed it on the corner of his desk. He glanced at his watch. He had five minutes, darkness would soon claim the skies and he hated to drive at night. Impatiently, he picked it up, flipped it around and searched its back for sender's details. He was surprised to find none.

Without further ado, he sliced the envelope open and emptied its contents on the desk. Intrigued, he stared at the two small envelopes; one of them padded. He decided to open the flat one. He raced through the words on the centre of an otherwise blank piece of paper, his heartbeat suddenly erratic. Impatient hands tore the other envelope open. The moment its content hit the desk, he understood the message, knew where he had to go.

Alexandra inspected the envelope the receptionist had handed to her, the moment she arrived at the office with curiosity. The fact no sender's details had been included seemed odd. She was not expecting any urgent mail and had no idea who might have sent it. Swiftly, she tore it open and an eager hand searched inside it. She retrieved two small envelopes. One of them was padded. She placed the two envelopes on the desk in front of her, swinging her eyes from one to the other. She opened the flat one. As she unfolded the neatly folded sheet of paper, read the four words printed in its exact centre, her heart skipped a beat. Nimble fingers tore the padded envelope open and she emptied its content on her desk. The moment the mysterious item was revealed she stood up, snatched the note from the desk, placed both items in her handbag and fled the room in the direction of her apartment.

The minute she got home, she headed for her bedroom, packed essentials in an overnight bag and headed for the shower. As massaging jets kneaded her tense body, she processed the stream of thoughts. The message was clear. She knew where she had to go. Who was expecting her or what she must do, she had no idea. Opposing emotions fused; she was equally apprehensive and thrilled at the uncertainty.

As Alexandra drove towards destiny, the words printed on the mysterious note ricocheted unremittingly; *the time was nigh...the time was nigh.* Her questions were about to be answered. The end of the journey was imminent. She had waited long to unravel the message the feather had left behind...

She had been driving for a while when her cell phone rang, it was Michael, calling to tell her he would be away on business for a few days. The moment she hung up, relief washed over her. She did not have to lie.

Marcus sat in his home office, his dark eyes fixed on the large padded envelop. His agent's receptionist had been adamant; the courier had insisted it was crucial the delivery reached him no later than noon. Whilst probing fingers inspected the cushioned package, he questioned the nature of its urgency, why it was vital he collected it before noon. He had been in no mood to make an early trip to the city, but her insistency had sparked his curiosity. Marcus had no idea who had sent him the envelope, the absence of sender details added to the mystery. He had been tempted to open it the moment it was in his possession but a sixth sense alerted its contents should be inspected in the privacy of his home. As he had driven home, he had glanced at the padded envelope repeatedly, speculating if its contents had anything to do with Quill. The last envelope had revealed a life-changing content, perhaps this one did too. Marcus had learned through own experience that reality could well surpass fiction.

He was about to open the envelope when the phone rang. It was Kian Hansen, his literary agent, informing him the contract for his new book was ready for inspection. Marcus thanked him briskly and agreed on an appointment for the following week. His current novel was in its final stages, he had been writing like a maniac not wishing to break the rhythm. The last chapters of a novel were always the most difficult. A fitting climax must be delivered. Since his first best seller, 'The Magic Feather', Marcus had published two other novels, 'Miracle' and 'Synchronicity' both had of which had topped the bestsellers lists. He was proud of his success; his novels translated into more than a dozen languages, eagerly awaited by devoted readers.

He had never lost sight that he owed his success to Quill, to Ethan. He had not been able to thank him; the publishing contract prohibited any mention of the matter to anyone. 'Anyone' included Ethan. Marcus had understood the request, the lesson. He had been reluctant to accept Ethan's gratitude and Ethan had denied him the same. Still, he wished he had been allowed to express his appreciation. Ethan had repaid his act a hundredfold, had made his lifelong dream a reality. At only twenty-three years of age, he was an internationally renowned author and, though he acknowledged he was talented, he was conscious of the fact that without Ethan's help he would never have achieved overnight, continued success. Most of all he wished he could have explained the real reason that had made him refuse Ethan's gratitude. He had felt he did not deserve it. He had not been defending Ethan, but a young orphan named Charlie.

Marcus did not cross paths with Ethan during their respective years at the university. Destiny had it they never met again. Marcus had returned often to the pub, hoping to find him. He never showed up.

The moment his novel achieved widespread recognition, hit number one in the bestseller list, Marcus became the most famous student at the university. His popularity soared, everyone wished to be his friend. Girls flocked around him as if he was some kind of superstar. Party invitations inundated him. Whilst the sudden stardom would have been any student's dream, Marcus hated the fact he had become so visible.

His teachers were extremely proud of his achievement. He could do no wrong. His grades had always been extremely good, suddenly, they were excellent. Despite his reluctance, Marcus was forced into a more sociable life. During his life at university, he had several sporadic relationships but none of the willing females managed to tie him down. When Marcus returned home, he had no recognised girlfriend. Some of the girls he had dated had been charming companions, but he had not managed to fall in love.

The royalties from his novel made him considerably wealthy and, against Alexandra's advice, he purchased a beautiful twelve bedroom, eight bathroom detached villa, ten minutes by bus from the children's home. Alexandra had argued the property was inadequately large, expensive, but

Marcus had been adamant. He needed a spacious home, one big enough to accommodate his family.

The bedrooms were extremely spacious and Marcus instructed an interior designer to equip and decorate each of the ten rooms destined to allocate four children. Disney themes: Little Mermaid, Beauty and the Beast, Finding Nemo and Toy Story decorated the younger children's bedrooms. Fantasy movie themes: Avatar, Harry Potter, Lord of the Rings and Narnia, the older children's. Every room enjoyed the latest gadgets: plasmas, game consuls, laptops... and a vast array of educational toys. A large bedroom, decorated in warm tones, containing two double beds and en-suite bathroom, with hydro shower and Jacuzzi, was destined to Care Workers accompanying the children. The luxurious bathroom a reward for their zealous dedication to his siblings.

His large master suite, on the top floor, enjoyed another en-suite bathroom with Jacuzzi and double shower. The remaining six bathrooms were destined for the children; three for the boys, three for the girls. Each bathroom contained three showers, three washbasin units and three toilets. The girls' decorated in a dusty pink, gold and white vaudeville theme, the boys' a navy blue and white nautical theme.

The first weekend Marcus moved into the house, forty of the children stayed over. Since then, the children had taken turns staying at Marcus'. They all counted the days until it was their turn again.

Marcus adored his new independent life. During the week, he worked on his writing and went out occasionally with friends he had made in the literary circles he frequented. He had recently begun dating someone. A stunning brunette named Dionne, who was the editor of a Fashion Magazine and frequented the creative ambience. Dionne had a special quality about her. She was highly intelligent and stunningly beautiful, yet unassuming. The combination lured him. Slowly, but steadily, she had begun to grow on him. It was too soon to mention love, but he had no intention of nipping the budding romance. Dionne was not only intelligent but highly intuitive. After a couple of dates, she had infiltrated Marcus' 'cold' facade, understood the reason for the algid barrier. His past inhibited his emotions, condemned him to be an introvert, one with a sensitive, generous soul. She could not wait to meet Marcus' large 'family'.

She had fallen for him the instant she had laid eyes on him, his handsome dark looks, his compelling eyes... yet his talent being what initially attracted him to her. When she had discerned the man behind the 'mask', she had been gladly surprised to find a deep, caring human being. Dionne was a patient woman. It did not matter that Marcus wished to pace the relationship, that he was not overtly expressive with his emotions. She could wait. He was worth it.

Marcus devoted weekends exclusively to the children and had been pleasantly surprised Dionne understood his commitment. She was fast becoming a very special woman.

The children enjoyed swimming in the Olympic sized pool that had been fitted with two slides, or watched movies in the large movie theatre he had installed in the basement. The theatre enjoyed a soft drink's dispenser, a soft ice-cream dispenser and a pop corn machine. Marcus had wished to compensate them for the drab and paltry existence they had endured in the past.

Alexandra often reminded him of his words to her the first time they had met, when he had assured he would become a famous writer and buy a large beautiful house. He had achieved his lifelong dream but had never imagined his home would be full of so many people that loved him, he loved.

The moment Marcus hung up the phone with Kian, he opened the envelopes. As soon as he inspected its contents, he headed to his room, packed a small bag and raced to his car.

Marcus was eager to reach his destination, could not wait for the awaiting mystery to be resolved. Once again, reality surpassed fiction, his only wish as he drove down to the coast was for a fitting climax.

Ethan was in the boardroom, waiting for his marketing team to arrive. New companies had shown keen interest in advertising on Quill's user interface and they would be deciding on the most interesting options offered. As he waited, he scanned the portfolios on his desk, marvelling at the outstanding creativity of his graphic designers. He had chosen them well. Every one of them was fresh out of university and top notch. Their ground-breaking ideas were unrivalled, ensuring the continued prestige of his company, its progress. Quill prided itself on scooping up fresh talents before rival companies snatched them. Ethan's lucrative remuneration packages made the latter easy. New recruits felt privileged at the chance offered. Becoming part of the successful, challenging and generous company was the ambition of those wishing to embark on a prosperous career.

The company thrived under Ethan's direction. The number of advertising contracts expanded as the user interface continued to be the leading search engine in the world. Innovative software packages were developed, including email utilities that were full proof to nuisance spam and malicious viruses. The company extended its acquisitions, investing in realty, communications, and so forth. Under Ethan's leadership, and in only one year, the number of employees tripled and another building housed the expanding corporation.

Ethan became the most sought-after bachelor in the country and the media was continually hunting for information on his private life. Ethan detested media exposure, limited his public appearances to business-related events. Michael had taken great pains guaranteeing his friend's intimacy. His private address was a mystery to even his private secretary and loyal bodyguards ensured his whereabouts were secret, with the exception of Ethan's close family circle which included Alexandra and him. The women he dated signed confidential agreements. If the relationships did not blossom, the company compensated them generously for their discretion. Ethan wished his private life exceedingly separate from his business.

Outlandish strategies from paparazzi failed to intrude on Ethan's privacy; the elite security team assured his personal life remained impenetrable.

On weekends, he traded the frenetic beat of the city for a country or seashore destination. He needed to unwind, be a normal person with an ordinary life. He chose destinations scrupulously, travelled under a false identity. He worked twelve-hour days from Monday to Friday, the intervals of detachment allowed him to sustain sanity.

He was currently dating a woman he had met on a seafront restaurant, located in one of his favoured coastal refuges. She was the daughter of its owner. One night, after enjoying a succulent meal, he noticed her sitting on the sand, pensively staring ahead at the dark ocean. Her fresh beauty had immediately caught his attention.

Battling timidity, he had walked up to her uncertainly and introduced himself. The moment she had raised her head, her childlike blue eyes had smiled at him, his heart had thundered in his ears and could have sworn he had heard hers fluttering in her chest. He was secretly chuffed she had allowed him to sit beside her on the peaceful beach. When she had agreed casually to dine with him the following night, his euphoria was comparable to that of a teenager taking the most beautiful girl in school to prom.

During the next couple of months, he had made the beautiful seaside town his only destination. Ethan had not wished to reveal his 'real' life; he had wanted her to fall for the man, not the company. The sad realisation every single woman, who had professed undying love to him, had simply been after his money, had aborted the burgeoning relationships. Sydney seemed different, genuine. He had begun to fall in love with her and hoped the nascent romance withstood the test of time. He hoped that by the time he revealed his identity, she was truly in love with the man and the company was merely a bonus.

A knock on the door announced it was time for the meeting. Ethan was expecting his team of young experts, but it was his secretary who appeared through the door, carrying a padded envelope. Excusing herself for the interruption, she placed the package diligently on the polished boardroom table and informed him the courier had insisted the envelope reached him no later than noon. The minute he was alone, he opened it.

The moment he viewed its contents he called his secretary and instructed her to cancel the imminent meeting, his meetings for the week. Rashly, he ordered the competent assistant to call Michael, inform him he had gone to help a friend with a personal problem and would possibly be away for a couple of days.

Michael would deduce he had gone to see Sydney. Alexandra and Michael were the only ones that knew of her existence. He had no other 'friend'. Without losing time, he retrieved a set of car keys from the filing cabinet and headed hastily for the secret riser.

When Ethan left the building, he was wearing a security uniform. His usual escorts did not accompany him. Careful no one followed him, he got into the small inconspicuous car, parked in a parking lot, two blocks away, and drove to the nearest gas station. Retrieving the travelling bag he kept in the boot, he headed for the rest room. In minutes, he was back in the car wearing a jogging suit, cap and sunglasses.

As he drove towards the familiar destination, he thought of Michael. He knew his friend would be concerned, would find the fact he had not called him personally, told him the nature of the problem, uncharacteristic but he had no choice; there was a part of his life he had not shared with him, with anyone...

Barely minutes from the jam-packed highway, he received a text message from Michael informing him an unexpected business proposition had materialized and he would be away from the city for a couple of days. Ethan was thankful for the opportune coincidence. He hated having to lie to his friend. As he negotiated traffic, he thought of Sydney and the secrets he kept from her.

Marcus's question about Ethan's involvement with 'Quill' was answered a couple of years later. He had just finished a public signing of his recent bestseller, at the usual city bookshop, and had not felt like going home. The day was pleasantly inviting and he decided to have a cup of coffee, relax on the sunny terrace of a coffee shop, in the bookshop's vicinity.

As he had sat, drinking his espresso, analytical eyes roaming over the sea of people flooding the street, he reflected again on his overnight success, the curious events that had led to the publication of his best seller. He could not believe people wished to queue up for hours to obtain a copy of his signed book. The first time his literary agent had arranged a public signing, he had felt anxious. He was not accustomed to the open admiration from strangers. Most of his life he had chosen to be inconspicuous and the brutal exposure unnerved him. Part of him felt like an imposter.

. Absentmindedly, he gazed through the glass facade at the plasma TV, situated at the corner of the long room, when Ethan's face suddenly filled the screen. In seconds, he was inside the cafe and without stopping to ask the bartender for permission, turned up the volume. He stared at the screen in shock. He had gathered Ethan was somehow connected to the multimillion corporation, but he had never expected him to own it.

Before he had time to absorb the image in detail, the enraged bartender switched channels and lowered the sound.

As Marcus recalled the short-lived scene, an image surfaced; the man in the dark grey suit, standing beside Ethan, was none other than Alexandra's Michael.

The realization uncovered a distant enigma; Marcus remembered Alexandra's reaction when he had relayed the exciting and extraordinary news. Logically, she had been overjoyed, but he had sensed something unnatural in her manner. Briefly, he had wondered if Alexandra knew of Ethan's involvement but had immediately ruled out the farfetched possibility.

He had been wrong.

Arianne was on location with her filming crew, when her secretary called. A courier had left an envelope for her at the reception and it was imperative she collected it before noon. The company driver was already heading her way; the package would reach her well before midday. Arianne was surprised. She was not expecting urgent mail. As she stood outside the old church, waiting for father Damien, she thought of the events that had led her to him.

A few weeks earlier, one of her reporters had received a mysterious call. A young woman claimed to have witnessed a miracle in her neighbourhood parish. Other calls followed, every caller, parishioners of the same church, claimed the same. None of the callers had offered an explanation other than a miracle had occurred in their parish. The nature of the miracle remained an enigma. When Arianne and her crew set out to visit the small congregation, on the outskirts of the city, they had no idea what they would find. Once again, she had not needed to cover the story, could have delegated fieldwork to a junior reporter, but she had been enticed by the mystery, had felt oddly compelled to visit the burgoise neighbourhood.

Arianne stood impatiently, with her two-man crew a short distance from the church. She had been waiting for forty minutes and there was still no sign of the priest. She kept eying her Rolex exasperatedly until, finally, he appeared, in the distance, across the park, an excited entourage trailing behind. The eager parishioners strode across the stone path, leading to the church, making the sign of the cross in tandem. The moment father Damian reached the arched doorway, he gesticulated excitedly, indicating Arianne, and her crew, followed him into the small Gothic church. The accompanying congregation remained at its foot. As Arianne walked into the holy building, she felt a shiver of anticipation. She was dying to find out what the old priest was so eager to relay.

As they sat down on one of the front pews, a glimmer of sadness shading his furrowed hooded eyes, he told her of the violence that had plagued their streets, how they had been condemned hostages to panic. How the neighbourhood's children had no longer been able to play in the park, in their own gardens. How curfew at sundown had made them prisoners of the dark. The moment night had enveloped the neighbourhood, they had became prisoners of their own homes, barricaded to limit violent trespassers.

Their precarious situation had been unsustainable and they had turned to fervent prayer. Every dawn, they had congregated in church, beseeched God for divine intervention, for his divine hand to cleanse their streets of the rampant malevolence. For weeks, nothing had happened. On the contrary, the wave of corruption had fast expanded to become a tidal one. Many had contemplated selling their homes, depart the nightmarish neighbourhood.

Parishioners had hit the zenith of despair when the miracle happened. It was still dark; they had only just begun to pray when a rustling sound, resembling the flutter of wings, had echoed the old sanctuary. Everyone had been startled. The confused crowd had kept searching the doors, the windows, whilst a diaphanous light begun to sprout from the ground, at the foot of the steps, leading to the altar.

The sheer white light had twirled slowly up to the ceiling, until the translucent tornado had hit the convex roof. A small sum of parishioners had rushed out to the street, the rest had remained within the church's protective walls. After a few moments, one of the parishioners, who was brave enough to face the menacing streets returned. Agitatedly, he had urged the rest of the worshippers to abandon the church, witness the miraculous event. One by one, they had left the sacred haven and the astonished crowd had gazed at the lucent column filtering the ceiling, reaching up to the heavens. The extraordinary spectacle had induced the mass of awed men and women to kneel on the grass and pray fervently.

After approximately ten minutes, the column had begun to fade, disintegrate, and an awestruck congregation had returned to the confines of the church, where they had continued praying passionately. As they had prayed, everyone had felt the buzz emanating from where the column had emerged. The pulsing energy had uplifted their souls, and some of the parishioners had begun to cry as an intense feeling had inundated their hearts. A small crowd of people had ventured to the sacred spot, at the foot of the altar. One of them had stooped down and picked up something from the floor. When the emotional group had returned to the pews, they had realized the young man carried a perfect white feather in his hand. Everyone agreed an Angel had visited the church. Since then, the neighbourhood returned to the peaceful locality it had always been.

Arianne watched her crew; their awed expressions told her they had believed every word. A priest, a whole congregation, could not be lying.

Arianne thanked Father Damien for his time, his account and told him she would be back to see him the following day. The moment they left the church, Arianne instructed one of her crew to make some calls, check the crime rate of the neighbourhood, interrogate the townspeople. She did not doubt the Father, but it was her duty to check the veracity of the story, compile facts. As she sat on the steps of the church, waiting for the 'evidence', the Channel's driver arrived and handed her the envelope. She had forgotten all about it and without paying much attention to the exterior of the package tore it open.

The moment she viewed its contents, she excused herself vaguely, got into the car and instructed the driver to take her back to the city, home. Three hours later, she was heading towards the coastal town, two hundred kilometres away.

As she drove down the congested highway and remembered the feather the priest had shown her, she thought of her own feather. It was not a coincidence she had felt drawn to visit the church. She had been destined to witness another miracle. She believed the old priest. She had felt the exulting energy. She believed in angels. The time for the final revelation was nigh.

Michael drove down the coiling road. He could already distinguish the sea. Dancing lights skimmed its peaceful surface, adding a dreamy quality to the inviting landscape. Soon, the beautiful cove, shadowed by the familiar structure, appeared in the distance. Ten more minutes and he would reach his destination. A sweet nostalgia invaded him as he remembered the day he had met Alexandra, the unforgettable night they had shared. He could not get over the uncanny coincidence. The word replayed in his mind, *coincidence...coincidence...*There was no such thing; experience had taught him coincidence did not exist...

Quickly, he parked his car in the empty parking lot, slung the overnight bag on his shoulder and hastily climbed the steps to the hotel. When he had reached the double glass doors, he hesitated. Suddenly, the confidence that characterized him faltered, he panicked. For a moment, the urge to turn around, get in his car and leave invaded him. Realising it was not an option, was not what he truly desired, he took a deep breath and headed towards the reception. As he traversed the lobby, the ghosts of his past, the man he had once been, the fleeting feeling of unworthiness, evaporated.

The moment he reached the polished wooden counter, a friendly '*good afternoon Mr. Jenkins*' greeted him. He studied the smiling receptionist, wondering how she knew his name. **Who** had told her his name? If she was part of the 'plan'... resisting the temptation to question her, he accepted the small white envelope she handed to him with a smile and sat in the terrace bar, as she suggested. The energetic, young woman could not be more than twenty years old and her polite demeanour had been typical of hotel employees. She was simply doing a job. She was not part of any plan. The thought was ludicrous.

He made himself comfortable in a corner table, at the far end of the bar by the veranda, and gazed out at the silent cove. The breathtaking scenery again prompted thoughts of Alexandra. As his eyes rested on the placid seas, he mulled over the strange happenstance; of all the places in the world, the cove had been the chosen destination, a place so close to home, a place where he had found love. There was a connection, it was evident the choice of venue would have otherwise been improbable. He could not wait to find out what the mysterious link was. He was thirsty and asked for a pint of beer. In minutes, the waiter returned with the pint and a bowl of mixed dry nuts. Michael took out his wallet and was about to pay him, when the waiter informed him politely that drinks and snacks were courtesy of the hotel. As he quenched his thirst, as the cold drink gushed down his parched throat, he wondered who was playing host.

He was about to take a mouthful of nuts, when he suddenly remembered the envelope he had placed in the pocket of his jeans. He retrieved it carefully and placed it on the table. He lit a cigarette, took a few nervous puffs and without further delay opened it. The folded piece of paper contained a short message, a feather, a smaller version of the one he had received that morning. As he read the words '*the others will arrive soon*', he wondered with increasing curiosity, who the 'others' were.

Arianne felt calm, unfretted by the unknown. She was convinced that, whatever it was that lay ahead, was part of God's plan. Since the day she had received the feather, she had felt special, had waited eagerly to be 'summoned', to discover what she had ultimately been chosen for.

The grief, the tragedy of her past was long forgotten, God had recompensed her generously for her ordeal. He had not forgotten her, had been waiting to save her. She had come to understand; her suffering as a child was the sacrifice she had paid to be chosen. Given the chance, she would have it no other way. The encounter with the feather had erased every recollection of pain. Sorrow, anguish, no longer contaminated her memory, her heart.

As she neared the cove, her thoughts travelled back to the past, to her mother. A slither of melancholy invaded her as she recalled how her mother had never made the slightest effort to make her feel special, loved. Her thoughts returned to the last time they had spoken, a couple of years before, and regretted that she had been reminded again that her mother did not love her. Thankfully, the cruel rebuff had no longer possessed the power to cause her pain.

Despite everything, she had loved her mother, still loved her. That she could forgive, love her mother regardless, was what was important, made her special. Perhaps, her capacity to forgive was the reason God had chosen her...

Her mother had called a couple of times since then, each time her sole intent had been to ask her for money. She was always in need of cash; always going through a rough patch. Arianne had sent her the money, had agreed to keep sending her money on a monthly basis. Her one condition was that she never called her again. She no longer harboured resentment against her mother, but had realised there was no point in holding a 'fake' relationship, one that was, and had always been, one sided. She wished her no ill, did not mind helping her but from a distance. Her mother had never called again.

Except for a few cars, the parking lot was empty. *Strange*, she thought. *It was high season.* As she walked up the steps she felt a rush of exhilaration. She was about to discover why she had been summoned, who had summoned her. She could not wait.

She was halfway down the lobby to the reception, when a chirpy blonde-haired, young woman popped out from behind the counter and beamed at her. '*Good afternoon Miss Saint Clare,*' she greeted professionally. Arianne stared at the buoyant woman, wondering if she knew the host's or hosts' name. Before Arianne could speak, she disappeared under the counter, popped back up and handed her a small white envelope, the perfect smile pasted on a face inviting no questions. Politely, she informed Arianne whilst she waited, complementary drinks and snacks were available at the terrace bar. As Arianne headed towards the sunny terrace, she wished to scream, *waited for what?*

The moment she set foot on the warm veranda, she recognised the man sitting on the corner table, overlooking the beach. She had met him once, a long time ago, whilst covering a murder trial. Damian Roffe, the Electronics' tycoon, had been accused of murdering his young wife. Everyone had thought him guilty, but was declared innocent.

The brilliant young lawyer rumoured to employ 'unorthodox' methods, who had defended him, was Michael Jenkins, the man sitting a few meters away from her. Weeks after the sensationalist trial, he had disappeared from Ryman and Barns, the most prestigious firm in the city, without trace. Arianne had wondered then, what had made him leave his brilliant career, his promising future? Ignoring the coincidental presence of the lawyer, and without waiting for her order, she opened the envelope and smiled. Finding another feather had not surprised her, but she was dying to know who the 'others' were.

John watched his wife's beautiful, sleepy face on the pillow beside him. As he watched her peaceful expression, his heart overflowed with joy, love, gratitude. He could still not believe how fortunate he was. He had everything a man could wish for. An amazing family, a job he loved, good friends, the miracles that touched his life...he could not bear to think he had nearly lost it all. Every night he thanked the feather, he thanked God. Every night he slept peacefully. He would never forget the second chance given. He would never stray again. Since the extraordinary encounter, the astonishing events that ensued, he no longer thought of himself as a man who served the law, but a servant of God.

John had been ecstatic when he had been promoted to Commissioner, overjoyed his family was proud of him. The unexpected honour had meant more than money, status. Becoming Commissioner awarded him something more valuable: the power to change things. In only six months, he had achieved many of his goals. Two weeks into his post, he had set up a new Criminal Investigation Department; one which incorporated the latest technology; investigative advances.

The Mayor and he had become good friends. They visited the same church on Sundays, lunched together with their families, after the midday service, and conversed extensively on spiritual matters. Like he, the Mayor was a recent 'believer'. An extraordinary event had given him a different perspective of life, he had confided to John, without awarding details. John had been curious, but had refrained from asking the nature of his 'awakening'. He kept his own secrets.

The Mayor's support had been instrumental in the pursuit of his goals. With his aid, the department's annual budget had been extended. Both men held the same vision; making the erosion of crime the city's priority. The Mayor trusted John, shared his beliefs, his high intentions.

Under John's leadership, the city's crime rate had fallen to unprecedented levels. Justice was swift and citizens began to trust in the law again. They had begun to feel safe in a city that had once been corroded with violence. A sophisticated Internal Affairs Department was set up to ensure corruption no longer infected law-enforcing agencies. Other cities were astounded at the cleansing operation initiated, and successfully undertaken, by Commissioner Taylor. Many followed suit. Police Commissioners, from every city, adopted equal strategies and, one by one, the crime rates in those cities descended. Everyone congratulated the young Commissioner for his remarkable achievements, everyone praised his dedication and mastery. John was proud of what he had accomplished but understood he was merely a tool in God's hands.

His thoughts returned to the second time he had witnessed a miracle, to the day he had saved two innocent angels from the clutches of their depraved father. He had been working at his desk, going over investigative reports, when, out of the blue, he decided to get himself a sandwich from the snack bar, across the street from the station. He had suddenly changed his mind as he had made his way to the small bar. He had turned around and had begun to walk in the opposite direction, towards the police car park. Trancelike, he had sat in a patrol car, turned on the ignition and had begun to traverse the city robotically. With no recollection of the route, he found himself parked outside an elegant town house, situated in a private and luxurious residential complex, on the west side of the city. He had stared at the three-storey, white brick house wondering how he had gotten there, what his purpose was.

Children's shrieks had suddenly disrupted the placid neighbourhood, the terrorized screeches originating from a room on the second floor. He had flung the door of the patrol car open, bashed his corpulent body against the front door and rushed up the stairs. The piercing trill voices emanated from a bedroom, at the end of the long corridor, to the right of the landing. He had kicked the door open and stood petrified on the threshold, gun in hand, as he had engaged the repulsive scene. Two little girls cowered upon their respective beds. A man stood at the foot of the bed naked, a lascivious expression in his eyes, a rope dangling from his hand...

He had thrown up on the baby pink carpet. His gun pointed steadily at the depraved perpetrator. The abuser had turned around slowly, raised his arms, until they stretched high over his head, and fixed his stare on space behind John. John had searched his vacuous eyes for a flicker of emotion. He had found nothing. Disgusted by the condescending smile that had begun to curve his thin lips, the arrogant stance of his body, the decadent intention still lurking in his eyes, brought him close to throwing up for a second time.

As if on cue, police sirens had suddenly filled the ignorant hush of the neighbourhood and, seconds later, two officers rushed the stairs to the room.

What had ensued was still a blur in John's memory. He could barely remember fragments of the arrest. The only thing he could recall vividly was the two frightened, tear-filled eyes, staring at him from the rear window of the police car, that hurriedly took them away to the nearest hospital. Luckily, the degenerate savage had not had time to inflict any damage.

A couple of hours later, John had sat in his office with the two innocent angels. As he had watched them, watched the beautiful faces, draped by amber ringlets, his heart had gone out to them. He could not understand how anyone could wish to harm them, rob them of their innocence, especially their own father. The thought was unthinkable...

The girls had curled up quietly on the couch, settled in the corner Neither of them had spoken a word. Stricken by terror, uncertainty, they held hands tightly. John had ordered a fellow officer to bring them ice creams and as he offered the two pink and white cones, they had finally managed a dull smile. John could not help blink back tears as he had confronted their eyes. The coy gratitude had had nothing to do with the melting cones in their tinny hands; the timid baby blue eyes told him they were grateful he had saved them.

As they had sat, engrossed, licking the cream melting down the wafer cones, John had dialled Alexandra's number. He had worked with the competent young Social Worker in the past and knew how dedicated she was to her job, what a caring person she was.

Alexandra had rushed to embrace the girls the minute she had caught sight of them. They had buried their heads in her belly, their fragile shivering arms circling her tightly, their tears wetting her skirt, refusing to let go of her. Alexandra had wrapped them with her arms, spoken words of comfort, reassured them that this time, they were truly safe, that their father would never hurt them again. It had taken time and effort to convince the girls her words were sincere, that the system would not let them down a second time. Gradually, they had relaxed their iron grip and, holding tight to Alexandra's hands, accompanied her to another office.

On the verge of tears, Alexandra had thanked him profusely for saving the girls. After she had finished with bureaucratic procedures, she had left, with one of his men, to return them back to the safety of the Children's Home.

John had brooded over the afternoon's events. He was baffled; he had not worked in that particular case. He knew nothing about it, had no idea how he had ended up on that precise doorstep, at the exact moment. He could not remember driving there, having called for backup. When he had asked the police officers who had so opportunely appeared on the scene, how they had known, he was disconcerted by their puzzled expressions. Of course, he had called for backup. They were in the vicinity when they had heard him call for assistance over the radio.

What the two officers never told John was that they had no clue how they had been in the immediate vicinity of the thwarted crime. How they had gotten there. They could not remember having left the station or getting into the car.

What John never told anyone was that he had seen the patrol car he had driven in, towed away by the department's mechanic, the following morning. That when he had casually enquired about the nature of the repairs, he had been told the radio had been broken for days.

It was only seven thirty, when John left the house. He had not wished to wake his wife. It was Sunday and she always slept a bit longer on weekends. Quickly, he had gone to his study, tore a page from the note book he kept beside the phone on his desk and, scribbled a quick note, informing her an urgent case had arisen, one that would keep him away from home for a few days. He had showered quickly, changed into a jogging suit, packed a small overnight bag, with a change of clothes and other essentials, grabbed his wallet and picked up his car keys from the chest of drawers. Before he left the room, he kissed his wife gently on the forehead then headed down to the laundry room in the basement, where he picked up the uniform his wife had brought home from the cleaners the previous day.

As he headed towards the garage, the small bag in one hand, the plastic covered uniform in the other, he made a mental note to call the station the moment he arrived at the cove. He had already briefed his men vaguely, sworn them into secrecy, without divulging unnecessary information. He had not needed to, his men would follow him to the end of the world if necessary. They trusted John Taylor. He had shared the bare specifics; the time, location and that they should pack a small suitcase. He did not know how long he would, they would, be away. He did not even know if the cove was the final destination.

As he left the picturesque town behind, turned the junction to the cove, he thought of Sister Julia and the secrets she kept. He thought of miracles past, of those to come. He thought of his family, of the many blessings in his life, in his world. He was ready. He could not wait to repay God.

As he descended the snaking road to the sandy inlet, he checked the items on his list; walkie-talkies, fluorescent barriers, megaphone, blank ammunition, flashlights... *He had everything... knew what he must do. What Slade must do.* Sister Julia's orders had been clear. Neither Slade nor he knew what would happen at the cove, what the 'others' must do.

Slade and he had become fast friends, trusted each other. They had connected instantly. The bond had strengthened after they had stayed in the hotel. As he neared the cove, he wondered if his new friend had met the feather, if the people, they had been following for days, had also encountered the magical talisman. He had said nothing, but had seen the expression in Slade's face when he had taken the distant shot of Arianne. The beautiful woman walking into the chrome and black glass building that housed Channel 6, clearly fascinated him. Slade had never mentioned her, yet John sensed the famous newscaster was no stranger, that his friend felt more than admiration for the ravishing woman he had captured so intently with his lens.

Slade left his attic early, the time was finally nigh... After a hurried shower, and a quick change of clothes, he popped next door to visit his sister, who was having breakfast on the terrace, as usual. He had wished to spend some time with her before leaving for the cove; he had no idea when he would return, if he would return. He had no clue as to what awaited at the end of the mysterious expedition. Slade was not afraid; fear was an emotion he had stopped feeling a long time ago. He was ready; felt he had been ready for the mystical moment all his life.

His sister looked radiant; the rays of sun, filtering through the dense trumpet vine ceiling of the spacious porch, cast a subtle misty aura around her. Flared her beautiful deep-set, hazel eyes in emerald hue and, for a second, he wished he had time to immortalize the dreamy moment.

Sadie kept talking incessantly about her wedding plans, flashing the diamond solitaire ring, proudly exhibited on the wedding finger of her left hand. Slade was happy for his 'kid' sister. She deserved all the happiness in the world. He admired her, admired her strength, felt pride at how she had survived the past, been able to resume her life. After the tragedy, he had been afraid for her, terrorized of what she might do to herself. It had taken a lot of therapy, many months of seclusion in the private clinic, to piece her together. As he watched her cheerfully eating scrambled eggs on toast, he thought of the time when she had refused to eat, to speak. Mercifully, those days belonged well in the past. Thankfully, his sister now led a happy life, a fulfilling one, had learned to smile at her future.

Slade was immediately taken with the young man who had stolen his sister's heart. Sean, her fiancé, resembled their father, both physically and in personality. He had his warm smile. Slade did not have cause to doubt that the young man loved his sister. He seemed to adore her, seemed perfect for her. Slade prided himself on being an excellent judge of character, but he had needed to be certain. His extensive travels, encounters with people from every walk of life, had taught him to be cautious.

Sean was an accountant in the company and he had met Sadie at the company's Christmas party the previous year. Although Slade detected nothing to make him suspect the young man's intentions were dishonourable, he was still wary. Without Sadie knowing, he had summoned Sean to his office. The one next to his sister's, the one he had never used. They had remained locked in the office for two hours. The following day, he had summoned him again and the young man had signed every page on the pre nuptial agreement he had had his lawyers draw up. Sean was deeply in love with his sister; money was not the reason that had lured him to her.

Secretly he felt shame for having distrusted him, for going behind his sister's back. He had had no choice. His sister had suffered enough. Sean never told Sadie of their encounter, never betrayed his soon-to-be brother in law. He had understood Slade only wished to protect Sadie.

They would be getting married in two weeks and, as Slade kissed his sister affectionately on the cheek, as he said goodbye, he hoped he would be back in time for the wedding. Hoped to take the happy pictures that would become part of the 'life' assembled on his shelves.

As Slade sped down the fast lane of the highway to the cove, he thought of his own metamorphosis, the spectacular changes in his life. He had finally begun to feel he 'belonged'. His attic had fast become a home, the sanctuary he retired to after a hard day's work. He no longer felt the urge to escape the city, to hop from one country to another. Sadie was thrilled he had finally settled down, remained close to her but, above all, she was overjoyed he finally seemed at peace.

His prestige as a photographer had soared; marketing companies inundated him with offers. Celebrities hunted him; they all wished to be immortalized by Slade Alston's expert eye. Soon, he would be fulfilling a lifelong dream, a photographic exhibition in a prominent art gallery. Amidst, the shots chosen, there were images of his 'other' life.

His nightly ritual continued. He still flickered through the pages of his history. He had grown to cherish the memories. The visual remnants now gave him strength. He was grateful for his happy childhood, grateful he had been blessed with such wonderful parents, grateful that they had been great role models to emulate in the time they had had together. His parents had instilled the moral foundations, the values, that allowed him to be the man he was. That because of his parent's legacy, he had had the exceptional fortune to be 'chosen' was a constant thought.

Slade no longer delved in his other obsession. He no longer indulged in rancorous thoughts, in vengeance. He was certain the two monsters who had killed his parents had paid their due. Karma was a bitch.

As he neared the cove, as he rolled down the steep windy road, his thoughts drifted to the feather, the miracles he had witnessed. He felt enormously privileged that the fluffy fellow had chosen to insist over the terrace, enter his life, chosen to save him.

When Sister Julia had given him the list of names, he had been shocked to find two people had already crossed his life path. He had photographed Marcus on a number of occasions; the handsome smiling face that appeared at the back of his bestseller books were his creations. Arianne, he had not met, but she was the woman he loved. It seemed bizarre that one could love a person they had never met, but stranger things happened...he should know...

The extraordinary awaited, *the time was nigh, he had been summoned and he had come*...but the mystery's impending resolution was not what made his heart race. He could not wait to meet Arianne.

*Before Amanda headed for the temple, she flew back to the valley. Anton slept, the valley slept. For a moment, she stood by the garden gate, the Sacred Book close to her chest. She looked up at the quiet heavens.* **Perhaps she would be lucky... perhaps there was still time**...

*Swiftly, she ascended the steep face of the mountain. Her wings nearly brushing the limestone cliff, she glided over the dark plateau, to the heart of the shadowed woodland, and floated down to the entrance to the temple. Warily, she opened the heavy gilded door and sneaked down the long glowing corridor to the Golden chamber. The door was slightly opened, just as she had left it. Quickly, she tiptoed across the ivory marble floor to the glass cylinder resting on the white column, located at the centre of the room, her heart pounding. The glass door remained open.*

*With extreme care, she nestled the book on the gold, silk cushion, closed the curved, glass door and pressed the three-digit code on the small, golden panel at its feet. Amanda had not meant to memorize the secret code when the elders had retrieved the book, at the Circle of Light meeting, her eyes had unintentionally fixed on his finger and she had automatically registered the numbers to memory. With hindsight, it seemed odd that the Elders had not taken stringent precautions. The moment the book was safely locked in the cylinder, she took a deep breath. The gulp of air still filled her lungs when she heard the door creak faintly behind her.*

*Three pairs of slit eyes fixed on her, watched her from across the circular room. The imposing angels studied her in silence, then looked at each other. Amanda stood rooted to the spot. She dare not move, speak, was dangerously close to tears.* **No, she would not cry, would not plead. She would face consequence with dignity. The Supreme Masters of light would not understand, would refute her 'feeble' excuses, they would not find justification in her acts. They would never understand she had had no choice. She had to help her son...she would**

***tell them nothing...*** *She braced herself for darkness, for exile again...*

*She stood in the centre of the cold room. Her eyes closed, listening to the dooming silence, thinking of her son, of how much she would miss him, miss their world. Once again, there was a sacrifice to be made. This time there would be no recompense. For an eternity, she stood there, wings pasted around her torso, eyes closed, waiting. The room remained silent. No one moved. No one spoke.* **The statuesque angels had left, had locked her in the chamber***... She was about to open her eyes, when a deep voice resounded in her ears...* **She doesn't know***...*

*At the sound of the words, Amanda opened her eyes and, forgetting her fear, confronted the looming angels.* **'Don't know what?** *She whispered, her eyes ablaze. The angels ignored her. She felt suddenly weak, her legs turned to jelly, her vision fuzzy.* **'Where is my son?'** *She whispered again, fighting the rising scream. The seraphim faced each other, their backs to her, and began to whisper between them, disregarding her frail assertion.* **'She hasn't found her yet... the extent of her sacrifice... Seth has met her...no... he doesn't know....'**

*Amanda did not need to listen further; the broken sentences had already revealed the terrible secret. By the time the three powerful angels had turned to face her, she had raced out the chamber, shot into the heavens, through the ceiling of leaves.*

Alexandra was the third to arrive. She had been driving for two hours. She was exhausted. Tension had provoked a migraine; the sharp pain over her left eye would not subside. She felt sick; nausea always accompanied the acute pain. Her neck felt stiff and she longed for Michael's strong massaging hands. She missed him, wondered when she would be able to see him again. Guilt weighed heavily. She detested lying to him. She wished she did not feel the compulsion to keep part of her life secret.

Before she got out of the car, she searched her bag for the migraine tablets she always carried. She put two tablets in her mouth and washed them down with a small bottle of water. She hardly noticed the few cars in the parking lot. She did not see the red mini among them. Flashing lights over her right eye blinded side view; she could only see the path in front of her.

She had already climbed the last step leading up to the hotel when, on impulse, she turned around and headed towards the beach. She needed to placate the agonising pain. She could not face whatever it was she was about to face until the pain had eased off. The flashing lights were gone. The pattern of her migraines was always the same; pain, flashing lights, more pain. The only way to avert a full-blown attack was to take the tablets, at the onset of pain, and lie in the dark, in silence for a while. Using the key in her pocket, lying down on a bed was the logical option, but knew somehow it was not what she was supposed to do.

She took off her shoes and barefooted walked a few meters into the sandy cove. She lay down on the empty sands and closed her eyes. Despite the pain, she found herself relaxing, smiling feebly, as the familiar location prompted an image of Michael, walking down the beach the day he entered her life. *It was strange*, she thought, *of all places, the small beach where she had found Michael, love was the chosen destination. It was highly improbable that the latter turned out to be a mere coincidence...* As she nestled deeper into the moulding ground, her mind grappled to find an explanation. *Why the cove, what was the connection*? As she pressed her palms on her forehead, her trail of thought changed course. She thought of the feather, relived the miracles, the message, that had ultimately returned her to the magical shore. Initially, she had questioned why the feather had chosen her, why it had not chosen someone worthier of its blessings, someone special. As time had elapsed, she had come to believe the children, that surrounded her life, were the cause.

Her headache began to settle. The thorny pulse dulled. A few more minutes and it would vanish. She only needed to rest for a little while longer...

Ethan was edgy, impatient. He could not wait to reach his destination, discover what awaited him in the quaint hotel, resembling a huge beach house he had visited when only a boy. He could not imagine the reasons for the coincidental venue, his hyperactive mind conjuring a string of farfetched possibilities. He had no idea why he had needed to deliver a generator to the hotel that afternoon, purchase the hotel. The email had baffled him, but his instructions had been clear, the sender, 'The feather', allowing no contest, no procrastination. It had taken him minutes to convince the Hotel owners. He had tripled the market value for the Seaview, had secretly given its staff a sumptuous retirement check. None of them would have to worry about money again in their lives. They all signed contracts that claimed monies belonged to a timely inheritance. The lawyers had seen to it that paperwork was 'legal'.

Though he had to admit, the instructions seemed bizarre, he had learned to go with the flow a long time ago, realised he should not question the providential coincidences that had shaped his destiny. There had to be a fundamental reason for the chosen destination. He only needed to wait for a little while longer. He suspected Quill was a key element in whatever was about to happen. To the world, he was the sole creator of the revolutionary software that had made Quill a reality. He knew otherwise. Divine inspiration had filled in the blanks.

As he sat in the lobby, he kept glancing surreptitiously at his watch. Fifteen minutes had elapsed and still no one had appeared. For a moment, he wondered if the hotel was empty. Key number seven swung impatiently in his hand. He had been tempted to use it, go up to the room, but instinct warned he should not. In an effort to distract his high-strung mind, he steered his thoughts to Sydney. Her beautiful face, her warm eyes, appeased him. She was his haven, her arms the peaceful abode where he recharged his spirit. Quill was his baby. It was his duty to nurture it. Many depended on him. Sydney gave him the strength.

He harboured high expectations for their relationship. He hoped the feeling was mutual. One day he would bring her to the mysterious hotel, overlooking the perfect beach, reveal his truth.

Marcus could not get the words out of his mind. *The time is nigh* kept haunting him. *Why now?* He questioned silently. As he watched the vast ocean stretching boundless to his side, he wondered whom, or what, awaited him. He thought of his first novel, 'The Magic Feather', and speculated if there were more parallels with his story, if the tale would have a similar revelation. As he neared the cove, memory spiralled to the night he had visited the hotel, gone to see Arianne. To this day, he had never quite understood what had impelled him to visit her.

He thought of her often. He had felt the urge to contact her but never had. He had been afraid. She was a highly successful woman, a famous TV personality. He was only an orphan. They belonged to different worlds. The craving to see her remained strong and, when he had become successful himself, he had nearly plucked up the courage to contact her. He had sat in his office all morning, his hands resting on the keyboard, staring at a blank Word document, until he had finally picked up the phone and dialled her office number. The moment Arianne's secretary answered the phone he had hung up.

The gap between their worlds had narrowed but, deep inside he still believed himself to be the orphan he had been when they had first met. Another chance had cropped up to see her after the night he had visited her at the hotel. Alexandra had commented, casually, that Arianne would be spending a couple of days in her office. He worked in the office a couple of afternoons a week. He had not turned up until she had left town, claiming he was ill. He had already suffered enough rejection in his life. He felt guilty about lying but had no alternative; the real reason would have sounded bizarre.

The moment his car turned into the parking area, Marcus saw the receptionist was waiting for him at the entrance of the Hotel. *How did she know he would arrive at that precise moment? Who had told her to wait for him?* He thought. His imagination running riot, he controlled himself. He had waited all these years, he could wait a little longer. He followed the bubbly receptionist, through the back entrance of the hotel and into a cosy dining room adjoining the kitchen. The diligent young woman, told him to sit down, make himself comfortable and handed him a small white envelope, before she disappeared through the kitchen. The moment she was gone, a polite waiter appeared with refreshments and snacks.

Marcus stared at the envelope in his hand for a few moments, then opened it. Placing the small feather on the dining table, to one side, he read the accompanying note. As his long fingers caressed the symbolic clue, he was intrigued. Suspense his natural habitat, he could not wait to discover who 'the others' were.

*Seth stood near the window, looking out to the sea. Julia stood behind him. Neither of them spoke, they did not need to. After their last meeting, outside the convent, room number seven had become their meeting point. The portal, the room, had reinforced their affinity.*

*Thoughts of his mother suddenly invaded Seth. His mother had not mentioned the cove, the room, to him when she had confessed his atypical conception. Describing the location, had seemed a mere triviality to her. It was not until he had confided his strange connection to the room, how thinking of Julia immediately transported him to the elegant silver room to her, that she had told him. Amanda had not understood the young nun's connection to the room but had wished to see it again. She had been eager to show her son where his father had travelled to save her, given him life. She had wished to share the part of her 'other' life, she could.*

*The moment mother and son had walked into the room, they had felt the uplifting vibration. The pulsing beat in the room was different to that of their world, the mortal world. Room number seven had witnessed his conception, the fusion of two worlds. The essence of that union lingered in the room. The ethereal had synthesised with the earthly, creating a limbo space, holding the strengths of both worlds. That was why Seth felt empowered, enlightened, within its walls. Why visualising Julia took him there remained a mystery...*

*As Julia and Seth continued to watch the cove, the empty sands submersed by effulgence of moon, each knew what the other one was thinking. The time had finally arrived. There was no turning back, in only a few hours...*

*A cloud of unease hovered over Seth. The fact there had been no reaction from the realm daunted him. He was not ignorant of the ways of his world. The eye of the realm was sagacious. He had been watching the skies assiduously, but there was no trace of the celestial legion. A subtle sensation that someone was watching him, had been for some time, had recently been unnerving him. Still, he had no evidence on which to base his suspicions. He was fully conscious of the repercussions his defiance would carry. Transgressing the divine laws, this second time, would condemn him a 'fallen angel'. The supreme beings would exile him, segregate him from his family. A mortal, he would share the same world as Julia, but they would have no recollection of each other...worse still, the angelic realm would take it out on humankind. Unleash the apocalyptic riders...*

*Julia empathised with Seth as they watched the dark sea mirroring their thoughts. She felt his apprehension, his doubts, his fears...his solitude and wished she could pacify his soul. As her eyes roamed his back, her eyes rested on the flaccid wings, she felt his vulnerability, his faltering courage. Gently, she encircled his waist, rested her cheek on his back and held on to him tightly.*

*She had been holding his drooping torso for a while, when his body suddenly tensed and he stood tall, rigid. As his arched back had straightened, his wings had become taught, she could have sworn she could hear blood coursing his veins. For a moment, she wondered if angels had veins, blood...and realised how little she knew of the angel standing in front of her, the angel she loved...*

*Eventually, Seth turned around to face her, his eyes aflame with unparallel passion. His wings became alive, extraordinarily lustrous, its tips silver metal. As Julia moved away, his wings fanned then curved upwards, to float imperiously above him. Julia watched, fascinated, as Seth's body began to radiate light. White rays shot from his chest and his eyes blazed with cerulean flame. She delved deep into the concentrated sapphire light; she had never witnessed such zeal, fortitude. The transitory weakness was gone. He was ready.*

John concealed his patrol car behind the rubbish room, shaded by trees, at the far end of the parking lot, and waited impatiently for Slade to arrive. Fifteen minutes later, Slade's Porsche curved into the parking. The two men hurried into the Seaview. Hastily, they climbed the steps to a room, on the second floor, and waited impatiently for Sister Julia to join them. The moment she walked into the room, Slade handed her the envelope. One by one, she scanned the black-and-white prints, her back to them. As her intelligent eyes lingered on them, a hint of satisfaction touched her lips. Carefully, she placed the photographs back in the envelope.

John had no idea his photograph was one of the six concealed in the envelope. Slade had taken the secret shot the night they had slept in the cove, whilst he was asleep.

Slade had no idea his photo was in Julia's possession, that she had taken the clandestine shot a day before she had instructed him to capture 'the others'. Unlike Slade, John had not understood the Sister's curious request. Slade had told him nothing of the mysterious transformations.

Slade had been curious to discover if his photo transformed, anxious to see what the alteration would illustrate. None of the shots he had ever taken of himself had altered.

Slade had inspected the photos Julia had requested repeatedly and, though the pictures remained intact, he suspected they would not remain unchanged for long. He could not wait to find out what the miraculous mutations would depict. Before Sister Julia left the room, she handed them a second set of instructions. With nothing left to do but wait, they made themselves comfortable on the twin beds.

As both men stared up at the ceiling, they hypothesized about the extraordinary event about to befall the cove, pondered on whether they would see the feather again. The last relics of sunlight filtered obscurity, when Sister Julia returned and informed them it was time.

Minutes after she had left, John headed midway up the road, off the cove, in his patrol car wearing his uniform. Slade headed for the beach. As each was left alone at their respective posts, they wondered if the 'others' had already arrived.

Julia walked diligently down the steps to the lobby and hurried out the hotel, towards the beach. She needed a breather, a moment of solitude to untangle her feelings. As she walked down the narrow, stone path leading to the cove, she analysed the mystifying emotions that assailed her when she was close to her angel. The more she saw him, was near him, the more the feelings seemed to intensify. As she had watched his magnificent wings fan regally, hover proud, she had felt suddenly envious of the glorious plumage with silver tips, shimmering like sheets of pleated foil that gave Seth the freedom of flight. She had only travelled by plane once and the experience had been an exhilarating one. She could not wait to soar high in the heavens again. Since the liberating experience, she had felt somewhat claustrophobic being earthbound. It was a ridiculous sensation. Only birds could fly and she was no bird.

She had stepped on the sand when she saw Alexandra, curled on the beach. She seemed to be asleep. She took off her shoes, walked slowly over the humid grains in her direction, knelt down and placed her hands on her temples. She had felt her reviving migraine the minute her feet had touched the beach. After the encounter with the angel, Julia had developed 'healing hands', she could disperse her own migraines the moment her palms pressed her pounding temples. When she was certain the headache no longer threatened, she stood up over Arianne's stretching body and whispered her name.

Alexandra fluttered heavy eyelids and sleepy eyes squinted into focus. A spark of recognition lit her beautiful eyes at the sight of the black and white habit. *What was a nun doing on the beach? How did she know her name?* Uncertainly, she whispered *'who are you?'*

'*My name is Sister Julia... the time is nigh my dear*', was the curt answer. *'Please follow me',* she continued. Without waiting for Alexandra's retort, she spun around on her slender heels, swiftly tread over the damp earth and speedily ascended the dusty stone path to the hotel.

The minute Julia had begun to walk away, Alexandra rose unsteadily, dusted the sand that smeared her clothes and followed the mysterious nun inside the hotel, *'the time is nigh'* humming her ears.

She scanned the lobby for a sign of her, the nun had disappeared. A young man sat at the far end of the lobby, to the right of the counter. He seemed to have fallen asleep on the comfortable armchair. She stared at him, rubbed her eyes, then focused on him again. It was impossible. Her recent migraine was making her hallucinate.

She approached him tentatively, the hammering in her chest rocketing dangerously. She felt her knees weaken... *'It couldn't be...' 'What was Ethan doing here?'* She voiced, dumbfounded. Fighting the wave of fatigue sweeping her body, she placed a clammy hand on the reception counter in an attempt to steady herself. The moment the question had left her lips, Ethan opened his eyes. At the sight of Alexandra, he jumped in his seat, his eyes wide in disbelief, as he realized he was not dreaming. That the woman standing over him, evidently shocked, **was** Alexandra. Her eyes mirrored his confusion, as she fought for the words that remained stuck to her vocal cords. *'Alexandra is it really you? What are you doing here?'* Ethan whispered at last, his body stuck to his seat.

.Before she had time to answer, a familiar voice startled them. *'Alexandra? Ethan? What are you doing here?'* Astounded eyes darted in its direction, probed each other's in shock. They stood numb, mute, eyes swinging between each other as they tried to rationalise the implausibility of the encounter. Before their minds had time to unravel the confusing scenario, a young man appeared from a corridor at the far end of the room.

He stopped dead in his tracks as he took in the surrealist scene. They watched him in amazement until, eventually, they realised he was no longer not looking at them, but behind them. Before they had time to turn around, and find out the reason for his consternation, they heard a woman question in a tremulous voice, *'Marcus is that really you?'*

Before any of them had time to react, Julia descended the steps to the lobby and all eyes swung her way. Arianne, who had shortly managed to unlock her eyes from Marcus', froze. '*Sister Julia*' she whispered brokenly, '*what are **you** doing here?*' No one heard her. They were too engrossed watching Julia, watching each other, trying to come to terms with the outlandish coincidence, the realization they had all been concealing the same secret, that 'the others' had never been strangers... quite the contrary.

Julia rushed to the dazed group and, before anyone could voice a word, firmly instructed them to follow her. They ignored her. She had suddenly become invisible in their midst. They remained unmoving in the deafening quietude, threatening reproach. Guilt, apprehension, shaded their eyes as they questioned each other, justified themselves silently.

Julia repeated the command, her tone inflexible and, one by one, they extricated themselves from the cord of tension binding them. Slowly, they turned to look at Julia who was already climbing the stairs.

No one spoke, asked where they were heading. The five keys in their possession revealed the destination. As Julia led the stunned group up the steps to room number seven, she smiled inwardly. As expected no one had used the key, had learned to wait, to trust. Every one of them had been a good choice.

As Michael trailed behind the confused, yet expectant group, he struggled to remember where he had seen Sister Julia. Her face seemed extremely familiar.

*Seth remained by the window. As he watched the undisturbed night, inhaled the tangy sea breeze, listened to the nigh time chorus of waves, gently crushing on the shore, he had never felt so alive. His heartbeat pounded fiercely in his chest as the planet, that had witnessed his creation, whispered encouragement. He had never felt so revitalised, his soul resplendent, as he harmonised with universal calling.*

*The time had come to put the final part of the plan into action. Julia had been a formidable executor, had carried out his bidding to perfection. Her advice had been invaluable. Angels understood the spiritual connotations of the mortal world, prosaic matters were out of their depth. He would have been unable to accomplish the quest without her. She was a surprisingly knowledgeable and judicious woman. Her investigative work had been diligent, faultless. Seth had given Julia clues to their identities, but she had accomplished the rest. She had followed each clue meticulously, until she had finally tracked them all down. Arianne had been the exception. Julia had not needed to search for her. She had known from the onset who Seth had been referring to.*

*Her investigations had revealed secrets, secrets about to be exposed. Julia had discerned the immediate pattern. They were all connected. She had scanned records, travelled to the places where they had lived, still lived. Met the people they had known, knew, until she possessed an exact blue print of their lives. She was also a link in the chain of life that connected them. The fact they all resided in her immediate world, were connected to the same city, was not coincidental.*

*Seth could not wait to meet the seven mortals that had visited him in his dreams. He could not wait to meet the men and women who were about to help him propagate his vision for the world. Julia had shared with him every detail of the mortals' lives. He was aware of the repercussions his feather had had on their lives, how his unsuspecting 'ally' had changed them, the world around them.*

*He understood the choice. They were good people. Good people in essence, who had strayed from their truth, the light, for a while...some, more than others.*

*The pain of the past had determined the paths they had embarked on, the wrongful choices they had made. Their suffering, the suffering of those around them, had made them lose faith...*

*The feather, had shown them another way, had rekindled hope. The divine gift had touched their soul, awakened them to the distant memory of the source. As they had changed course, stepped on the path of the light, their true nature, their innermost dreams, had materialised. The realisation of those dreams making them key players in the mission they were about to accomplish.*

*However, the tragedy they had suffered as children was the 'real' connection. The common denominator would ultimately enable them to understand the reason, the climax, of the journey. The blue prints of their lives had given Seth the definitive clue.*

*His feather had cleansed their souls, eliminated tormentuous childhood memories, all trace of pain. Darkness, the negative pall, lifted from their souls, their spirits had elevated unrestrained to a higher spiritual frequency, been 'awakened'.* **They** *were the testimony, the living proof that the vicious cycle could end.*

*Ethan had been the exception, been blessed with an ideal childhood. He was the testimony that environments, relationships, life experiences, shaped the men and women every child would become. Ethan had been chosen to reaffirm this insight. He had also been chosen for his privileged mind.*

*A sudden stir in the night made the sheer curtains, partly covering the window, usher a gust of warm air into the room. Soon the gentle breeze would turn to gale and the winds of change would finally blow a miracle of over the earth.*

*Seth braced himself for the covert mission that would be his last. For a moment, he wished his mother stood at his side. She was his pillar of strength, had always been. She was the reason he stood in that room about to defy the realm, battle to save the Earth. He would never have been able to fathom his destiny without her, her guidance had been instrumental. He was proud of his mother. Her courage reaffirmed his conviction. He wished he could have asked her to accompany him; at her side, he felt invincible. The selfish petition was out of the question, he would not allow her to sacrifice her life again. This was his war, his moment.*

*The mortals were approaching; he could sense them. The time was nigh...*

*He searched the heavens for a hint of burning light; a caution that warrior angels lurked the darkness, and then his thoughts returned to his mother. He hoped she was safe. He fervently hoped he lived up to her expectations.*

Julia climbed the wooden steps to the first floor, a silent entourage followed. She turned the key in the lock and walked inside. The moment each of them stepped into the room, they felt the purifying vibrancy suffusing the air, the peculiar resonation that had enticed them, uplifted their spirits, the first time they had set foot inside its dreamy walls. The room was exactly as they remembered, except for the hundreds of candles edging it. For a moment, they forgot their turmoil, questions, and lost themselves in memories each held of the inviting chamber.

Alexandra held her breath as she took Michael's hand. Michael held it tightly. Arianne could not get her eyes off Marcus. Marcus' eyes alternated between Arianne and Ethan. Ethan watched Marcus earnestly. No one moved, the low short breathing echoing the quiet rush of the room.

Quickly, Julia headed for the wall to the right side of the bed, retrieved a knife from the top drawer of the night table, felt the wall with her free hand and proceeded to cut a rectangle; the shape of a door. Her delicate hands tore at the silver wallpaper, peeled the layer, defined by the rectangle, to reveal a white door. Everyone stared in surprise as the word 'nursery' printed on a wooden plaque at its top. A second key turned its lock and Julia disappeared through it. The curious crowd followed her into darkness.

The moment Julia turned on the light, they scanned the room. The sign on the door had misled them; seven chairs circled the centre of the room. On each seat was a large envelope. Computer equipment stacked a desk at the far end of the room. Above it hung twelve plasma TVs, and filming equipment was propped against the wall.

They looked at each other puzzled. No one had the slightest clue what the equipment was for, what they must do, what was about to happen.

Julia instructed them to pick up the envelopes with their name and sit on the allocated chair. One by one, they sat down, waited curiously, eyes engaged on Julia, envelope in hand. A nod from Julia signalled they should open them. The unanimous expression was one of sheer confusion. The envelopes contained photographs of them, taken a couple of days before. Ethan's envelope also contained a list of written instructions he understood to perfection.

*Why did Julia have their photographs? Who had taken them?* They thought perplexed, as they studied the black and white prints. Before anyone had time to ask questions, the miracle happened.

Simultaneously, the photographs began to blur. Black and white merged to a grey mass, which lightened, sharpened, to become perfect images of their past. They stared in awe at the photographs illustrating the misery of their early lives. As sad faces stared up at them, each was reminded of the heartache, the loneliness, that had afflicted them then.

Marcus sat under a lonely tree, in an empty stone yard, his grey uniform matching his sombre expression. Arianne stared out of a window in a dilapidated building, her eyes screaming desperation. Alexandra stood haggard on the doorstep of her childhood home, dressed in black, her grief-stricken eyes fixed on oblivion. Michael was perched on the edge of a beat up sofa, in a dim lit room, desolation aging his eyes.

Julia opened the two remaining envelopes. One illustrated a boy sitting in a classroom; he was the only child in the room that did not smile, the other, a boy holding a younger girl's hand. They were dressed in black, both held red roses in their hands, their expressions reflecting excruciating sorrow.

Ethan's photo remained intact. He was the only one except of childhood trauma; his parents had been decent, loving people. Had loved him unconditionally, instilled moral values, supported his dreams. He was the perfect example of a child's sound evolution to adulthood, a noble young man with a generous soul.

Ethan looked sheepishly around the room. He felt awkward that his photograph had not altered. Guilty, he was the only one that had been spared a tragic childhood. No one noticed. They were deeply engrossed in their own images; immersed in memories of the past. Their eyes riveted on the images, they shared equal thoughts. They could no longer feel pain, the memory of pain, the destructive emotion obliterated. They were no longer those children; all trace of anguish had evaporated.

To their amazement, the images began to haze, transform again. Joyful, laughing eyes now stared up at them, all trace of sorrow expunged. Alexandra had witnessed this kind of miracle before, still, she was as stunned as the others were. They had all witnessed miracles, knew they existed but none of them had been prepared for the eloquent depiction of emotional transformation. The miracle they had just shared was testimony of their metamorphosis; the feather had purged them all.

Julia's heart warmed as she watched their spellbound expressions. Soon, they would understand the photographic phenomenon was a prelude of the miracle about to seize the world.

Julia disappeared again into room number seven, locking the door behind her. The minute they were alone, Michael, who was staring intently at Alexandra, placed his hand in the front pocket of his jeans and retrieved the tiny white feather. '*This is not the first feather...,*' he broke off, the timbre in his voice shaky. Taking a deep breath, he continued. '*I suppose it is not the first for you either*', he added, his eyes circling the room to fix on Alexandra's tear filled eyes. '*The feather came into my life a long time ago, changing my perception of the world, of life, changing me...I became a better man...*' he carried on, emotion drowning his words. '*Since then, the miracles have been many...*' he continued in short breaths. '*One of them is standing by my side...*' he trailed off. As he had uttered the last words, he had walked towards Alexandra and lovingly clasped her hand.

Alexandra had begun to cry discreetly the moment Michael had began to speak. At the touch of his hand, she had begun to cry openly. Michael placed a protective arm over her shoulder, pulled her to him so her head rested on his chest. He held her tight, her breath on his heaving chest, the room vibrating with the intense and pure emotion that bound them. Arianne had also begun to cry as she held Marcus' gaze. Ethan thought of Sydney, wishing she were standing next to him.

Suddenly, they were all speaking at once, confiding their particular encounters with the feather. As they interchanged individual experiences, everyone marvelled at the parallels in their accounts. The feather had transformed their lives, filled them all with hope, changed them into the people they should be. Miracles had been bestowed on them, on those they loved. Lifelong dreams had materialized. They had achieved success, love, and most importantly, a serenity of spirit they had never dreamt possible.

As they pondered on their journeys, they understood their life connections. They had been walking the same frequency, shared the same hopeful vision, and it was inevitable their lives had become intertwined. It was evident they had all had the chance to tell each other about the feather, and none of them had. An unspoken alliance had been forged; they had all waited for the 'right' time.

Alexandra and Michael understood they were **truly** a match made in heaven. Ethan and Marcus embraced unashamedly. The time had finally come for them to express mutual gratitude. Arianne and Marcus comprehended their connection; peace invaded their hearts as the haunting confusion dispelled.

They had been destined to meet, protect, help each other. The common journey beginning the moment the feather had touched their lives. The time was fast approaching, very soon they would find out why, what destiny had in store. Anticipation pumped their veins; they could not wait to discover what the ultimate plan was.

They had been so engrossed in their own photographs, the unexpected miracle they had just witnessed, the secrets they had unburdened, they had forgotten to enquire about the two people missing in the room. The group was incomplete.

Alexandra revealed one of the identities. She had recognized John Taylor before the photo transformed. Had collaborated with the dynamic police officer a long time ago, shared a miracle. Marcus revealed the other. The photo belonged to Slade Alston, the famous photographer. The accomplished photographer had taken his photo for several of his books. Marcus wondered fleetingly, if Slade Alston had taken the shots...if he had witnessed the miracle before.

When Julia returned, everyone inundated her with questions. She urged them gently to be patient. She understood their keyed up curiosity but they would have to wait a little while longer, until midnight.

When Julia disappeared again, they returned to their seats, tried to calm down. It was impossible; the time was 'nigh'. Michael sat beside Alexandra, an arm over her shoulder, when he suddenly remembered the dream memory had suppressed, the day he found the feather... the feather found him. The images were as lucid as day. He had dreamt of Alexandra, of the children they would bear. All trace of apprehension disappeared, whatever happened that night, they would face it together. They would be together for the rest of their lives.

Alexandra's thoughts wondered back to the Children's Home, to the image of children, flying colourful ribbons, hanging over its entrance. The involuntary image sparked her lost dream. She reached for Michael's hand, whatever happened she would never be alone.

Ethan sat alone reading the list of instructions. Something extraordinary was about to happen, something so monumental, he would be emitting it to the whole world. That he was the 'exception to the rule' was not the only reason he had been chosen. Finally, he understood why he had been divinely inspired to create Quill. He could not wait to find out what he would be transmitting to the planet at midnight.

Arianne sat beside Marcus and finally confessed the orphanage's investigation had been a ploy to see him again. Marcus confessed he had feared rejection and had deliberately stayed away. Shame no longer inhibited them. The instinctive feeling they had felt for each other finally made sense. A strong connection had existed between them. The truth revealed they felt lighter, finally at peace.

Arianne kept gazing into Marcus's dark eyes. He had changed, matured, but his eyes remained the same. They still held the broody, boyish allure she remembered. She regretted not having contacted him before, wasted time... She had been ecstatic at his success. She had bought all his books, secretly acquired every article on his many accomplishments as a writer. She had seen all his TV appearances, recorded them, seen them a hundred times. She had been tempted to interview him again, but had resisted the temptation, deciding to let sleeping dogs lie.

She felt what she had thought to be exaggerated pride at his achievements. The constant curiosity with his life did not seem so bizarre anymore. As Marcus shared the plot of his current novel, she marvelled at his enthusiasm, his passion. His books were an inspiration to humanity. Enticing narrations with a spiritual undertone, sublime messages intended to provoke inner reflection, filled with heroic characters. His first novel, 'The magic feather', was a good example. A story about an orphan girl who finds a magic feather and is taken on an exciting journey, throughout the five continents, in search of a treasure that will be of great consequence to mankind. Throughout her journey, the magical talisman empowers her to stir soul-awakening in everyone who crosses her path, in order to help her in her quest. The similarity in the story with the miraculous events in Marcus's own journey, all their journeys, was evidently no coincidence.

As Marcus continued narrating the intricacies of his new novel, she impulsively reached for his hand and caressed it gently. She studied it unconsciously, her eyes lingering on the base of his thumb. Marcus was surprised when she suddenly jerked it towards her, lowered her head to inspect it closer. Abruptly, she let it drop, nearly toppled the chair as she stood up and rushed towards the window at the end of the room. Marcus remained seated; the baffled expression on his face signifying he had no idea what had spurred her stampede.

As he watched her standing by the window, her back to him, the spastic movement of her shoulders indicated she was crying. Soon, everyone in the room was watching her, watching him. Alexandra stood up quickly and hurried towards her.

Marcus became more anxious by the minute. Arianne was inconsolable. Both women kept looking at him, whispered secretly. Michael rushed to Alexandra's side. She seemed to know the reason for Arianne's sudden distress and wished to help. Minutes later, he returned to his chair, his face shaded a mixture of incredulity and concern. He sat edgily beside Ethan, muttered something to him in a low voice and both turned to stare at Marcus.

Marcus was on the verge of screaming: '*why are you staring at me?*' Before he had the chance to voice the rapidly escalating frustration, Julia entered the room. She hurried over to the two women, clutched in a comforting embrace, and stated with unfaltering conviction, '*Yes Arianne, Marcus* ***is*** *your son.*' Marcus thought he had misunderstood her outburst but the look on everyone's faces told him her words spoke the truth.

John waited impatiently for his men to arrive. He had already barricaded the road, laid the flashlights, 'fake' guns and walkie-talkies on the open boot of his car. Julia had been adamant. No one was to trespass into the cove; if necessary, he could fire the blanks. The walkie-talkies were a backup, in case of power failure.

Julia had felt the intensifying vibration, emanating from Seth, and was unsure of the consequences his energy could have on power supply. Hence, she had instructed Ethan to purchase the powerful generator 'waiting' in the hotel's basement.

As John sat in his car, he kept eyeing the photograph Sister Julia had given him. The image had surprised him. Sister Julia was an extremely resourceful woman. He had no idea how she had been able to unearth the photograph, he could not recall the shot ever being taken. He was certain the distant image held hidden intention

Surprisingly, the image did not disturb him. He felt no hate, no rancour. The pain had disappeared; the visual recollection could not revive it. As he pondered on his early life, the life he had learned to bury, the image began to alter before his astonished gaze. The sombre expression mutated magically and a smile, mirroring those of the children sitting around him, illuminated his face. John was unprepared for the amazing transformation but was not shocked. It was not the first time darkness had been erased from his past.

Slade sat on the shore, his camera ready. As he listened to the hiss of the ocean, Arianne filled his thoughts. He hoped she had already arrived, had come. He wished to see her desperately, could not wait another minute. A sudden unnerving thought gripped him; perhaps it was another near miss... Thoughts of the impending happening were dismissed, as he reflected on the 'unlucky' possibility. He must see her. make her part of his life. He visualised her face, her eyes... For the first time in a long time, he prayed, asked his feather to grant him the possibility, counteract destiny's cruel jokes.

As he searched his bag for a spare set of batteries, he realised he had not opened the envelope Julia had given him. Trembling hands ripped it open. The photograph showed Sadie holding his hand at their parent's funeral. His eyes fixed on the red roses they carried...their mother's favourites...and he smiled. As he absorbed the image, he felt no pain only bittersweet nostalgia. He did not understand how Julia had unearthed the photo; no one took photographs at funerals. Before he had time to analyse the puzzling observation, the images began to transform.

Smiling, happy faces stared up at him and red roses now contrasted the pure white clothes that had replaced the mourning attire. Slade held the image close to his eyes; the image, evidence of the tragedy, trauma eradicated. Sadie and he had come a long way. They were no longer those children. They had learned to forgive, keep only the good memories, the love they bore the two wonderful human beings who had raised them, made them the people they were. As he inspected the image closer, he realised two cloudy, smiling faces hovered above them, and he began to cry like a child, shed the first tears since his parents had died. He gazed in wonder at his mother and father's gentle eyes. They had always been watching, protecting them from heaven. At that instant, he realised he no longer feared death. His parents would be waiting for him when his time came...

As he lingered on his mother's face he realised, in astonishment... Arianne had her beautiful eyes...

*Seth was sitting on the bed when Julia entered the room again. He was deep in meditation, elevating his vibration, preparing himself for the strenuous exercise he was about to perform. The spectacular vision awed Julia; silver lights danced around him, swept over his body, over his outstretched wings. The silvery shimmers merged to form a single glowing, white light that floated above his head. For a while, it hovered there, and then elongated vertically to spear him, eyes closed. Slowly, his body began to elevate. He hovered in the lotus position, approximately a metre from the bed, as the light contracted then stretched to form a translucent bubble around him. Silver and white lights began to dance inside the floating bubble until both hues merged to become an intense white light. After a few moments, the blinding light shrank to become a glowing, silver orb, twenty-five centimetres in diameter.*

*The resplendent ball floated to the centre of his chest, then suddenly disappeared inside it. Slowly, Seth floated back on the bed and opened his eyes. The moment he partly lifted his eyelids, sapphire beams shot under them, to illuminate the room a bluish hue. When his eyes had opened wide, the beams contracted, and his iris became sapphire flame.*

*In one thrust, his wings spanned, curved up to the ceiling, his chest roaring with the thunder of a hundred drums. Julia was afraid it would explode in his chest. His wings moved up and down to the rhythm of the thumping beat, until the flapping and pounding became one. Unexpectedly, the wings dropped, hang inert at his sides. The beating in his chest settled and the room returned to silence. Still mesmerised by the magical scene, Julia stood quietly by the door, gazing at him, oblivious to the fact she had just witnessed Seth's two worlds merge into one.*

*Julia suddenly began to feel faint thus stood against the wall. She felt warm. Her own chest had begun to beat fiercely and her body to shudder. Seth watched her aghast. He knew the mortal shell was fragile...something was wrong with Julia. He rushed towards her but, before he could reach her, Julia slumped to the floor.* **This could not be happening, not now. It was his fault. Julia had been standing too close. He had been careless, had not anticipated the intense vibration could harm her...***he thought to himself desperately, as he placed his hands on her chest.*

*Remembering the healing technique, he had learned on the Islands, his palms travelled up and down her body shedding a violet light. Julia remained unresponsive and panic gripped him. He needed her. She was vital to his plan, to him. Julia lay on the floor, unconscious, her breathing a whisper her heartbeat a murmur. Seth placed his hands on her chest, closed his eyes tight and the light intensified. Julia remained corpse still.*

*He was about to scream her name, when the sound of flapping startled him. Alarmed, he swung his head in the direction of the window.* **They had found him...**

*Seth feared the warrior angels had finally emerged from their hideouts, intending to detain him... he was proved wrong. He was both shocked and relieved to find his mother standing in the room.*

*Amanda flew swiftly towards the edge of the sphere. She could not believe she had been so blind...Seth had spoken of her many times...*

*She was a fool. She would never forgive herself. The price she had paid for her reckless disobedience was higher than she could have ever imagined. She hoped it was not too late. She hoped there was still time... As she flew through the gritty layer, she kept looking behind her. No one followed her. She must reach the cove. She must find them before the realm found her....*

*She had just crossed into the mortal world, when a deep, and disconcerting, emotion wrenched her soul. The twisting, pulling feeling turned quickly to dread. Before she had time to process the confusing and disquieting sensation, a blinding light engulfed her and she had to shut her eyes. The moment she perceived the light had vanished, she opened them. She was floating over the cove, a short distance from the hotel. Without time to analyse what had happened, she darted in through the familiar window, on the first floor. The moment she saw Julia lying on the floor, she understood the force that had transported her to the room.*

*Quickly, she rushed over to Seth, pushed him gently to one side, knelt on the floor beside Julia and placed one of her hands on her forehead, the other on Seth's chest. To Seth's astonishment, Julia began to flutter her eyelids the moment her body absorbed the powerful light, emanating from his chest, sieved through his mother to her forehead. In minutes, Julia regained consciousness, breathing became regular and her heartbeat stable.*

*After she had absorbed the luminous energy for a few minutes, Julia felt strong enough to stand, and with Seth's help, managed to walk slowly towards the bed. Seth helped her lie down and covered her with the sliver bedspread. Her eyelids had suddenly begun to feel heavy and in seconds, she was peacefully asleep.*

*Seth starred at his mother questioningly.* ***What was his mother doing here? What was wrong with Julia? His***

**mother's propitious appearance could not be a coincidence.** *Seth sensed she had come to protect Julia.* **But why...?** *He thought, bewildered as he bolstered himself for more revelations. Confounded, he watched his mother caress Julia's face; an expression of absolute tenderness, revealed the nun was no stranger to Amanda. He did not understand why his mother had never mentioned her. He had told her about the dreams, his visions of her. He had told her of their encounters, how thinking of her had opened a portal to the earth, and she had said nothing. When his mother finally raised her eyes, confronted his baffled expression, answered his questions, he realised she had not known of her existence until very recently.*

*Seth could not believe what his mother was telling him. He could not comprehend why their lives had been riddled with so many secrets. His mother's rushed words, again, yielded understanding. The feather was not the only entity connecting him to earth. A stronger force had pulled him inexorably to the mortal planet. As his mother confided the feelings of emptiness, she had felt for so long, the unflagging sensation something was missing in her life, he had understood. An inexplicable void, a feeling of desertion he could not quite define, had accompanied him as long as he could remember. It was as if something life sustaining, a piece of him, was missing. At last, he understood the force of his emotion, the unfathomable magnetism, the furore of wholeness he felt in the presence of the young woman asleep on the bed.*

*He had been blind. He had neglected the signs. The truth had lain before him and he had been unable to see it. He had failed to recognise her, decipher the nature of their connection, remember they had been bound to each other before either of them had been born.*

*Amanda looked at her son with rising concern. For the first time in her life, she was unsure what to do, say. She knew Seth was having a hard time processing this last revelation, but it was crucial he knew Julia's identity, that Julia knew. They knew now. Culpability, anxiety, ravaged Amanda, she had defied the realm, had placed her family in jeopardy. Silently, she prayed that neither Seth nor Julia had to pay for her sins a second time…*

*Time was running out. The realm would be hunting her, hunting them. As she reproduced her last thought, she realised it was strange the Warrior Angels had not tried to curb their rebellion... time was their enemy. They must wake Julia. Tell her the truth...*

*When Julia opened her eyes, she saw the angels contemplating her. The female angel was as beautiful as Seth was. Her soft long feathers seemed more delicate, unlike Seth's, her airy appendages were wholly white. The resemblance between them was extraordinary; the same pellucid blue eyes, golden hair, except hers cascaded below her waist.* **Every angel must look like this...** *she thought dreamily. Heaven must be a beautiful place... As the female angel caressed her hand, she smiled up at her, musing what her connection to Seth was, what she was doing in the room...The featherlike fingers made her flesh tingle, and a mellow feeling invaded her heart. She closed her eyes and pandered to the gratifying feeling. She felt dizzy, strangely elated. After a while, the prickling sensation amplified. Deeper, more powerful emotions claimed her. The intense feelings equalled those Seth's presence induced.* **Angels had a potent effect on mortals,** *she thought vaguely, the commanding emotions feeling too overpowering for comfort.*

*Amanda strove to find the right words. As delicately as she could, she began to deliver the truth to Julia. Seth remained solemnly quiet by her side, his eyes on Julia. Julia listened in amazement to the words spouting from the angel's mouth. She did not understand...could not quite grasp what she was saying. The scene was surreal, was not happening. She was still asleep, dreaming. She shut her eyes tight, reopened them. The female angel was still there. It was no dream. Desperately, she looked at Seth, willed him to voice another reality. Seth remained silent, his dour expression confirming the female angel was saying the truth. It could not be. She was mistaken. She was Julia, had always been...*

*Amanda felt Julia's distress, denial, but her words kept deluging the room. By the time Amanda had imparted the full confession, Julia knew the angel was saying the truth, a truth she had held deep in her soul, a truth she had always known but had forgotten, been made to forget...*

*Seth and Amanda stared earnestly at each other then turned to search Julia's eyes. Julia sat on the bed, her eyes furrowed broodingly as her arms crossed over her chest, clutched her shoulders. A torrent of thoughts entered her head, never to return in the same way...*

*No one spoke; Julia needed to come to terms with the earth shaking admission. Her world had suddenly been turned upside down...her world was no longer her world.... Amanda knew the repercussions of knowing the truth, the transformation that would ensue, and hoped it was a timely one. Her son needed all the help he could get.*

*When she had managed to calm down a little, Julia got up from the bed, walked slowly towards the window and looked down at the familiar sea, the shadowed cove, embracing the changeless surroundings. Her world seemed intact on the surface...*

*As she crossed the room, she avoided eye contact with the angels. She was not ready... She took a deep breath, closed her eyes again and, for a moment, wished she was back at the convent. The convent...now more than ever she understood her calling, understood why she had been so different to other girls her age, but she could have never imagined those differences would turn out to be so drastic. As she endeavoured to process the truth of her nature, a sense of liberation engulfed her. Despite her confusion for the first time in her life, she felt wholly at peace with herself.*

*She had often wished she had not been a disappointment to her parents, that she could have fulfilled their aspirations, lived the kind of life they had wished for her. At that moment, she felt immense relief. Selfishness, stubbornness, were not the reasons she had defied them. She had never had a choice. The choices she had made were those she had been destined to make. Her early vocation had been no infantile whim; the reaffirmation of that vocation in adolescence had been no quixotic pursuit. Becoming a nun had felt her natural path, devoting her life to spiritual endeavours soothed her yearning soul. God had not been 'calling' her when he had whispered her name, he had been reminding her…her 'blind' faith was not the result of spiritual strength, constant prayer. She had never been blind. The feather entering her life suddenly took an entirely different perspective. It had found its way to her for a different reason to the others. It had been travelling home...*

*For a moment, Julia wished the revelation had been possible at another time, a quieter time. Her emotions were in turmoil. She wished to express, question, so many things...there was no time. She had a mission to accomplish. Seth needed her. Quickly, she turned around and faced her angels. 'We are running out of time' she stated, determined.*

When Julia returned to the room she headed straight for Marcus and Arianne. Julia understood they had much to speak about, resolve, but there was no time. The summit was about to begin. Arianne had stopped crying but remained distraught. Julia understood her frustration, her pain, her anger. She had thought her son safe, had believed he was living the life she had wished for him, the life she had been deprived of.

The immeasurable joy she felt knowing Marcus was her son was blackened by the knowledge of his heartbreaking childhood. She felt tremendous guilt for having abandoned him. She should have protected him, never have allowed her fears to blind her. Marcus' tragic past was her fault...her sacrifice had not only been in vain, it had condemned him...

Marcus could not believe Arianne was his mother. He had a mother. The feather could not have blessed him more. Arianne's explanations had been unnecessary. Her reaction exonerated her from sin.

Arianne's eyes burned into Julia's, explanations were necessary; she prayed she could exonerate her from all sin.

Julia ignored Arianne's accusatory stare. Explanations would have to wait. It was time.... As she explained each of their roles, they nodded in affirmation. They were ready.

Michael and Alexandra helped Arianne carry the filming equipment. Arianne was expecting her filming crew at any moment. Her text message had been clear. *Seaview Hotel, 11.30pm, tell no one, scoop of the century!* They would be the only ones crossing John's barrier. The filming equipment they had found in the room was the back-up plan. Michael prayed the camera men would make it on time; he was no expert.

Slade was busy on the beach lighting the hundreds of candles laid out near the shore. The steady flames, curving inwards towards the sea, suffered no threat, the eerie stillness a blessing. As he crawled across the sand, sparking the five-lined curvature, he was amazed to find that the level layer of sand surrounding each candle was intact. As John and he had dug the long, wax cylinders into the cove early at dawn, they had thought the monotonous task futile. The winds would bury them. The sea would swallow them up. People would steal them. The odd array would raise suspicions… Julia had laughed at their vehemence, reprimanded them gently for their lack of faith, and hung up the phone. It had taken them four hours to complete the task. The cove had remained uncannily windless, abnormally empty. The moment they had embedded the last candle in the sand, they had received a text message from Julia: *Another Miracle? Lol!*

There was a strange buzz in the air, the sea was extraordinarily still and the full moon unnaturally luminous. Her glowing face seemed to smile knowingly...hearts pumped with excitement as they headed impatiently for the candlelit shore. Arianne's distress had subsided. *She would have time to speak to Julia later…Julia was incapable of betrayal….there had to be a coherent reason for the cruel travesty..an absolving one ... She was thankful to God... he had saved her again, had imprinted her mark on her son, so she could find him...*

Marcus could not help a faint smile as he walked proudly beside his mother. His mother...the words were inconceivable. Marcus' imagination had concocted myriad, climaxing scenarios; none of them included finding his mother. He finally had roots, a surname...

Michael and Alexandra walked ahead, holding hands. Neither Michael nor Alexandra could get over the fact they had unsuspectingly been allies. That their journeys had been secretly parallel, that and were standing on the same cove where they had met, to witness the mystical journey's climax. They would have an amazing story to tell their children, their grandchildren, someday…

Ethan was busy up in the room connecting computer equipment. He had already instructed his team of geniuses to make the necessary adjustments to the user interface, Quill. He had called ten of his most talented recruits back to work. None of them refused.

The last time Julia had returned to the room they had been shocked to find she had discarded her habit and was instead wearing a casual pair of pants and sweater. To everyone's surprise, beautiful golden hair fell, in soft curls, below her waist. Her eyes seemed peculiarly resplendent. All of them agreed there was an almost ethereal quality about her, that she was too beautiful to be a nun.

Michael's mission had been the most challenging. He had succeeded. In only a couple of hours he had a fleet of executives at Quill acquire ten of the best legal firms in the country and merged them into one. The largest and most prodigious team in the nation, probably the world, awaited instructions inside the sophisticated realty acquisition Quill had ever made. The 'intelligent' colossus had coincidentally completed construction a month before. Quill's bid for the building had been the highest. The building had been empty, perfect, waiting... He had also hired expert personnel in a variety of fields and supporting services, i.e. elite security, caterers, cleaners, maintenance and so forth. The contracts required they live in the installations, and could not leave the building until further instruction, probably for months. The latter had deterred no one from making the commitment, in a few months they would earn what most earned in a lifetime.

*Amanda wished she could have remained in the cove, helped her son, help Julia, but knew it was better for all concerned that she return home, lured the celestial force to the valley. As she had flapped her wings noisily over the crimson field, the sparkling forest, Julia's confused eyes had haunted her. She had wished so much to take her in her arms, tell her how much she had missed her…she had wished to say so many things…sudden panic gripped her. She would never see her again….*

*When she reached the valley, there was no sign of commotion, the atmosphere intriguingly ordinary. As she entered the cottage, Anton's greeting told her he was blissfully unaware of any trouble. Strange, she thought, that no one had come, that there was still no reaction from the higher echelons of the realm.*

*As she sat on the porch praying, debating whether to shoot into the sky and return to the cove, she was unaware of the three pairs of eyes watching her, watching her son, watching Julia, observing humanity from the Sky Dwellings...*

Julia glanced at her watch; it was eleven thirty. They had exactly thirty minutes before the World Summit began. It would be a long time before the world saw an assembly of such calibre again. The intention was to 'gatecrash' the powerful reunion the moment it began. The media had been announcing the important gathering for months, had commented on the rumours echoing the corridors of powers, claiming unprecedented collaboration between countries was on the cards. Though everyone hoped radical, constructive changes ensued, that world leaders finally came up with 'the' master plan that would cure the rampant recession, the evils afflicting the earth, most were wary. Politicians had lost credibility a long time ago. History spoke for itself. The world was chaos.

Ethan was busy checking data on computer screens. The TV screens, hanging above him, displayed alternating news channels from across the world. The moment Ethan heard Julia come in, he swivelled on his armchair and informed her he was ready to go at a touch of a button. The truth was it had not been easy. He was fortunate Quill had the best minds on the field. Together with their genius leader, they had been able to alter the innovative software they had recently developed to suit Ethan's request. The latter was a powerful weapon, a destructive one in the wrong hands.

Ethan had already made plans for its extermination when the mission was over. He had taken drastic precautions, isolating his collaborators, so no one except him had the full version. He had tested the virus the night before and was amazed at how quickly the deadly parasite rid the cyber world of immorality; whole websites dedicated to the propagation, decadence, forever.

Julia checked skeleton staff had left, no one had intruded the hotel. When she had inspected every inch of the building she headed for the parking lot, secured the gates and made her way down to the beach to join the others.

When the emotionally charged group set foot on the cove, they noticed someone stood on the edge of the flaming shore. Marcus, who walked ahead of the crowd, recognised him immediately. It was Slade Alston. Slade remained on the edge of the sea, waiting for the silent group to near him. The moment he saw Arianne's beautiful face his pulse raced, and the familiar quiver usurped his heart. Despite the histrionic atmosphere, he racked his brain for a witty line...he could not find the words. As the silent group neared him Arianne rushed to catch up with Marcus and took his hand. He felt his heart drop and cursed destiny for scorning him again. Dark disappointment hooded his eyes as he stood, his feet immersed in the shallow and unusually warm waters, hoping Arianne would not detect his discomfort.

Slade watched their shadowed faces; they all seemed to recognise him. Sister Julia must have told them his was one of them that John was up on the slope, guarding the cove. Arianne was the third to offer her hand, speak her name. At the sound of her creamy voice, at the touch of her soft hand, his heart lurched and he felt himself blush. *Thank God for the darkness, he* thought, holding on to her hand longer than necessary. Quickly, Arianne, who did not realise the two men already knew each other, introduced Marcus.

As the small crowd walked away from him, to stand a short distance away from the shore, he kept reliving Arianne's words. '*This is Marcus…my son...*' The words had been manna to his ears. He would never have guessed. She seemed too young to be his mother.

Thankfully, Arianne's crew arrived on time and Michael kept voicing relief. The task mercifully delegated to expert hands. Everything was as should be. The crescent of flickering lights by the shore set the scene perfectly, thought Julia. Seth would be pleased. Her…..the female angel, would be pleased. She could not bring herself to voice the word….she was not ready.

They stood in a row in the centre of the cove. Their faces bathed in the soft glow sketching the shore a short distance away. Everyone kept glancing at Julia, who was standing a few meters from them watching the sky. They huddled closer, joined hands as the unnaturally quiet cove murmured quiet exultation.

As Julia kept vigilant eyes on the heavens she felt momentarily queasy. A strange sensation accompanied the woozy feeling. The shocking disclosure was taking its toll; ostensible serenity did not reflect the inner turmoil she grappled hard to conceal. A strange numbness spanned the length of her spine transitorily. *She must have hurt herself when she fainted to the ground,* she reasoned.

Everyone continued to side-glance Julia, trying to discern a flicker of anticipation, confirmation the 'happening' was imminent. Her stoical expression revealed nothing. Julia had been disconcerted at their reactions. She had been expecting them to bombard her with questions the moment they had set foot on the beach. Interrogations never came. She explored their faces; they were impatient yet calm, curious yet trusting. Their mystical journeys had begun a long time ago. They had learned not to question. Accept, flow with the will of the universe. Julia had instructed them to be silent, to look beyond the dancing lunate lights, the restful seas.

The filming crew was ready. Three cameras zoomed in on the sea, from different angles. Arianne reluctantly disentangled herself from Marcus' hand and positioned herself in front of the centre camera, barely meters from the kindling rows. Slade was eager, camera on tripod, ready to immortalise the miracle. Michael, Alexandra and Marcus continued to huddle, hold each other's hands. Julia could not help grinning as she noticed the white feathers pinned to their chests. A fitting homage, she mused.

*Seth bolstered himself for the imminent revelation. He had concluded another powerful meditation; he felt strong, determined to take on the greatest challenge he would probably ever face. The time for reckoning had arrived; humanity would soon face a choice of mammoth consequence, the most important choice they had ever had to make.*

*Thoughts of the dire consequence his deed would bear invaded him again. Without doubt, the aftermath would be brutal. He pushed the cataclysmic thoughts from his mind. He had already accepted his fate. That his mother and Julia suffered heaven's nemesis was the one thing clouding his resolve. He would do his utmost to protect his mother, protect Julia, when the time came. He would claim he had stolen the sacred book, that his mother was only responsible for returning it; protecting him…that Julia was unaware of her nature, a mortal he had coerced... he would spare them retribution. He would find a way…*

*As he stood again by the window, tracing the light delineating the shore, the backdrop to his earthen debut, he had no regrets, remained steadfast in his conviction. He was doing the right thing. Deep in his soul, he knew his actions served the highest intention. It was unfortunate the world that had seen him grow did not share his hopes for the world that had seen his soul born.*

*He had not chosen to be different, his destiny, to be part of two worlds. He loved his two worlds; the immaculate beauty and peace of the realm, the raw beauty and unpredictability of the earth; the serenity and excellence of angels, the passion and vulnerability of mortals.*

*He hoped to triumph, shake humanity. Awaken them to a higher understanding of universal law, help them take the first steps towards an optimistic future; put an end to earthly tribulation. He hoped to show the realm they were wrong…*

*To a mighty sweep of his wings, he jumped off the windowsill and darted high above the cove*

Muffled fluttering broke the calm hush of the beach. The flickering flames, the semi circle of candlelight, began to elongate, sway energetically despite the uncanny absence of wind. In seconds, the blazing lights widened, merged into one, creating a flaming crescent which reflected back from the sea to form an illusionary circle of fire. The flapping began to gather momentum and thunderous batting resonated above the ocean. No one moved; all eyes riveted on the jet-black horizon, the incandescent orb suspended in night cast with exotic shadows. In minutes, the beating sound hovered over the circling blaze unsettling the sea below, until its epicentre began to swirl frantically.

It was an unearthly sight; the sea outside the glowing edge was dead still, contrasting ponderously with the turbulent whirl. The new moon had shed its shadowing veil and a column of light beamed down the horizon, spilled onto the sea, travelling in a straight line to join the burning circle.

Arianne's crew had begun filming, the unusual landscape already delivering amazing footage. The enthralling scenery befitted the bewitching narrator, captivating the unprecedented audience with her velvety voice, readying the world for the unparalleled event about to be witnessed. As Arianne had repeated the words Julia had written minutes before, she wondered what her viewers would think if they knew she was as clueless as they were, as impatient to find out what the unimaginable event was.

The moment stifled flapping had broken the silence, they had suspected who the mysterious visitor might be. The rising, batting sound was a dead giveaway. They could not wait to confirm their suspicion as modest fingers caressed the feather on their chests. Soon, the flapping subdued and the peaked sea tamed until it was mirror still. The perfect dark ring, edged by fire, began to dye a golden hue, reflecting the glow that had suddenly appeared a few meters above it. The liquid mirror reflected the intense light, the sudden burst of blinding rays stretching to double its circumference. The dark silhouettes edging the fulgent shore stood motionless, holding their breath as they processed the amazing spectacle. Glad that of all the people on earth, they were the chosen.

The dazzling rays lit up the entire cove, transforming the sea a remarkably translucent turquoise, the night an electric orange and golden-streamed sky. Ivory sands were speckled with a twinkling allure. As the privileged witnesses drank the hypnotising scene, they all shared the same thought; they were standing on a tiny bit of heaven.

Everyone felt the swelling buzz in the air as a form began to emerge at the centre of the radiant star. Slowly, a tall white figure appeared at the centre of the scorching light and began to float leisurely towards them. As the image became clearer, they saw he was male. Golden curls floated in the nonexistent wind to reach his strong sinewy shoulders. He was nude except for the white cloth that swathed his hips. The perfectly chiselled body resembled that of a Greek God, except his smooth torso had no navel. The flawlessly contoured face, the aquiline nose, was that of an Adonis. A condensed blue glow emanated from under his eyelids. As he opened his eyes slightly, burning sapphire rays were unleashed and then dulled revealing mesmeric, translucent, turquoise eyes that matched the sea beneath him. He was the most beautiful being anyone had ever encountered.

He hovered above the fiery ring, staring directly at the centre camera for a few moments. He probed the lens, he probed humanity, then closed his eyes. Suddenly, he threw his head back to face the heavens and brusquely raised his arms. Two magnificent wings, tipped in silver sprung from behind him to float proudly over his head. The world stared in wonder at the impressive, pure wings that seemed to have been cut out of wax and dipped in silver. The stately plumage bowed high up over his head then out to his sides, to span the ten meters of burning circle. They levitated regally against the enthralling backdrop, gracefully in the warm breeze that gently rocked the ocean. All eyes remained fastened on the heavenly visitor, entranced by his spectacular beauty, his spellbinding eyes. He had the kindest gaze and the gentlest smile they had ever witnessed.

The camera crew had stopped filming, visibly nervous. They were about to deposit their cameras on the sand when a gentle nod from the mystical creature's head assured them they could continue recording. Slade was unperturbed, his mind still on Arianne, and the beautiful hands that had pinned a feather to his chest. The impromptu brooch had confirmed his suspicions that they had all received the feather. He was ready, camera in hand, camera on tripod, ready to catch the most momentous images of his life.

Seth's eyes roved over each of them and smiled conspiratorially as he noticed the feathers pinned to their chests. Arianne and Alexandra were crying unashamedly. The men were finding it hard to fight the tears threatening to spill down their manly cheeks. It was the most awe-inspiring moment of their lives. Everyone standing on the diamond-speckled sands was a lucky eyewitness to the final confirmation that heaven existed, that their lives did not end upon earthen soil.

Ethan watched the inspiring vision emerging from the monitors and plasma screens in the room, and wished he were standing in the cove with the others. Watching the angelic apparition on screen was not comparable. At the first hint of flutter, he had pushed the first button and had watched, in silent pride, as the breathtaking and astounding scene replaced every satellite emission in the world, every computer screen in the world. At the touch of the second button, the virus had been launched and the virtual highway almost immediately, radically cleansed of evil. One of the plasma screens remained tuned to Channel 6; the reporter covering the world summit had confirmed the crucial meeting had begun. Leaders of every nation had attended, were already deep in session.

In minutes, Arianne was the most famous newscaster on the planet. Her beautiful face captivated the billions of incredulous people engrossed on the magical landscape; her narration of the events, of the impending culminating moment, had all eyes glued to the cove.

As Ethan listened to leading radio channels, he was aware the commotion the images were creating, the furore unprecedented. Everything was going according to plan. The moment the visitor had begun to speak he had quickly turned up the volume. Within moments the mesmerising voice echoed throughout the room, resonated throughout the planet. On the basement stood the huge generator, plan B. The remote switch lay on his desk. Nothing had been left to chance.

Seth spoke carefully, deliberately, as he faced the cameras; his windows to the world. He spoke in their language, in all their languages, a faint, high-pitched sound echoing in its wake. His beautiful, pellucid, blue eyes were overwhelmingly gentle, yet overpoweringly intent, as he began to deliver his message.

Equably, he began to narrate his first contact with the mortal world to the rapt audience: he had only been a young angel, when he had his first glimpse of the earth, crossed the frontier into their world. What he had witnessed had perturbed him deeply, he explained...plunged him into unimaginable sorrow. As he had watched humanity his soul had bled, the devastating and incomprehensible images tormenting it to this day.

For a few moments, the Messenger remained silent as intent, turquoise eyes permeated the visual membranes, and the world held its breath. When he began to speak again, his tone had changed. It was deeper, graver. Solemnly, he told an astounded world of his desire. He wished every inhabitant in the planet, every single mortal, had stood in his shoes when he had intruded onto their world.

He wished they had witnessed the prevalent chaos. The atrocities committed by its inhabitants through objective, alien eyes...

Like him, they would have been appalled at the insanity, the unnecessary devastation, the self-inflicted and damaging emotions that inundated the hearts of men. Like him, they would have questioned the need for so much destruction, man's blindness to the futility of war, the capricious and malicious annihilation of life. Like him, they would have questioned man's permissiveness to the destruction of the planet, their only home... Like him, they would have been horrified at the failure of its inhabitants to protect the vulnerable, the innocent; their legacy, their only hope for a future. His tone lowered a few more decibels, became grimmer, as he cautioned he was alone in his quest, that he had no allies in the angelic realm. The Supermalls; non tangible beings of golden light closest to the source, to God, those that reigned in his world, no longer held hope for man, believed in their capacity to evolve, guide the world into a future of light. The conviction had proliferated. Humankind had no allies.

The angelic realm had waited and waited, had hoped the following century brought about the necessary change, the leap of man to a higher spiritual consciousness. The centuries had rolled by. One war had led to another. Powerful countries continued to prey on vulnerable ones. Greed and selfishness plagued the planet. A planet its inhabitants had not had the foresight, the inclination, to protect. Many species had been damned to extinction, contravening natural balancing laws. Oceans drained of life. The ozone layer destroyed due to pollution, despite advances in technology. Trees, the lungs of the earth, were unscrupulously torn from the earth they nourished. Mother Nature had begun to rebel, meteorological incongruities that had already resulted in multiple ongoing catastrophes across the planet were fast becoming a threat of apocalyptic dimensions...

A guilty world, a fearful and stunned world, listened to the soul-searching words, to the beautiful ethereal creature delivering the poignant message from the golden, streaked skies. Slowly, he hung his head, became silent once more as the gleaming feathery appendages drooped slightly. Again, the world held its breath...waited in suspense for the celestial messenger to lift his head, confront their eager eyes, to speak. Seth remained silent, looking down on the dead calm, on the smouldering ring that had turned as dark as his eyes. The golden light that surrounded him had begun to diminish, waver in intensity, until he finally whispered '*time is running out*' in a weary voice...

Collective dread gripped civilization as the dooming words echoed the planetary hush. Global hysteria lurked in every corner of the globe as humanity digested the veracity of his statement, as widespread introspection sustained his fatidic deliverance. *'The vicious circle must be stopped...'* he whispered, after what seemed to a despondent world as eons. *'...if man is to survive...,'* he continued, visibly drained.

Silence invaded the cove, the world again, and a multitudinous, multiracial audience gasped for breath once more. Mercifully, they did not have to suffer the agony of silence much longer. The golden light that surrounded the angel began to grow in intensity. In moments the spiking rays had lengthened, regained its initial luminosity. Fiery tongues sprouted the falcate shore until the golden light, hovering meters above the dark ocean, again mirrored its blazing core. The shadowy skies regained the heavenly sunset layered hues and the docile seas recaptured its cerulean vibrancy. In one brisk movement, the magnificent silver-rimmed wings spanned wide, taut as the spiritual advocate lifted blazing sapphire eyes to penetrate the world again.

His firm voice, echoing with a higher pitch, broke the daunting silence as the world braced itself for more revelations. He spoke clearly, unwaveringly, his tone gentle yet stringent... He had come to save the children...

He had trespassed into their world with a sole intent; he would deliver the vulnerable from the clutches of a dissolute world that no longer protected them. He must safeguard humanities' legacy if a world that swung on the precipice of destruction was to earn salvation, continue existing...

The earth's children had come to him, visited his dreams. The survival instinct of young souls had tuned to his spiritual resonance, to the vibration of pure love and hope he held for their world. The visionary catalysts had enlightened him, had helped him decipher where the only chance of humanity lay...

Children could not continue to grow up in a world beleaguered with violence, with depravity. They could not evolve into the same violent, depraved men and thus condemn humankind. The innocent could not continue to suffer, to die idle deaths, for it was in them that the goodness of humanity lay. It was in early souls, souls unconquered by the destruction of ego, souls that echoed with the truth of their origins, were attracted to the light of the source, that hope for the world prevailed...

If that light, surviving in early souls, continued to dim, afflicted by a world that did not encourage its propagation, the earth would remain the dark place it had become and ultimately cease to exist. Man must create a new world; attain the high-intentional global consciousness that would elevate the planet to the spiritual dimension that ensured its perpetuity. Adults no longer held the power to do this; they had long fallen prey to the egoistic antics of the ego, surrendered to the temptations of fallen angels who had infiltrated their world when its frequency was weak, when the light of their souls had dimmed down to a flickering speck.

For hope to manifest, he would erase all past suffering from children's memory, every recollection of violence, every negative emotion from their young souls so the light in their souls burned pure, burned unprecedentedly bright to become the resplendent beacon that would light man's path to a confident future.

Only children would be cleansed, man would not be exonerated of their responsibility; salvation would not be handed on a silver platter. The universe would not breach the timeless laws that dictated evolution; a consequence of lessons learned. Man would need to overcome the millenary decrees, would have to vow protection of the light, prove worthy of the divine gift. Failure to do so would result in dire consequences for humankind. He had seen the future and it was bleak.

The planet watched in trepidation as the dazzling apparition delivered his ultimatum. The purity of his wings was almost blinding as he lifted them to hover above his head, plunge them suddenly to lift him high in the air. Billions watched, enthralled, as he soared swiftly over the coral golden skies, as the silver tipped wings etched a glittering signature in the remarkable backdrop. He looped the sunset skies that had claimed night and then unexpectedly dived back to float meters above the water, nearer to the shore. A dumbstruck audience gazed at the diamond letters, suspended high above his head, and the world whispered the name of their one and only ally...

Myriad eyes darted up and down screens, traced his name high in the sky then sank down to the airy mass of feathers, suspended metres above the glassy aquamarine ocean. The sea swirled vigorously, creating a raging gust that extinguished the burning ring. As Seth flexed his wings high, a rain of feathers detached itself from his winged span. As the imposing wings plunged low, new feathers emerged instantly. The svelte, lambent plumes floated high into the sky and travelled at the speed of light in every direction. One feather split into thousands covering the cantaloupe-tainted sky in a shimmering wispy ripple that stretched to infinity.

A feather strayed towards the shore and stuck itself to the lens of one of the cameras filming the inconceivable. Quickly, Michael instructed the cameraman not to touch it, they were not meant to touch it... In seconds, a temperate current lifted the wandering feather up into the air. As it spiralled up the thermal column, it split to form a gleaming wave that soon joined the silken ripple which spread, unhindered, across the planet.

Michael, Alexandra, Arianne and Marcus huddled closer. Beads of joy streamed their faces as they watched Seth beat his glorious wings, as they watched the inverted rainfall ebb into space. Slade was absorbed behind the tripod, flashing intermittently at the rapturous vision, at the winged deity floating beneath the dense undulation. Wonder and confusion enveloped them; none of them could fully comprehend why the angel had chosen them, bestowed such honour. They had long crossed the threshold of innocence, yet, for some unfathomable reason the feather, Seth, had made them the exception to the rule; cleansed them in adulthood. A feeling of inadequacy infused the warm golden air as they silently questioned their fortune.

Humble gratitude filled their hearts as they watched the awe-inspiring miracle, watched the beautiful iridescent being shed hope on the world, send out the silken darts that would soon obliterate any recollection of suffering from children's hearts; memory of darkness from their young souls. As their eyes trailed the proliferating wave of feathers, thoughts of their own past tragedies invaded them again. The feather had saved them. Seth had saved them, salvaged the broken child inside them, released them from the chains that bound them to their heartbreaking pasts. Every child, on the face of the earth, was about to be blessed with the same fate and their hearts rejoiced at the indubitable purge that would liberate them.

John stood with his men on the cliff, midway up the twisty road. Ethan kept him abreast of every detail over the walkie-talkie but he could not help wish he were standing on the cove with the others. He smiled inwardly as he observed the deferential expressions surrounding him. Rapt eyes drank the segmented landscape, the patch of heaven stretching the entirety of the curved inlet, the intense light hovering feet above the turquoise waters, the glittering wings fluttering the golden air, the silken white cloud heaving over them far into space....

Shoulder to shoulder they stood, unmoving on the ledge overlooking the dark sea, edging the turquoise lagoon. The burly uniformed men cried like children as they listened to the soothing, mesmerising echo reaching them from below. John felt honoured he was one of the chosen, privileged he was able to share the historic moment with his loyal and cherished companions. None of his men had questioned the 'special' mission; they had blindly followed their leader to the designated destination. None of them could have imagined, in a million years, how 'special' the mission would turn out to be.

John glanced at the string of cars behind the barricade, at the human cord lining, lighting the sloping ridge candles in hand and smiled again. The moment the transmission had begun, people in the vicinity had flocked to the cove.

Mercifully, he had not needed to employ force. No one attempted to trespass the barrier. The curious string of people had peacefully abandoned their vehicles and, trancelike, walked to the cliff to stand silently as the messenger's mesmeric voice floated in the warm air to reach their yielding ears. John had known the end of the journey promised something spectacular, magical, but the enthralling apparition suspended in the surreal landscape, shedding hope on humanity, surpassed his wildest expectations.

The minute the transmission had begun, channels across the world had automatically tuned to the cove. Leaders of the world raised eyebrows when a nervous aide rushed into the room and interrupted the important meeting and whispered something to the speaker. The world summit came to a halt. A rush of suits headed out of the large conference room, hurried to an adjoining room where a fifty-inch plasma was broadcasting the earth-shattering event.

Everyone stared incredulous at the images spanning the screen and it took a while before they could make sense of the unearthly scenario, digest the transcendental implications. Word that an avalanche of reporters camped outside the building spread like wildfire. Phones began to ring like mad and, for the first time in history, none of the most powerful men in the world knew what to do, what to say, how to react...

Leaders of great nations were dumbstruck, men accustomed to take decisions of vast magnitude felt abysmally inadequate, insignificant, before the heavenly presence. The powers bestowed on them, by a majority of compatriots, seemed inconsequential at that instant. Countries, governments, had contingency plans for every possible threat, catastrophe, complex dilemma that assailed their nations. An invasion an alien encounter... but none of them was prepared for a totally unpredicted and unimaginable event that rendered them powerless.

God existed. Heaven existed. The elitist group could do nothing but watch, wait...

In barely thirty minutes, the feathery wave had covered the skies of the entire western and eastern hemispheres and had begun to roll vertically to cloak the rest of the globe. The lustrous wispy cloud hung low over the earth, waiting...

Seth kept flapping his wings laboriously. His eyes closed as a silent world watched, waited for the silken cumulous to pour the miracle. A stupefied audience remained ghostly quiet as the numinous creature continued to pour feathers into the heavens, continued to fill the skies with hope.

The regenerating healing technique, he had secretly perfected on the islands, was a strenuous task. Seth felt suddenly fatigued, faint, his wings becoming extremely heavy. Julia, who was standing alone a few meters from the shore, instantly sensed his lassitude and, visibly alarmed, rushed to the edge of the crystalline sea. The tingling sensation down her spine had returned. The pins and needles were on crescendo and she kept pushing her shoulders backwards in an effort to curtail the numbing sensation in her arms and neck.

The tumultuous revelation, the fainting episode, had debilitated her. She felt weird, giddy, oddly short of breath. As she waded frantically towards Seth, her arms oared the balmy waters, cupped hands spilled salty scoops on her face, her neck.... She was waist deep when she saw that Seth's was struggling hard to keep flaccid wings from dropping. His eyes, wide with panic, mirrored hers, as she burrowed the limiting density with all the strength she could muster, realizing Seth was about to drop into the ocean. She moved slowly, her limbs drained, numb. She would never reach him…

Dread enveloped the cove as everyone realised something was wrong... The angel's feathers had gone suddenly limp, drooped listlessly to his sides. The light surrounding him had dulled, flickered weakly. Fearful eyes remained fixed on Julia as she struggled towards him when, suddenly, the angel's convoluting body plunged into the ocean, extinguishing the fiery tongues lining the immediate shore. The world watched in horror as the beautiful angel plummeted into the water, and the planet held its breath again...

Michael and Marcus were the first to react. They rushed to the shore, tumbled into the sea and began to traverse the ten meters of ocean separating them from Seth. Overtaking a hysterical Julia, they groped at the mass of feathers sprawling the still waters. Quickly, they turned Seth face up; his deathly pallor filled them with dread. Fearing the worst, they dragged the semiconscious body with Slade's help, who had rushed into the sea after them, onto the damp sand. The ethereal creature was barely lucid. His eyes closed, his damp, dishevelled feathers shuddering feverishly in their powerless hands.

Marcus glued his ear to the centre of the wing covering his collapsed body. He had suddenly remembered reading once; wings were the lungs of angels. Michael and Slade knelt beside him perplexed but said nothing. No one knew how to save an angel. No one knew if angels could die...After moments of agony, uncertainty, hopelessness, Seth mercifully moved his head slightly and eyelids flickered as he brokenly whispered '*Julia, Julia...* '

Arianne, who had rushed to hold Alexandra's hand, tore away from her and rushed over the cold sands, in the direction of the crew, signalling them to stop filming. As she neared them, she realized the cameras no longer pointed at Seth but focused steadily on the ocean behind him. When she followed the recording trail, the vision she encountered stunned her. Without stopping to think, she picked up the microphone, dangling from the centre camera's tripod, and invaded the filming range….

She smiled at the world nervously for a few moments, turned her head in the direction of the ocean, then back again at the camera. For the first time in her professional life, she was lost for words…

Alexandra, who had remained rooted to the spot, finally reacted and rushed to Michael, who stood crestfallen over the feeble contorted body. She held tightly to his clenched hand in an effort to comfort him. Tears rolled down her anguished face as she took in the desolate scene. A rain of desperation speckled the chilling dampness; she cried for the angel, for the children...she cried for Michael. As she caressed his cold hand, she empathized with the impotence tormenting his soul.

Slade had followed Arianne to the camera crew and impulsively placed a shoulder over her delicate, quivering frame. His eyes darted back and forth between the astonishing scene materializing before them and the angel lying inert on the shore. The dramatic moment was slightly alleviated when a disconsolate Arianne plunged herself into his arms and clutched on to him with the force of titans. He fought hard to curb back tears as he felt her heaving chest against his racing heart.

Ethan could not believe what was happening. *Angels could not die,* he thought distressed, and began to dial Arianne's cell number. He had broken off transmission and awaited instructions... Slade finally answered his call, quickly cut him short instructing him to continue emitting the signal. The minute cameras changed angle again he understood why...

John and his men joined the gasping crowd. At sight of the angel tumbling into the sea, the endless chain of panic-stricken spectators had simultaneously dropped to its knees and begun to pray. John could bear it no longer, and leaving his men in command of the blockade, raced towards the cove.... As he sprinted over the twisting tar, one thought persisted; *angels could not die, angels could not die...*

All cameras focused on Julia, as she stood immersed in the dazzling, sea-green waters. A radiant, almost opaque light had begun to dance around her, enveloped her to cocoon her in a glowing white and silver trimmed, translucent bubble. She faced the shore, a haunting expression on her beautiful face, her soft curls cascading to dip, thread the ocean. She closed her eyes, slowly pulled her sweater over her head and thrust her head back as golden tresses floated to cover her naked torso. Unexpectedly, she turned around to face the horizon, tilted her head to the stellar sunset sky and raised her arms to the blaze of tongues that had spontaneously ignited to close the fiery ring again.

The luminous bubble began to broaden, then slowly began to ascend, lifting Julia a few meters above sea level. Suddenly, the floating globe swivelled, projecting Julia onto the shore. Her head was thrust backwards and her eyes remained closed, a glowing blue light filtering her eyelids. The scene was spectacular, Julia floated inside the diaphanous sphere, against the impressive dusk background. Lustrous locks covered her breasts and forked lightning rays flashed from behind her to become shafts of light, spanning over the golden mirror, circled by fire. No one had expected the second happening and the world watched in frenzied expectation at what would ensue...

Infinite eyes scurried from the ocean back to the shore, from the angel lying inert on the shore, to the mortal woman suspended above the unearthly tinged seas. The suspended globe began to tremble, quake violently, until the tremor halted abruptly. Julia began to radiate with the same golden light that surrounded her, languidly lifted long lashed eyelids and burning aquamarine eyes probed an enraptured world.

To a sudden jerk of the head, swing of arms stretching up towards the heavens, a pair of white silver edged wings sprang from behind her and the world caught its breath again. The delicate mass of feathers floated regally to her sides until they glowed pure and magnificent. She contracted them, gracefully fanned them open over the vibrant sea. Blazing, sapphire eyes reached up to the heavens as wings swooped the air to curve proudly over her head. Again, she stared at the world, this time her lips curved in the gentlest smile. The female angel was now the most beautiful creature encountered by man...

No one had expected the extraordinary permutation. No one had expected the mortal woman to transform into an angel. Especially the holders of the other five feathers who stood stupefied on the shore, sharing a disconcerting thought. Each had begun to worry the feather pinned to their hearts would have the same mutating effect on them. It was then that Michael realised where she had seen her before; the angel resembled the beautiful young woman he had seen in the painting, back at the cottage...

The moment Julia metamorphosed became the beautiful, ethereal butterfly, adorning the golden dusk, Seth's strength ebbed back to life and he regained full consciousness. Assisted by Marcus and Michael, he stood up uncertainly until, finally, he towered sturdily over them. His thinning mass of feathers began to dense at amazing speed and the dullness in his eyes quickly regained its glowing lustre. Silently, he stared at the two men standing beside him and gently nodded his head in gratitude. As he turned his head towards the ocean, he confronted the unexpected scene....

Enthralled, he watched Julia suspended in all her glory against sunset hues, the shades of red and yellow reflecting over the ocean making it look like coloured shards of glass. The moment his eyes rested on her beautiful face, delved into her liquid, turquoise eyes, a powerful surge of energy rushed through him and he emitted a deafening high-pitched sound that reverberated throughout the cove, the piercing ripples turning circles of light to reach Julia.

In one swoop, he was beside her. He floated to her right, feet away from her, and joyous eyes took in her celestial configuration. She could not be more beautiful... He stretched his arm, reached her hand and Julia smiled deep into his eyes.

Majestic wings waved in unison as the beat in their chests became one, as the light in their souls radiated with the same intensity.

Profound emotion seized him as he realized how much he had missed his beautiful twin sister. How he had carried the pain of her absence since they had been separated the moment they had abandoned their mother's womb. Destined to different worlds, neither had known of the other's existence, an elusive sense of loss shadowing them. Seth wished to know the reason behind the unjustified deed. He wished to know why he had been the one chosen to remain in their realm, and Julia exiled. His mother had not made the choice. Fleeting anger arose inside him as he wondered who had condemned them and why…

The mystical creatures, the divine messenger and his new ally, floated together, side by side, as the light around them intensified, bathing the cove in surreal daylight. Two pairs of gauzy, sapphire eyes now probed a soundless world, a waiting world. The flutter of wings gathered impetus and feathers from both their wings began to pour, regenerate, this time without faltering. Seth could not take his eyes of Julia. She had returned to his side the moment he needed her most. Their 'other' world needed her. The fusion of two worlds materialized again; the intention of two worlds, the unbeatable force condemning darkness.

The north and south hemispheres were soon covered in the snowy blanket, in the floating mesh of feathers waiting to flood the earth. Ethan smiled as he watched the satellite pictures appearing in the first screen. The blue planet resembled a huge snowball floating in the universe.

Within moments, the singular feathers cascaded simultaneously upon the earth's surface and inhabitants of the five continents took to the streets to watch the heavenly deluge. They had not understood exposure was unnecessary. The feathers would find their way to the children, through brick walls, glass, cement, wood...through any solid matter, over any earthly barrier, over any distance, its path unstoppable.

A staggered world watched as feathers found the young targets, with a promise to cleanse them, imbue them with immutable memory of the source. Children's faces, eyes, illuminated unparalleled radiance as feathers poured from the skies, darted across rooms, streets, desserts, jungles, snow, water...and pinned to their chests. Rainbow smiles adorned every inch of a planet that had begun to resonate with a unique and uplifting frequency...

Seth and Julia floated towards each other and as they smiled knowingly into each other's eyes Seth placed a protective arm over his estranged sister. Together, they watched the last two feathers, one from each of their wings, entwine, twirl away, leave the crepuscular patch of sky into the gem-flecked cosmos, in search of the two remaining children to be purified by its magic...

The moment the last two feathers disappeared in the distance, Seth thought of his mother. He wished she could have been at his side, their side. She would be proud of him, them. They had succeeded; humanity no longer rocked the precipice to destruction. They had been gifted with a second chance which he was certain would not be wasted. The seven mortals waiting on the shore would ensure the safe passage of the world into the future.

Luckily but surprisingly, celestial forces had not thwarted their mission but the euphoria of triumph was blemished by the unnerving realisation condemnation awaited their mutinous deed. The time had come for them to leave. They must return home. He needed to protect his mother... That the angelic realm had not impeded the covert mission did not mean there would be no repercussions. The moment they set foot on their world, Julia returned 'home', their defiance of the realm would be exposed and the consequences of their rebellious act revealed.

Seth wondered if he would be able to protect Julia. He had had no notion of her true nature, anticipated her transformation…he erroneously presumed she would be staying in the mortal world...would be safe... For a moment he wished she could stay behind, continue with the life she knew, had come to love. It was impossible. The metamorphosis was irreversible. Gently, he nodded at his sister. It was time…

Julia looked around her for a few moments, absorbed the world that had seen her birth, had seen her grow, wondering if she would ever return, if she would be condemned to return to a different life, in another lifetime… It was no time for regrets. The world was safe. She had found her family. She had done the lord's work. At least that was her earthly conviction; she had, after all, been an angel for a short while… It did not matter what the realm thought of her. She trusted Seth, her mother. Her mother...the word took a different connotation...Quickly, she delivered a prayer to the

Father. She must see her again, even if it was only for a moment. She needed to tell her what burned in her heart…

A nod of her head confirmed she was ready, as ready as she would ever be. In sync, they shot high into the air. Their silver tipped wings shedding a glittering trail in the recent night.

Grey twilight hues had begun to paint the sunset stretch of sky, soon the heavens would be a uniform black, silver-dusted ceiling. They stood in a row, like Moai statues on the hard edge of the shore. Confounded eyes had followed the tinsel spray vanish over the hotel into the vesper sky. The angel's abrupt departure had knocked them cold. No one spoke; no one voiced disheartenment, the collective disappointment... None of them had expected Seth, and even Julia, to leave without saying goodbye...They grouped closer in an effort to mitigate the profound sense of abandonment they all felt at that moment.

The exaltation of victory, the pride and euphoria they had felt at having helped the angels complete the mission successfully was marred by a strong feeling of disenchantment. They remained on the shore for a while longer, stony silhouettes against the darkening ocean, forgotten, minute grains of sand in the dessert of oblivion.

They moved closer, merged their bodies to a single mass, attempting to palliate the sensation of insignificance, until finally, Michael announced feebly they should all return to the hotel... go home...

Deflated, they traversed the humid sands, eyes fixed on the glowing window on the first floor. The women sobbed quietly. The men struggled to maintain composure, clearing their throats from time to time. No one understood the cold departure. They had all expected a more emotional finale to their journey; an intimate encounter with the angelic creature responsible for their wondrous journey, the miracles in their lives, the miracle for Earth...

Arianne could not believe she would never see Julia again, that Julia had not taken a moment to say goodbye to her, and was now crying inconsolably in Slade's willing embrace. Marcus trailed behind them; the worst writer in the world could not have come up with a more incongruous climax…

In silence, they climbed the dusty boulders to the empty hotel, to room number seven. None of them wished to be alone, to sleep. Sleep could not appease the mayhem in their souls. They felt lost in a world that had begun to feel alien. Without Seth, Julia, they were disoriented...

Ethan met them at the entrance of the Seaview, visibly affected by the unexpected and frosty culmination to their mystical odyssey. Enthralled, he had watched the angels soar high into the dawning night, the luminosity of their wings defying twilight, silver dust spraying the light, coal sky. His heart had raced with anticipation at the thought of meeting the heavenly guardian responsible for his privileged life, for the preservation of life. When he had realised they would not be returning, the screen remained a greyish square, he had nearly screamed his name, willing him to return.

They sat facing each other on the empty chairs, circling the centre of the room; oblivious to world channels emitting reruns of the momentous event... The room remained painfully hushed as each of them struggled to assimilate the unforeseen anticlimax, comprehend what they must do next...

A sudden blast of air swung the door of the room wide open and the subtle vibration in the room rose to an electrifying buzz. Ethan was the first to bounce off his seat, rush into the other room. The rest followed quickly. The brilliant light emanating from the door heeded the angels had returned....

Seth and Julia had never left the cove. They had vanished to the mortal eye. They had hovered invisible over the inlet, until everyone had returned to the hotel. They had wished to say goodbye in the intimacy of the magical room...

Seth could not wait to meet the seven mortals who had invaded his dreams to aid him in his quest. He had much to tell them, much to thank them for... They were about to discover his connection to the earth, to Julia, to room number seven. He would tell them of his mother, of his world, and they would share their visions for the future of their world...

Seth and Julia finally said their goodbyes at dawn. The night had been long, emotional, revealing. As Seth and Julia flew side-by-side, high over the clouds towards the frontier, they agreed the feather had chosen wisely...

The seven friends standing on the shore had held hands, held their breath, as they watched Seth and Julia, hover a few moments above the lulling sea, their eyes gleaming. As they floated gracefully in the gentle breeze, both nodded their heads and smiled at them one last time…melodious sound of wind chime echoing in the perfect cove.

They had become invisible, meters above the shore, and everyone had smiled up at the waking heavens as they remembered Seth's last words;. *'There is much to do...'*

# Epilogue

*High above the world three pairs of eyes watched as the feathers descended upon the children, watched their young hearts fill with ecstasy as their souls were cleansed; as they were reminded of their timeless nature. Light lit the world at it never had before. They had succeeded; humanity had surrendered to the realisation the world's demise was imminent, that they were the conscious perpetrators of its death.*

*For the first time, every inhabitant of the blue planet awakened to the same consciousness; they must change. Those that were spiritually elevated; 'light workers', had understood the need for change a long time ago and were overjoyed; they were no longer a minority. Tepid believers embraced the reaffirmation of their faith; God existed. Sulphur souls were simply terrified that the world, their life could end. The latter though, were not beyond hope; in time, the reason for change would be another; they would inevitably be 'infected' by the light.*

*They had chosen well. Amanda had been the perfect candidate. She had lived up to their expectations, so had her offspring. Since she had been a young angel, they had watched her. They had watched many young angels, but she had stood out from the rest.*

*Her boundless sensitivity made her 'different', the perfect candidate. It was virtually impossible for her to control the overwhelming compassion that emanated from her soul for all living things. They had seen the way she had reacted in the halls of growth, how the light of her soul had merged instantly with the forest's glowing energy, with every living creature's in the glittering bush. How she had harmonised with that life, understood their language the moment she had set foot on the multicoloured woodland. Her symbiosis with the universe the moment she had heard the whispers inside the tree of life.*

*They had known she would 'fail' her mission; they had thrust her upon mortal ground before she had been disciplined by maturity. She had reacted just as they had presaged...*

*Her punishment, her mortal impregnation had been the initial step. The moment they had set the scene, brewed the storm, they had accompanied a willing Anton to the southern turret and watched him fly off to save her, plant the first seeds of the plan.*

*The laws in the Angelic realm were indissoluble. No angel must guide, help a mortal, unless invited to do so. They had known she would 'get involved': her profound empathy had ensured that.*

*For a long time mortal pleas had become scarce. Humanity had lost faith, had fallen prey to fallen angels lurking in the shadows, and heaven was forced to watch as the world headed towards assured destruction.*

*The Cherubim had reported the abysmal state of affairs to the trinity of angels of the first sphere. After much thought, much prayer in the higher stratums of the realm, they had allowed the Virtues and Powers to interfere: angels of the second sphere responsible for maintaining the presence of the source throughout the whole of existence. Together with the help of Thrones, angels of the same triad, powerful conduits between physical worlds and the realm, they had found a way to change humanities' destiny, the world's debacle. Angels born upon earth, from a mortal womb, they decided would not be infringing the sacred rules.*

*The universe had done the rest, had rearranged itself to spur the coincidences, the miracles, that ensured a vision of such high intention. Julia had been an initial surprise, but they had immediately understood the ingenuity of the universe. Universal foresight had concocted a reinforcing ally to the plan from its onset. It had ensured the connection between the two worlds remained strong.*

*The moment Seth and Julia descended on the valley, angels, of the second sphere, escorted them to the Golden chamber. The moment they saw Amanda standing in the centre of the circular room, they rushed to embrace her. Sentinel Principalities guarded the doors.*

*They stood in silence, holding hands, their sombre expressions anticipating punishment. Amanda did not care what happened to her. She had predicted retribution. She had no regrets. She only wished her children spared. Seth did not care what happened to him. He only wished his mother and sister spared. Julia did not wish to be separated from her long-lost family. The instant the three Seraphim set foot in the chamber, Amanda and Seth were disconcerted; the towering, six winged angels were smiling. Confused, they looked at each other. Before Amanda or Seth could utter a word, the Seraphim in the centre began to speak.*

*As he delivered his speech, a wave of relief inundated the room. Amanda could not believe the words assuaging her anguish. Seth could not believe the words assuaging his guilt. Julia did not understand the melodious, piercing words mollifying the cutting atmosphere...*

*Mother and son continued to gaze at each other astounded. The Masters of light had known of their plan all along, were the masterminds behind it. That was why no one had tried to stop them… Providence had had nothing to do with the success of their mission. They should have known; nothing, however trivial, escaped the discerning eyes of the realm.*

*The realm* **had** *cared; ultimately decided humanity was not beyond hope, had believed in man's potential, his capacity to change at the edge of the precipice. Thus, they had conspired to create that precipice, knowing Seth would make humankind stand on its edge, look down on an abysmal future.*

*Seth marvelled at their perspicacity, the ingenious, intricate plan they had so patiently woven over time…since his mother was a young angel.*

*Contravening angelic laws had not been an option, so they had conspired to create hybrid angels. The universe had astutely conspired to place one in each world.*

*The sound of footsteps suddenly echoed the corridor leading to the chamber and all eyes turned in its direction. The moment Anton walked into the room Amanda rushed into his open arms.*

*Seth watched his father caress his mothers soft curls, her cheek, as he gazed lovingly into her eyes. Seth watched his father lift his eyes, look over his mother's shoulder at Julia, who was standing timidly beside him, tears welling in his eyes.*

*Julia watched her mother, her father embrace, in the knowledge she would not be separated from her family again. She had sensed her twin brother's fears in the cove, had accepted her fate long before they set foot on the realm. The realisation she had been spared, would be staying 'home', had an eternity to make up for time lost, filled her with immense joy.*

*When her parents had walked up to her, cocooned her in their wings, in love, she had felt blissfully at peace, complete.*

*She would be staying in the valley, at least for a while. She needed time to acclimatise herself to her new world, her new life. She had recently discovered who her mother was and had only just met her father…*

*Seth watched his parents embrace Julia in love and he fought hard to hold back tears. As he watched his family finally reunite, safe, his thoughts strayed to the seven friends he had left behind in his other world, wondering when the higher angels would allow him to visit them again...*

*He would be leaving the valley soon. He was to become an Arch Angel, the Guardian Angel of Young Souls. His dream of visiting the sky dwellings had become more tangible...*

## Afterword

*As Amanda, Anton and Julia watched Seth leave the valley, their hearts filled with pride. He would be gone for some time. An intense curriculum awaited him in the Halls of Light; the silver, glass temple midway off the cloudy highway connecting the Mountain Dwellings to the Sky Dwellings. They would miss him, but were glad he had received such an honour. When he had soared out of sight, Amanda smiled and Anton placed a loving arm over her shoulders, over his daughter's. Their family was complete. All the secrets had finally been unburdened…*

*The moment Julia had set foot on heavenly ground she knew she was home. She still missed her 'other home', but she did not have long to wait. An ex-teacher she was a disciplined student and had graduated, like her mother and brother, top of her class. Her missions to earth would begin soon.*

*Julia loved life on the realm. She loved being so near to her God, loved to fly like a bird.*

Michael hardly left the New World Headquarters building in three months. No one had left the building. There was still a lot to do. Treaties between countries to be signed, new environmental, commercial, civic laws to be enacted and so on. Overnight, the world became a single democracy. Religions ceased to separate humanity, wage wars in the name of God. Every inhabitant of the planet became a 'follower of the light'. They were well on their way to creating the utopia idealists had only been able to dream of.

Alexandra became Ambassador to the Children of The World, within months, safe, loving environments embraced orphan children of the earth. Most were adopted, the rest placed in 'Rainbow Homes' funded by either governments, munificent companies, charitable organizations or generous benefactors all over the world. A picture illustrating children flying coloured ribbons, circling the earth whilst holding hands, hang over the entrance of the children's residences. Like Michael, she had only left World Headquarters for three days: one to get married, two to honeymoon at the cove. Room number seven was again witness to a twin conception.

Marcus Saintclare's new books, 'The Messenger' and 'The Children of light', became instant best sellers, this time without the need of a powerful marketing machine. Arianne took a well-deserved break after her world debut with the documentary 'The Message'. She moved in with her son and together they cared for Marcus' 'other' family.

Slade won the Pulitzer Prize for his photo; 'The Messenger'. The image of the ethereal being suspended in all his glory, resplendent wings floating majestically at his sides whilst pellucid eyes spellbound the world against the magical backdrop, was impossible to contest. (The image spurred Marcus's bestseller and blockbuster film) On his night table, another prized photo, Arianne's, was proudly displayed. At the foot of the photo frame, scribbled on a small piece of paper was her private phone number. The nine-digit number firmly anchored to Slade's memory, he rang her a dozen times a day. Still, the crumpled note remained a cherished memento that rekindled the memory of her beautiful face the day she had coyly agreed to go out with him.

John retired early from the police force and became CEO of W.P.O. (World Peace and Order); a subsidiary company of Quill that had become the world's number one watch dog. Ten floors of the 'Cyclops' accommodated the sophisticated technology that kept a vigilant eye on the world. Hanging over the desk in his office, situated on the last floor, was the medal awarded to him by law enforcing authorities, from across the world for his dedication to world safety and peace. On the desk was another cherished possession, a photo of his wife and children.

Quill continued to be the number one search engine in the world, the leading IT Company under Ethan's masterful leadership. Slade's images of 'The Messenger' and Arianne's narration and filming of the event was posted in the user interface so the world would never forget its promise. The lethal virus was destroyed. All but for a small 'infection' that ensured no corruptive images ever invaded the virtual highway again. Numerous multimillion companies followed Quill's altruistic example and dedicated substantial profit percentages to 'The Children Fund'. Sydney and Ethan got married the moment the hectic pace of the first months slowed down and a sense of normality was restored. Their honeymoon suite was room number seven. Ethan had wished Sydney to fall in love with the man and not the company; she had preferred the Hero…

In the heart of the city, on the wall of the most prestigious art museums of the world, hang a magnificent painting, 'Amanda'. A beautiful woman was immersed in the sea, near the shore, in a perfect cove overshadowed by a quaint hotel. On closer inspection, one realised the froth stretching behind her depicted two wings.

The famous artist's signature spelled Claire.

## *Angels that weep.*

*Delicate as a butterfly's wing, are their bones,*
*Innocent as cherubs their eyes,*
*Soft is their skin, like the petal of rose,*
*And lonely the spirit that cries.*

*Small is the heart that loads so much pain,*
*Tiny the hands that defend,*
*Little the feet that scatter away,*
*From enemy days without end.*

*Lonely the world where they pray,*
*Hidden the nights where they weep,*
*Tormented the games they must play,*
*Vile is the bed where they sleep.*

*Can't you hear them?*
*Screams that echo your street,*
*Can't you see them?*
*Children weary on feet,*
*That are dragged, as they look to the floor,*
*Don't look up, when they pass by your door,*
*Lest the monster, that is lurking in shadows,*
*Finds out,*
*They've allowed you to hear,*
*What their soul cannot shout.*

*Listen careful for those angels that weep,*
*Make them safe in their sleep.*
*For the laws of mankind are too lenient,*
*For the monster convenient,*
*They're not just,*
*Uncontrollable lust,*
*Must be proven,*
*Without shadow of doubt so extreme,*
*That most die,*
*Without voicing their scream.*

*Fragile like china dolls', are their bones,*
*Blameless like saints' are their eyes,*
*Dark is their skin, like mantle of night,*
*And desolate the spirit that cries,*

*Pure is the soul that screams with starvation,*
*Tiny the hands that will hunt,*
*Little the feet bitten by cold,*
*In streets that are deaf, to their desperate chant,*

*Indifferent the world where they beg,*
*Hungry the nights where they weep,*
*Uncertain the days they must face,*
*Cardboard the beds where they sleep,*

*Can't you see hear them?*
*Wails that echo the earth,*
*Can't you see them?*
*Children famished from birth,*
*In lands that are barren, ravaged by hate,*
*Early death, is the sentence of fate,*
*Lest the veins, of the earth that have frozen,*
*To ice,*
*Melt to generous stream,*
*And destroy famine's scream.*

*Listen careful for those angels that weep,*
*Don't condemn them to sleep,*
*For the eyes of the world have been blind,*
*Distribution of wealth, ill designed,*
*'Feed the world'*
*Must be promise upheld,*
*Hunger killed,*
*Without generous hearts vowing dream,*
*They will die,*
*By the hand of your sin.*

*Jackie Canessa*

# Coming Soon…

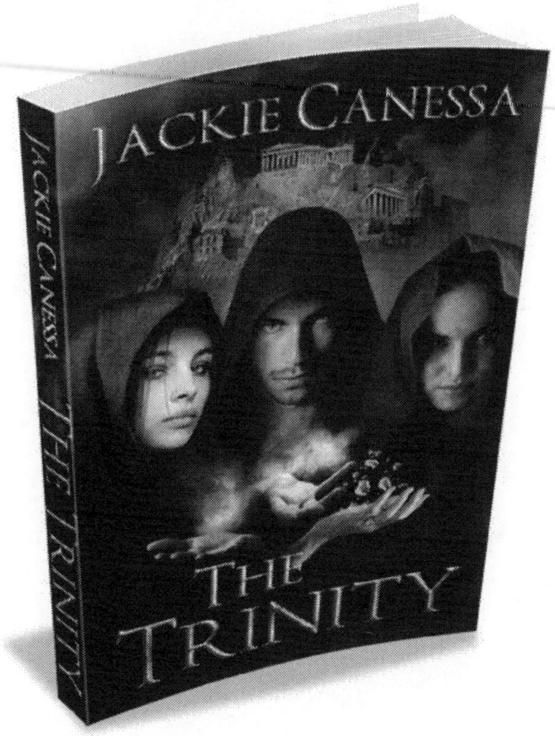


The Trinity, a pulse-pounding contemporary fantasy novel envisaged to hit book stands early autumn... For an update on the Author's work and contact details check out

**www.jackiecanessa.com**

12230319R00228

Made in the USA
Charleston, SC
21 April 2012